THE Lioness OF Morocco

THE Lioness OF Morocco

JULIA DROSTEN

Translated by Christiane Galvani

This is a work of fiction. Names, characters, organizations, places, events, and incidents are either products of the author's imagination or are used fictitiously.

Previously published as *Die Löwin von Mogador* by Kindle Direct Publishing in 2013 in Germany. Translated from German by Christiane Galvani. First published in English by AmazonCrossing in 2017.

Published by AmazonCrossing, Seattle

www.apub.com

ISBN-13: 9781503941922
ISBN-10: 1503941922

Cover design by Rex Bonomelli

Printed in the United States of America

Table of Contents

Part One

The Blue Pearl of the Atlantic

1835 to 1840

Nothing shall ever happen to us except that which God has ordained for us. And if you put your faith in God, He will guide your heart. For God knows all things.

—the Koran

Chapter One

London, June 1835

The fifteen clerks taking their lunch break in the counting house of the Spencer & Son Shipping Company almost choked on their food.

There at the door stood Sibylla Spencer, visibly out of breath and pressing an envelope against her chest as she looked from one startled face to the next. The boss's twenty-three-year-old daughter normally visited only once a year, when she and her stepmother distributed Christmas presents.

Yet it was not Christmas but the middle of June. It did not bode well that Sibylla had appeared unannounced, distraught, and, it would seem, unaccompanied in the rough masculine world of the Port of London. At least this was what Mr. Donovan, the lead accountant, feared. He stepped away from his desk with some hesitation.

"Your father is in a meeting with the dock committee, Miss Spencer. He should be back within half an hour. Do you wish to wait for him? Peter"—he motioned to one of the apprentice clerks—"get a chair for Miss Spencer."

As Sibylla impatiently shook her head, another voice came from a desk near the window. "This seems urgent. I shall escort you, Miss Spencer, if you will allow me. I was on my way to the docks anyway."

A tall young man with an elaborately tied silk cravat, stylishly tight vest, and highly polished shoes took a briefcase from his desk, walked over to Sibylla, and bowed briefly, folding his tall frame in half like a pocketknife.

"Benjamin Hopkins," he said in a slightly nasal, vaguely arrogant voice. "I'm your father's leading purchasing agent."

Relieved, Donovan retreated to his desk. Benjamin heard muttering and felt the piercing eyes of his coworkers on his back. All of twenty-eight years old, he had managed to become the right-hand man of shipping and business magnate Richard Spencer. And he never missed an opportunity to make the boss aware of his colleagues' smallest mistakes. That, along with his fastidious attire and affected speech, led to widespread dislike and ridicule.

Yet if Benjamin was sweating under his high-collared shirt, it was not because of the palpable hostility from his coworkers, but rather the scrutiny of Sibylla's sapphire-colored eyes. She studied him for some time without uttering a word and, just as he feared he would be turned down, she nodded. "Very well, Mr. Hopkins."

Benjamin breathed a sigh of triumphant relief. "I certainly hope that you are not bearing bad news," he said, looking at the envelope in her hand.

"That's hardly any concern of yours, Mr. Hopkins." She turned on her heel and hurried down the stairs.

As Benjamin snatched his coat off the hook and slipped it on, he overheard someone say quietly, yet distinctly, "Just look at that bootlicker; now he's going after the boss's daughter."

"What's keeping you, Mr. Hopkins? I'm in a hurry," Sibylla called.

Benjamin strode through the door with his head held high.

Sibylla was already settled in her elegant two-seater. "Come on, Mr. Hopkins! Or are you averse to a woman holding the reins?"

"Oh, on the contrary, I would consider it an honor to be your passenger!" he exclaimed, climbing in next to her.

"Let's not exaggerate now, Mr. Hopkins." She clicked her tongue and the brown hackney mare pulled so forcefully that Benjamin lost his balance and fell against the seat. But even Sibylla's disdainful look was not enough to shake his confidence.

Over the course of yearly company Christmas parties, he had seen Sibylla turn from a child to a graceful young woman. She'd had many suitors, but her willfulness and sharp wit had proved too daunting for all of them. Before long, she had gained a reputation for being intent on controlling a man, and this deterred many. Benjamin, on the other hand, saw an opportunity. Company gossip was swirling around Richard Spencer's fear that his daughter might end up an old maid. And the greater that fear, the less likely he would be to object to a son-in-law like Benjamin, who had neither an impressive family tree nor a fortune of any note.

"What is this meeting my father is attending?" Sibylla asked as she maneuvered through the hustle and bustle of carts, stevedores, sailors, dock agents, laborers, and employees of the surrounding offices.

"I'm certain a lovely young lady such as you would rather talk about more entertaining subjects," Benjamin replied with his most charming smile. Alas, what had proven so effective with other women earned him no more than a look of annoyance.

"Would I be asking if I weren't interested?"

Benjamin laughed sheepishly. "Well, it's about trade with the Maghreb, that is to say, trade with Northern and West Africa. Your father, as president of the West India Dock Company, received a letter from the general consul of the British government in Morocco. The sultan is extending an invitation to British and Continental traders. His coffers are empty after many years of war against the rebellious Berbers.

Trade with the Moroccan Jews has stimulated the domestic economy, and now we are supposed to improve overseas trade."

"Isn't it dangerous there? I've heard of pirates taking Christians hostage and selling them as slaves."

"I'm impressed by your knowledge, Miss Spencer."

"I read often. Most of all about foreign lands I'll probably never see."

He nodded as he wondered if she might be satisfied with the carefree society life of attending tea parties or receptions wearing the latest fashions and exchanging the latest gossip.

"Fortunately, the pirate problem along the coast is under control," he explained. "Some local rulers have been effectively bribed and others intimidated by our navy. The sight of our battleships is very impressive, I can assure you. And Sultan Abd al-Rahman's invitation means lucrative business."

"So the members of the dock association are deciding whether to send ships to Morocco?"

"Yes, they're discussing the port of Tangier on the Mediterranean and Mogador on the Atlantic. The trouble is that it's difficult to find people willing to work in an uncivilized Arab country."

"Mogador," Sibylla muttered to herself. "How mysterious!"

Benjamin eyed her surreptitiously. She was slender, with a straight back, and almost too tall for his taste. The wind played with her hat and the lace flounce of her dress that stuck out from under her light coat. Her blonde hair blew a bit around her face, but he was able to see her lashes and her elegant nose. Her delicate white skin and wind-reddened cheeks intensified his impression that this English rose belonged at an elegant ball rather than at the loud and dirty Port of London.

"Well, Mr. Hopkins. What's your verdict, having examined me so intensely? Do you judge me with a businessman's eye, assessing the same way you do barrels of rum and sacks of coffee? Do you deem me a pretty but useless package?" Her tone was mocking but her look was searching.

"F-f-f-forgive me," he stammered. "But if I may say so, you are a balm to the eyes of any man, and it would never occur to me to compare you to a barrel of rum or a sack of coffee. That would insult not only your beauty but also your integrity, which you have once again demonstrated to me."

"What a shameless flatterer you are, Mr. Hopkins!" she said, shaking her head.

Benjamin wisely decided to dispense with any further compliments. "Turn left up ahead and then go along the high brick wall."

Sibylla guided the gig from the frontage road onto a narrower path running parallel to a canal that connected the Thames with the West India Docks.

"My goodness!" she exclaimed as they passed a hall from which emanated the pounding noises of steam engines. "This place is nearly as busy as Oxford Street."

"And the urgency to unload wares is the same, only in much greater quantities," Benjamin added.

Her eyes sparkled with excitement. "Now I understand why my father always says that the port is London's *raison d'être*."

Three- and four-mast barques—big, stable West Indian ships—were lined up close to each other. The entire dock was on a peninsula, the Isle of Dogs, surrounded on three sides by a wide bight in the Thames. Thirty years ago, the West India Docks were built as part of the first commercial harbor installation in London separate from the river, with two large basins that could accommodate a total of six hundred boats and were connected to the Thames by a sophisticated system of canals.

"Here, on the east side, is the entrance and exit passage for the ships," Benjamin explained to Sibylla. "First, they go to the import dock to unload their freight. Then they go on to the export dock to take new freight on board, and then on to a wider canal to head out into the world."

"How marvelous to think that, thanks to these ships, people all over England are able to enjoy coffee, tea, and sugar from the Caribbean."

Benjamin nodded absentmindedly, his mind back on the young woman's letter. "Surely it must have been very urgent news that prompted a respectable young lady to set foot in this place?"

"Nicely put, but still much too inquisitive, don't you think?" she retorted.

Miffed, he turned his attention to some gulls fighting over a dead fish and missed Sibylla's amused glance. She looked at him sitting there sulkily, leather briefcase cradled against his chest. His face was pleasant, if a bit soft. His eyebrows and eyelashes were fair, his eyes light blue, his lips small, and his nose rather long and protruding. He was clean shaven with neat sideburns, an impeccably knotted cravat, and highly polished shoes, all of which suggested a penchant for luxury and vanity.

Some of her previous suitors had attempted to treat her like a child. Others had offered advice and, when she did not obey, retracted it in indignation. One had even acted impudently with her, and she had boxed his ears. It had been this questionable candidate who spread the rumor that Sibylla Spencer wanted to control the men in her life.

Ever since leaving the Lady Eleanor Holles School for Young Ladies at sixteen, Sibylla had been expected to marry and start a family. No one seemed to take into account her wishes, which were to experience life in all its richness and to see the world's wonders with her own eyes. Left to her own devices, she would not marry for a long time. But she was twenty-three now and almost all of her friends were married with their own children while she was still at home, living by the same rules as her sixteen-year-old half brother, Oscar. She was well aware of the fact that an unmarried woman was treated the same as a child. Perhaps marriage was indeed the only way to win more freedom.

She guided her carriage past the eastern gate to the docks to get behind the wall surrounding the entire area.

"This letter is from my half brother, Oscar," she began without prompting. "He says that he's going to be able to play in the cricket match against Harrow on Sunday after all. He's been working very hard to be able to do this. And now he wants us to stand on the side of the field and cheer him on, of course."

"Of course," Benjamin echoed. Though flattered that Sibylla had shared the content of the letter after all, he could not make out why this message was important enough to warrant her urgent trip.

"I could have waited until this evening to tell Father the news, it's true," she continued. "But we have all wished so fervently for Oscar to make it onto the team. As a child, he was weak and so often ill that Father feared seeing his company without an heir. And besides," she said, with a mischievous smile, "I was in the mood for a little adventure."

At a click of her tongue, the mare picked up speed. In no time, they had left behind the fire station, the barrel makers, rope makers, and cabinet makers, the passenger waiting area, the wood merchants' offices, a blacksmith's, and the stables for the workhorses, and arrived at the ledger house. The building housing the offices and administration of the West India Dock Company was a striking edifice, with its yellow and maroon bricks and shiny copper roof. It held not only the conference room for the partners, but also a writing room, a canteen, and offices for harbor police and dock security. There was a group of gentlemen standing under the arches, engaged in intense discussion. While Sibylla recognized several members of the dock association, she did not see her father.

One waved animatedly as he rushed over. "Dear Miss Spencer, what on earth are you doing here? Your family is well, I hope? Surely nothing has happened at home?" He scowled at Benjamin as though he were to blame.

"Everything is fine," Sibylla replied curtly. "Is my father still here?"

The man shook his head. "I'm afraid not. He has gone to the dock to ensure that we have enough warehouse space for the merchandise coming in from Morocco. I can send a messenger, if you'd like."

"Many thanks, but I'll go myself." Sibylla clicked her tongue and the mare began to pull. As they reached the west gate of the docks, she turned to Benjamin. "Would you like me to let you off anywhere in particular?"

Benjamin responded with a look of indignation. "Surely you don't think I would leave you alone? Your father would have my head!"

The day laborers who gathered outside the gate every morning looking for work as porters were long gone. In their place stood several horses and carts waiting to be admitted. As Sibylla joined the line, her gaze wandered over the large memorial plaque on the wall, commemorating the founding fathers of the dock association. It filled her with pride when she recognized the name of her grandfather, Horatio Spencer, one of the men who, at the end of the previous century, had realized their vision of the largest dock installation in England with boundless patience and foresight, and in the face of great financial risk.

The guard at the gate stared at Sibylla and her elegant little gig in disbelief, but when he recognized Benjamin, he gave a quick nod and waved them through. Before them lay a long street. To the right was the harbor basin, in which so many ships lay anchored that Sibylla wondered how in the world they didn't constantly ram into one another. To the left were the warehouses, five-story brick buildings with ramps, cargo hatches, and rope hoists.

"The heaviest wares, such as barrels of rum, are stored at the bottom, above that, the sacks of coffee and sugar or bales of cotton, and at the very top are the lightest deliveries, normally spices. A total of nine warehouses are filled with merchandise from the import dock. At the moment, two of them are being leased to the East India Company, which uses them to store tea," explained Benjamin.

The dock was bustling. Sibylla caught snippets of all the languages of the world, and barrels rumbled over the cobbles. Workers in shirtsleeves pushed carts laden with bulging brown jute sacks back and forth between the pier and the warehouses, and the metal chains of the massive cranes rattled and squeaked. A group of flaxen-haired sailors disembarked, laughing and singing, from a ship bearing the flag of the kingdom of Denmark. The next boat over, an officer was bellowing in Portuguese at some dark-skinned sailors as they scrubbed the deck. There were dozens of barrels set along the pier, waiting for transport. The air smelled of pine tar, sticky-sweet rum, and fishy, brackish water.

Sibylla would have loved to take in every detail, but she had her hands full trying to calm her horse. The mare was overwhelmed by the great number of smells, the relentless noise, and the flurry of activity. She snorted, pricked her ears, and made several attempts to bolt.

"Fear not, Mr. Hopkins. I've got her under control!"

"Thank the good Lord," Benjamin muttered as he clutched the armrest.

Finally settling her horse, Sibylla noticed a crane lifting a pallet with a half dozen sacks of coffee, and asked, "How long does it take for them to unload a ship?"

"Well, a great West Indiaman holds nearly five hundred tons, if not more. It takes four days at most to unload. When cargo traffic was still handled in the river, it used to take weeks."

"Which would drive up the cost of the merchandise," noted Sibylla. "Plus, there's no protective wall along the Thames to keep away thieves."

"Why, Miss Spencer, how extraordinary."

She gave him another of her mocking looks. "So surprised, Mr. Hopkins? Am I to deduce that you think me incapable of such acumen?"

He laughed awkwardly. "You must admit that business is not the usual sort of thing to interest a young lady."

"I daresay that you, Mr. Hopkins, have no idea what a young lady might be interested in," she replied, looking at him with one eyebrow raised.

This time, Benjamin was unable to withstand her piercing gaze and turned swiftly away. "Oh, I see the *Queen Charlotte* up there! She arrived this morning and I have to check the cargo," he tried to declare firmly, blushing when his voice cracked like a boy's. "But first I shall take you to your father. Warehouse three is directly across and so you can leave your carriage here. I shall get one of the workers to mind it for you."

Sibylla looked in the direction Benjamin was pointing and saw a splendid ship. Her two broad and massive quarterdecks, intricately carved and colorfully painted, towered over the harbor basin.

"What, no figurehead, no naked mermaid?" she asked, looking at Benjamin provocatively.

Again, he felt the perspiration starting to build under his shirt, but controlled himself. "If there is one, then it would be in the front at the bow. Shall we go and look?"

Instead of answering, she smiled, leaned back, and took in the sight of the three sky-high masts with their rigging pulled and their crow's nests at dizzying heights. Suddenly, a stubbly man appeared next to them and barked, "Why don't you do your gawking somewhere else? We're trying to unload here!"

Sibylla clicked her tongue and urged her skittish horse on. This time, they stopped by the long, thin gangplank of the *Queen Charlotte*, which seemed taller the closer they got. Sibylla determined the ship to be no less than one hundred and fifty feet in length. She regarded its broad body, carved from dark wood, its sturdy and well-fortified appearance. The six cannon barrels pointing straight in Sibylla's direction only enhanced this impression.

"That's Nathaniel Brown up there. He's the captain," Benjamin said, pointing to a broad-shouldered man wearing the Spencer Company's navy blue coat and a black bicorne over his brow.

Sibylla took a good look at the man. His features were harsh and weathered, betraying no emotion. He stood at the railing, watching intently as another net full of rum barrels hung in midair on its way from the *Queen Charlotte* to the pier.

Benjamin cleared his throat. "We should try to find your father. I'll ask one of the men to mind your carriage for a mo—"

"Watch out!" Captain Brown shouted as he leaned over the railing. "Get away from there! Quickly!"

Chapter Two

Richard Spencer and two other gentlemen stepped out of warehouse three. One of them was the deputy chairman, second in command of the West India Dock Company. The other was an engineer whom Spencer had asked to check whether the warehouse needed any remodeling to ensure that the temperature and humidity required to store grain and leather, the two main imports from Morocco, were appropriate. When the screams began no more than twenty yards from him, Spencer at first paid them no heed. Shouting was commonplace at the docks. But then he squinted with irritation. What the devil was a little gig like that doing at the docks? It was the same kind of lady's carriage his daughter drove!

"What in God's name?"

Two workers were running toward the gig, screaming with all their might and gesturing upward.

Spencer cried desperately, "Sibylla! Look out!" He began to run, knowing it was too late.

At exactly that moment, Benjamin heard the net creak. What he saw took his breath away. The hoist of the crane hovered almost directly above them, and from its massive hook dangled a full net. It contained six barrels, each made to hold one hundred liters of rum and each as tall as a grown man's hip. Suddenly, the net jolted and tilted dangerously to one side. Benjamin realized that at least two of the overly taut ropes had already snapped. He was gripped with fear.

"Let's go!" he bellowed, leaning toward Sibylla and trying to wrest the reins from her. "Go!"

That's when the top two barrels slipped from the net. They came down on the pavement directly next to the gig with a deafening crash. Wood splintered and rum splashed all over the pier. Sibylla cried out, the horse bolted, and Benjamin only just avoided being thrown out into the narrow space between the ship and pier. The gig flew up the gangway on one wheel and briefly became airborne before coming down hard and sliding over the pier wall. It was only the side of the *Queen Charlotte* that prevented carriage, horse, and passengers from landing in the harbor basin. Sibylla yanked on the reins and leaned all the way back. But the spooked mare fought her. The iron of the axle grated on the stone and caused sparks to fly as they careened along the quay wall. Sibylla again pulled on the reins, but by now they had left the ship's wall behind and tipped closer to the harbor basin. As Benjamin lost his balance, Sibylla cried out and reached for him. The reins slipped from her hands, and Sibylla and Benjamin plunged headlong into the water.

The water was cold and painful as it swallowed Sibylla. Flailing toward the surface, she felt her right foot come in contact with something soft. Benjamin, perhaps? She was surrounded by slimy green water. She kicked vigorously, but her coat and ample petticoats threatened to drag her down. Her lungs ready to burst, she feared a pitiful death by drowning. Fear giving her strength, Sibylla kicked free of some of the heavy fabric and finally broke through the surface.

"Help!" she gasped. "Help! I can't swim!"

Wet strands of hair covered her face and eyes. In her effort to move them aside, she again went under and began to swallow the fetid, brackish water. All of a sudden, someone was pulling her up by her hair. She emerged, gagging and spitting.

"Stop kicking, damn it!" she heard Benjamin's voice. "Otherwise we'll both drown."

He had one hand under her chin to keep her above water and his other was moving them both toward the quay. He moved with excruciating slowness, hampered not only by her weight but that of his own soaked clothing. Yet Sibylla's breathing became calmer. She could see papers from Benjamin's folder, the ink running off in rivulets before going under. And over there was her hat, dancing in the swill. Green algae had managed to wrap itself around the brim like some malicious decoration. The figurehead of the *Queen Charlotte* seemed to be mocking her.

She heard excited voices above and made out her father and one of his terrified associates standing at the edge of the pier. And she also saw the petrified crane operator, a worker, and Captain Brown. A few sailors had been following the drama, hanging over the ship's railing. One shouted, "That's the newest way to catch mermaids!"

The insolent remark snapped the captain out of his shocked trance. "What the devil are you gawking at?" he bellowed. "Off with you, get to work! Go and scrub the decks! I want them clean enough to eat off!"

The smirking men slinked away.

Meanwhile, Benjamin had reached one of the many iron ladders along the quay wall and pushed Sibylla toward its rungs. She climbed as fast as her wet clothing would allow, reassured by the fact that Benjamin was right behind her. When she had reached the top, she felt indescribable relief at finally being on terra firma again.

Her father's face was ashen as he took Sibylla in his arms and wrapped his coat around her shoulders. "What on earth are you doing here, child?" he asked in disbelief.

"It was because of Oscar," she whispered, feeling ridiculous. "I wanted to tell you about his match on Sunday."

Richard looked at her incredulously for a moment. "That's why you came to the harbor? Are you quite . . . ?"

Cognizant of the curious listeners all around, he did not complete the sentence. Yet his admonition stung. Even though she had mere moments ago been in serious danger of drowning, still her father wasted no time in finding fault.

Sibylla looked around and was relieved to see one of the workers caring for her mare, who had managed to avoid taking a plunge. Even the gig looked to be intact, if a bit scratched.

Benjamin joined them on the pier. Water dripped from his coat, there was algae clinging to his shirt collar, and those carefully polished shoes were ruined.

Spencer pressed Benjamin's right hand. "You saved my daughter. I am deeply in your debt, Mr. Hopkins."

Benjamin bowed. "Any gentleman would have done the same, sir," he said, the cold of the harbor water making his teeth chatter.

Sibylla was unable to suppress a smile. "My heartfelt thanks to you as well, Mr. Hopkins."

"Are you well, Miss Spencer? Do you need a doctor?"

She shook her head. "I am not hurt, thank you. I'm afraid I did hit the water rather hard, but it's likely no more than a few bruises." She sneezed.

"If all you get is a cold, you'll be lucky, silly girl," her father grunted. He waved over a dockworker and pressed a few coins into his hand. "Take two uniforms to warehouse three. Sibylla, you will have to be content wearing men's garb until you get home."

He placed his arm around his daughter and bade Benjamin to follow. "Come with us, Hopkins! We'll find some sacks of coffee behind which you can dry yourselves and dress yourselves."

"I'll follow in just a moment, sir," Benjamin said as he pulled out his handkerchief to wipe some algae from his shoes.

"Some nets just tear at the right moment, hey, Hopkins?" he heard someone say behind him.

Benjamin looked over his shoulder and saw Nathanial Brown, captain of the *Queen Charlotte*, looking at him with his cold black eyes.

"What do you mean? Did you have something to do with this?" Benjamin instinctively stepped away.

"Quite a clever way to cover up our little business, don't you think?"

Benjamin gasped. "You almost killed us, damn it!"

Nathaniel Brown smiled disdainfully. "Is it my fault that you turn up at the wrong moment with the owner's daughter? If you're smart, you'll report to Spencer that all six of the barrels fell and were broken."

"All six?" Benjamin looked at the crane. "But it was only—"

"Six, you idiot! Two plus the four we unloaded on the Thames earlier. Spencer will never notice. He was so preoccupied with his daughter that he never even looked at the nets."

Benjamin looked around nervously. But Richard Spencer and his daughter had long since disappeared into the warehouse.

He and Brown had a long history of cheating the shipping company in petty ways. They'd make a few barrels of rum or sacks of sugar, or maybe a few sacks of tobacco or coffee, disappear while the ship was still on the river, and then sell the goods illegally. Benjamin would simply tell Spencer that the missing merchandise was rotten, damaged, or had gone overboard at sea.

"You'd better run along behind your master like a good spaniel, Hopkins." Brown laughed. "Collect your reward."

Benjamin shot him a look of annoyance, then headed for warehouse three.

"Who would have thought the two of us would go not only for a ride today but a swim as well?" Benjamin called a few minutes later, drying his hair behind a stack of brown sacks.

"This situation seems to amuse you to no end, Mr. Hopkins. I prefer to bathe at home in clean, warm water." Sibylla's head appeared from behind a wall of bulging burlap sacks labeled *dos Santos—Café da melhor qualidade*.

"So a dip in the harbor basin was not the little adventure you had hoped for?" Benjamin quipped, encouraged by her teasing tone.

Sibylla's eyes roamed the large hall in search of her father. In vain. She began to examine Benjamin. His body, though concealed up to his waist by coffee, was bare. His shoulders were narrow, his skin pale, and his wet hair thin. His appearance in no way aroused in her the consuming desire experienced by the heroines of the romance novels she occasionally borrowed from her stepmother.

She sneezed again. "There is a draft in here," she stated, turning away from Benjamin and stuffing her wet hair under the bowler hat a dockworker had brought her along with a striped flannel shirt; a pair of rough-textured, dark blue cotton pants; and an oversized pair of boots.

"The air has to circulate," Benjamin explained, pointing to the louvered windows. "Light and warmth spoil coffee and destroy its aroma."

Richard had taken them to the second floor of warehouse three and sent all of the workers outside. Having assured himself that his daughter and Benjamin were not changing clothes behind the same sacks of coffee, he had walked to the other end of the hall, which measured at least one hundred feet in width and twenty feet in depth, in order to inspect a new delivery.

Sibylla bent over to try to lace up the heavy boots. Benjamin, now dressed, stepped out from behind his stack. "It would be an honor for me to assist you, Miss Spencer."

She hesitated at first, but then accepted his offer with a smile. "That's very kind, thank you."

He heaved a sack onto the floor for her to sit on, then kneeled before her. His fingers did not touch her as he got to work, and yet this action seemed much more intimate than earlier in the harbor basin, when he had held her above water.

"There is still some algae in your hair," he said softly.

"Where?" she asked, just as softly.

"Here." He reached up and pulled it from the strand of wet hair that had slipped out from under the hat.

"Ahem." Richard was standing behind them.

Benjamin scrambled to his feet.

Richard looked his daughter over with a furrowed brow. "You look frightful! I will have the cover put up on the carriage for your ride home lest someone recognize you."

But she did not look frightful to Benjamin at all. At first glance, she might have been mistaken for a man. Her soft features, however, betrayed her indisputable femininity. His heart began to beat faster as he rushed to help his boss into his coat.

All the rustling of papers and scratching of pens at the shipping company's counting house came to a stop the moment Benjamin stepped over the threshold. Fifteen unabashedly curious pairs of eyes took in the sight of his peculiar getup.

Benjamin smiled. He'd always rather liked being the center of attention.

"What happened? Why are you dressed like that? Where is Miss Spencer?"

Benjamin stopped the questions with a wave of his hand. He relished keeping his coworkers in suspense and knew the tale of his adventure was sure to spread like wildfire anyway. This way, he'd appear a hero to his coworkers and the soul of discretion to the Spencers.

At last, Donovan, ever proper, admonished everyone to get back to work and leave Hopkins alone.

It was with some reluctance that the buyers and scribes, bookkeepers, and clerks finally returned to work.

The door to the counting house opened and Richard Spencer stuck his head in. "Hopkins, would you please come into my office for a minute? Donovan, have two cups of tea sent in."

The boss's office was a large square room. In front of the window stood a desk with an inkwell, pens, folders, and a gas-powered desk lamp, rather than one of the old oil lamps in the office next door. The boss also worked seated comfortably at his desk instead of standing like his clerks. The walls were lined with shelves filled with documents and scrolls of paper containing ship designs and, on one wall, there was a cabinet, secured with three locks, in which money and important documents were kept. A simple rectangular table with four chairs stood in one corner.

From the workshops in the courtyard below, muffled voices, hammering, and sawing could be heard.

There was a knock. An apprentice entered, placed a tea tray on the table, poured the steaming brew, and was gone.

"Please, be seated," said Spencer, motioning to the table. He was an imposing man, with his meticulously trimmed salt-and-pepper beard and a corpulence bespeaking a fondness for fine food and wine. His eyes were clear and penetrating under their bushy brows.

Benjamin happily obeyed. This, after all, was the first time in thirteen years' employment that he had been invited to tea with the boss.

Spencer stirred his tea several times, took a sip, and came straight to the point. "How many barrels did we lose today?"

"Six, sir," Benjamin replied anxiously. But seeing Spencer nod, he ventured to add that the insurance company would surely compensate them for the loss.

"Excellent, Hopkins, excellent." Spencer seemed well pleased. "Go ahead and add the four barrels we lost from the *Unicorn* last year. What are we paying such horrendous premiums to those cutthroats for, anyway?"

Benjamin nodded but wondered about the real reason he had been summoned. Had there been too many losses in recent months? But he was taken unawares by what Richard Spencer said next.

"My son is taking part in his first cricket match next Sunday."

"Your daughter had mentioned it, sir."

Spencer cleared his throat. "Ah. So you know. Very good. Then perhaps you will join us at St. John's Wood on Sunday and cheer the boy on. I'm sure my daughter would be pleased to see you."

"It would be my honor, Mr. Spencer!" Benjamin shot out of his chair to take a bow. "It would be a great honor to see your charming daughter again."

Spencer emptied his cup. "That's settled, then. See you on Sunday."

Chapter Three

St. John's Wood, June 1835

Benjamin Hopkins watched Sibylla, who looked very pretty in a cornflower blue dress, noticing how the color brought out her eyes. The blonde hair visible under her hat was coiffed in tight ringlets and the hat was secured with a coquettish side bow. The ladies with their parasols, colorful dresses, and patterned silk scarves resembled birds of paradise, and the gentlemen in their dark dress coats, top hats, and long slender pants seemed very elegant.

Three thousand Londoners had assembled at the cricket ground at St. John's Wood in Regent's Park on that warm Sunday in June in order to attend the most important social event of the season: the annual cricket match between Eton and Harrow, the two best schools in the country.

The game had been going since morning, and now Sibylla's younger brother, Oscar, had just scored the winning run for his team. Time for tea.

Looking as proud as any family member, Benjamin stood next to the Spencers and received the congratulations of the other spectators. Today, he was no mere observer of the rich but one of them.

With a smile and a bow, he escorted Sibylla to a picnic area the servants had set up in the shade of an ancient plane tree. There were blankets spread out on the lawn, silverware and crockery on a folding table, and a jug of lavender lemonade and a bowl of fresh strawberries sat prepared. Richard opened the wine and champagne bottles, while Sibylla handed out ham-and-salmon sandwiches and her stepmother, Mary, sliced the cheesecake.

The enjoyment of these delicacies in the open had been made popular by Princess Victoria, and Lord's Cricket Ground, a green oasis right in the middle of London, was excellently suited for it.

"Would you please get the tea, Oscar?" Mary asked.

"Why me? I want to celebrate!" Oscar replied, holding his champagne glass for the servant to fill. He looked sweaty, his white cricket uniform dusty, his hair disheveled, but he was beaming with pride. Having spent the previous year as a substitute, he had not been thought capable of such heroics.

"If you continue guzzling champagne like that, we will have to keep you away from the kerosene cooker," Sibylla teased.

"Says the woman who fell into the harbor," he retorted.

"A piece of rather good fortune, I daresay. For, had I not saved your esteemed sister, I would not be present here today," Benjamin boasted.

"Incredibly good fortune, indeed," Oscar said under his breath. He wondered whether his sister could really like this tall, pale Hopkins or whether he was just another hapless suitor whom she would scare away before long.

"Mr. Hopkins, if I might ask you to take care of the tea, please?" Mary sighed as Sibylla attempted to swat her brother with a napkin. "And, Sibylla, did you bring your father his sandwich?"

Mary had married Richard shortly after Sibylla, then just four years old, lost her mother in a riding accident. She had raised Sibylla and loved her no less than she did her biological son, Oscar. But her gentility had not rubbed off on her stepdaughter. Sibylla was mercurial, quick witted, and difficult to manage. Richard did not approve of her behavior and was constantly trying to rein her in. Yet the older Sibylla became, the harder she fought to make her own decisions.

Mary threw a furtive glance at Mr. Hopkins. Perhaps, she thought, he might be a husband for Sibylla at last.

She did have her misgivings, though. Richard had shared with her that Hopkins came from an honorable but humble background, and she knew well that a man who rose in society as a result of his marriage was rarely taken seriously.

A business associate approached Richard and clapped him on the shoulder. "What a splendid son you have there, Spencer! Someone who can truly follow in your footsteps one day."

"That he is," Richard agreed as his face lit up with pride.

Sibylla pursed her lips. Everyone was behaving as though Oscar had just single-handedly defeated Napoleon. But it was just a game, a leisure activity! She immediately regretted her bitterness, though. When she was a girl, she had often played cricket with Oscar in Hyde Park. She had been good, but then her father and Mary deemed it unseemly for a young lady to break into a sweat and scream and pant trying to hit a small ball. Of course, Oscar, not even particularly fond of cricket, was encouraged to practice.

But it was not in Sibylla's nature to give up. If she was not going to be permitted to play cricket, she was going to attract her father's attention by some other means. And today she had a particular kind of surprise in store for him.

"Look, Father," she told him with gleaming eyes as she reached into one of the wicker baskets. "I've grown these myself in the greenhouse."

"Tomatoes?" he asked impatiently. "What for?"

"To eat," she replied and then took a hearty bite out of one of the red fruits.

"What, are you mad?" Richard leapt over, tore the tomato from her hand, and cast it into the bushes. "Spit that out at once! Or do you want to kill yourself, you foolish girl?"

Sibylla's eyes filled with tears as she turned away to spit the piece of tomato into the handkerchief that Mary had quickly handed her.

"They aren't poisonous," she sputtered. "A Colonel Gibbon Johnson has proven that by eating them in public. They're quite palatable, in fact. You could make a lot of money if you sold them, to city dwellers, for instance, because they have no time or space to grow them themselves."

"Nonsense!" Richard said. "And terrible business sense. Even if they weren't poisonous, people would believe they are. It is difficult to eradicate superstition."

"If Oscar had come up with this idea, you would have been thrilled," she replied furiously.

"Enough!" Richard roared. "Stop it with your foolish schemes and adventures. Accept your station in life."

"Richard, please," Mary admonished him quietly, because he had attracted the attention of several people. She signaled Benjamin, standing by the kerosene heater, to start pouring the tea.

"Sibylla, dearest," she began gently. "Won't you pass your father a cup of tea?"

Sibylla obeyed without comment or expression. The festive mood of that summer's day had been dashed. Oscar went off with his teammates to celebrate. Mary's spirits only lifted once two of her lady friends came over to inquire in detail about the young man accompanying Sibylla. Richard had fished the *Times* out of a picnic basket and was studying a report about the progress of the Commercial Railway, set to link the western part of the docks to central London.

Sibylla watched Benjamin, who was reading the label of one of the champagne bottles. Presumably, he wanted to remember the name in order to show off at the next available opportunity. She had been noticing how much he tried to impress her, only she was not sure whether to find this ridiculous or touching.

She sighed softly, then took out the book she had brought along. It was the account of a marvelous journey that an English merchant named Mr. James Curtis had taken to Morocco. He had even been a guest at the sultan's palace.

The ruler's invitation had been discussed at length in the Spencer office. Richard, gleeful at the thought of an untapped market, had sent one of his traders, a Mr. Fisher, who had previously worked for Spencer & Son in Algeria, to Mogador. To Sibylla, the very idea of an exotic country like Morocco was thrilling. She would have loved to be in Mr. Fisher's place, but she was well aware that was out of the question. So she had gone to Lackington, Allen and Company, a large bookseller in Finsbury Square, and purchased not only James Curtis's but also James Grey Jackson's travelogue, as well as a translated edition of *One Thousand and One Nights*.

She became so engrossed in Curtis's description of the colorful bazaar in Tangier that she forgot all about her quarrel with her father.

"Might I persuade you to accompany me on a walk around the cricket field, Miss Spencer? Your mother assures me that she would have no objections." Benjamin stood in front of her expectantly.

Sibylla, caught up in her reading, was on the verge of declining his invitation before thinking differently. She would never be able to evaluate Hopkins's potential as a husband who would grant her freedom and value her opinions if she did not afford him an opportunity. She closed her book and flashed a radiant smile. "With the greatest pleasure, Mr. Hopkins. Would you be so kind as to help me up? My legs have grown stiff from sitting."

"But of course!" Benjamin quickly offered her his arm.

"Do you believe that this time it will come to anything?" Richard asked his wife, watching the pair walk away arm in arm.

Mary smiled dreamily. "We should allow them the opportunity to find that out for themselves."

London, February 1836

"We make a beautiful couple, my love. Everyone who sees us together says so." Benjamin stood behind Sibylla in the hallway of their home and smiled at his reflection in one of the full-length crystal mirrors.

It was thrilling being able to visit the high-end tailors, hatters, and glove makers, and order whatever one's heart desired, then simply have the invoice sent to *Hopkins, Stanhope Gate* in the exclusive Mayfair district.

Benjamin had managed to acquire quite an impressive new wardrobe in the ten weeks he'd been married to Sibylla. Each time yet another package was delivered, Sibylla would tease that they would soon need to build an addition to the house in order to accommodate everything.

Now, too, she was looking at him archly. "Could it be that I have mistakenly married a peacock?"

Benjamin smiled uneasily. He wasn't fond of her teasing because he could never be sure if it was meant to be loving or derisive. But he was very fond indeed of being able to count himself among the rich. Many people exhibited a new reverence for him. He had his own office and his former coworkers tried nearly as hard to please him as they did the boss.

That evening, he and Sibylla were going to visit Sibylla's parents. Richard Spencer had invited a special guest to dinner, a Scotsman by the name of Liam Moffat, who had traveled to North Africa on behalf of the Royal Geographical Society of London. Richard was keenly interested in any information that might affect his trade with Morocco.

"Your carriage is here, sir," the butler announced.

Benjamin placed Sibylla's cape over her shoulders. He arranged the collar and nodded with satisfaction when her amethyst necklace sparkled in the light from the wall sconces. Even though it was just a family dinner, he had insisted on selecting her gown and jewelry. She had humored him to a point because his childlike delight in luxury amused her, but when he had tried to instruct her maid on her hairstyle, she had protested, saying, "You are treating me like a doll. I don't even recognize myself anymore!" His face had been so crestfallen that she regretted her objection at once.

It was the same look he'd given her that June afternoon at Lord's Cricket Ground when he asked permission to call on her soon and she hesitated. They had not discovered many things in common during their walk. Sibylla feared that, if married, they would live parallel lives. Then she remembered the unpleasant quarrel with her father and felt a renewed determination to break out of her circumscribed existence.

"I would be delighted if you came to call," she'd said, and Benjamin's bright smile had eased her doubts.

In August, he had asked for her hand. In December, when they were married, the one thing that Sibylla knew for sure was that she did not love him.

Benjamin seemed to her like a boy in a giant toy shop allowed to choose whatever he liked. They had been married in the elegant St. George's in Hanover Square, although Sibylla would have preferred a modest ceremony in a simple church. He had compiled a very long guest list, which she would dearly have loved to reduce by half. And yet she could not find his parents' names anywhere.

He had been very embarrassed when she pointed it out, hemming and hawing, saying that they lived very private lives and did not take pleasure in lavish fetes.

"Are you ashamed of your parents? Don't you even want to invite them?"

Benjamin had fallen silent, his face a deep red. Sibylla ended the conversation by adding his parents to the list and telling him that, if they were honorable people, she would be happy to welcome them.

Sibylla would never forget that moment. It revealed much about the character of her future husband and so, while Benjamin was busy choosing menus, engaging musicians, and hiring a dance instructor to teach him the Viennese waltz, Sibylla asked her father to place her dowry in a trust. It was a rare occasion when she and he were of the same mind. A trust was the only way for a woman to retain the fortune she brought into her marriage. Otherwise, every penny went to the husband.

It took them ten minutes to get from Stanhope Gate to Sibylla's parents' at Hamilton Place. It was snowing, and the cold dampness crept through the cover of the landau in which they rode. Sibylla snuggled into her fur blanket, which Benjamin had carefully tucked in around her. It was gestures such as these, unexpected and rare as they were, that made her feel a fondness for him. Had it not been for the blanket and a coal pan provided by the butler, she would surely have frozen to death in her silk evening gown and thin satin shoes.

She leaned her head back and listened to the steady beat of the horses' hooves. Park Lane was almost deserted. People did not leave the warmth and comfort of their homes without good reason in weather like this. The snow was now accompanied by a dense fog. Pea soup, Londoners called the impenetrable fog that rose up from the Thames and mixed with the sulfurous smoke of countless fires.

They arrived at her parents' house, an elegant white building with pillars on each side of the black, lacquered entrance.

"I can't wait to hear what Mr. Moffat has to say," Sibylla gushed, stepping out of the carriage. "I have already read so much about the Orient, but how much more exciting it will be to hear a first-hand account."

"I just hope it doesn't get around that I'm married to a genuine bluestocking," Benjamin replied with a shake of his head, thinking of the books and magazines stacked on Sibylla's nightstand. "The gentlemen at the club might begin to think that I'm henpecked."

Once they had entered the house and been welcomed by Sibylla's parents, Richard whispered to Benjamin, "Hopkins, I must have a quick word with you."

Liam Moffat had arrived just behind them. While Mary and Sibylla were greeting the guest of honor, Richard pulled his son-in-law into a corner of the dining room.

"I'm afraid I've had some bad news. Our man in Mogador has died. It appears he fell victim to a typhus epidemic." Richard pulled out an envelope and handed it to Benjamin.

"It's very bad for us, indeed," he continued as Benjamin scanned the letter. "Considering all we have spent on the gifts for the sultan and his court alone just to ensure our business goes smoothly. And now this!"

"We must quickly send someone in his stead," Benjamin agreed. "Our ventures in Morocco have been going so well. It would be a terrible pity if we had to pull out."

The butler opened the dining room's double doors and Liam Moffat entered with Mary on one side and Sibylla on the other.

"Why have you two been huddling together?" Sibylla whispered as Benjamin took her arm.

"Your father has just informed me that our commercial agent in Mogador has died."

She looked at him pensively. "So we need someone to take over the business there."

A fire crackled in the marble fireplace. A large rug lay on the hardwood floor. Chandeliers hung from the ceiling and crystal mirrors graced the walls. The long rosewood dining table was surrounded by delicate chairs on slender legs. The food was arrayed around a splendid silver centerpiece. There was carrot-and-potato soup with parsley, turbot fresh from Billingsgate, cutlets and game pie, French cheese, and exotic fruit for dessert. Benjamin served Sibylla, and Mr. Moffat insisted on serving the hostess.

"Of course, compared to this sumptuous meal, my fare in Morocco was rather plain. I would live for days on nothing but dates, flatbread, and goat cheese," Mr. Moffat commented.

"I so wish I could see the places you have visited with my own eyes!" Sibylla said.

"I am quite sure that an intelligent and energetic woman like yourself can realize such a plan," Moffat replied chivalrously.

"And I suppose you wouldn't mind assisting my wife in implementing this plan," Benjamin nearly spat.

Sibylla looked up in surprise. It was the first sign of jealousy her husband had shown.

Moffat inclined his head. "*Inshallah*, as they say in the Orient: if God wills it."

Benjamin's face began to blaze, and Mary quickly took over. "Please, Mr. Moffat, do share some of your adventures with us."

While the Scotsman was talking, Benjamin leaned over and hissed in Sibylla's ear, "What a showoff!"

Moffat was a cartographer and land surveyor whom the Royal Geographical Society had sent to Morocco at the behest of Sultan Moulay Abd al-Rahman because the Alaouite ruler wished to modernize his country. By collecting data on boundary lines, river valleys, mountain ranges, oases, and deserts, Moffat had made the mysterious country in northwest Africa somewhat more accessible to foreigners. Richard wanted to know all there was to know about trade goods and natural resources, and Sibylla was captivated by the description of the old caravan routes that led through the Sahara from the Mediterranean to Timbuktu.

When Moffat reported that some of the most important items being traded in the country were slaves taken from the heart of the continent, the table grew quiet. Richard's father, Horatio, had founded the family shipping company with funds derived from the slave trade. His captains had used glass beads and colorful cotton cloth to buy young men and women from local tribal chiefs along the coast of Guinea and sold them to sugar plantations in the Caribbean. Horatio had been a respected businessman at the time, but no one spoke openly of this blood debt anymore. The slave trade had been outlawed in England for almost thirty years now.

"What happens to the Africans who end up as slaves in Morocco?" Sibylla finally asked.

"Many of the men become soldiers. Some become farmworkers, and the ablest among them gain influential positions at the sultan's court. Many become domestic servants, but the most beautiful women are sold into harems."

Mary's eyes grew wide. She had learned about harems in her novels. "Did you ever visit such a place, Mr. Moffat?"

He shook his head. "That would surely have cost me my life. No stranger is allowed to see a Moor's women."

"So one must acquire one's own harem to find out how it works." Benjamin chuckled, swirling his wine.

Richard, seeing that Benjamin was ready to launch into cruder remarks, shifted the topic back to business. "As you know, our commercial agent in Mogador has passed away. Do you know anyone who could be entrusted with that post?"

"I'm sorry, but I'm afraid the local British consul is in a much better position to help you with such matters."

Richard furrowed his brow. "I fear it'll take us a good six months before we're back in business."

"But, Father, we already have someone for Mogador," Sibylla announced, placing her hand on Benjamin's arm. "My husband."

Chapter Four
Mogador, early May 1836

"Why, it's like we never left London." Benjamin peevishly handed the binoculars back to Captain Brown. According to Captain Brown, the *Queen Charlotte* was within striking distance of Mogador's harbor, but dense fog obscured everything.

The captain placed the binoculars in his pocket. "Like I've been tellin' ya. Foggy a lot along the coast here. The Canary Current cools the Atlantic air and the result is this damned mess."

"Captain, we've been anchored out here for two days now. How much longer can this last?" Sibylla stood at the railing between Brown and her husband, fighting the impulse to retch. She'd been battling a debilitating case of seasickness ever since coming aboard at the end of March.

"It's clearing. We'll reach port today."

Surprised, she and Benjamin followed his outstretched arm and were able to make out a thin tower through the swirling curtain of fog.

"Minaret on the big mosque," Brown explained. "Only thing that can stop us now is a northwest trade wind. But I should think a British West Indies sailor can handle it!"

"The wind is strong here, but nothing like those storms in the North Sea." Sibylla shivered as she recalled the first days of their voyage.

Brown laughed. "Well, if you can't handle a bit of a breeze, you're in the wrong place. Mogador's windy year-round. Excuse me, I best speak with my helmsman if we're to get the *Queen* to port in one piece." He gave a brief bow and hurried away.

The next wave came and the ship bucked like a horse. Sibylla retched and clutched Benjamin's right hand.

"You ought to go and lie down in the cabin."

She shook her head vehemently. "Absolutely not. I have spent the entire journey there, with the exception of the time ashore in Lisbon when we had to wait for the wind to change."

"I had thought it would be much hotter here, so close to the Sahara," said Benjamin. "But spring in England is just as mild, only with more rain."

Again, the ship lurched in the strong swell. Sibylla closed her eyes in resignation.

In the night, the watchman's yells had roused her from restless sleep. She had heard orders being shouted, the sound of boots tromping across the deck, and shrill whistles. After two days at anchor, the ship had finally begun to move again, only not forward, as expected. Instead, it seemed to go in circles. Benjamin, worried, had hurried on deck to find out what the matter was and returned to the cabin to tell her that the anchor chain had broken; they had ended up on a shoal and were now spinning in an eddy. Only he had not been able to finish explaining all this to Sibylla, who had begun vomiting again into the bowl that was always next to her bunk. At least by dawn the *Queen Charlotte* was once more securely anchored by means of a spare chain.

Sibylla heard a loud screech above her head. Two seagulls had alighted on the yardarm of the foremast. The curtain of fog was thinning above their white heads, and she caught a promising glimpse of blue sky.

"Could you ever have imagined actually being here so soon when Mr. Moffat first came to dinner?" she asked Benjamin.

Richard Spencer had expressed no objections to Sibylla's suggestion that he send Benjamin to Mogador. On the contrary, he had wanted him to depart as soon as possible.

However, Richard had been categorically opposed to the idea of Sibylla accompanying her husband. He had only reluctantly given his consent once Moffat assured him that many European ladies lived with their husbands in the foreigners' quarter, safely separated from the rest of the city.

Sibylla and Benjamin were the only passengers on the *Queen Charlotte*, which was laden with tea, cotton cloth, and hardware. Their London servants, upon hearing that they would henceforth be required to live among Moors, had quit their service. The couple had very little luggage. Sibylla's consisted mainly of boxes of books, among them her copies of *One Thousand and One Nights* and the Koran. Benjamin, for his part, had stocked up on French wine, Scotch whisky, and smoked ham, aware that these delicacies were prohibited in a Muslim country. Knowing they would be moving into Mr. Fisher's already-furnished house, they had brought no furniture, and instead packed an abundance of gifts. The sultan, his court, the tribal chief of Mogador, several sheikhs, and various Arab merchants must all be taken into consideration in the interests of good business.

"That old sea dog was right," Benjamin grumbled. "The fog is lifting. But it remains to be seen if we can make it into the harbor. I wonder if it might not have been wiser to approach from the south."

"I'm confident the captain knows what he's doing better than we. This is not his first time here," Sibylla countered.

The *Queen Charlotte* slowly fought her way forward against the waves. The closer the entrance grew, the narrower it seemed. The heavy ship had to squeeze between the harbor mole on the left and the small Isle of Mogador on the right. Waves crashed against the rocks. A fortress emerged out of the last wafts of fog. Suddenly, the wreckage of a frigate appeared. Sibylla grabbed Benjamin's hand and gave Captain Brown a horrified look. He was standing at the bow next to a sailor, measuring the depth of the water with a plummet. The first officer was on his other side awaiting his orders and shouting them to the helmsman at the stern. It seemed like an eternity to Sibylla, but they finally made it through the narrow passage and saw the harbor of Mogador extend before them like a long, thin crescent. As it was filled with sand, they had to drop anchor at quite a distance from the mole.

"We'll have to change boats." Benjamin pointed to the vessel heading their way from the shore. There was an Arab standing at the stern, shouting one command after another to the twenty black-skinned men rowing in tandem. As the boat came alongside theirs, the first mate shouted an order to lower the ladder.

Sibylla peered down. "He can't be serious."

"I'm afraid he is, dear."

"No!" She grabbed his arm. "I could lose the baby."

He looked at her in disbelief. "What baby?"

She bit her lip. This was not how she had planned to tell him. Her doctor in London had warned her not to embark on the strenuous sea voyage, but she had sworn him to secrecy. She wanted to get to Mogador at all costs, and neither Benjamin nor her doctor was going to stop her.

She had been wanting to inform Benjamin of his impending fatherhood ever since they departed, but kept silent for fear he would send her back from one of the ports where they stopped for provisions along the way.

"We are going to have a baby," she said so softly he could barely hear her above the wind and the waves. "In the fall."

"And when were you planning to tell me? When the midwife was on her way?"

She blushed. "You and Father would never have permitted me to go on this journey had you known! I planned to tell you as soon as we were safely in Mogador."

Benjamin shook his head. After thinking for a bit, he told her, "We're going to do it the way we did it that day at the London docks, only in reverse. I'll climb down first. You follow right behind and hold on to both ropes." She nodded bravely but looked pale.

"Don't be afraid," he reassured her. "It'll be all right."

Half an hour later, they finally reached terra firma. After so many days at sea, Sibylla felt the ground sway under her feet. Still, she was overcome by a feeling of solemnity.

I am in Africa, she thought. *How many English can claim to have been here? I am sure I can count the women on my fingers!*

She looked up to the fortress with its brightly colored flags flapping above the towers and battlements. Mogador—the Blue Pearl of the Atlantic, as the Arabs called it—rose up behind the ramparts. Cube-shaped houses with no more than two stories were lined up close to each other. Their whitewashed walls gleamed in the sunlight. The tall tower of the minaret rose into a sky so blue as to make the recent fog seem like a dream. The national flags of the foreign consulates were hoisted high above the roofs. Seagulls screeched above. The wind tore at Sibylla's dress and tousled her hair. Tiny grains of sand stung her skin.

There were other high-sea ships besides the *Queen*. Sibylla recognized French, American, Spanish, and Prussian ensigns, but compared to the bustling Port of London, they were few. Several smaller boats were berthed at the mole. Fishermen sat along the water's edge, mending their nets. There was also a small wharf where the wooden frame of a fishing boat was being readied. Sibylla noticed a group of men emerging from the darkened arches of one of the massive entrances to the city.

"The welcoming committee," remarked Captain Brown, who had accompanied them to deal with the customs formalities.

At the head of the small troop was an Arab with a carefully trimmed silver beard. He wore a white turban, a white tunic under an open black *burnoose*, and flat slippers. His suntanned face radiated the confidence of a man accustomed to power.

"Is that the *qaid*?" Sibylla wanted to know.

Brown nodded. "A high-level official. One of Morocco's ruling elite, the Makhzen—a frequent visitor to the court."

The other younger Arab, similarly dressed, hung back, as did a man in a black kaftan and turban. The fourth man, a middle-aged European dressed elegantly in a fine tailored suit, stepped forward.

"Welcome to Mogador, Mrs. Hopkins, Mr. Hopkins," he said with a bow. "William Willshire, British consul, at your service. I am accompanied by His Excellency Qaid Hash-Hash, governor of Mogador; his translator, Nuri bin Kalil; and Mr. Philipps, the harbormaster." As he spoke, Willshire gestured to the two Arabs and the man dressed in black.

Sibylla's excitement rose. She had resolved to make the best possible first impression, not merely out of politeness, but for the benefit of her father's business.

She smiled at the *qaid* and said slowly but clearly, "*Assalamu alaikum*, peace be upon you."

Expecting the governor to be delighted at being greeted in his mother tongue, she was shocked when the man looked right past her—as did his translator. Had she somehow offended the *qaid*? She had practiced the greeting so carefully. She turned to Mr. Willshire, who shrugged his shoulders and said quietly, "It is not that His Excellency wishes to offend you, Mrs. Hopkins. Quite the contrary, he would never consider being so disrespectful as to address you or even look at you in the presence of your husband. This is his way of honoring you both."

"Oh," she whispered. Her first faux pas.

Benjamin was annoyed by Sibylla's forwardness. Did she want the governor to think that, in England, women considered themselves the equals of men? He stepped forward with his right hand extended. "My pleasure, Your Excellency. My name is Hopkins, of Spencer & Son."

The governor did not take Benjamin's hand, but he did bow slightly. "*Assalamu alaikum*, Mr. Hopkins." He continued in Arabic. "You have brought us a stiff breeze, as they say at sea. Many a ship has wrecked on our breakwaters. But not the English, kings of the seas."

Bin Kalil translated and the *qaid* smiled at every word. But Benjamin felt slighted nonetheless. He turned and asked the consul, "Why the devil didn't he shake my hand?"

"Well," said Willshire, clearly embarrassed as bin Kalil translated every word. "His Excellency would never touch an infidel."

The *qaid* smiled even more broadly and had the translator tell them, "His Excellency hopes that you will feel at home in Mogador and is looking forward to receiving you in his residence soon."

The two Arabs bowed and returned to the city. Captain Brown went to the customs station with Mr. Philipps and the rest of the group headed for the city gate.

Having overcome her nausea, Sibylla now watched the bustling port with fascination. Just like in London, the harbor here was teeming with sailors. Some loaded and unloaded ships, using the yardarm of the mainmast as a hoist, while others were busy cleaning or carrying out repairs. She could hear hammering and sawing, and she saw sailors filling holes in ships' hulls, restoring broken masts, and mending torn sails. Small rowboats in the harbor basin transported crates and barrels of wares and provisions to be checked by the harbormaster's clerks before disappearing into warehouses or the belly of a ship.

On the other side of the city gate, two adolescent Arab boys held the reins of the donkeys that Mr. Willshire had arranged to transport the new arrivals. Benjamin made a face and muttered that they would look foolish. Exhausted as she was, though, Sibylla was grateful for the opportunity to ride.

They entered the city from the south and rode across the square behind the city gate.

"This gate is called the Bab El Mersa," Mr. Willshire explained. "There are, of course, other entrances to the city. The caravans from the northeast, for instance, enter through the Bab Doukkala because of its easy access to the *souk*."

They passed the *qasbah*, the fortress. Sibylla noticed some cannons on the fortifications and a pair of storks nesting on one of the towers. The birds, busy feeding their young, made Sibylla think of the baby in her belly. Benjamin also spotted the storks and, when his eyes met hers, they smiled at each other.

The *medina* was behind the *qasbah*. Hardly any sunlight reached into the narrow alleys. This form of construction offered protection against the heat of the midsummer sun and the unrelenting wind. Sibylla was surprised by the plainness of the buildings in the *medina*. The walls were unadorned and whitewashed with unwelcoming blue doors without windows. No sounds could be heard from behind the thick walls. She was disappointed, having pictured palm trees and citrus groves, fig trees and fountains. Yet all she saw here were stray cats, children playing on the well-trodden clay, and a few gaunt beggars cowering on the ground. "In God's name, please give me something to eat!"

"Is it just me, or were the streets here drawn with a ruler?" Benjamin remarked.

"You are quite right," Willshire answered. "A French architect designed Mogador on a drafting table seventy years ago. He was the sultan's prisoner, but after his work found favor with his captor, he was allowed to return home."

"And why did the sultan want to build this city?" Sibylla inquired.

"Sidi Mohammed Ben Abdallah, the sultan at the time, wanted to turn Mogador into his country's biggest port. And he was successful!"

The deeper into the *medina* they went, the livelier the alleyways became. Sibylla stared in amazement at the dark-skinned women in colorful garments carrying purchases from the *souk* on their heads as they made their way back to their masters' homes. Arabs were returning from prayers at the mosque, and bearded Jews, with their dark turbans and dusty black kaftans—which, according to Willshire, the sultan required them to wear—hurried past with their heads bowed. The visitors also saw several Berbers, dressed in brown woolen wraps with sables flung over their shoulders. Mr. Willshire told them the Berbers from this region belonged either to the Chiadma or the Haha tribes. The former had settled down, practicing agriculture on the plains, while the latter were nomadic cattle herders in the Atlas region. At times, the tribes waged war against each other.

Mr. Willshire explained that the residences of the European merchants were situated around the governor's palace, not far from the western fortification and the port. Indeed, in no time they stopped in front of one of the plain whitewashed buildings. The open door was guarded by a tall, broad-shouldered black man.

"This is Hamid," the consul said.

Hamid bowed before allowing them to enter a narrow, dimly lit hallway.

Looking to Sibylla, Willshire said, "I trust that you won't object, but my wife had everything cleaned and polished for your arrival. Incidentally, we're your neighbors to your right. The Silvas are to your left: a Portuguese merchant family. We also have some French, Spanish, Dutch, and a few Danish families here. Oh, and there are some Brazilian families. Altogether, we are almost two hundred foreigners, a tight-knit community in a city comprising some ten thousand Arabs and Jews each."

"How do you all communicate?" Sibylla marveled.

Willshire smiled. "We all speak a little bit of everything, mainly English, French, and Spanish. Ah yes, and you should know that your predecessor's servants are still here. You have already met the gatekeeper. There is also a cook, a gardener, and two female servants. The women are former slaves who have worked in various English households and are, therefore, acquainted with our customs and language. But you do owe the servants back pay. They have not been paid since Mr. Fisher's death."

"You mean to say that our servants are not slaves?" Benjamin wanted to know.

Willshire shook his head. "The cook and the gardener are Arabs and, as such, not slaves. The others were freed because the sultan has forbidden foreigners in his country to keep slaves. And as a good Christian, one should not indulge in such barbaric customs anyhow," he added sternly as he led them down the hallway.

Finally, they stepped out into a surprisingly large inner courtyard ringed by a colonnade and several rooms. There was an ornately carved wooden staircase leading to yet another walkway and more rooms above.

Sibylla was enchanted. At last, the Arab garden of her dreams! A shallow basin with a babbling fountain stood in the shade of some orange and lemon trees. The flower beds were bordered by marble pathways. Lizards sunning themselves on the warm stones scurried away as the new tenants approached.

Birds were singing in the trees and delicate violet blossoms climbed up the bannisters.

"This is the *riad* you will call home," said Willshire. "It is excellently suited to this climate. The kitchen wing and several housekeeping rooms are downstairs. The living quarters are upstairs and on the roof is a terrace with a magnificent view of the city and the ocean."

Sibylla whispered, "It is like something out of a fairy tale."

Benjamin, unimpressed, remarked that it lacked the comforts he was accustomed to.

Willshire smiled. "Of course, it lacks the modern conveniences of an English home, but, believe me, the Arabs know a thing or two about comfort. Ah, here comes my wife."

A young woman appeared at one of the doors on the first floor and hurried over. "There you are at last! We've been waiting for days, but that ghastly fog just refused to lift. I'm Sara Willshire. Welcome to Mogador. You look like you could use a glass of tea. I have had it prepared in the Moroccan way, but not to worry, it's delicious!" Sara clapped her hands and a black woman emerged from the house. She was carrying a silver tray with glasses and a teapot that smelled of mint.

Sibylla found it outstanding, but Benjamin said that he would have preferred a cup of good English tea.

"I know exactly how you feel." Sara laughed. "Everything really is very different from dear old England."

Chapter Five

Mogador, mid-May 1836

"Allahu akbar! Ash hadu an la ilaha illallah!"

"Damn caterwauling! They just don't let up, do they?" Benjamin shot up in bed.

Nine days had passed since their arrival in Mogador, and he was exasperated every time he heard one of the *muezzin*'s five daily calls to prayer. Especially the predawn call.

Sibylla too had been awakened, but she was not upset. "At home we have the church bells that ring, and here they have the *muezzin*. They don't seem so different to me."

She stretched out contentedly under the covers and thought about the new, most likely bright and windy day dawning. She couldn't see anything because the windows of their *riad* were small and faced the courtyard. But in the evenings, she enjoyed standing on the flat roof of the house just like the locals and watching the bright orange sun disappear over the western horizon. The days here did not fade gradually. Velvet blue night followed the sunset seamlessly and, once the moon had risen and was surrounded by the brightly shining stars, it seemed to Sibylla much closer than in London.

"This caterwauling—which I sincerely hope you are not comparing to the ringing of church bells—wakes up innocent people before six in the morning. Extremely rude is what I call that!" Benjamin grumbled as he lit a candle, climbed out of bed, and threw on a robe over his nightshirt.

Muttering angrily, he disappeared behind a screen where the wash-stand was. He and Sibylla were using the bedroom previously occupied by Mr. Fisher. Like all the other rooms in the *riad*, it was smaller than those in their London house. While Benjamin slept in Mr. Fisher's small bed, the Willshires had arranged a divan for Sibylla, and she found it reasonably comfortable. Besides the beds, there were several colorfully painted chests and chests of drawers, which looked somewhat out of place next to the heavy English oak armoire from Mr. Fisher's estate. Sibylla had hung mirrors and family portraits, but she did not really feel at home in this hodgepodge of a house.

There was a knock at the door and the housekeeper entered with a pot of steaming tea. She placed it on Sibylla's nightstand and lit one of the oil lamps. Sibylla and Benjamin were still trying to get used to the fact that, unlike in London, there were no gaslights in Mogador. Benjamin disguised his discomfort and homesickness with a bad mood.

"Good morning," the housekeeper said in the melodious English that Sibylla so appreciated. Like every day, she was wearing a dress made of brightly colored cotton tightly wound around her ample hips, a turban covering all of her hair, and heavy gold earrings whose sparkle contrasted beautifully with her ebony skin.

"Thank you, Nadira," said Sibylla, accepting the steaming glass. She had quickly realized how beneficial mint tea was for her morning sickness and made a point to drink it in bed every morning. Benjamin did not like the sweet brew, but he had unearthed some of Mr. Fisher's finest Indian Darjeeling and reserved it for himself.

Nadira bowed and left to set the breakfast table. Sara Willshire had told Sibylla that Nadira did not know her exact age, but as Sibylla observed the housekeeper's smooth face and swift movements, she concluded that Nadira could not be much older than she. And Firyal, the other servant, was even younger.

"I must say, I'm surprised that I have also been asked to the first official visit at the palace today," she said. "After all, Qaid Hash-Hash ignored me quite completely when we arrived, and I cannot imagine that his attitude has changed."

"Perhaps he wants to make up for his discourtesy." Benjamin emerged from behind the screen. He was freshly shaved and had donned his best tailcoat and a burgundy cravat.

"You look very elegant."

"Well, that's because I know what is proper, as opposed to this Moor, who summons us on a Sunday to discuss business."

"As you know, Sunday is a business day here and Friday is a holy day instead," Sibylla calmly replied.

"And Saturday, because that's when the Jews celebrate their Sabbath. No wonder this country's economy is such a mess!" And with that, he was gone.

Sibylla watched him leave, concern evident on her face. Ever since their arrival in Mogador, he had made her feel his discontentment as though it were her fault. He also still held a grudge over her keeping her pregnancy secret for so long. They had not been intimate since boarding the *Queen Charlotte*, and Sibylla longed for some expression of tenderness, even as sparing and clumsy as Benjamin's. She was stung by his rejection whenever she tried to kiss or touch him.

Their wedding night had been disappointingly unemotional. Benjamin had lain on top of her without so much as a kiss or a caress. He had lifted her nightgown only far enough to penetrate her. The process itself had been hasty and painful and left her feeling that something ineffable and awkward now stood between them. Afterward, Benjamin had pulled up his blanket, turned away from her, and fallen asleep. Sibylla, on the other hand, had long lain awake, asking herself what, if anything, she meant to him.

She had read exciting and enigmatic descriptions of lovemaking in the pages of *One Thousand and One Nights*. There were virgins with breasts like pomegranates and fluffy rabbit's fur between their legs. There was mention of tender bites and kisses, of debauched orgies with dozens of male slaves to whom the wives of mighty rulers surrendered as soon as their husbands turned their backs. She had hidden the book under her pillow and read it secretly. And sometimes she caught herself lying in the dark, caressing her round belly and swelling breasts while her husband lay softly snoring in Mr. Fisher's narrow bed.

Breakfast consisted of warm flatbread with syrup, fresh oranges, dates, and a specialty that Nadira called *laban*, goat's milk sprinkled with sugar. Sibylla enjoyed the combination of sweet and acidic flavors. Benjamin had made a face when tasting it for the first time, mumbling something about understanding why Mr. Fisher had died. From then on, he stuck to his imported ham and some flatbread.

"I feel completely isolated from the rest of the world," he complained as Sibylla entered the breakfast room. "The newspapers from England still have not arrived, the spoken language is a mystery to me—not to mention the written language."

"We ought to learn Arabic," suggested Sibylla. "That way we would feel more at home here."

Benjamin stared at her, then broke into laughter. "Why not Hebrew as well while we're at it, so that we can speak with the Jews?"

Mr. Fisher had furnished only a few of the many small rooms in the house: a dining room, an office, a salon, and the one bedroom. The walls of the rooms were painted white like the exterior, some adorned with elaborate Arabic calligraphy. The wooden ceilings were decorated with colorfully painted carvings, and sumptuous carpets with red, blue, and green designs covered the floors.

It is obvious that a bachelor lived here, Sibylla thought as she meandered through the rooms.

Nothing matched, everything seemed lifeless, almost abandoned. But she was sure that, once she had turned the house into a cozy home, Benjamin would begin to feel better. Especially once children's voices filled the now-empty rooms.

Sibylla had chosen a green dress for the visit with the *qaid*. She had read that green was the Prophet's favorite color and hoped to please her host with her choice. Yesterday, she had let out the seams in the waist to accommodate her expanding girth.

Because the governor's palace was no more than a few hundred yards away, they went on foot. The *qaid* had sent his translator to escort them. In addition, Sibylla asked Nadira to accompany her. She felt more at ease in the company of another woman, particularly one familiar with both foreigners and Arabs. Hamid also came along to carry the gift. Sibylla had realized at the last minute that, while they had a carefully chosen gift for the *qaid*, they had overlooked his family.

"Take some of the Indian tea, my lady. People here love tea as much as they do in England," Nadira had suggested.

For the women of the house, Sibylla had plucked some colorful shawls and embroidered handkerchiefs from her chests.

As they walked through the alleyways, passersby and street vendors stared in amazement. Word had gotten out that two new *Engliz*, as they called them, had arrived. Although Sibylla wore a hat, a few blonde curls peeked out, and in no time, curious onlookers came running. A few very bold, giggling children even came up and tried to touch her before being chased away by Nuri bin Kalil.

Sibylla's hair caused quite a stir in Mogador. Benjamin too had blond hair, but it was short and sandy, not as golden as Sibylla's. Nadira had told her that there were some who thought her a *djinna*, a female demon, while others believed her hair color protected her from evil spirits. She was careful to cover it every time she left the house.

The *qaid* lived in the stateliest building in town. The guards stationed in front of the tall, arched gate regarded the visitors with stony expressions, before one deigned to lead them into the front courtyard, which was covered with shiny marble tiles. A wide stone staircase led halfway to the upper floor before splitting in two and rising to a colonnade with exquisitely chiseled columns.

The *qaid* appeared to greet his guests. Sibylla noticed that he was dressed as simply as on the day of their arrival. Only this time, he wore a dagger in a striking silver-studded buckle. His Excellency was accompanied by several Arabs, as well as an older man with round wire-rimmed glasses and the mandatory black attire of the Jews. Nuri bin Kalil introduced the Arabs as the governor's relatives. The Jewish man, called Samuel Toledano, was a *tujjar al-sultan*, a merchant working for His Holiest Majesty Sultan Moulay Abd al-Rahman, explained bin Kalil.

Benjamin, Qaid Hash-Hash, and the relatives bowed and exchanged greetings. The governor gave Sibylla's green dress an interested glance, but then acted as he had done at their first meeting and ignored her. The small group moved to one of the reception rooms, and Benjamin thought it a good time to present his gifts.

"Your Excellency, on behalf of the Spencer & Son Shipping Company, I would like to thank you for the warm welcome to your country and ask you to accept this small token of our appreciation."

He motioned to Hamid, who handed the governor a small package wrapped in silk. Even before bin Kalil had finished interpreting, the *qaid* passed the unopened package to one of the servants.

Sibylla wondered with some irritation if he was disappointed at the gift's size. After all, the silk handkerchief was wrapped around a small leather box containing an expensive gold watch.

Sibylla signaled to her husband to distribute the packages of tea. Once all the gifts had been presented, the *qaid* clapped his hands. A slave entered and beckoned Sibylla and Nadira to follow her.

"Where are we going?"

"Mr. Hopkins's wife will have the honor of welcoming the ladies while the gentlemen discuss business," explained bin Kalil.

Sibylla was stunned. She had been prepared to be ignored, but to be sent away . . .

"His Excellency put our gifts aside so quickly," she said quietly to Nadira as they hurriedly followed the slave. "Do you think that they did not please him?"

"Do not be concerned, my lady," her servant whispered. "It would have been extremely rude for him to open them in the presence of his guests."

Sibylla soon realized that, despite his modest attire, the *qaid* was fond of splendor and luxury. The chambers and corridors were bright and airy, the ceilings adorned with white stucco and the walls tiled with tiny mosaics. The floors were covered with thick silk rugs in vibrant colors, and everywhere there were inviting embroidered cushions and intricately carved coffee tables. Although there were no pictures, Sibylla noticed the variety of weapons on display. Knives, daggers, sabers, and swords in the choicest sheaths made of silver and even gold. Two firearms were displayed in one of the rooms. They were simple shotguns such as Sibylla's father possessed for partridge and rabbit hunting, yet a servant stood guarding them like valuable treasure.

"Now we are leaving the public area of the house," Nadira explained. "The women's quarters are behind this door. No man may enter here, save for His Excellency and a few next of kin. If one of the women falls ill, a *hakim* is permitted to enter and examine her."

"How have you come to know all this?" Sibylla asked.

Nadira replied that, before she was emancipated in order to serve Christians, she had been a slave in the household of a court official in Marrakesh.

The guards opened a double door and the slave guided them to a large room. She indicated to the guests that they were to wait and disappeared. Sibylla looked around with curiosity. The room seemed no different from the many others they'd passed through. Large windows opened to an interior courtyard. The shutters were open, allowing the fine muslin drapes to flow in the breeze. Somewhere outside, a lonesome peacock cried, but otherwise it was still. Trays covered with rose petals and fragrant herbs sat on low, exquisitely carved tables. A door opened and a group of women entered. Aside from the female slaves, the only local women Sibylla had seen had been completely veiled and scurrying through the narrow passages of the *medina*. But here in their living quarters, the women did not conceal their faces. They returned Sibylla's curious smile and looked at her with expressive kohl-rimmed eyes.

They were led by a diminutive old lady leaning on a cane of carved ivory. Though she appeared fragile, her lined face revealed kindness and intelligence. She wore a loose garment of silver-gray silk ending halfway down her calf. Below that Sibylla was able to make out pants of the same fine material and pearl-embroidered slippers. Her arms, neck, and ears were adorned with striking gold jewelry. The other women were far younger. They too were wearing kaftans with pants in all colors of the rainbow, as well as opulent jewelry. Some had covered their shiny, dark hair with translucent scarves, but most wore it loose down to their hips. A dozen chattering children ran about, the smallest among them carried by their nursemaids.

The elderly woman stepped forward to greet Sibylla. Nadira translated for her. "El Sayyida Rusa Umm Hash-Hash, My Lady Rusa, mother of His Excellency Qaid Hash-Hash, welcomes the honorable lady from the land of the *Engliz*."

Sibylla bowed respectfully and gave her name. Next, the *qaid*'s chief wife greeted her.

"Princess Lalla Jasira is a member of the sultan's family, may God grant him a long life," Nadira said.

After the first wife, who was most likely Sibylla's age, there were three other wives, all very young and pretty. The fourth and youngest was in the late stages of pregnancy and had her hands proudly folded on her round belly. The concubines were also introduced to Sibylla.

"They come from Abyssinia, where the women are renowned for their beauty, and are Christian slaves," Nadira explained.

With their soft brown eyes and delicate limbs, the concubines reminded Sibylla of gazelles.

The greetings concluded, Rusa gave a short speech, while smiling at Sibylla encouragingly.

"El Sayyida and the other ladies have heard that their esteemed guest from the land of the *Engliz* has hair that resembles the fur of a desert lioness. They respectfully ask their guest to remove her hat so they may see for themselves." Nadira gave Sibylla an awkward look.

Sibylla was amazed that news of her hair color had reached even here inside the harem.

It was a harmless enough request and it would be impolite to turn it down, she thought as she untied the bow under her chin. Cries rang out from all corners. Some of the women giggled, others covered their mouths with their hands, the children squealed with excitement.

"They are saying that they have never before seen golden hair," Nadira translated over the din. "They believe that you must be an angel of heaven."

Sibylla shook her head resolutely. "Tell them that, in my country, many people have hair like mine."

The incredulous murmurs grew loud. Rusa at last managed to call everyone to order.

"The honorable Sayyida Rusa asks you to undo your hair," Nadira relayed.

"Very well." Sibylla pulled the pins out of her hair so that it fell over her shoulders. The women whispered reverently. One asked if the curls were made of spun gold. Another wanted to know if her hair had magic powers over men.

Sibylla laughed. "Tell them that men in northern countries have hair like this as well and that no one has more power than God has given him." Then she waved for the woman who had asked the question to come closer and touch her hair. The woman approached almost timidly and then proclaimed proudly in Arabic as Nadira translated, "This is human hair, only its color resembles gold."

"Or the fur of a lioness," another added.

Little by little, the women calmed down and Sibylla was able to distribute her gifts.

Next, they partook of some refreshments in the garden. To Sibylla, it seemed like paradise, with its floral fragrance, fountains, and birdsong. They all settled on brocaded cushions around a rectangular pool in which ornamental fish swam. Rusa, Lalla Jasira, and the others urged her to try delectable peaches and pieces of melons, raisins, and candied blossoms. One servant held a parasol over Sibylla while another fanned her.

But the party erupted again when they learned that Sibylla was already twenty-four and had not had a baby yet. This was shocking, indeed! Nadira translated rapidly as the conversation surged.

"You ought to make a pilgrimage to the grave of Sidi Magdoul on the outskirts of the city," Wahida, Hash-Hash's favorite concubine, advised. "He will help you to have many children, just as he helped the Prophet Ibrahim and his wife, Sara, to become parents many times over even at an advanced age."

Sibylla laughingly assured Wahida that she did not require Sidi Magdoul's assistance as she shifted her dress to allow the women a glimpse at her round belly. They rejoiced and showered her with advice for an easy pregnancy and a successful birth. The fourth wife wanted to send her midwife to Sibylla, while the third gave her an amulet, a small silver hand with an engraved eye. "If you wear this over your heart, Fatima's hand will protect your unborn from the evil eye."

As the eldest and the *qaid*'s mother, Rusa was the senior member of the harem and respected as such. Lalla Jasira was second and did justice to her name, which meant "the gentle one." After her followed the second, third, and fourth wives—and only then the concubines. Wahida was granted a special position and the title Umm Walad, the mother of her children, for already having borne her master two sons.

Rusa had wrapped the shawl Sibylla had given her around her shoulders. She was not seated on the cushions, but on an easy chair to the left of their guest. Lalla Jasira was perched on a thick, round cushion on Sibylla's right. Nadira stood behind her, ready to translate. Rusa clapped her hands and a slave appeared with a bowl of baked goods, which Rusa broke into small pieces and threw to the fish. Sibylla was impressed by her graceful movements and her soft, manicured hands.

"The *qaid*'s women are just like these fish," Rusa told her. "They live together in a beautiful home, lovingly cared for by a benevolent master. They want for nothing."

"That is true, no doubt," Sibylla countered. "But does this basin not obscure the fish's view of the open ocean?"

As soon as the words left her mouth, Sibylla wanted to kick herself for offending her delightful hostesses. She wondered if she would ever learn to hold her tongue.

Yet Rusa merely smiled and Lalla Jasira replied, "One need not summit the mountain to look into the distance. If we desire, the world comes to us here in the palace. For example, thanks to you we are learning how women live in faraway England."

Her dark eyes scanned Sibylla's light hair, her European-style dress, and came to rest on her thin silk stockings and the flat satin slippers.

"Those *babouches* you're wearing," said Lalla Jasira, "are really very pretty. Do all the ladies in your country wear them?"

Nadira translated and Sibylla nodded with a smile. "With your permission, I will present some to you. Tonight I will write a letter requesting a shipment for you and the other ladies."

Rusa and Lalla Jasira exchanged meaningful glances and asked to take a closer look at the shoes. They examined the workmanship and spoke to one another for several minutes. Then Rusa returned to her easy chair and addressed Sibylla.

"El Sayyida Rusa and Princess Lalla Jasira would like to make a business proposition to the honorable English lady Mrs. Hopkins," Nadira translated. "They would like to order five hundred pairs of the English slippers and they are offering to pay thirty gold *benduqui*."

"Are these women permitted to engage in trade? Do they even have their own money?" Sibylla could not help her astonishment.

Rusa wanted to know what Sibylla's question was and once Nadira had translated it, had her reply, "The Prophet, in his infinite wisdom, has granted women the right to manage the wealth that he has put at their disposal. El Sayyida and His Excellency's four wives have free access to their dowries. In addition, His Excellency pays every one of the ladies in his harem one *falus* per day."

The question piqued Lalla Jasira's interest, prompting her to inquire if the honorable Mrs. Hopkins herself did not have a bride price.

"Oh, I do," Sibylla mumbled and thought of the trust with her dowry. "But it took some doing for me to have the right to manage it myself." She turned to the two women. "It would be an honor for me to do business with you. But thirty gold *benduqui* will make me lose money. One hundred *benduqui* will just about cover my costs." She smiled shrewdly. Sibylla did not really know whether that was a fair price, but she had heard that bargaining was considered something of a sport in the Orient.

Rusa and Lalla Jasira nodded approvingly before making a counter-offer using flowery language. They eventually agreed on sixty *benduqui*.

Lalla Jasira clapped her hands and gave an order to a slave. The woman hurried back to the palace and quickly returned with two little leather sacks, which Lalla Jasira then ceremoniously placed in Sibylla's hands. "Count it, Mrs. Hopkins; you get half now and the other half when the *babouches* arrive."

Sibylla took a look into the little sacks. The idea of engaging in trade without the permission of her father or husband thrilled her. Back home in London, this would never have been allowed, yet somehow, here in a harem in Morocco, it was possible!

"For whom are the five hundred pairs of slippers intended?" she inquired.

"Princess Lalla Jasira is certain that the ladies in His Esteemed Majesty Sultan Abd al-Rahman's harem will be interested in this fashion. She is acquainted with many of the ladies since she comes from one of the ruling houses of the Alaouites."

Sibylla nodded slowly. Five hundred women for one man. Sara Willshire had been right in saying this place was very different from England.

She pulled herself together and said, "Nadira, please inform the ladies that I agree to their proposal. I shall make all the necessary arrangements."

Benjamin was waiting for his wife in the reception courtyard of the governor's palace as the *muezzin* called the faithful to afternoon prayers from the minaret of the mosque. The *qaid*, his relatives, and his translator had already taken their leave. Only Samuel Toledano remained.

"I don't suppose you or those damned Moors have ever heard of fair play, or have you, Toledano?" Benjamin was in a filthy mood. "And don't try to look so innocent. After all, it's your fault that the governor is unwilling to sell me the exclusive rights to the leather trade. I saw how you signaled him to turn down my offer."

The meeting had begun harmoniously enough. Qaid Hash-Hash had proudly shown his guest his weapons collection, his gyrfalcons, and his Arabian horses. But later, when they sat together over tea and Benjamin presented the contracts drawn up in England, Hash-Hash had rebuffed him.

"Toledano is quite capable of handling the leather trade. Furthermore, His Majesty's decisions are sacrosanct. They need not be put in writing by a peddler," Hash-Hash had declared with disdain.

Toledano had looked utterly innocent during that exchange, and at this moment too, the merchant appeared equanimous. "Do not give up so easily, Señor Hopkins. Here in the Orient, one seldom comes to an agreement after the first meeting. Come to see me at my home in the *mellah*, directly behind the *souk*. We will find a way for you to do profitable business as well."

Benjamin made a face. Toledano was speaking to him in Spanish, a language Benjamin spoke well, having been responsible for Spencer & Son's Caribbean trade, but this man's archaic dialect irritated him. It did not matter that Nuri bin Kalil had tried to explain that the Moroccan Jews had retained the language of their Spanish origin since having fled from the Inquisition in the fifteenth century.

"I strongly suggest that you not waste your time dispensing advice," Benjamin grumbled, thinking of his impatient father-in-law back in London.

Toledano remained friendly. "You are impatient, Señor Hopkins. If you want to do business in Morocco, remember this: you Europeans have clocks, but we in the Orient have time."

Chapter Six

Mogador and Marrakesh, September 1836

"Please pardon me for being so frank, dear Sibylla, but your plan is pure foolhardiness!" Sara Willshire frowned with disapproval while threading a needle.

Sibylla folded the diaper she had just finished seaming. "No, it isn't," she declared. "We'll be gone a mere twelve days, and I am still six weeks from giving birth. And besides, I'm feeling quite well!"

The two young women were sewing baby clothes in the interior courtyard of the Hopkins residence in the shade of an olive tree. It was warm and still with the soft scent of roses and mimosa flowers filling the air. Sibylla and Sara met almost daily and talked about everything and nothing while the mound of gowns, bonnets, and diapers in the basket at their feet grew. Sibylla had just told the consul's wife that she planned to accompany her husband on his trip to Marrakesh. Sultan Abd al-Rahman had invited Mogador's merchants for an audience.

Qaid Hash-Hash, who was accompanying the group, had explained that His Most Gracious Majesty wanted to assure himself that the infidels entrusted to his protection were not lacking for anything.

Sara shook her head. "Morocco is not England," she warned. "We don't travel on established roads in a comfortable stagecoach. We sit in the saddle and at night we sleep on the floor in a tent or, if we're lucky, in a *caravanserai*! What's more, the interior is hotter than the coast. Even in September, the temperature in Marrakesh is above eighty-five degrees. I have made the journey several times and, believe me, I don't relish having to go again. We'll be riding five consecutive days from morning till night! If the stress were to bring about premature labor pains, you would find no doctor or hospital."

"I'm a good horsewoman," Sibylla replied stubbornly. "And I'm not as fragile as all that. Besides, I'll have Nadira with me."

Just then, the servant appeared with a jug of orange-blossom water, glasses, and a plate with fresh figs. Sibylla smiled gratefully. Nadira had become indispensable to her in the four months since she had arrived in Mogador. During her many years in the service of foreigners, the young woman had developed a feel for their wishes. Sibylla spent far more time with Nadira than with anyone else. Thanks to her, she was learning everyday customs. During the last few weeks, she had even begun to learn Arabic. She would point at an object and her servant would tell her its name.

"Does your husband accept your desire to accompany him?" Sara asked.

The question angered Sibylla. It was her decision alone whether and where she traveled! "Of course. And why not? After all, we English are a sporting lot."

Benjamin had, indeed, expressed the same concerns as Sara. But once he saw how irritated Sibylla was, he had quickly backed down. She rarely saw her husband anyhow. He was busy either in the port or at the customs station, meeting with ship captains or inspecting merchandise.

He complained constantly that Arabs were unreliable business partners whose every move he personally had to monitor in order to avoid being swindled. Unlike Sibylla, he was making no attempt to acquaint himself with the habits of the people. Yet Richard sent long letters praising his engagement. And although Benjamin had not succeeded in obtaining exclusive rights to the leather trade, Toledano was supplying him with leather of outstanding quality from Fez in return for a commission. In addition, Benjamin was trading in gum arabic, crucial to the production of paints and medicine, and in grains from the fertile northern plains and the ancient royal city of Meknes.

"The baptismal water arrived yesterday," Sibylla reported.

Consul Willshire, who conducted Bible readings at his residence on Sundays in lieu of church services and who was responsible for the salvation of the English souls in Mogador, was to baptize the baby.

"I have also received letters from home. My brother, Oscar, finished school last summer and Father has made him an apprentice clerk. My stepmother writes that he hates having to rise so early in the morning." She smiled to herself, lost in thought for a moment. "I was determined to get out of London, but now I realize that I do miss my family. They are so very far away. Sometimes I yearn just to hear their voices."

"Oh yes, and how I miss the shops!" Sara exclaimed. "Wouldn't you just love to look through the sewing patterns at Debenhams or wander through Covent Garden?"

"I would rather attend the theater," Sibylla replied. "I do find it strange that there is absolutely no public life here in Morocco, no theater or opera, no balls or sporting events." She rummaged in a box until she found a small button and held it against a tiny white cotton gown to see how it looked.

"Social life takes place behind thick walls in this country. It took me a while to become accustomed to that as well," Sara admitted.

"And that is precisely why I have to escape from this confinement for a few days!" Sibylla persisted. "I spend almost all day in this house with its tiny windows or else in the courtyard. When I go out walking, I reach the city walls within ten minutes at most. I've seen nothing of the countryside!"

"I do understand you, my dear Sibylla." Sara said with a sigh. "But I think it is a very bad idea."

The foreign merchants and their consuls from England, Spain, Portugal, France, the Netherlands, and Denmark had joined a caravan arranged by Samuel Toledano. It consisted of fifty heavily laden camels, five camel riders, and several assistants, who took care of the animals. Once in Marrakesh, they would join other caravans to become a giant caravan, consisting of several hundred animals, that would then head through the Western Sahara to the legendary city of Timbuktu. The caravans traveling south transported dates, oil, henna, salt, cotton cloth, glass beads, metal products, rugs, and ceramics. On their return, they brought ostrich feathers, ivory, gold, and, most important, slaves.

To protect the small caravan from bands of thieves on its way from Mogador to Marrakesh, it was escorted by thirty riders from the sultan's cavalry. The governor of Mogador himself rode along on a magnificent Arabian stallion, his most prized gyrfalcon on his arm.

The road to Marrakesh, a dusty, well-trodden path, led directly eastward. Not far outside the walls of the city, they rode through groves of argan that, according to Sara Willshire, grew nowhere else. These primeval trees with their wide crowns bore plumlike green fruit with kernels from which the natives extracted a nutritious, gold-colored oil. Apparently, the fruit was popular with goats as well—to her great amusement, Sibylla spotted several grazing up among the branches.

The argan groves were followed by juniper bushes and low-growing shrubs. Every now and then they saw some abandoned, dilapidated mud huts and small harvested fields. They crossed through brooks that were almost completely dry after the long summer and offered just enough water for man and beast. Intoxicating oleander bloomed along the banks. Nadira pointed out grasshoppers and chameleons to Sibylla and Sara, and once, even the papery skin out of which a snake had slipped. The farther east they traveled, the sandier the ground became. Finally, the Atlas Mountains became visible in the blue haze.

The first two nights, they pitched tents. Dozens of little campfires sparkled in the darkness. Nadira made tea and ricelike couscous, to which she added olive oil and butter. Sibylla sat next to her husband on a flat stone near the fire and thought it very exciting to be traveling in a way which had long been relegated to the past in Europe.

"This is our second picnic together," she whispered to Benjamin, scooping up her couscous with a piece of freshly baked flatbread, as per local custom.

"True," he replied and glumly regarded his tin bowl. "Only back then the food was better."

The second night, they were awakened by loud shouting and rifle shots. Horses neighed, camels howled, and donkeys screamed.

"Hyenas," Consul Willshire explained when Benjamin and Sibylla stumbled out of their tent. "No need to worry. The sultan's riders have shot a few and chased off the rest."

Heading out the next morning, they were confronted by the bodies of the large predators, which the cavalry had laid out as deterrents around the edges of the camp. Sibylla shuddered at the sight of their powerful fangs.

By the third day, she began to feel the effects of the heat. She felt exhausted and dusty when, toward evening, they rode through the arched gate of the only *caravanserai* along the route. The lodging for travelers and traders was no more than a plain building made of rammed earth, its four walls surrounding an interior courtyard with enough room for two caravans the size of theirs. Storage rooms and stalls for the animals were on the first floor and the travelers slept in simple windowless rooms on the second. There was also a small prayer room. The gate was locked at night for protection.

Nadira was building a fire to cook over when a group of women came into the courtyard. They immediately attracted Sibylla's attention as they were not veiled. They circulated among the travelers with baskets filled with flatbread, eggs, goat cheese, and dried meat for sale. Sibylla was fascinated by their proud, open faces. The skin on their suntanned foreheads and chins was tattooed. They were barefoot, their wide skirts decorated with multicolored braids and tassels. They wore blouses and colorful scarves on their dark hair.

"These women are members of the Chiadma tribe," Consul Willshire explained to Sibylla. "They are Berbers, the people who lived in this area for years before the Arabs."

"Chiadma," Sibylla repeated. "I have heard you mention them before. You were talking about feuds with another tribe—the Haha, if I'm not mistaken."

"That's right," Willshire agreed. "Berbers are hotheads. They do not respect authority and one can never be certain that their intentions are peaceful."

Sibylla watched the women's skirts swaying around their hips. Several of the travelers, especially the foreigners, who had not seen such an unfettered display of femininity in some time, stole desirous glances.

"They are here alone, without men. They seem to enjoy more freedom than Arab women," Sibylla observed and was astonished to see the consul blush.

He cleared his throat. "One could say so, Mrs. Hopkins. Indeed, one could say so." He cleared his throat again. "Now, if you will excuse me, I have to check that our boy has seen to the mules. Because as always, if you want a job done well—"

And he was gone.

"Do you think we ought to buy some meat for dinner from them?" Sibylla asked her husband, who merely shrugged.

"If you insist, but don't be surprised if they try to sell you a boiled cat as rabbit stew!" He turned and took their luggage to their room.

Her curiosity aflame, Sibylla asked Nadira to teach her more about the Berber tribes that made up much of the rural population of Morocco. But Nadira had always lived in the city and had come into contact with Berbers only when they were selling fruit or sheep's wool in the *souk*. She could not understand the Chiadma language.

More Berber women arrived when night came. They were young and beautiful, had gold and silver coins woven in their long black hair and shining belts and heavy silver bangles around their wrists. Some of them sat in a semicircle, singing and clapping. Others began dancing in a way Sibylla had never seen before. They stamped their feet into the ground, their hips vibrated, and their arms moved in serpent-like motions. The flames of the fires were reflected in their kohl-rimmed eyes and made their skin shine like bronze. Sibylla was glad that the dark concealed her glowing cheeks. The best word she could think of was "voluptuous," and yet they were also exciting and elegant.

Others seemed to feel the same. "*Como las gitanas*, like gypsies," one of the Spanish traders whispered and softly clicked his tongue.

Sara Willshire wrinkled her nose. "Shameless!" she muttered. "Simply shameless! Come, William, let us retire."

She rose and gathered her skirts high as though she feared coming in contact with something filthy. Her husband uttered a reluctant sigh and obediently followed.

Benjamin couldn't take his eyes off the performers. Sibylla watched as he stood with a group of traders, his jaw hanging open. She felt embarrassed at seeing him like that, while at the same time wounded by the fact that he had never once looked at her with such desire. She rose and pushed her way over.

"I'm tired."

It was as if he didn't quite recognize her. "Well then, go to sleep," he retorted and turned once again toward the dancers' hypnotic hips.

Sibylla was not surprised when he came back very late, creeping like a thief into their small room. Feigning sleep, she wondered if he had approached one of the dancers to do the sort of things for which men paid women. She instantly felt ashamed. How could she accuse those women of being prostitutes merely because they danced in a way some found provocative?

She listened carefully as Benjamin took off his jacket and untied his boots.

Never suspecting Sibylla might be awake, Benjamin lay down on his narrow cot, wrapped himself in a blanket, and pulled it up to his ears. He found himself in turmoil. Furtively, he began to touch himself, his imagination taking him to the seductive Chiadma, whom he found so much more arousing than his wife.

The following morning, Sibylla felt ill. The baby in her belly had been kicking relentlessly. She was suffering from the heat, which became worse the closer they got to Marrakesh. Her back ached and her legs felt leaden. Benjamin had to assist her in dismounting from her mule for the lunchtime break. Not even the rest in the shade of some date palms provided any relief. For the first time, she feared that Sara Willshire might have been right.

When they continued that afternoon, it was all she could do to stay in the saddle. The *scirocco*, the desert wind of the Sahara, had blown in, and red desert dust, which the animals' hooves raised, enveloped the caravan like a cloud. In an effort to protect herself, Sibylla had followed the example of the natives and wrapped a shawl around her head, leaving only a small slit for her eyes. Still, the tiny grains of sand got between her teeth, in her ears, eyes, nostrils, and hair. Nadira and Sara Willshire, riding beside her, had also wrapped themselves in their shawls. Sibylla wondered how Benjamin could tolerate it in his English riding attire. He refused to don a "Muslim costume" and was wearing solid leather boots and a top hat, and clutching a riding crop, as though he were on a leisurely outing on a rainy English day instead of braving the stifling heat of southern Morocco.

"You can blame this wretched *scirocco* if my head explodes," lamented Sara.

"And I feel so nauseated," Sibylla groaned. "Nadira, how do you say 'I'm sick to my stomach' in Arabic?"

Her servant, clutching her donkey's scruffy, short mane, answered tersely, "*Am bjejani batne*, my lady."

"Perhaps I should follow your example and dress like an Arab woman. It looks quite comfortable," Sara declared, eyeing Sibylla, who was wearing a loose silk kaftan and wide silk pants, which allowed her to straddle her mule.

Sibylla had never before ridden like a man, but found the mule easier to control that way. Her outfit was a gift from Rusa and Lalla Jasira after the "English *babouches*" had arrived. The ladies had been delighted by the shoes, and Lalla Jasira had wondered aloud about next ordering the beautiful silk stockings she had seen the *Engliziya* wear.

"Arab dress is very comfortable indeed. I haven't yet decided if I'm even going to go back to wearing a corset after the baby comes," Sibylla replied as she looked at Sara's tight-fitting bodice. She could see dark sweat stains under the long sleeves, and the skirt with its many petticoats must have been as warm as a woolen blanket. Sara and Nadira were both riding sidesaddle.

Benjamin was riding next to Toledano and Consul Willshire. He had been finding it hard to look his pregnant wife in the eye for fear she might somehow see the effect the Chiadma dancers had had on him. And anyhow, riding at the front of the caravan put him in an excellent position to discuss business and avoid women's topics like babies and clothes.

By now he was aware of Toledano's position as the most powerful of the Jewish traders in Mogador. No one looking at the elderly man, dressed in his faded black kaftan and slouched on his donkey—the sultan did not allow Jews to ride mules or horses—would have believed it. But Benjamin had been a guest at his house, where, behind an inconspicuous facade, Toledano lived in charming luxury with his wife and several children.

In the afternoon of the following day, when the walls of Marrakesh appeared on the horizon, Sibylla was so relieved she almost began to cry. She had been feeling a pulling pain in her belly, not too severe, but persistent enough for her to begin to worry. The ground was uneven and every stone gave her an unpleasant jolt. She clenched her teeth and tried hard not to think about what it would be like to be delivered of her child along a caravan route.

She directed her gaze to the cornered minaret of the Koutoubia Mosque, which towered over a sea of rooftops. Sunlight glittered in its gilt spheres. In the distance, one could see the violet-blue and white colors of the High Atlas.

"Is that really snow at the top there? So close to the desert? What a fantastic country!" she exclaimed.

The caravan crossed the Al-Haouz plain, a fertile region of olive and pomegranate groves, which the Arabs called the Sultan's Gardens. Sibylla saw goats, sheep, and cattle grazing in green meadows. Along the roadside there were granaries built out of the red mud typical of the area, and colonies of sparrows nested in the trees. She could hear a mysterious rumbling and rushing underground.

"Are there underground rivers here?" she asked.

"In a way, yes," explained Sara. "These are *rhetaras*, or canals that the natives dig into the mountains until they strike groundwater. This water is carried to the fields and even as far as Marrakesh."

Two hours later, Sibylla, Benjamin, the Willshires, Nadira, and the *qaid* with his entourage rode toward the Bab Doukkala, a city gate on the northwest side of Marrakesh. Samuel Toledano remained behind to oversee the caravan's unloading. Cypresses and date palms towered overhead. The city wall, fortified with battlements and massive bastions, easily twenty-four feet in height and seemingly endless in length, impressed Sibylla deeply. Next, some poles driven into the ground directly in front of the gate caught her eye. On the tip of each pole was a shriveled brown orb. As they rode past, she realized with horror these were human heads, which appeared to grin at her through lifeless eyes and exposed teeth. She felt a wave of nausea and quickly placed her hand over her mouth.

"What's the matter with you?" asked Benjamin.

"Did you not see, there, in front of the gate?"

Benjamin squinted. "Well, I always knew the people in this country were barbarians."

"Those are the heads of executed criminals," Consul Willshire said. "The sultan has them preserved in salt."

"How terrible," Sibylla gasped.

"He really is quite a peaceful sort," Willshire assured her. "But there are many who envy him and would like nothing better than to depose him. The Alaouites may be holy, but they are not inviolable. The heads of the executed serve as a warning to all those who would think to conspire against His Majesty."

"Has he displayed the heads of Christians as well?" Benjamin's voice sounded a little thin.

"Sultan Abd al-Rahman would much prefer a hefty ransom to full-blown diplomatic conflict. He witnessed what happened in Algeria because of some outstanding wheat payments. The Dey of Algiers wound up in exile and the French took control of the country. That is something Abd al-Rahman does not want to risk on any account."

A broad earthen street led to a mosque in the southeast, and the alleyways of the *medina* branched off from there. Worshippers coming out of the mosque looked at them with curiosity. Sibylla noticed how the Jewish members of their group quickly dismounted and removed their slippers as they approached the mosque.

"The sultan's orders," Sara whispered to her. "This is how Moroccan Jews must show their respect to the true believers. But it does not apply to us Christians. We're foreigners in this country and are permitted to enjoy the Orient's holy hospitality."

Sibylla soon noticed that, even in this big city, foreign infidels were something of a novelty, especially in the company of an Arab dignitary and escorted by the sultan's own cavalry. She was grateful to have her blonde hair shrouded. People came running from all directions. Some gave friendly waves or smiled shyly. Others circled them silently or made a sign to ward off the evil eye. Sibylla found the people gaunt and poorly dressed.

"Am I wrong in thinking that the royal city of the south seems somewhat run-down?" she asked Sara softly enough to avoid being heard by Nuri bin Kalil.

The consul's wife nodded. "There was a terrible pestilence here a few years ago and, shortly thereafter, an outbreak of the pox and cholera."

A group of children tried to push toward Sibylla's mule. They were thin, dressed in rags, and had their dirty hands outstretched. "*Dju*, good lady, hungry!"

Sibylla was about to search for her purse, but Nadira quickly drove her donkey between her and the little mendicants, and Nuri bin Kalil chased them away with all kinds of ugly insults.

"Nadira, how could you be so cruel?" Sibylla was horrified.

"If you give them alms, my lady, in no time you will be surrounded by so many that you would not be able to go on. They would cling to the harness of your mule and would not let go until they had taken everything from you, like rats gnawing on a carcass."

"I appreciate that you wanted to protect me, but it is unchristian to chase away the hungry, most of all children," Sibylla insisted.

"Islam too instructs the true believers to give alms, Mrs. Hopkins," Nuri bin Kalil said. "But it does not expect the lamb to sacrifice itself to the lion."

Sibylla fell silent, shaking her head emphatically. She thought of the innocent baby in her belly and how no child should ever have to beg for food.

The group reached the center of the city, the sultan's riders mercilessly forcing aside anyone who did not clear the way immediately. Sibylla took in the dilapidated facades, empty shops, the entire streets that seemed abandoned. Rats and stray dogs were foraging in the heaps of trash outside small homes, and the odor was so foul that she pulled up her shawl tighter against her mouth and nose.

It was only when they approached the *souk* that the city came to life. There were slave traders roaming through the streets with their "merchandise" in tow. The smell of freshly baked bread and roasted meat wafted from the communal kitchens. One could hear the rhythmic tapping of the metal-artists' market. Berbers were unloading wool rugs. A mysterious scent of cinnamon, vanilla, and cloves filled Sibylla's nose.

The *fondouks*, or city inns, were located behind the markets. The *fondouks* were much like the *caravanserais*, but they also housed workshops and sales rooms in which the merchants could display their wares.

"There is a splendid *hamam* behind our inn," Sara told Sibylla as they dismounted in the courtyard of their *fondouk*. "It is part of a mosque with a Koran school, but the *hamam* is open to all. I always go there to get thoroughly cleaned after the long trip. One ought to be nicely washed for an audience with a sovereign, don't you agree?" She winked at her friend.

Sibylla heaved a big sigh. "I can't imagine anything I would like more right now. We'll take Nadira and let ourselves be pampered!"

If there was one thing she had learned to appreciate in this country, it was the *hamam*. Back in England, she'd had her own bathtub, which had stood in her bedroom behind a screen. But to wash oneself in Morocco, one had to go to a public bath. The women's section of the bath was also the only place—aside from a harem—where Sibylla encountered her Arab counterparts as they dedicated themselves to their beauty routines and exchanged the latest news. She had been quite inhibited during her first visit, not knowing what to expect. But she soon learned to relish the uninhibited, relaxed atmosphere and quickly forgot that she was covered by nothing more than a cloth around her hips. By now, her pregnancy was decidedly visible, but she was not the only one in this place who was with child, and all the women, pregnant or not, were happy for her, inquiring about her condition and showering her with advice.

Benjamin, needless to say, did not share Sibylla's love of the *hamam*. While he did not try to dissuade her from going, he made no secret of his distaste and declared that not the Devil himself could get him to bathe with naked strangers. Sibylla had reconciled herself to the fact that she and her husband had little in common.

Chapter Seven

The audience with Sultan Abd al-Rahman took place the following day, the first day of the sixth month, Jumada al-Akhira, of the year 1252 after the Prophet's departure from Mecca. The Gregorian calendar indicated that it was September 13, 1836. On her way back from the *hamam* the previous evening, Sibylla had learned that the city's *muezzins* had announced the new month with the appearance of the tiny sliver of the new moon.

For her audience, she wore an outfit made of purple silk material interwoven with gold threads that she had found at the *souk* in Mogador. It was cut as wide as an Arab kaftan but as long as a European dress and concealed her pregnancy almost entirely. Following her directions, Nadira had sewn it together with a shawl that allowed Sibylla to conceal her hair.

She had slept soundly after her visit to the *hamam*. She felt well and rested and wildly relieved that the pulling in her abdomen was gone. The group from Mogador went on foot to the sultan's palace, which was located in a large garden in the southern part of the *medina*. Most of the gifts had been loaded on a donkey, and Benjamin carried the special one for the sultan.

Once the *souks* lay behind, they crossed a large square filled with tents and stalls. Under the canopies, the city's executioners waited for business alongside itinerant doctors and other traveling people. It was the place to have one's teeth pulled or one's future foretold.

After not quite half an hour, they reached another square ending in a hefty red sandstone wall with a closed wooden gate. The sultan's green flags were flying on the bastion. There were guard tents on both sides of the gate. Sibylla was surprised to see the guards not standing at attention like their counterparts in London but sitting idly on the ground, sipping tea and playing cards.

Besides the merchants from Mogador, there were supplicants from Tangier, Rabat, and Tétouan, altogether several hundred people waiting to pay their respects to the sultan. Consul Willshire spotted James Butler, his counterpart in Tétouan, and Edward Drummond-Hay, the British consul general in Tangier. Sara introduced Sibylla to the wives of the English merchants along the Moroccan coast. While Mrs. Willshire and the other ladies lamented the strange food and hot climate, Sibylla went to look for Benjamin. Her husband was talking animatedly to Samuel Toledano. She knew Benjamin had high hopes for the audience. Most of all, he hoped his gift to the sultan, a valuable silver-studded hunting rifle made by England's finest gunsmith, would impress the ruler of all the faithful.

Sibylla observed the Black Guards, the sultan's slave army, with curiosity. They were lining up on both sides of the gate. These tall men were distinguishable not only by their uniform, a white kaftan and a red *tarboosh*, but also by their hard, unflinching expressions. Consul Willshire told them of the Black Guards' undying loyalty to the Alaouites for almost two hundred years.

The Berbers too were represented in the square. The riders sat proudly on their beautiful Arabian horses and got the lively animals to perform all kinds of tricks.

Sibylla hoped that His Majesty would not keep them waiting too much longer and dabbed her forehead with a corner of her shawl. It was time by now for the noonday prayer and the sun was unrelenting.

"I believe there is some movement at the gate," said Mrs. Butler, the wife of the consul of Tétouan.

The guards had finished their card game and stood at attention on both sides of the gate. The riders had taken their positions behind the perfectly straight lines of the Black Guards while the merchants eagerly waited at the other end of the square.

"Come with me," whispered Benjamin, who had suddenly appeared next to Sibylla. "Let's not miss this moment." He took her hand and led her to the front.

As the massive wings of the gate opened, Sibylla held her breath. She had never before met a ruler face-to-face. She had seen King William IV in his box at the opera once, but that did not compare to this moment.

A single rider on a magnificently decorated white stallion came through the gate with measured steps. A bodyguard walked close to the horse and was closely followed by a eunuch carrying a giant carmine sunshade.

"That's him," Benjamin whispered. He had removed his hat, as had all the other gentlemen in their delegation, and his voice sounded solemn. "Toledano told me the parasol is his symbol."

Sibylla took a closer look at the man. He was middle-aged, not particularly tall, with round, bearded cheeks and a gentle-looking face. His horse seemed more spectacularly decorated than he himself, she thought as she looked at his simple white kaftan. He wore neither medals nor rings, no chains or other regalia. Were it not for the red umbrella, he might have been any random subject. But then she remembered the impaled skulls she had seen by the city gate and told herself that it would surely be a mistake to underestimate this man.

"His Royal Majesty Moulay Abd al-Rahman bin Moulay Hicham bin Sidi Mohammed bin Moulay Abdallah bin Moulay Ismail, Imam of all Believers, Caliph of the Islamic Community and Sultan of Morocco of the Holy House of the Alaouites, who are descended from the Prophet's daughter herself," Consul Willshire intoned. He and his wife had fought their way to the front of the crowd to join Benjamin and Sibylla.

"May God bless our ruler's life," the Black Guards shouted in unison. They took a deep bow and touched their right knees as a sign of their devotion.

The sultan stopped in front of the delegation of merchants and it was only then that Sibylla caught a glimpse of the man riding a few feet behind him. At first, she took him for an Arab, not only because of the black hair visible under his turban but also the traditional kaftan and long pants he wore. Yet his suntanned, lean face was clean shaven, his features less aquiline, and his eyes less dark. He was also tall like a European. At least, his legs were a little too long for his petite Arabian mare.

"Who is that man on the brown horse?" she whispered to Sara.

The consul's wife immediately knew who she meant. "That's Monsieur Rouston. So he's back at court," she added wryly in her husband's direction.

"What do you mean?" Sibylla was curious to know. "Is he a foreign diplomat?"

"Rather a French misfit," Willshire said reflexively. He, like most Englishmen, had a strong dislike for the French. "Rouston used to be an officer with the Chasseurs d'Afrique and served in Algeria. However, the past few years, he has preferred to dwell in a mud hut with the Chiadma. Because he persuaded them to resolve their longstanding feud with the ruling family, the sultan holds him in the highest regard. Abd al-Rahman particularly seeks out Rouston's advice when it comes to the reform of his army, which, between you and me, is in deplorable condition."

"Military advice from a Frenchman!" Benjamin huffed. "Apparently, the sultan has never heard of Abukir, let alone Waterloo, or he would know of the military superiority of us English."

Sibylla turned her gaze back to Rouston. She took him to be about thirty, a few years older than she. He sat calmly and confidently on his prancing mare while he looked into the crowd.

What sort of man prefers to live in the desert with a Berber tribe rather than with his own kind behind city walls? she wondered. Was he married to one of their women? She shook the improper thoughts from her head.

At that moment, Rouston looked her way and their eyes locked for several seconds. He smiled subtly and Sibylla's heart leapt. She was startled. Never had she experienced anything of the sort—with Benjamin or any other man. What could have gotten into her? She was a married lady, after all, and a pregnant one at that! She quickly lowered her gaze and moved closer to Benjamin.

Meanwhile, the sultan's interpreter had translated his master's greeting into all the languages of those present. "His Imperial Majesty Abd al-Rahman, Sovereign of all the Faithful, renews and reinforces the friendly alliance that his ancestors have built with the rulers of the European countries. His Imperial Majesty will do everything in his power to intensify and expand this alliance, with the help of God."

At a signal from His Majesty, the consuls general stepped up one by one and answered with well-chosen words. After Consul General Drummond-Hay had spoken, a eunuch and several slaves approached to collect the gifts for the sultan.

"But I wanted to present the gun to His Majesty myself," Benjamin protested. "This way I know neither that he really received it nor that he knows it is from me."

"You may rest assured that His Majesty is informed in detail about the provenance of all the gifts," Consul Willshire told him.

Yet Benjamin refused to hand it over. The delay caught the sultan's attention and Drummond-Hay felt compelled to explain. A short exchange with the translator ensued.

"His Imperial Majesty the Sultan permits the merchant Hopkins to hand over his gift to his favorite eunuch, Feradge!"

Benjamin looked at Drummond-Hay uncertainly and the latter nodded emphatically. So he unwrapped the gun from its protective cloth. Before handing it to the eunuch, he held it up for the sultan to see. A murmur went through the lines of soldiers as the silver studs sparkled in the light. Even His Majesty seemed interested. Benjamin was satisfied. He was sure that the sultan would reward him for this valuable gift, maybe even with exclusive rights for the export of leather!

Benjamin pondered how to make his request as the eunuch handed the gun to his master and the sultan examined the workmanship. He would speak of the amicable relations between their countries, of lucrative deals, rising exports, and rising profits.

But he never got the chance.

"His Imperial Majesty Sultan Abd al-Rahman thanks the merchant Hopkins for his valuable gift. It is only a merchant who disposes of extraordinary wealth who can make extraordinary gifts. His Majesty esteems this generosity highly. But His Majesty's heart is saddened because his unfortunate people are suffering from hunger. Yet now, thanks to the generosity of the merchant Hopkins, His Majesty can aid his people by raising export taxes by a mere ten percent. Ten percent, the same as the churches of the infidels levy."

"What?" Benjamin gasped. "That's the thanks I get? A ten-percent increase in tariffs?"

"Hopkins, be still!" Consul Willshire took hold of Benjamin's arm. "If you don't play along, he'll raise the tariffs even more!"

Benjamin blanched. He had never felt so tricked. It was all he could do not to scream in anger at this greedy ruler of the Muslims.

Just you wait, he thought, clenching his fists. *He who laughs last laughs loudest! Whatever you take from me now, I'll get back penny for penny later!*

"Come," Sibylla whispered and took his clenched hand. "Let's go back to the inn."

At that moment, the translator's voice rang out once more. "His Majesty would like to know if the lady whose hair resembles that of a desert lioness is among his guests."

Sibylla could not believe her ears. How could the sultan know the name the *qaid*'s wives had given her? What did this mean?

She stepped forward hesitantly and bowed her head. She heard the sultan's deep voice, which was always soft, whether assuring the merchants of his friendship or raising the tariffs for her husband.

"His Imperial Majesty says, So this is the merchant's wife with the lion's hair who has sold English *babouches* to our wives. Our wives were very pleased and thank the lady with the lion's hair."

A murmur went through the crowd. Sibylla raised her head in surprise. The sultan nodded gently and turned his horse. A few seconds later, the palace gates closed behind him.

Benjamin glared at his wife. She had told him of her business deal with the slippers, but he had dismissed it as frivolous. But now his wife had been honored by the sultan in front of everyone while he had been humiliated—also in front of everyone.

"Stop! Stop this instant!" Sibylla drove her mule between the man with the whip and the two slaves. The slave driver reined in his mount and stared at her furiously, his arm raised, ready to deliver the next blow. The two men struggled to their feet. Blood was streaming down their backs, and their skin was broken and covered in welts. It hadn't even been two days, but the extravagance and ceremony of the scene at the gate seemed to Sibylla to have happened in another world.

Their wrists were bound, and their necks were held inside two forked branches tied together at their throats and attached to each other at the end. Whenever one stumbled, the other was pulled to the ground with him.

Sixty male slaves and twice as many women, some with children, accompanied the caravan that had set out from Marrakesh for Mogador one and a half days ago. The women were tied to each other with ropes only. Like the men, they were dressed in nothing more than loincloths, which barely covered their nakedness.

When the caravan had made camp the previous evening, the slaves had begun to sing, sadly and plaintively and with such profound despair that Sibylla broke out in goose bumps. They seemed so broken, so haggard and exhausted. It filled her with impotent rage to look on as the drivers beat them and drove them on. The only thing that enraged her even more was the undisguised lust with which the male travelers, both European and Arab, gawked at the poor women. She yearned to go after them with her riding crop the way the slave drivers wielded their whips.

The slave driver grudgingly lowered his whip, unwilling to strike the English lady. Sibylla, her heart racing with triumph and fear, turned her mule away.

How can Toledano permit this? she wondered, for the slaves were his. He had purchased them in Marrakesh from a northbound caravan and marked them with his brand. Sibylla had been racking her brain as to how anyone could treat other human beings worse than pack camels.

She jumped at the ugly curse flung by another slave driver swinging his whip above the heads of several women. Nadira, riding next to her mistress with her head hung low, flinched as well. Sibylla suspected she suffered not only at seeing her sub-Saharan compatriots humiliated so but was also reminded of her own history.

"Where do they come from?" Sibylla asked her. "Do they belong to your tribe?"

Nadira answered with a sad look. "These people are Igbo. I am Mandingo. But in our suffering, we are all brothers and sisters."

Igbo and Mandingo. Sibylla had never heard of either. Nor had she any idea where these people lived, or that they might be from many different places, different tribes. She realized how little she knew of the inhabitants of this continent.

The slave driver again raised his whip to beat the two stumbling men, but he was seized by the arm by a rider galloping up from behind. The surprised man fell off his mule with a cry.

"*Arrête-toi!* Stop it!" André Rouston bellowed and spun his brown mare in such a way that her hooves stamped on the ground mere inches from the frightened driver's head. The man quickly rolled out of the way and sprang to his feet, but the Frenchman was next to him again in no time and grabbed his arm again. "Your slaves are your brothers—that is what the Prophet commanded! The next time I see you or one of your friends mistreating these people, I will tie you together like these poor devils!"

The driver gave him a look filled with hate and tried to free himself. Disgusted, Rouston pushed him away so hard that he almost fell down again.

Sibylla watched with bated breath. At last, someone had found the courage to fight for the captives!

Rouston had joined their caravan in Marrakesh because he was on his way back to the Chiadma. Sibylla had not had the opportunity to speak with him herself since he rode a little apart most of the time.

"Is there a problem?" Toledano asked. He had hurriedly trotted up on his donkey from the head of the caravan. One of the slave drivers must have alerted him.

"Stop your men from mistreating these people!" the Frenchman snapped at him.

"With all due respect, Señor Rouston, I acquired these Negroes legally and, if they are obstinate, they will be punished. Only then will they appreciate the power of their master."

He spoke in measured tones. Yet his attitude left no room for doubt that he resented the interference.

"They're not being obstinate, Señor Toledano, they're exhausted!" Rouston shouted, but the merchant merely nodded politely and rode away.

Meanwhile, Benjamin had ridden up to Sibylla. He was annoyed by the way his wife was admiring the Frenchman.

"So your heroic representative of the *grande nation* is trying to introduce these Negroes to the concept of human rights, is he?" he remarked smugly.

"No need to be so rude. You, after all, are in business with a slave trader," Sibylla responded calmly.

He glared at her. "And aren't you rather sanctimonious for someone whose grandfather made a fortune from the slave trade? Besides, Toledano is one of the sultan's merchants. It's impossible to do any business around here without him. Unless, of course, one is selling shoes directly to the sultan's harem."

"One might think you're envious."

"Envious? How ridiculous. I'm just reminding you to mind your own business. The Negroes are Toledano's. He has paid for them and can do with them as he wishes."

Before Sibylla could respond, Benjamin had pointedly guided his mule toward Toledano. She watched him ride away, her lips pressed together. Benjamin had been curt and irritated with her for the last several days. She had very much wanted to explore Marrakesh with him, but he had avoided her as though it were her fault the audience with the sultan had not gone as he had hoped. That same evening in their room in the inn, she had even told him how sorry she was, but he had cut her short and stormed out of the room.

In a few weeks, we are going to be a family. But even this child does not seem to be bringing us closer to one another, Sibylla thought glumly.

She knew Benjamin had come to Morocco full of ambition, anxious to impress his father-in-law and be rewarded with a management position back home. Yet one disappointment followed on the heels of another, first with Qaid Hash-Hash and now with the sultan.

Perhaps she was not doing her duty to help her husband gain a foothold here? Sibylla sighed softly. She felt no real desire to support him.

She much preferred to act autonomously, to learn about both business and local culture on her own. She had bought several bolts of silk cloth at the *souk* in Marrakesh, which she planned to offer to merchants in London. Benjamin knew nothing about this and, judging by their latest row, he was not going to be at all pleased once he found out.

If I really want to heal the rift between my husband and me, I should stop trading, she thought. As difficult as it was, Sibylla resolved that this would be her last deal. She would soon become a mother and have no more time for business anyhow.

Irritated, she shooed away some flies buzzing around her face and, at that moment, was racked by a piercing pain.

"My lady? Are you all right?" In an instant, Nadira was by her side.

"No!" she gasped, holding her abdomen. "Get my husband! Quickly!"

Chapter Eight

"Don't be troubled, Señor Hopkins. Even the sultan himself—may the Almighty grant him eternal life—knows that one cannot skin an ox twice." Riding next to Benjamin, Samuel Toledano studied him. "Believe me, there is good business to be done anywhere you want."

Benjamin looked morosely at the slaves stumbling along one after the other. "That is surely not the case with your Negroes," he grumbled. "I don't suppose that these rawboned characters here will fetch much."

Toledano bowed his head. "You are right, of course, Señor Hopkins. The proceeds are hardly worth the barley groats I have to feed them to fatten them up," he lamented.

Then he looked around and rode closer to Benjamin's mule. "Over in America, the prices are still quite decent: seventy pounds for a healthy man and fifty for a woman. But unfortunately, you English have prohibited overseas sales."

"Seventy pounds!" Benjamin stopped his mule and looked at Toledano in disbelief. His father was grateful to make about twice that sum a year at his job as a bank teller.

"I assure you, Señor Hopkins, and if you will allow me . . ." Toledano once again looked around in all directions.

Nadira came up galloping.

"Master, master!" Her face was distorted with worry. "Please come! The mistress is in great pain."

Sibylla screamed in anguish, dropping her reins and grasping her abdomen. Disoriented, her mule took off at an irregular trot. Sibylla groaned. Every step felt like a stab. She collapsed in the saddle and clung to the animal's mane.

"Sibylla, for heaven's sake, don't fall!" Sara Willshire guided her mule next to her friend's and tried to take the reins, but the startled animal flung its head back and forth and made it impossible.

"Help! Stop! We need help!" Sara screamed.

Eventually, the pain in Sibylla's abdomen subsided, allowing her to reach for the reins and stop the animal.

"What's the matter with you?" Sara asked, profoundly alarmed.

Sibylla shook her head. Her face was white. "I just had a horrible pain in my belly and back. It's much better now."

"Your child! It's coming!" Sara gasped, crossing herself. "Here, in the middle of nowhere!"

"Nonsense!" Sibylla replied. "I still have four weeks to go."

"You had better dismount in any case," said a French-accented voice behind her.

Sara and Sibylla turned and stared at Monsieur Rouston. He leapt off his brown mare, walked over to Sibylla's mule, and took the reins.

"Madame Hopkins, *n'est-ce pas*? My name is André Rouston." His voice was soft and reassuring, and yet she blushed.

"*Alors*, madame, don't be afraid. I'll help you." He extended his hand to Sibylla. She tried to stand in the stirrups, but was overcome by a new wave of pain.

"Stay calm, madame," she heard Rouston say. "Give me your hand. I have you."

As the contraction subsided, Sibylla took the hand offered to her. Rouston's hand was warm, tanned, and callused on the inside.

The nervous mule suddenly stamped its hooves and she fell against Rouston with a cry. Quickly, he caught her in his arms.

"I am going to carry you into the shade now, Madame Hopkins. Can you see the palm tree with the three trunks over there by the dry riverbed?"

She nodded silently and clenched her teeth in pain.

He noticed this and continued. "You were so concerned about the well-being of the blacks, you must have forgotten all about your own."

"Fortunately, you, Monsieur Rouston, seem always to be in the right place at the right time, whether to help maltreated slaves or a woman in distress," she replied. She noticed how flippant the words sounded and was annoyed with herself. She wanted to convey to him how very grateful she was.

"Stubborn girl was determined to undertake this trip even though I warned her against it!" Sara had gotten down from her mule and was trailing behind the Frenchman and Sibylla, looking anxious.

Sibylla shook her head. "I'm fine. The pains will go away. I've had them all along."

Sara placed her hand on her friend's arm. "What? Since when?"

"Since we left Marrakesh," Sibylla replied softly. "And a little bit before, but not so severely."

"And you said nothing? At least in Marrakesh we would have had doctors and midwives!"

"The child is due in four weeks? Did I hear that correctly?" Rouston asked.

He was carrying Sibylla as gently as a porcelain doll. She felt safe and sheltered in his arms, and the pain no longer frightened her so. When they reached the palm tree, Rouston knelt down and delicately placed her on the ground, careful to ensure she was entirely in the shade of the sprawling tree. Sibylla heaved a sigh of relief. Even the afternoon heat was more tolerable here. The Frenchman looked at her pensively.

"Perhaps the journey has been too stressful. Your child may indeed come sooner than expected."

Alarmed, the women looked at each other.

"No! Not here!" Sibylla implored. What a nightmare, to be delivered of a child along this caravan route without any help! She turned her head and looked over to the chained slaves, the heavily laden camels, to the slave drivers and the riders on their donkeys, mules, and horses, who marched by in a long line without taking much notice of her. And to think she was to blame for her own misery! Tears welled up in her eyes. "Oh, if only I were at home!"

Rouston went to his mare and fetched his rolled-up blanket from behind the animal's saddle. He returned to Sibylla and pushed the blanket under her head.

"You must not get upset, Madame Hopkins. I am afraid that, by the time you arrive home, you will have a baby in your arms. We cannot help that, but we are going to get you safely to the *caravanserai*, at least. You cannot ride, so I am going to build a stretcher for you. Toledano will have to lend me four of his strongest men, and they shall carry you for the next few hours. Can you hold on that long?" He scrutinized her face.

"I'll try."

"Build a stretcher? But how?" inquired Sara Willshire.

"I learned it as a soldier. A few strong branches and a blanket is all I need. It's best if I start looking at once. Finding good trees is the hardest part." He looked at the almost treeless plain, which was covered in sand and stones. "There are some young jujube trees on that knoll over there. Perhaps I can use them." He jumped on his horse and galloped off.

Sara sighed. Then she took a handkerchief from her skirt pocket, found the water bottle hanging on her mule's saddle, poured lukewarm liquid over the cloth, and sat down next to her friend. "How are you feeling?" She gently dabbed Sibylla's forehead, face, and neck.

"Better right now, thank you." Sibylla's eyes followed the small dust cloud making its way up the hill. "Monsieur Rouston is a gentleman, isn't he? I mean a true gentleman, not one who just pretends to be polite to a woman but in fact thinks very little of her."

They watched as Rouston reached the top of the hill, took his scimitar from his saddle, and began hacking away at the trees.

"Watching him attack those trees just to be of service to you, my dear, one might almost feel pity for the poor plants," said Sara.

"What do you mean?" giggled Sibylla.

They could hear rapid hoofbeats approaching. Benjamin jumped off his mule and threw the reins to Nadira, who had followed on her donkey.

"Sibylla!" His face was pale with worry. "What's happened? Are you all right? You didn't fall from your mule, did you?" He squatted down next to her.

"No, but she has pains in her belly. It's possible that the child is trying to be born," Sara informed him.

"But not here, not now!" Benjamin stammered just as Sibylla had done.

"I'm afraid that that is for the child to decide. I just pray it will be patient until we reach the *caravanserai*." Sibylla smiled weakly.

"You can't possibly ride that far," Benjamin replied incredulously.

"Monsieur Rouston is building a stretcher," Sara said. "Fortunately, he was nearby and able to assist your wife."

Benjamin's expression darkened. "I told you not to travel to Marrakesh, but you knew better, of course!"

"And you were right, of course." She placed her hand on his arm. "I should have listened to you."

Benjamin looked almost mollified. "Do you remember when we fell into the harbor basin in London? I was there then and helped you. And today I am going to help you reach the inn safe and sound."

◆ ◆ ◆

Blue velvet darkness was swiftly falling when the contours of the *caravanserai* appeared before them. Sibylla was at the end of her tether despite the stretcher that Rouston had fashioned. The pain in her abdomen had hardly let up. It came in inconsistent intervals and was so severe that it took her breath away.

"These contractions are preparation for the birth. They are stretching your body for your child's head to pass," Nadira explained. She had not left her mistress's side.

"Are you a midwife?" Sara Willshire, also riding at Sibylla's side, was astonished.

Nadira shook her head. "I am not an expert, but I have assisted with many births. My mistress need not be afraid."

"If nothing happens to her or the child, I'll give you an extra month's salary," said Benjamin. He felt uncomfortable not only because he had no idea how to console his wife, but also because he himself was terrified for her and for his unborn child. Not knowing what else to do, he repeatedly admonished the stretcher bearers to be careful and alerted them to every stone on the path.

Rouston had not stayed with them. No sooner had Sibylla been safely placed on the stretcher than he galloped off to the *caravanserai* to make arrangements for the birth. Nadira had told him they would require a quiet room, boiled water, clean towels, and thread, plus torches and candles for light.

When the exhausted bearers came staggering through the arched gate four hours later, Rouston ran to greet them. "I have readied a room in a remote corner. Madame Hopkins can be taken there immediately."

Benjamin lifted Sibylla from the stretcher. Her eyes were closed and her forehead covered in sweat.

"How are you?"

"Afraid," she whispered without opening her eyes.

So am I, he thought. But he tried his best to sound confident. "Women have children every day. My mother had five!"

She smiled faintly. "I hope not to have to endure this pain five times."

"I can hear the heartbeat," Nadira said. "It's strong and regular."

Sibylla was lying in a tiny room on a thin mattress. The thick, windowless mud walls kept out the heat of the day. Nadira had lit two torches and placed them in sconces on the wall. Then she had squatted next to Sibylla, lifted her kaftan, and placed one ear just above the navel on the bulging belly. Now she lifted her head.

"Your child is strong, my lady. If you permit, I am going to feel its position."

Sibylla nodded. She had neither doctor nor midwife to assist her, but Nadira seemed more experienced than she'd let on. Sara Willshire's presence consoled her as well. The consul's wife was kneeling next to her and tirelessly shooing away mosquitoes. Ten minutes before, when a rush of bloody water had come from between her legs, Sibylla had been convinced there was something wrong with the child.

But Sara had soothed her. "That's only your bag of waters breaking. That always happens before the child is pushed out of the mother's body."

But for the time being, there was no sign of that. In fact, the contractions had stopped. But even that was normal, Sara had assured her. She urged Sibylla to use this respite to gather her strength.

Nadira's hands were palpating her mistress's belly inch by inch. Finally, she explained, "The child is lying the wrong way around, my lady. His head is up top and his backside at the bottom. But don't worry," she added quickly, seeing Sibylla's frightened expression. "For the mother, it is almost the same." She hesitated. "Though it might take a little longer and hurt more."

Sibylla nodded bravely. "So long as you are here to help me. They all come out eventually, don't they?"

"Is your mistress in danger?" Sara asked.

Nadira shook her head. She did not tell the ladies that a breech birth was more likely to endanger the life of the child. If the umbilical cord were to be compressed and the child deprived of the mother's blood supply, it might die. But Nadira was going to do everything to prevent that from happening.

"Ahhh!" Sibylla groaned and jolted upright.

Sara took a firm hold of her friend's hand.

Benjamin anxiously paced the courtyard of the *caravanserai*. He kept looking up at the closed door behind which his wife had disappeared several hours earlier. The eastern sky announced the night's end. The refreshing cool air would soon be simmering in the first rays of sunshine. The doves on the roof of the inn greeted the morning with soft coos. The travelers too were slowly awakening. Several Arabs had rolled out small prayer rugs in one corner of the courtyard and said their morning prayers in the direction of Mecca.

The camel drivers were seeing to the needs of their animals. Small flames were flickering in several hearths. The scent of mint and freshly baked bread wafted over to Benjamin. He had not eaten since noon the day before, but he did not feel hungry.

"Still no news?" Rouston appeared next to him.

Benjamin shook his head. "I can't imagine why it should take this long."

"Yes, well, we men expect quite a lot from women, don't we?" Rouston remarked. He reached into the inside pocket of his jacket, pulled out a flat silver flask, and handed it to Benjamin. "You look like you could use some."

Benjamin looked at him with some uncertainty at first, but then accepted the flask and took a long draft. "Oh yes. That is good." He wiped his mouth with the back of his hand. "Even if I do prefer whisky to cognac." He was about to return the flask to the Frenchman when Rouston said, "Finish it, Hopkins."

Benjamin was more than happy to comply. "Do you have a family, Rouston?"

The Frenchman shook his head and grinned. "Not that I know of."

"A bachelor, I see. Well, I have done well for myself by giving up bachelorhood. All sorts of opportunities have become available to me since I married a shipping company, so to speak." Benjamin giggled, the alcohol and anxiety loosening his tongue.

As muffled screams reached the courtyard, his demeanor changed. "Though I must confess I am quite concerned," he muttered. "Because, you know, the child is very early. I told my wife not to undertake this journey, but she can be stubborn."

Rouston nodded silently. He liked independent women. They had a certain pride and confidence that he found attractive. He thought of Idri, the Chiadma woman with whom he had shared his life for two years. They had met during a *moussem*, a festival in the mountains, during which the whole tribe was gathered. There was much celebration, music, and dancing. Idri was a pretty widow with coal black eyes, breasts like ripe apples, and swaying hips. According to Berber custom, widows and divorced women determined for themselves who their next husbands would be, and how long they would be permitted to stay, for divorces were as simple as marriages. André and Idri had sealed their union before the *qaid* of their tribe as well as five male and five female witnesses. Afterward, André had paraded his wife on a donkey across the festival square.

He jumped at the earsplitting scream above him. The men looked at each other, wide-eyed. Then they heard the soft bawling of a newborn.

"My child," Benjamin whispered. "It's here!"

The door to Sibylla's room was flung open and Sara Willshire appeared.

"Mr. Hopkins, come and welcome your son!"

Chapter Nine

Mogador, December 1839

"Tom! Give it! Mummy!"

Sibylla sighed, laid the letter she had just opened on the table, and went to the gallery to find out what was happening. "What's the matter now? Tom, are you teasing your little brother again?"

Three-year-old Thomas looked innocently at his mother. His two-year-old brother, John, stood beside him, wailing miserably.

"I want!" He pointed accusingly at Tom, who was holding the morsel out of his little brother's reach.

Sibylla had to suppress a smile. The two looked so adorable in their little kaftans over their long pants, especially Johnny, who had not yet lost his baby fat. Everything about him was chubby and soft, and his tearstained eyes looked so pitiful. Like his brother, he had light blond curls and deep blue eyes. Tom was taller and slimmer, with delicate features that made him appear older than his three years.

John was only fifteen months younger than his brother. Sibylla had told Benjamin she wanted another child, and was delighted when, shortly after Thomas's birth, she found herself pregnant again. The baby had turned out to be a boy and, when she held the rosy little creature in her arms for the first time, she completely forgot that she had wished for a girl.

"Tom, did you take your brother's pastry?" Sibylla asked.

"No, Mummy!" Tom shook his head vehemently. "It's mine. He dropped his in the water and Daddy's carps ate it!"

"Is that right, Johnny?" Sibylla looked into the pond in which the fat gold-colored carp, Benjamin's pride and joy, were lazily swimming their rounds.

The little boy nodded through his tears. Eating was one of his favorite activities, and the sweet gazelle's horns filled with almond paste, which Nadira had given the children, were one of his favorites.

"How many times have I told you to sit and eat your food in peace, John? If you do that, you won't drop anything," Sibylla admonished her younger son.

"Hungry," Johnny replied plaintively.

"You'll have to wait until lunchtime, darling. Run along and play now!"

The little boy made a face as though he was about to start crying again.

"Here." Tom broke the remainder of his horn in two and gave a piece to his brother, who immediately stuffed it into his mouth.

Sibylla was touched. "That was a wonderful thing to do, my love."

Tom's affectionate concern was not only for his little brother. He was always anxious about everyone's well-being: his mother and father, Firyal, Nadira, and all the servants. He even asked his mother whether the beggars in the alleyways had food to eat and a bed to sleep in like he did.

Sibylla was grateful that her firstborn was growing up so healthy and kind. After his birth, she had been unable to nurse him, and Thomas had been raised on donkey milk fed to him drop by drop. Rouston had purchased a female donkey while Sibylla was still recovering in the *caravanserai*. He had also transported her and the newborn safely back to Mogador. Benjamin, expecting some ships from London, had been unable to stay with her. She herself had urged him to go, although she had been quietly disappointed that he had actually left her behind in the *caravanserai*. But if he hadn't, she would never have discovered what a diverting travel companion André Rouston was. While she was lying on the stretcher—this time with her baby—being carried by four slaves, he rode next to her and chatted. So she learned that, after the Algerian War, he had traveled all over the Maghreb. His descriptions of his encounters with belligerent Berber tribes, sage Arab scholars, and Oriental princes living in unimaginable splendor were so lively that Sibylla felt like she'd been there herself. She particularly liked the story of how he had visited Moulay Idriss, Morocco's holiest city in the northern part of the Atlas Mountains on the pilgrims' route to Mecca, disguised as a Muslim.

"John!" Sibylla shouted, leaning over the bannister. "Be sure to thank your brother for sharing with you."

"Thank you, Tom," the little boy said with a full mouth. Then he extended his sticky hand. "More!"

Tom laughed mischievously. "Come and get it!" He ran off, John at his heels.

Sibylla watched them run around the old olive tree and then charge up to the sundial that Benjamin had bought two years ago to celebrate a particularly lucrative deal. To Sibylla's great amazement, he had even dug a base for it himself. Her husband was not normally a big enthusiast of physical labor. Once the sundial had been assembled, polished, and set in the courtyard of their *riad*, he had planted the Union Jack in the ground next to it and invited the *qaid* for a viewing. Sibylla remembered how proudly he had shown off his valuable sundial. His sons saw it mostly as a jungle gym, much to Benjamin's chagrin.

"You boys leave the sundial alone, do you hear me?" Sibylla called. Benjamin was not at home—the better business was, the less time he spent with his family—but she did not want to risk any trouble.

Fortunately, the boys could romp outside all year round. Even now, in early December, it was as mild as England in the springtime. The roses were in bloom in the *riad*'s courtyard, the flowers still exuded their intoxicating scent, and the little orange trees that Sibylla had had planted on both sides of the staircase bore succulent fruit. She thought it was wonderful to be able to forgo boots, muff, fur cap, and long coat. All she needed was a shawl around her shoulders. In turn, she gladly tolerated the sand and dust that the constant wind drove into the house.

She returned to her room. In her native England, the chimneys would be lit, but here in Morocco, all that was needed was a copper pan with a little coal. She took a small piece of scented resin from a bowl and threw it into the embers. The room filled with the scent of amber and nutmeg. Sibylla closed her eyes with pleasure. She loved her life here—unlike Benjamin, who even now regarded everything with suspicion.

She sat on the divan and took out the letter again. It was from her stepmother and had arrived on the mail boat the day before, together with various issues of the *Times* and a box filled with books. Mary was Sibylla's most reliable connection to England. She kept her stepdaughter up-to-date on all the latest news in London. Currently, everyone was preparing for the social event of the century, the wedding of young Queen Victoria and the German Prince Albert of Saxe-Coburg and Gotha. Every week, Mary and Richard were invited to balls and receptions given in the couple's honor, and Mary complained that her seamstress and milliner could not keep up with the design of all her trains, gowns, hats, and gloves. Also, she was concerned about Richard's health. He had celebrated his fiftieth birthday the previous year, but suffered from dizziness, shortness of breath, and poor sleep. She was planning to take him to have the cure in Bath the next summer, she wrote, since the new rail connection had made it easier to reach.

Sibylla folded the letter and laid it on the table. Then she got up, moved the divan away from the wall, and removed a loose board from the back of the wooden frame. Hidden behind it was her secret compartment. She reached inside and pulled out a rectangular box made of rosewood and mother-of-pearl. There was a little lock on the front. This box was where she kept the money she made from her business transactions. First, the sixty *benduqui* that Rusa and Lalla Jasira had paid her for the English slippers. Once word had gotten out that His Sovereign Majesty's wives dressed their feet in English *babouches*, the wives of important courtiers, *qaids*, and *viziers* wanted to be a part of the new fashion trend. Business grew without Sibylla's having to pay too much attention to it, and the resolution she had made before Thomas's birth to stop for the benefit of her marriage was quickly forgotten.

Rusa and Lalla Jasira brokered much of her business and received a small commission for their efforts. Sibylla used part of her proceeds to pay for the goods she exported to London. Thanks to Lalla Jasira, she had contacts to merchants who provided silk, brocade, and damask of the finest quality, materials much in demand in England. Although Benjamin complained when she took up cargo space on the boats, Sibylla enjoyed her trade too much to give it up. No one except Sibylla knew about the little box, not even Benjamin, who regarded her business as nothing more than silly dalliances on which she squandered her dowry.

Sibylla carried the box over to her desk, pulled a thin chain holding a small key from under her dress, unlocked the box, took out a leather-bound notebook, and opened it. Then she dipped her quill and wrote: *December 5, 1839.* Underneath, she recorded the expenses for five boxes of velvet shawls that had arrived that day in Mogador and that were meant to warm the shoulders of London ladies this raw English winter. The merchant had sworn that his wares came from Kashmir, and begged God to strike him with blindness if he had dared deliver inferior quality to the *Engliziya*.

Sibylla spread sand on the wet ink, closed the notebook, placed it back in the box, and locked it carefully. As she pushed the divan back to the wall, she could hear the coins jingling behind it and she smiled contentedly.

There was a knock at the door and Firyal entered, carrying a tray with a glass of warm almond milk and a plate of sesame sweets. She placed it on the flat table in front of the divan.

"There you are, my lady," she said, looking uneasily at her feet. "Will there be anything else?"

"Thank you, Firyal, that will be all," Sibylla replied warmly.

The servant quickly disappeared. Sibylla noticed that she was wearing a colorful new dress wrapped tight around her hips. Presumably, the material was a reward for the nights she spent in Benjamin's bedroom.

Benjamin had taken the servant into his bed shortly after John's birth, when he and Sibylla had moved into separate rooms. She had long noticed the lascivious way his eyes lingered on Firyal's bottom or her ample breasts whenever she leaned over to pour his tea. At night, she had heard the telltale tapping of feet on the wooden planks and the soft opening and closing of doors. The following day, Firyal always avoided her. And yet Sibylla did not hold a grudge against her husband; quite the contrary, she was glad that Benjamin acted out his male desires with the servant. She had never appreciated the physical side of marriage, and she did not mind forgoing it. She had long ago abandoned the notion of finding romance with Benjamin.

"The *Engliz* can make horses fly! What's next, a flying ship?" Qaid Hash-Hash shaded his eyes from the sun and squinted at the magnificent red animal. As the gangway was too narrow, the sailors had harnessed the horse to the pulleys of the main yard, and now the precious cargo was floating halfway between the *Queen Charlotte*'s deck and the dock. The spectacle was so remarkable that Benjamin, the *qaid*, and the harbor-master were surrounded by a fast-growing crowd of onlookers. Nuri bin Kalil translated because Benjamin, in contrast to his wife, had managed to learn almost no Arabic, despite having already spent more than three years in Morocco.

Benjamin answered with a hearty laugh. "What's next, you ask? Why, a flying carpet, of course! No offense, Your Excellency, but since the sultan offers his guests only tottery mules for transportation, I had to arrange for a decent horse for myself!"

The governor studied the arrogant Englishman. A conspicuous sundial, carp from another part of the world, clothing tailored from the finest cloth, and now this magnificent stallion. He was deeply interested to know how the Englishman acquired the means for such luxuries.

I am going to set one of my informants on him, Hash-Hash decided as he enviously eyed the horse, which had by now been deposited on the quay. Benjamin proudly walked up to the animal and was about to take hold of the halter when a seagull swooped in close, spooking the horse and making it rear.

"Hey there, what's the matter? Calm down." Benjamin jumped back. As he did, his tall top hat, which gave him the appearance of a long, thin reed among the shorter Arab men, fell off.

The *qaid* croaked with laughter. "Your horse wants to fly again, Englishman. I think it knows the Koran. There it is written, Thou shalt fly without wings!"

But Benjamin could not hear him. He was busy chasing his hat, which the wind was driving along the quay.

The governor slowly approached the horse. *By God, what a wonderful stallion*, he thought, congratulating himself on having offered the Englishman the use of his stables. He would mate the magnificent animal with one of his mares and ride it without the Englishman's knowledge. The man's equestrian skills were like those of a monkey riding a camel, and he was using the horse only to show off anyway.

"Be careful, Your Excellency!" Benjamin called out as the stallion shook its flame-colored mane.

But the *qaid* was undeterred. Speaking mellifluously and softly, he took hold of the halter and reassuringly patted the animal's neck. The stallion snorted but held still, and Benjamin watched in disbelief as the Arab stroked the flanks, then squatted and felt the legs while a sailor carefully removed the straps.

"He has the chest of a lion, and his legs are as muscular as those of a wild ostrich," the *qaid* declared with admiration.

Flattered, Benjamin adjusted his top hat and replied, "He comes from Earl Godolphin's stock and has won many important races in England. I'll wager a hundred pounds that he could leave any of your little Arabian horses in the dust."

The *qaid's* eyes sparkled, but unfortunately, the Prophet had strictly forbidden games of chance. With a heavy heart, he replied, "I will forgo the competition for your sake, Mr. Hopkins. An Arabian horse is unbeatable."

"You jest!" cried Benjamin. "Even my three-year-old son would come in first on an English stallion such as this!"

The *qaid* bared his teeth furiously. "Before you mount this stallion, you are going to pay the import tax, or else I shall be compelled to confiscate him."

Benjamin swallowed back an angry reply. That cutthroat Hash-Hash was capable of anything. These Muslims were probably so foul-tempered because it was Ramadan. After all, denying yourself even the most basic necessities throughout the day and then gorging after sundown was surely not very healthy. No wonder they awakened in the morning with an upset stomach and in a bad mood! Benjamin, smirking to himself, watched as the *qaid* trudged away without any acknowledgment.

"So this time it's a racehorse that you're rubbing the Arab's nose in. Didn't anyone ever tell you that it's stupid to show off like that?" a voice behind Benjamin whispered.

He spun around. "Brown! For God's sake! I hadn't noticed you. Do you have to creep up on me like that?"

The *Queen Charlotte*'s captain grinned. Benjamin looked at the man's decayed tooth stumps and grimaced in disgust. Brown resembled a crow with his dark frockcoat, stringy graying hair, and dark, piercing eyes.

"We should leave now," he declared. "Or have you forgotten that we have an appointment with old Toledano? This was a devil of a trip, by the way. I'll tell you about it when we get to Toledano's . . ."

André Rouston placed both hands on the remnants of a three-hundred-year-old stone wall that had once been part of a small church built by the Portuguese when they had had a trading post here. At one time, it had been possible to stand on the brick floor and see the beams of the steeple with its bell. Now, however, both the roof truss and the bell were gone, and André enjoyed the wide view of the Atlantic. Far to the southwest, the pale gold December sun had broken through the veil of mist and sparkled on the water like diamond dust. In the north, the color of the waves alternated between ink blue and stone gray. Whitecaps danced on the surf. It was low tide; the ocean was slowly retreating, exposing the wrecks of fishing boats run aground outside the harbor entrance, and leaving behind shells, driftwood, and a wavy impression on the wet sand.

Whenever André had business in Mogador, he came to this place, secluded from the noisy, bustling harbor. He watched two three-masted sailing ships, one flying the red-and-green banner of Portugal, the other with the French tricolor. They had rounded the promontory and set course for the open seas, their sails inflated.

Whenever he stood in the ruins of the old church, listening to the seagulls screeching and the eternal rushing of the water, he pictured the ships that carried their cargo to every corner of the earth and then took the exotic wares of distant countries on board in return. He was fascinated by the way shipping connected all the continents of the world. Years before, during his brief stint as a sailor, he had not yet seen things that way. He had experienced brutality, cruelty, oppressive confinement, and draconian punishment. And as soon as his ship had reached its homeport in northern France, he had run away. To the army.

He could hear the jeering laughter of children below the walls. Next, the reproachful voice of a little boy called out in English, "Mummy, you're doing it wrong! It keeps falling down!"

Curious, André leaned over the parapet. Directly below, a half dozen Arab boys were jumping up and down, screaming something about stupid infidels. At some distance from them in the sand stood two little boys with curly blond hair. The younger hopped excitedly around the older, trying to snatch a ribbon, which the older one clutched tightly. At the other end of the ribbon was a diamond-shaped kite made of red and yellow parchment paper being held by a woman.

André was elated when he recognized her. The wind had pulled a few golden strands out of her long braid and was playing with the hem of her kaftan. She jumped in the air, trying to launch the kite. He noted with a grin that she was barefoot. For a few seconds, the paper kite spun helplessly in the air, sagged, then crashed to the ground while the Arab boys jeered and whistled.

André's eyes wandered from the kite to the woman. She was kneeling before her distraught son and trying to dry his tears with her handkerchief. But Tom crossed his arms and turned away from his mother. He obviously blamed her for the fact that the kite would not fly.

It did not take André long to spot the cause of the problem. After all, he was a farmer's son from the Causses region in the south of France, and he'd grown up building and flying kites on the high, windy plains near his home. How lucky for Sibylla and her boys that he was there to help! He pushed away from the rough tower wall and hastened toward the beach with a spring in his step.

André knew it was unwise, but he had longed to meet Sibylla Hopkins again, without her husband, servants, or Mrs. Willshire. And now *le bon* Dieu—the good Lord—had granted him this opportunity. Who knew when He might see fit to do so again!

Chapter Ten

"Monsieur Rouston! But what on earth?"

Sibylla tried to smooth her windblown strands of hair only to have the wind tousle them again. He noted with delight that she blushed and tried to hide her bare feet in the sand.

He had found her looks remarkable more than three years ago when she had stood before the sultan in Marrakesh. Tall and slender, light haired and light skinned, she stood out in this country like a rainbow over the desert. Yet it was her face that captivated him. It was only at first glance that Sibylla looked like a delicate English rose. If one looked more closely, as he did, one noticed the headstrong line around her mouth and her keen, intelligent eyes. This woman took an interest in everything happening around her and always wanted to get to the heart of the matter.

He'd understood immediately why they compared her to a lioness—it was not only because of the color of her hair, but because of her determined personality. What heavily pregnant woman would undertake the arduous journey from Mogador to Marrakesh? His friend Udad bin Aziki, sheikh of the Chiadma Berbers, had tried to warn him. "If you find a great treasure, beware of the fearsome snake that is hiding." The reminder that Sibylla was a married woman and a mother had not dimmed André's fascination.

And now this absurd joy at seeing her again.

"*Bonjour*, Madame Hopkins." He extended his right hand. "I didn't mean to startle you. But it seemed to me that these charming boys could use a little help." He winked at Tom, who was sheepishly wiping away his tears.

"I'm afraid you're right," Sibylla said. "Benjamin built this kite for the children, but it simply won't fly."

John came toddling over on his little legs to investigate. André leaned toward the children. "You two are Tom and John, no? I will show you how to make your kite fly."

The brothers nodded happily.

"Bon alors, garçons," said André. "Now listen to me. John, you go and get the kite. Tom and I are going to cut off a piece of the line and you, little rascals over there," he said, switching languages as he turned to speak to the Arab boys, "go and get me an armful of halfa grass over there by the fortress wall."

The boys scampered off, Johnny ran to fetch the kite, and Tom helped cut a piece of the line with André's sharp knife.

Sibylla had put her shoes back on and was trying to put her hair in some kind of order. She listened as Rouston showed the children how to make a tail for the kite using tufts of halfa grass by knotting them at regular intervals on a piece of line. With his black jacket, shirt belted at the waist, and wide pants tucked into his leather boots, he reminded her a little of an Ottoman officer she had met at the Willshires'.

"A kite needs a tail to prevent it from spinning on its axis and crashing," André was explaining to the children. He turned the kite over so that the cross that Benjamin had built from thin wooden sticks was on top, and slightly shortened the line that was attached to it.

"Now all we have to do is knot the tail onto the kite and then you'll see how wonderfully it flies. *Bon*!" He got up. "Promise not to fight and to take turns holding the line?"

The boys nodded earnestly. André handed the line to Tom, beckoned one of the Arab boys to come closer, and gave him the kite. "What's your name, son?"

"Sabri bin Abdul bin Ibrahim bin Ridwan bin Nurredin al Mogadori," the little boy proudly answered. "But you can call me Sabri."

"Pleased to meet you, Sabri. This boy here is called Tom Hopkins. You two are going to make this kite fly. You are going to take it and run as fast as you can while Tom holds the line. When I give you the signal, you'll throw the kite as high as you can, *oui*?"

The boy nodded seriously, then ran down the beach, kicking up sand behind him.

"Now!" shouted André, as the line grew taut in Tom's fist and the colorful kite rose into the blue sky, accompanied by the joyful cries of the children.

"Be careful not to let it fall into the water," he warned.

Then he turned to Sibylla, who had been shouting encouragements to the boys as well, placed his hand on his heart, and bowed with exaggerated gallantry. "Now we'll have some time to chat."

"Why not?" she replied.

The wind tore at Rouston's short black hair and Sibylla found herself wanting to touch it. She blushed again and reminded herself that this was madness. It would only end up making her unhappy.

And yet she could not stop her heart from pounding in her chest. She felt powerfully drawn to this Frenchman with his suntanned skin, laugh lines around his dark eyes, and wavy hair.

They had crossed paths several times since his heroics in the desert. She had seen him at New Year's receptions at the European consulates and now and again at the *souk*, where he would be selling the Chiadma's orange crop in spring and summer, the date crop in fall, and saffron and olives in winter. They had never been alone together and, still, every single one of their encounters was burned into her memory.

She had told no one about her disturbing feelings, but at night, when she heard Firyal tiptoe into Benjamin's room, she would find herself thinking about Rouston and wonder if he had a Chiadma wife, perhaps even children, or if he preferred a life without attachments.

The strong wind carried them snatches of the *muezzin's* call to *asr*, the afternoon prayer. André took off his jacket and laid it on the sand. "Please." He smiled at Sibylla. "Do have a seat." He sat down on the ground next to her and held out a paper bag. "Do you like roasted pistachios?"

"I do!" She reached into the bag. "I love Moroccan cuisine. We just don't have all of these delectable tidbits in England."

Rouston looked at her and a smile crossed his face. He too had felt an invisible bond from the first moment they met, and it made him happy in a way he had never known. He longed to tell Sibylla that he found her body, which her pregnancies had made fuller and more feminine, beguiling, and that the warmth radiating from her face made her the most beautiful woman in the world. But that was impossible. André had often wondered how fussy Hopkins, whose undiplomatic and grandiose demeanor had made him so unpopular with the Moroccans, could have been blessed with such an extraordinary woman as his wife.

"Monsieur Rouston?"

He cleared his throat. "Excuse me, dear madame. What was it you said?"

"I asked you what brought you to Mogador. Do you have business in the *souk*? I'm there myself quite a bit. It's a wonderful place, isn't it? All the aromas and sounds! One alleyway smells of soap and perfume, the next has Persian carpets and Indian silks, and the next camel heads and freshly skinned sheep. How marvelous!"

André tore himself away from her glistening blue eyes and answered, "You are correct, I was at the *souk* to sell the saffron harvested in November. The merchants were expecting it. But, of course, I had to deliver some to the sultan's private chef before anyone else."

"Morocco's red gold," Sibylla said with a smile. "That's what my father calls it."

"Because it is the world's most precious spice," André replied with excitement. "It is a secret in most of the world, but the Chiadma taught me how to grow it."

"And how is it that you, a European, came to be privy to this secret?"

"I arbitrated between the sheikhs of the Chiadma and the sultan, and was thus able to resolve a feud. As an expression of their gratitude, the Chiadma initiated me into the cultivation of saffron. Because, you see, the feud between them and the Alaouites had persisted for centuries and had brought their people to the brink of destruction. So now they prefer to pay him the *ushur*, the agricultural tax, rather than try to usurp his throne."

"Perhaps one day you will sell the Chiadma's saffron to us."

"I would, but your husband refuses to buy. He tells me the export taxes are too high and that he has other merchandise he can export at a lower price."

Sibylla looked him straight in the eye. "If you had negotiated with me, we would have found a solution satisfactory to all."

He gave her a mischievous smile. "I do not doubt it. One day, when I grow my own saffron, I shall come to you first, my lady."

"Benjamin had a hard time of it at the start," Sibylla said, feeling the need to apologize for her husband. "But then, after Thomas's birth, business began to take off. Now he is so busy that we hardly see each other."

She glanced over to the children. It was little Sabri's turn to hold the line, but John was already impatiently tugging at his kaftan.

"Benjamin did want to fly his kite with the boys," she mused. "But then the *Queen Charlotte* came in earlier than expected." Sibylla took another handful of pistachios. "Is it true that Sultan Abd al-Rahman often seeks your counsel? The rest of us foreigners are no more than useful infidels as far as he is concerned."

André laughed. "Well, I do allow His Majesty to beat me at chess. But to speak seriously: Abd al-Rahman is a great admirer of Napoleon and I was a major in the Chasseurs d'Afrique—though I did not join until 1823, several years after his death. And I am not certain that the sultan truly trusts me. I shall find out soon, though. The Berbers in Algeria and their leader, Abd el-Kader, have issued another *jihad* against us French. I have no doubt the sultan is having me watched to see if I will join my native country to wage war against the true believers."

"And? Will you?" Sibylla's heart skipped a beat.

"*Mon* Dieu, no!" André crumpled the empty pistachio bag. "I took my leave of fighting a long time ago. If I could, I would purchase a piece of land here and grow my own saffron. Unfortunately, the sultan does not permit Christians to own land."

Sibylla studied him with curiosity. Was this a good moment to ask if he planned to live in this country with a woman? Or if he perhaps already had a wife?

They were interrupted by loud shrieks coming from the beach. John was lying flat on his stomach in the sand and bawling at the top of his lungs. Tom had one of the Arab boys by the collar and was yelling in Arabic. "Let go of the string, you swine, or the *djinn*'s curse be upon you!"

The boy had apparently taken the kite's string away from John, and Tom was coming to his beloved brother's aid.

"Dear me!" Sibylla laughed awkwardly. "I must remind the servants to watch their language in the children's presence. Boys!" She jumped to her feet. "You are not to fight!"

She ran to the children, and André followed. John scrambled to his feet and she picked him up. The little Arab boy had fallen into a clump of sea pink and had dried petals all over his clothing and in his hair.

His face was very angry as the Frenchman gave him a stern talking-to. Eventually, he returned the line to Tom, his head hung low.

"However did you manage to appease them so quickly?" Sibylla asked once they were sitting in the sand, watching the children play peacefully once more.

"I threatened to unleash the ghosts of the Christian slaves who were walled in when this fortress was built," André answered with a grin.

"What? Immured people? That's the kind of talk with which you frighten children? You can't be serious!" Sibylla shuddered.

"I'm not. To be honest, I am not sure if this old wives' tale is true. In fact, I asked the boy if he was such a weakling that he felt it necessary to take things from a much smaller boy. And I could not help but notice, madame"—André scrutinized her with feigned severity—"Thomas can curse alarmingly well in Arabic."

Sibylla was embarrassed. "He must have picked it up from some playmates or the servants. There are some disadvantages to having your children learn the local language."

"You must plan to stay in Morocco for some time."

She laughed. "In truth, there is very little that would entice me back to London. And what about you? What keeps you in this country? Is it a woman?" Sibylla reddened as the last question slipped out. "Please forgive my curiosity!"

"Madame, there is nothing to forgive." In fact, with those four jealous little words, she had just made him the happiest man in Morocco.

If any woman could keep me here, it would be you, Sibylla Hopkins, though it is precisely because of you that I should leave as quickly as possible—after all, what could we hope for beyond a few stolen moments?

But he said, "You're wondering if I have taken a Chiadma wife. The answer is: no, I have not." He was delighted by the relief on her face. He paused for a moment and then continued, his voice tinged with mischief. "But one might say that a Chiadma woman has taken me for her husband."

"Oh? Really?" She could hardly disguise her disappointment. "These Berber women seem to have rather loose morals," she added a little disapprovingly.

"No, no," André countered unsmilingly. "That is far from true, madame. They are merely different from European and Arab women. The Berber tribes hold women in high regard. They are strong and free and make their own decisions. There are even some famous warrioresses among them. Have you ever heard of al-Kahina, the sorceress? When the Arabs invaded the Maghreb more than a thousand years ago, she united the tribes of the Zanata Berbers and led them against the intruders. The Zanata made her their queen. A captured Muslim she had adopted betrayed her to the enemy, and it cost her her life."

"She must have been a fascinating woman, a true Amazon," Sibylla said quietly. How sheltered and uneventful her own life seemed by comparison—even if she had managed to escape her father's strict supervision. Rouston, on the other hand, had married a Berber woman, who most likely was a second al-Kahina. Sibylla felt her heart sink at the thought.

"Why does your wife never accompany you to Mogador? Do you wish to keep her from us foreigners?" She bit her lip. She had not meant to sound so resentful.

"Sibylla," André said softly, making her blush as he used her given name for the first time. "I am no longer married to that woman. She moved in with her oldest daughter, who married a man from the Rif Mountains. She wants to help her set up her household. And so she asked me to consent to the dissolution of our union."

"She can divorce you? Just like that? Just because she wishes it?"

André nodded. "Idri was a widow when I met her. As a widow, she was entitled not only to choose all her subsequent partners herself, but also to divorce them."

"How unusual!" Sibylla marveled. She studied the floral pattern on her kaftan intently while trying to control the thought that was taking hold in her mind: *If only I could get divorced so easily and simply!* Yet she knew it was impossible. She had pawned her life to Benjamin in exchange for a little freedom, and nothing would change that until one of them died. She fought to suppress a deep sigh.

André gently turned her chin so that she was forced to face him in spite of the tears filling her eyes.

"Sibylla," he began, and her heart nearly leapt out of her chest.

"Yes, André?" she whispered.

"Sibylla, if only you . . ."

"Mummy! John let go!" they heard Tom shout. "And now it's gone! The kite is gone!"

Sibylla and André jumped up guiltily.

The group of children was standing at the beach not far from them, looking up at the kite as it fluttered off into the blue sky. Little Sabri stood next to Tom. They were about the same height and both held one hand over their eyes as they watched the red-and-yellow toy grow smaller and smaller.

Sabri said something to Tom and gave him a huge smile before running off with the other Arab boys. John and Tom raced over to their mother.

"Mummy?" Tom asked as he snuggled up to her. "Is the kite really going to fly to Mecca like the storks?"

"Who told you that?" The question took Sibylla aback.

"Sabri. He's my friend," Tom replied earnestly.

Sibylla laughed and took both her boys by the hand. "Well, then I suppose it must be so. Come now, let's go home."

André, who had shaken the sand off his jacket and put it on again, said, "If you permit, I shall escort you, Madame Hopkins."

She only nodded, but over the heads of the children, they locked eyes for a very long time.

Chapter Eleven

"And this is the sweet that the English serve to celebrate the birth of their highest prophet, the festival you call Christmas? It is certainly delicious, but should it not be sweeter, softer? Should it not be more exceptional for such a sacred occasion?" Lalla Jasira's face belied her polite words of praise.

Sibylla smiled. "I know what you mean. I used to adore gingersnaps. Our cook baked them for Christmas every year. But I must admit that three years of living in Morocco has refined my palate."

"Nonsense!" Rusa protested. "These pastries are very interesting. Can it be that I taste cloves and honey? Yes, and a hint of vanilla as well."

"You are too kind, Rusa," Sibylla replied and set her unfinished biscuit on her plate. "But I only wanted to present you with a little something that has to do with Christmas at home."

"Would you rather be there now, celebrating with your family?" Rusa looked at her guest compassionately. She had known the *Engliziya* for more than three years, during which the Christian woman had become more than just a reliable business partner. She saw the woman with lion's hair almost as a daughter.

Sibylla watched the *qaid*'s many children playing on the lawn. Nannies and governesses sat nearby and made sure that the children played nicely and that none of the little ones fell into the fishpond. Normally, she brought Tom and John with her to the harem. But today, both had complained of a tummyache and so she'd left them at home in Nadira's care.

"Rusa, my family is here in Mogador," Sibylla answered. "I am happy."

"Perhaps your family will grow soon, Sayyida Sibylla. You are able to give *el Sayyid* many more children," Wahida said.

When Sibylla had first met the *qaid*'s beautiful Abyssinian concubine, Wahida had already borne her master two sons. Now she had two daughters as well.

Sibylla thought of Benjamin and Firyal. If there were to be any more babies in the Hopkins family, they would certainly not be hers.

"Things are fine as they are," she said without bitterness. "Two boys keep me busy enough."

Wahida contemplated her. It must have been a long time since the *Engliziya* had shared her husband's bed. After all, her youngest child was already two years old. Of course, if she served her husband dry sweets like these, it was no wonder her womb remained empty.

Wahida knew many secrets with which a woman could hold a man captive. She knew how intoxicating fragrances affected him and which ingredients in a man's food not only delighted his palate but also enflamed his desire: "lady's navel," a moist, ring-shaped pastry with a flirtatious dab of whipped cream in the middle, for instance, or "lips of beauty," which tasted sweeter than a kiss.

But the *Engliziya* did not appear sad that her husband no longer wanted her in his bed. That could only mean that he either was very inept or preferred the company of boys. Or did the beautiful blonde *Engliziya* perhaps care so little about her spouse because she had taken a lover herself?

Today, the end of Ramadan, was especially well suited for finding this out. Yesterday, the *muezzin* had announced the appearance of the new moon, signifying the beginning of the month of Shawwal and, with it, the end of fasting. For thirty days, the *qaid*'s Muslim wives had fasted and prayed, honored their dead, and given alms. And as a reward, the Prophet, in his infinite wisdom, had bestowed upon them the gift of *Eid al-Fitr*, the Feast of Breaking the Fast.

When Sibylla had entered the harem's garden shortly after noonday prayers, the mood was already festive. She had intended only to leave the silk stockings and ginger biscuits as gifts, but Rusa and Lalla Jasira had invited her to join in the celebration.

Now she was resting on comfortable pillows by the water basin with the two most important ladies in the harem and the concubine Wahida. A slave had served Sibylla dove pâté and date ragout, lamb with pomegranate sauce, and swordfish wrapped in fresh mint leaves. Afterward, she had drunk tea flavored with cinnamon and cardamom, and, for dessert, the slave had brought apple sorbet with candied rose blossoms.

My word, Sibylla thought as she savored one delicacy after another. *No wonder these women find gingersnaps dull! I must take care not to get fat. I don't suppose André's Chiadma widow is fat.*

Ever since her encounter with the Frenchman on the beach three days earlier, she had been referring to him in her mind by his first name. She was sure that he had been on the verge of confessing something very personal, something concerning the two of them. But with the children's interruption, the moment had passed quickly, and all that was left to her now was a wistful memory and thrilling words unspoken.

She sighed and plucked a dark purple plum from the platter in front of her.

How delicious the fruit here is, she thought, closing her eyes with pleasure. It was as if they absorbed the sun's warmth, day in and day out.

When she opened her eyes, they met Wahida's. Her mahogany-colored eyes flashed. Lalla Jasira too was watching her with a little smile.

"Look at our esteemed guest nibbling at this plum," Wahida began. "Is it not as though she were stroking a man at his most sensitive place?"

Sibylla's cheeks grew hot. She knew the women in the harem were sometimes given to suggestive conversations. Rusa usually saw to it that these never turned too coarse, but during this special feast, they were permitted to get carried away a little. In any case, the *qaid*'s mother had nodded off after the sumptuous meal and was not paying attention to the salacious turn things had taken.

"The woman with the lion's hair is blushing like a girl before her first night of love, is she not?" Wahida continued. "And yet our *Engliziya*'s rosebud has opened and given her two strong little rose stems." She picked a juicy golden grape and consumed it gracefully.

Sibylla had no idea what to say, having had no experience with this kind of thing. Nervously, she looked to Lalla Jasira. The *qaid*'s first wife was holding the tip of her veil over her mouth and chuckling softly. Sibylla resolved not to betray the fact that she hadn't understood even half of Wahida's words. She could guess what the concubine meant by "rosebud," and that was shocking enough. But what on earth did the plum have to do with a man's body? Her mind reached back to *One Thousand and One Nights*, but she could recall no story in which the eating of plums had anything to do with making love. Besides, during the few intimate nights she had shared with Benjamin, she had noticed no sensitive areas.

If anyone knows where they are and if he even has any, then it is Firyal, she thought soberly.

"If you ladies will excuse me." Unsettled by the concubine's teasing, she nodded to Lalla Jasira and Wahida, stood up, and walked toward the stage that had been set up beneath a bright silk canopy.

To celebrate the *Eid al-Fitr*, Rusa had engaged some traveling musicians, ten women and one blind man, who were dancing and singing provocative songs. Sibylla joined a group of women standing in a semicircle, cheerfully singing along and beating small copper cymbals in time. Three young concubines swaying their hips pushed past Sibylla toward the blind musician, who was strumming the *al rababa*, a one-stringed instrument.

"Are you truly blind or do you secretly enjoy looking at forbidden fruit?" one of them whispered so close to his ear that her breath touched his wrinkled neck. Another giggled as she took her veil and tied it over his dim eyes. He too seemed to be enjoying the fun because he suddenly reached out one arm and took a few steps forward, making the young women screech and scatter. Sibylla had to laugh. What did it matter that Wahida had teased her a little? Today was a holiday, after all!

Boom, boom!

Sibylla started. The women stopped their conversations, the children their play, and the musicians their performance. Rusa sat up in her chair and looked about in a daze.

"Gunshots. They're coming from the beach!" one of the women shouted.

"Let's go to the rooftop to see," another suggested.

All of them hastened up the stone steps, pulling their veils over their hair and faces so that, from afar, they resembled a flock of birds. The older children excitedly ran ahead; the younger ones were carried by their nannies. Sibylla, Lalla Jasira, and Wahida followed together with Rusa, who walked with the aid of her personal slave.

"What a terrible racket!" the *qaid*'s mother said with concern. "I hope nothing has happened down there."

"I believe I know why they are shooting," Sibylla replied. "This morning, my husband told me he had to go to the beach this afternoon because His Excellency wanted to test the guns he had ordered for His Majesty."

Boom, boom! came the confirmation.

The spectacle from the roof proved exciting indeed. Ten men, among them the *qaid*, were galloping across the sand, their *burnooses* blowing in the wind. Their horses were adorned with splendid bridles, and long colorful fringes dangled from their saddle blankets. The men held their weapons in one hand, twirling them skillfully above their heads, while driving their horses with the other and uttering battle cries. Once the group split up, Sibylla noticed a structure consisting of two wooden planks that had been driven into the ground and a third laid across the top. This third plank had some strange-looking objects hanging from it.

"Are those melons?" Rusa asked and squinted in the direction of the beach.

"I think they're animal bladders filled with water. They seem to be using them as targets," Sibylla answered. "Look there, the sand underneath is wet." Then she recognized Benjamin. "Ah! That is my husband down there."

Benjamin was sitting on his red stallion well away from the scaffold and the Arabs with their guns. He himself was not armed. His horse was prancing nervously and he was busy keeping it under control.

"Is this what Englishmen wear when they ride into battle?" Lalla Jasira asked incredulously as she looked at Benjamin's top hat, his bobbing coattails, and his knee-high leather boots.

Sibylla shook her head. "The cavalry wears a uniform. If you would like, I'll have a picture sent. My husband is wearing the riding costume of a civilian, a gentleman, as we say in England."

Wahida lifted her veil slightly to better appraise Benjamin. She had long wondered what Sayyida Sibylla's husband might look like, and she was distinctly disappointed. The pale man was tall and thin like a reed, certainly not strong and sanguine enough to keep up with this lioness. She felt pity for the *Engliziya* as she thought about how unsatisfactory her love life must be. She lowered her veil and leaned over to Sibylla. "The next time your husband calls you, take him a cup of wine seasoned with a pinch of saffron. This will invigorate his loins and make him hungry."

But Sibylla was not listening. She was mesmerized by something on the beach. Wahida followed her gaze and understood at once.

"So it is the *faransawi* whom you desire," she whispered to Sibylla. "A beautiful man, by God. He makes a woman's heart sing, does he not?"

Sibylla had not noticed André Rouston right away. But now, as he ran toward the scaffold followed by some of the same Arab boys who had played with her sons and their kite, her heart skipped a beat once again.

Stop it, she thought and pressed her fingers against the stone balustrade. *Stop indulging in these improper fantasies!*

Still, she was unable to avert her eyes as André carefully checked that the riders had loaded their rifles properly. Even the Arab riders showed their respect and bowed their heads when he returned their guns to them.

"Sayyida Sibylla." She jumped as Wahida gently touched her arm. "If you wish, I can have my slave take a message to the *faransawi*."

Sibylla jerked away in alarm. "You are mistaken, Wahida. I am a married woman and a mother!"

She was terrified to learn that her feelings for Rouston were so apparent. Unsure, she looked to Rusa. Fortunately, the *qaid*'s mother had eyes only for her son, who was trying to keep his horse under control. But Lalla Jasira's dark eyes met hers and Sibylla felt as if the woman could read her thoughts. Sibylla blushed, and the woman placed her hand reassuringly on Sibylla's shoulder and nodded discreetly.

All Sibylla could do was nod back and look to the beach again. In anticipation of a great spectacle, the Arab boys had sat down in the sand. Rouston pulled his pistol from its holster and took a step back from the scaffolding. He raised his right hand and held it up for several seconds. When he finally fired, the riders began to charge with their rifles held high. The horses' hooves tore up the sand and screams filled the air.

Boom!

The animal bladders exploded with dull thuds. Water squirted everywhere, and the smell of gun powder permeated the air. The women around Sibylla exploded into laughter. The children on the roof ran around, gleefully imitating the sound of gunfire. Yet Sibylla felt suddenly alone and dejected. She bade farewell to Rusa, Lalla Jasira, and Wahida, and was escorted out of the harem by a slave.

"The lady with the lion's hair is a virtuous woman," Lalla Jasira said reproachfully to Wahida.

"Certainly," the concubine replied, looking at the beach, where the riders had taken their positions again. "But is the well not dry when it lacks water?"

"Sibylla!"

She spun around. André had suddenly appeared behind her in the narrow street.

"What are you doing here? Why are you not at the beach?"

Instead of replying, he took her by the arm and guided her behind a small bakery. A massive oven stood in the middle of the courtyard. It resembled a large beehive constructed of dried-mud- and-straw tiles. The oven belonged not only to the baker but the local residents as well. Every morning, neighborhood women would bring their freshly kneaded dough on large wooden planks. Now, in the late afternoon, the courtyard was empty. Two cats preening themselves on a pile of wood scurried away as the humans approached. Voices could be heard from several doorways, and the air smelled of the food the baker's wife was preparing for dinner.

André pulled Sibylla into a dark passageway. "I spotted you on the rooftop—your hair was uncovered. And then you disappeared. I thought you must be on your way home, so I came to find you." His voice was so tender, and still he held her arm. Sibylla's knees trembled.

"I apologize for the ambush," André continued. "I had to see you."

He was standing very close. She could feel the warmth of his body and smell the masculine scent of his skin.

"Why?" she asked quietly. "What are you planning to do now that you have—ambushed me?" If he was planning to take her into his arms and kiss her, she would not object at all.

"I want us to meet in peace and take the time to speak our hearts truly. Will you meet me at the old Portuguese church, Sibylla? We would be completely undisturbed."

Sibylla burned to hear the truth of his heart. And yet the idea of meeting this dashing Frenchman in the ruined church troubled her.

"Monsieur Rouston, I am a married woman and cannot slink through the alleyways like a thief to meet with a man! What if we're seen?"

"I will wait outside your house after evening prayers," André responded. "No one will see us in the dark. Not even the moon will betray us. The crescent is still very small."

"Truly, you have thought of everything. But I have not even agreed to meet," she said sharply. It annoyed her that he had made a plan before consulting her. If this Frenchman thought she could be had so easily, he was mistaken!

André, however, was undeterred. "Please, Sibylla! I know you feel that there is something special between us."

He gently placed a loose strand of hair behind her ear, making goose bumps rise all over her body. Benjamin might have shared her bed, he might be the father of her children, and yet none of that had created a bond between the two of them. André only needed to touch her lightly and she was ready to forget her marital vows.

"You may be right," she admitted. "But is that reason enough for clandestine meetings?"

"Is this not all we have?" he asked urgently. "In two, maybe three days, I will be riding back to the Chiadma, and months will pass before we see each other again."

She looked into his eyes. "If we had met earlier, under different conditions. But that was not to be . . ." She stopped. "It'll be dark soon. I must go. *Au revoir*, André."

Before she could have second thoughts, Sibylla forced herself to cross the courtyard. But André rushed after her.

"I will wait in front of your house, Sibylla," he whispered emphatically. "Will you come?"

She couldn't help but smile as she looked into his face. "I do not know. But please do not wait in front of the house. The gatekeeper will see you. Wait by the little gate to the back alley."

"God is great, God is great. There is no god besides God!" the *muezzin* intoned.

It was almost midnight. Sibylla wrapped the shawl around her head and shoulders, took her shoes in one hand and a candle in the other, and tiptoed out of her room. She paused for a moment in the corridor, but the house was silent. She heard the distant rolling of the waves and the wind rustling through the leaves of the olive trees. Outside the window, a few stars were twinkling in the sky, and a few gray clouds drifted past the silver crescent moon.

I am twenty-seven years old, she thought, as she padded along the wooden floor. *And here I am, in love for the first time. What a wonderful feeling.*

Over dinner, while Benjamin told her more than she'd ever wanted to know about guns, Sibylla had put aside all her misgivings. She had persuaded herself that she would give in just this one time and go to André. Then she would carry the memory of these few hours forever in her heart. Maybe it was wrong. But just once in her life, she wanted to know what it felt like to be held by a man who truly desired her and whom she desired.

Having made her resolution, she felt a happiness and freedom she had not felt for a long time. She even began to take pleasure in the notion of doing something so profoundly forbidden to women. Adultery was said to be a sin for men as well, but just how little this mattered was evident by her husband's indelicate behavior.

When she reached the children's room, she stopped, and could not resist stepping inside. The candle revealed her darling boys sleeping soundly in their beds. Tom sighed and furrowed his brow in his sleep. She leaned over and stroked his head. Rosy-cheeked Johnny clutched the little donkey she had sewn him.

She was suddenly struck that one of her boys might wake up with a tummyache. That they might cry for their mother, who would be gone—off seeking her own pleasure. Benjamin would wake up and discover that she had left the house in the middle of the night.

What sort of uncaring mother was she? While her marriage was not worth the paper on which the license was printed, her children meant everything to her!

No, she could not go. She would have to forgo her own short-lived happiness with André Rouston, no matter how great the pain.

Chapter Twelve

Mogador, January 1840

"Should a fully loaded ship not sit deeper in the water, Philipps?" Qaid Hash-Hash furrowed his brow as he looked at the *Queen Charlotte*'s stern.

The harbormaster was also watching the great sailing ship, which was slowly being maneuvered through the narrow harbor exit, and nodded pensively. "I agree, Your Excellency, a fully loaded ship should sit much lower in the water."

"Is there any danger of her running aground if she takes on all the freight in her capacity?" The *qaid* knew only too well that the harbor basin was sandy and in urgent need of being dredged. But, by God, who was going to bear the costs of such an undertaking? The sultan had already made it known that he could not spare a single *dirham.* That left the merchants, but they were terrible misers who sat on their money like brooding hens.

"That might indeed be a possibility at low tide, but right now it is high tide and she has sufficient water under her keel," Philipps answered.

"Perhaps it's the type of freight?" the governor pressed. "Ostrich feathers are light; elephant tusks take up a lot of room. That might explain the missing draft in a fully loaded ship."

Still, the harbormaster shook his head. "She has mostly leather and barrels of palm oil, in addition to a few crates filled with spices on board."

"Hmm." The frustrated *qaid* scratched his black goatee. "Destination?"

"Baltimore, Your Excellency, in the United States of America."

"You are certain of that?" The black raptor eyes focused on the harbormaster.

"Quite certain, Your Excellency. Is something wrong?" Philipps felt himself breaking into a sweat in spite of the cool December breeze. He quickly ran through the *Queen Charlotte*'s clearance process to rule out any mistake he might have made. Qaid Hash-Hash did not take kindly to mistakes of that nature. More than a few had found themselves in the fortress dungeon on the governor's mere suspicion that he might have missed out on some duties or taxes.

The *qaid* beckoned the boy who was carrying his water pipe for him and took a long puff. As he slowly exhaled the smoke, he again considered the mighty West Indian sailing ship. The wind carried the sound of whistles and bellowed commands to his ears. Sailors were climbing the rigging and running back and forth on deck.

The *qaid*'s onboard spy had told him the ship was heading south. The governor puckered his lips in disdain when he thought of the man's eagerness to talk when threatened with a few spoonfuls of molten lead in his stomach. And he had spilled another secret: the ship's carpenter had received orders to add two steerage decks as soon as they reached the open seas.

Hash-Hash snapped his fingers and the boy quickly took the hookah pipe from him. "Philipps!"

The harbormaster started with fright. "Your Excellency?"

"Why would a ship sail southward if it should be sailing westward?"

Philipps frowned. "It could have to do with the wind or the ocean's currents, but not here in Mogador, Your Excellency. All ships sail westward from here. So perhaps it is picking up more cargo in another harbor before crossing the Atlantic."

The *qaid*'s nostrils twitched like those of a bloodhound that has picked up a scent. "What kind of cargo could a ship like the *Queen Charlotte* take on from the Saharan coast?"

"None," Philipps replied without understanding. "There aren't even any decent harbors down there. The *Queen* would have to head much farther south, say to Guinea or the Gold Coast, but down there the cargo is mostly slaves."

Qaid Hash-Hash folded his hands behind his back and looked out to sea. The *Queen Charlotte* had left the narrow harbor exit behind her. Seagulls were circling above her masts. Her sails billowed in the wind as her pointed bow slowly headed south.

Finally, it all fits, the governor thought with satisfaction. The secret meetings that Hopkins and Toledano had been having with the *Queen Charlotte*'s captain, the half-loaded ship, and the riches that vulgar Englishman had amassed—the latest an odd bowl with gilded lion's feet, which he called a "bathtub."

Hopkins was obviously realizing profits for which he paid neither taxes nor duties. But it was not until now that Qaid Hash-Hash could be certain how he did it: slaves.

Not that the *qaid* objected to the slave trade as such. He might even have consented to having an infidel engage in it. But if this infidel thought he could smuggle all his proceeds past him and His Majesty Sultan Moulay Abd al-Rahman, he would soon learn otherwise. And to think that cursed Toledano, who had always enjoyed His Majesty's protection, was in cahoots with the Englishman!

Hash-Hash trembled with excitement at the prospect of arresting the ostentatious Englishman and acquainting him with the most select instruments of torture. But then he reminded himself that Hopkins was a foreigner, an *Engliz*, the subject of a powerful queen who ruled half the world. If he mishandled one of her citizens, he might very well attract this queen's wrath to Morocco and cause him to fall out of favor with His Majesty. After all, the sultan took great pains to stay in the good graces not only of the English queen but also the other rulers of Europe. Under no circumstances was Morocco going to suffer the same fate as Algeria, which was now nothing more than an unworthy vassal of the French!

No, the *qaid* sadly shook his head. He would have to leave the Englishman to the sultan. Oh, but the treacherous Toledano was his to deal with! He turned to the harbormaster, who remained at his side, awaiting further orders.

"Come to the palace this week to share some *shisha* with me," he ordered. "I am very pleased by the loyalty you show His Most Gracious Majesty. You have always kept in mind that an infidel can never be greater than the true children of God."

André Rouston leaned down to the Arab boy and handed him a basket full of sweet-smelling oranges. "You are to give this to the English lady, not the cook or any of the servants, you understand?"

"Yes, sir!" The boy looked at him innocently.

"And what are you going to say to the lady when you give her the oranges?"

"At the time for noon prayers, she is to come to the place of which the *faransawi* has told her," the boy repeated.

Rouston smiled. "Very good!" He opened the leather pouch attached to his belt, took out a few coins, and gave them to the boy.

"I'll wait here. When you come back and you tell me that you have spoken to the lady, you'll get another reward."

At midday, Rouston had already waited for two hours for Sibylla. When the Arab boy returned and proudly reported he had done just as the *faransawi* asked, André had hurried from the French consulate, where he stayed whenever he was in Mogador, to the little church. He was aware that he was early, but perhaps Sibylla would be early as well, and she might leave if she did not find him!

He had placed a small rug with just enough room for two people on the elevated stones beneath the steeple. He sat down on it and gazed at the golden ribbons of light that slipped through holes in the roof.

It really is quite ludicrous, he thought, shaking his head. *I am thirty-three years old. I have seen far more of the world than most and I have known plenty of women. And here I am, excited as I was at fourteen when the innkeeper's daughter allowed me to reach under her bodice when we were hiding behind the shed.*

His eyes roamed the interior of the small church. The last priest had left when the Portuguese had to abandon their trading post in the middle of the sixteenth century. The structure had been falling into ruin ever since. There was no more holy-water basin by the entrance for the faithful to dip their fingertips into, no more benches on the cracked stone slabs to allow the prayerful to kneel, the glass windows were broken, cobwebs hung suspended from the walls, and pigeons were nesting in the corners. Pirates, seeking refuge along the coast, had stolen the organ pipes and bells for scrap, leaving the steeple to the bats. It was peaceful here. André heard the wind whistling in the drafty corners, the cooing of the pigeons, and the scuttling of mouse feet. Were it not for the headless statues of Portuguese patron saints Anthony and Isabel, dressed in the habit of the Franciscans, no one would have guessed this ruin had once been a church.

He wondered why Sibylla had failed to come that night four weeks earlier. Someone or something must have prevented her. Her husband, perhaps, who had chosen that particular night to share her bed? It was almost unbearable for André to imagine Benjamin holding and loving

Sibylla. Or perhaps she had not wanted to meet him at all—an idea he liked even less. Perhaps she'd lost her nerve? But a woman like Sibylla did not lose her nerve. She did what she thought was right.

That night, when he had waited for her in vain, he had resolved to leave Mogador until the fall when it was time to sell the date harvest. Perhaps by then his feelings for this married woman would have cooled.

However, the days had passed, he had not left, and now he found himself sitting in the ruins of this old church, praying to the heavens that Sibylla would not strand him there a second time. Next to him sat a basket with red wine, dark and thick as syrup, truffle pâté, and ham that tasted of the oak forests of his childhood home—delicacies he had bought from the French consul's cook. He wished to spoil the one woman who captivated him more than any other.

But where was Sibylla? He tried to gauge the time of day. It had been at least half an hour since the *muezzin* had called midday prayers. *I'll wait another half an hour*, he decided desperately. If she had not come by then, he would never again impose on her.

He froze. The door latch clicked, the rusty hinges squeaked, and a figure squeezed through the gap. Sunlight flooded into the church for a moment and he made out a woman's backlit silhouette. Then the door fell shut.

"André?"

"Sibylla!" He stood up and went to her. A pigeon flapped its wings and disappeared through one of the holes in the roof. All at once, they were in each other's arms.

"Tu es là!" he whispered. "*Mon* Dieu, how I have waited for you!" He took her face in both hands and kissed her, and his happiness knew no bounds when she threw her arms around him and kissed him back.

"Pardon," he uttered once they had finally released one another. "I couldn't help myself."

She shook her head and placed her fingers on his lips. "Thank you for the oranges," she whispered.

"Did anyone follow you? Your husband perhaps?" He anxiously looked to the door.

"Benjamin has been on a business trip to Fez and Marrakesh for weeks. There were a few merchants in the alley outside. They were looking for the Portuguese consulate. I hope they did not recognize me."

He reached out and pulled the shawl off Sibylla's hair. As always, she was dressed like the local women: an embroidered, silver-gray damask tunic and a loose-fitting pair of pants, the *chalwar.* Her tousled hair made for a charming contrast. Never before had a woman cast such a spell on him!

André cleared his throat. "If anyone recognized you, it was because of your blue eyes. But they would lose their minds as soon as you looked at them, just like I did."

She did not know what to say. Benjamin seldom paid her compliments. Did André really find her so beautiful, even seductive?

He took her palm and covered it with kisses. "I am so glad!" he repeated. Then he led her to the stone pedestal. She looked around curiously.

"All these years in Mogador and I never knew this church existed."

"Hardly anyone does. And that is why we will be completely undisturbed," he assured her.

"Goodness!" she exclaimed as she noticed the rug and the basket. "What have you done?"

He just laughed and, in one fell swoop, swept her into his arms.

"Ooh!" She wrapped her arms around his neck and beamed as he carried her to the dais and gently lowered her onto the rug. He pulled the wine bottle and corkscrew from the basket.

"What shall we drink to?" he asked as he filled two glasses.

She took hers and held it up to a beam of light so that its contents sparkled like garnets. "I'll drink to having met you," she answered quietly and looked into his eyes.

◆ ◆ ◆

The sunlight had all but disappeared behind the westwork of the church, and still they found it impossible to part.

Sibylla sat on the rug, André's head in her lap, playing with his black curls. They had partaken of the contents of the basket and kissed each other endlessly. André had not tried to urge Sibylla any further, and for that she was grateful. She would gladly have surrendered to him because the wine had made her cheerful and relaxed. But at the same time, she was anxious. Whenever Benjamin had shared her bed, the process had been so pedestrian, even painful. What if the same thing happened with André? That would destroy everything between them. But instead, André had inquired in great detail about her life, how she had grown up. She told him how secure and sheltered her life in London had been.

"I had a good life and yet I was never satisfied. I never understood why my younger brother had all sorts of freedom while all I ever heard was what a young lady could and could not do. I wanted to travel the world and see and touch for myself all the things I only knew from books. That's why I encouraged Benjamin to take the position in Morocco and insisted that I be allowed to come with him. One day, I will be able to say that I lived in a world straight out of *One Thousand and One Nights*. That is something not even many men can claim."

"You could write a book about it—the true and extraordinary adventures of an English merchant's wife in Morocco," André suggested with a smile.

She tousled his hair. "Don't you make fun of me!"

"I am quite serious!"

"So you think I could write something like Lady Montagu, whose husband was ambassador to the Ottoman court in the last century?" Sibylla asked, thrilled at the notion.

"I am not familiar with Madame Montagu's writing, but *bien sûr*, why not? You have seen and experienced a lot . . ."

He kissed each of her fingertips. She leaned over and, with her lips, caressed his hairline, temples, ears, and neck. He groaned, pulled her to him with both arms, and hungrily pressed his mouth on her soft, warm lips. When he finally released her, he shook his head and smiled as though surprised.

"I still remember marveling at how you stood before the sultan in Marrakesh and had the courage to return his gaze. I would never have thought that we would one day be this close."

Sibylla sat up and smoothed her hair. The intensity of his kisses and her own hunger for them had her completely befuddled. Her doubts returned.

"The governor's favorite concubine was standing next to me on the rooftop when you were shooting on the beach. She immediately knew that you meant something to me. Was it imprudent of us to meet here?"

He sighed. A small dark shadow fell over their carefree afternoon. "True, in the eyes of society and the church, what we are doing is wrong. But I, for one, would like to proclaim before the whole world that you are mine." And now he could no longer restrain himself from asking, "Do you love your husband?"

Sibylla uttered a brief laugh. She leaned over André and he could feel her sweet, warm breath on his lips. "André Rouston, you are jealous and that makes me happy," she whispered.

He wrapped one arm around her waist and pulled her even closer. "Why don't you answer my question?"

Love, she had long ago realized, had had nothing to do with Benjamin's and her decision to marry.

"At first, I thought we might become partners," she explained after a long pause. "Particularly here in this country, where there are so few foreigners. But the more time passes, the more estranged I become from Benjamin. I don't understand it myself."

She pulled off a piece of the flatbread André had brought. "But enough about me. Tell me something about yourself. What sort of a man are you?"

He propped himself up on one elbow and drank the last drop of wine in his glass. The taste evoked long-forgotten memories of France.

"I did not have such a sheltered upbringing as you," he began, struggling for words. "Life in France during the Restoration was not easy for a poor farm boy. Say what you will about Napoleon, but under him, commoners had a chance. After he was gone, the Bourbons turned back the clock. In my home, we were short of everything: food, clothing, leather for shoes and boots, warm coats. And this despite the fact that my parents were emancipated farmers. Our family has owned a small farm in the Lot area for seven generations. And still, we never had enough to eat, especially if the harvest was poor. I worked like a horse ever since I can remember, but without black truffles, we would have gone hungry during many winters. My father knew the secret spots in the forest where they grow. Truffles meant for us what saffron means for the Chiadma: money for a rainy day."

By now, the church was almost completely dark. André could see only the outline of Sibylla's empathetic face. Now that he'd started telling his story, it was as though he could not stop.

"I am one of nine children," he continued. "I still shared a straw mattress with two of my brothers when I already was old enough to attend village dances with the girls. I didn't miss any chance to drink and that made me eager to fight. I was as strong as a young ox and just as moody. I probably was not easy to get along with at that time. I realize now that I was desperately unhappy. What did I have to look forward to? Life as a farmhand, because only the eldest son would inherit—"

"But you left," Sibylla said softly. "You took charge of your life."

He laughed. "It certainly did not look that way at first! At sixteen, I fled. I had sold one of father's truffles and felt rich and bold. I made it to La Rochelle and was going to sign on as a sailor and conquer the world . . . Sibylla, I fear I am boring you." He felt for her hand in the dark.

"Not at all, André. Please tell me more!"

She knew it was time for her to go home. The children were surely waiting. But she could not tear herself away from André and his soft, dark voice, which made his past come alive as though she had experienced it herself.

"And so you were hired on a ship?" She picked up his story.

He cleared his throat. It was such a dark chapter of his life, a year of which he was not the least bit proud. Still, he did not want to withhold anything from Sibylla. He wanted her to know everything and decide for herself whether she truly wanted him.

"I was abducted," he said. "Carried onto a ship and forced to be a sailor."

"That's slavery!" Sibylla exclaimed. "But you didn't become a slave, did you?"

"In a way, I did, yes. I was a stupid country boy, and one with money in his pocket. I drank myself into a stupor in the first harbor bar I found. There was a man who saw to it that my glass always had rum in it. The next thing I remember was waking up on the high seas and the mate holding a piece of paper in my face that said that I had been hired as a sailor."

"What a dirty trick!" Sibylla snorted.

André nodded. It was all true except for one particularly embarrassing detail. He had been snared not in a bar but in a brothel. He had gone with a prostitute who had taken all his money and promptly turned him over to a press gang for a bounty.

"At first, I was not that upset," he continued. "I had wanted to go to sea anyhow. But then I realized that I was working for a slave trader."

"How despicable!"

He had no idea whether her words referred to the slave trade or him. "Sibylla, know that I would never have done this work willingly. What I saw on that ship, how those poor devils were treated . . . I'll never be able to forget that! And to my great shame, I must admit that I participated, if only to avoid the cat-o'-nine-tails myself. Do you despise me now?"

He felt for her hand.

Sibylla thought about her grandfather's own dirty business. "God shall grant them repentance so that they may know the truth—isn't that what the Bible says?" She squeezed André's hand.

"I would gladly give my arm if I could erase that time," he professed. "When we berthed in La Rochelle one year later, I fled without even waiting to be paid."

"And what did you do next?"

"I had three options: a career as a harbor gangster, to enter into service as a farmhand for my brother, or to enlist in the military. I chose the military and that turned out to be a good decision. For the first time in my life, I met people who did not regard me as a scoundrel. I gradually climbed up to the higher ranks that were ordinarily reserved for the aristocracy. In 1830, I was transferred to Algeria and fought against Abd el-Kader there. After my discharge, I came to Morocco and here . . ."

"Is where our paths crossed," Sibylla finished thoughtfully. "It's late, André, I really must get home."

He stood up. "I'll accompany you."

While he rolled up the rug and placed it on his shoulder, she packed the empty wine bottle and the rest of their picnic into the basket.

"How I wish we didn't have to part," she said with a sigh when they reached the church door.

"Will you meet me here again?" he asked, his heart beating fast.

She wrapped her shawl around her head so that her hair was completely covered. "Of course, I want to. But it doesn't feel right to sneak around in this old ruin."

"We have no other choice at the moment," André replied, unsmiling. He opened his arms and pulled her close. "Let us leave the future up to fate. *Inshallah*, as the Arabs say."

She looked at him and nodded solemnly. "*Inshallah*. God willing."

Chapter Thirteen

"Get away from here, you good-for-nothing. What are you doing in front of my house?" Benjamin guided his stallion directly at the beggar crouching in front of the wall. The man ducked to the side, uttering a frightened cry.

Benjamin laughed and made his riding crop slice through the air. "There, see how able-bodied you still are?"

The man cowered against the wall and pulled the hood of his moth-eaten cloak over his face.

"All right now, I don't want to be too harsh; business in Fez and Marrakesh was good, after all." He reached into his jacket pocket, threw down a handful of coins, and watched with a shake of his head as the man scratched the coins out of the dust.

"That's just how you Muslims are: a bunch of idlers. You'd rather beg than work!"

He swung one leg over his horse's back, slipped out of the saddle, and tossed the reins to the servant who had accompanied him on the journey. "Take the animals to the stable and take good care of them. Put a blanket on my stallion so he doesn't catch cold. If you forget, I'll hold you personally responsible."

"Very well, sir," the man answered obediently.

Benjamin entered the house cheerfully whistling a tune. Had he turned around, he would have seen the man spitting contemptuously in his direction before disappearing down the alleyway with astonishing alacrity. A few moments later, the supposed beggar was standing in front of the walls of the governor's palace. He carefully peered in all directions and knocked on a narrow side door, which was immediately opened a crack.

"To the *qaid*, quickly!" he ordered the slave. "His Excellency is expecting me!"

"Daddy, Daddy! What did you bring us?" The two little boys came running across the *riad*'s courtyard and boisterously threw their arms around their father. Benjamin laughed, leaned forward, and picked them up, one in each arm. "Well, check inside my pocket, boys!"

He did not have to tell them twice. They squealed with excitement when they found two small horses carved in wood. "Wow, Daddy! Thank you!"

Benjamin looked around. "Where's your mother?"

"Dunno," said Tom.

"You mean 'I don't know,'" Benjamin corrected him.

"Mummy is gone!" Johnny shouted.

Benjamin frowned. "What do you mean? Nadira, where is your mistress?"

The servant stepped closer. "Mrs. Hopkins is not at home, sir. She has gone out."

"Gone out? Where?"

"I do not know, sir."

Benjamin scrutinized her ebony face.

Like hell you don't, he thought. But Nadira silently stood her ground.

"Well, I'll know soon enough." He put his sons down and gave them each a pat on the bottom. "Run along and play, boys. But don't throw the horses in the fishpond!"

He went to the stairs that led up to the living quarters. "I intend to take a bath," he informed Nadira. "See to it that everything is made ready. And tell Firyal to bring me soap and towels."

When the servant appeared bearing the requested items, clouds of steam were already wafting from the claw-footed porcelain tub in Benjamin's bedroom. Just like his sundial and horse, the imported tub had caused quite a stir when it was unloaded in the harbor, but that did not bother him. He found the Arab custom of visiting a public bath unnatural—especially for a man. To avoid ever finding himself in that dreadful situation, he had had a cistern that always contained enough water for a bath installed on the roof of the house.

"*Sayyid?* Sir? Are you there?" Firyal called.

Benjamin stepped out from behind the screen. He was wearing nothing more than a towel wrapped around his waist. "What took you so long? Don't you like me anymore?"

"I do, sir." She stood in the middle of the room, her head demurely bowed, pressing the towels against her chest. He was happy to see the little smile at the corners of her mouth and to think that she was looking forward to their rendezvous as much as he.

"Put that down and come here," he commanded.

She obediently placed the towels and soap on a small stool and walked over to him. He looked at her silently. She was just a Negress, a former slave, but damn it, she was a hundred times more enticing than his wife!

With two fingers of one hand, he stroked the delicate, warm skin between her breasts. Next he placed both hands on her breasts. They were full and heavy and it aroused him to see them bob and sway under her cotton dress. He spread his fingers, kneading the soft flesh, pinching the nipples until they became hard and he felt his own pleasurable arousal.

"Did you close the door properly?" he asked her quietly.

"Yes, sir." Her black eyes sparkled.

"I have brought some gifts." He nodded to a dresser on which lay a small folded package of cloth and a pair of gold earrings.

"You are very generous, sir." Firyal pressed herself against his hands. "Do you wish to bathe now or later? I think the water is still too hot. It should cool off a little."

He grinned. "I need to do the same and you are going to help me do it, aren't you, Firyal?"

In response, she felt for his towel and loosened the knot. He placed his hands on her shoulders and pressed her down. "Oh, you little hussy!" he panted hoarsely when he felt her mouth. "How I've missed you!"

"Harder! That's better!" Benjamin sat up in the tub so Firyal could scrub his shoulders. "Ahh, yes, wonderful! You can't imagine how much my back hurts after three weeks in the saddle and every night spent on those hard cots at the inns."

"I'm sure it was very stressful, sir." The servant set down the sponge and began lathering Benjamin's wet hair.

"Make sure to use plenty of soap!" he ordered. "I feel as if the stench from the tanneries is clinging to me. If the fine ladies and gentlemen who wear boots and gloves made from my leather only knew how tanneries smell! The fires of hell could not be any worse! But no matter—I concluded some excellent deals." He turned to Firyal. "Do you know what makes a good businessman?"

"No, sir. Please lean your head back now. I am going to wash out the soap."

Benjamin carefully leaned back and continued. "A good businessman knows how to buy the best merchandise for the lowest price and to sell for the highest price. That is how I convinced my father-in-law of my qualities and I—what was that?" Benjamin sat up with a start. "Do you not hear it? What is that racket?"

"Yes, sir. It sounds like someone trying to kick in the front gate."

Benjamin listened anxiously. There were crashing sounds coming from downstairs, a door slamming, men's voices hollering commands. And in the middle of it, he could hear Nadira and his children, squealing and frightened.

"Damn it, what on earth? Are we being robbed?" Benjamin got up hastily, water dripping from his hair and running down his body. "Come on, hand me a towel!"

The servant fearfully reached for the towels. But when she heard heavy steps coming toward them up the stairs, she froze.

"Good God, are you stupid or what?" Benjamin ripped the towel out of her hands.

The bedroom door flew open and crashed against the wall. Firyal screamed. Benjamin dropped the towel and instinctively tried to cover his nakedness with his hands.

Not three yards from him stood a black man with a red *tarboosh*, white kaftan, and the scimitar of the sultan's guards. His massive body filled the doorway. He scrutinized Benjamin with a stony expression.

"Benjamin Hopkins?"

"That is who I am. But who might you be and how dare you intrude here? I shall complain to the *qaid* personally!" Benjamin spat, determined not to be intimidated by the giant.

Instead of answering, the man stepped aside. Two others appeared behind him. Benjamin was speechless when he recognized them. One was Qaid Hash-Hash's personal secretary, the other Nuri bin Kalil. The secretary was holding a scroll of paper, which he handed to the interpreter. Bin Kalil bowed to Benjamin. "*Assalamu alaikum*, Mr. Hopkins."

"Bin Kalil!" Benjamin exclaimed. "What's the meaning of this? Why do you dare intrude in my private rooms? And armed at that."

He stepped out of the tub and leaned over to reach for a towel. The guard blocking the door placed his right hand on the handle of his scimitar. Benjamin flinched, but demanded, "Call off your dog, bin Kalil! Or is this your famous Arab hospitality?"

The interpreter gave a signal to the soldier, who took a step back. Benjamin wrapped himself in the towel as best he could.

Nuri bin Kalil unrolled the paper and a beautiful red seal became visible at the lower end. "Mr. Benjamin Hopkins, by order of His Imperial Majesty Sultan Moulay Abd al-Rahman, Imam of the all the Faithful, Ruler of Marrakesh, Fez, and the Sous Plain, you are hereby arrested for treason and fraud. The arrest is being carried out by His Excellency Qaid Hash-Hash. Until a verdict is pronounced, you will be held in the bastion of the Island of Mogador."

Benjamin burst out laughing. "Treason? Fraud? Are you joking? Now I have really had enough of this spectacle. Get out, all of you! I shall inform the British consul general in Tangier of this outrageous violation, and you may rest assured that they will submit a formal diplomatic grievance!"

The guard grunted something in Arabic and Nuri bin Kalil nodded. Then he looked directly into Benjamin's eyes.

"Put on some clothes, Mr. Hopkins, and come with us. If you resist, the guards will intervene. Believe me, it is better to follow the sultan's command."

Sibylla had bid farewell to André when they reached the alleyway. She was lost in thought as she walked toward her house and noticed the two guards at the gate only when she almost collided with them.

"What are you doing here?" she asked anxiously when they both stepped forward. "Let me by!"

Looking uncertain, the soldiers stepped aside.

"Hamid, who are these men?" she asked.

The gatekeeper shrugged his shoulders helplessly. "The Black Guards wanted to see the master. I had to let them in."

Sibylla raced inside. The hallway was dark and empty. An indefinable sense of fear and apprehension came over her as she hurried to the courtyard. Nadira was standing in front of the water basin and had one arm protectively wrapped around each of the children. All three were looking up anxiously at the colonnade.

"Nadira! What has happened? Why are there soldiers in the house?"

"Mummy!" Johnny and Tom ran to her. "The soldiers are taking Daddy!"

Sibylla stared at her servant in disbelief, but Nadira only shook her head helplessly. "I swear by the Almighty, my lady, I know nothing!"

She could hear a door being opened, then steps. Sibylla spun around and saw Benjamin coming out of his bedroom with a guard. He was followed by the *qaid*'s translator and another Arab man. Tom squeezed his mother's hand and Johnny began to cry.

The small parade came down the stairs. Benjamin's hair was wet, his shirt untucked, and his jacket unbuttoned. He avoided Sibylla's fixed stare.

She let go of the children and resolutely stepped into the guard's path. "Leave my husband in peace and get out of our house!"

But the man pushed her aside without a word.

"Benjamin!" Sibylla cried in disbelief. "What do they want? You are a subject of the queen. They are not allowed to treat you like this!"

He stopped and, for the first time, looked at her directly. There was fear in his eyes. "Inform Consul Willshire at once! There has been a grave misunderstanding."

The guard grabbed his arm and hauled him forward. She watched numbly as he disappeared into the dark.

◆ ◆ ◆

"If there is so much as an ounce of truth in the *qaid's* accusations, then we're talking about your husband's head, Mrs. Hopkins." Consul Willshire sank wearily into the divan.

It was long past midnight. Many hours had passed since the Black Guards had led Benjamin away, since a distraught Sibylla had burst into her neighbors' house with news of the arrest. The consul had not wasted a moment before leaving for the governor's palace. In the meantime, his wife had gone back to Sibylla's house to take care of her while they awaited Willshire's return.

"All of this is going to be cleared up, you'll see. By tomorrow, the whole thing will seem like nothing more than a bad dream," Sara had insisted, but Sibylla could sense the other woman's fear.

Now, Sibylla looked into the unsmiling face of the consul and said with strained calm, "Please, Consul, take a seat. May I offer you a cup of tea? I'm sure you could use it." She picked up the pot and a cup from the tray Nadira had brought and placed the steaming beverage in front of the consul. Then she took a seat opposite and waited for him to take a few sips before she asked, "What is my husband being accused of?"

Willshire took a deep breath and placed the cup on the table. "I'm not going to mince words, Mrs. Hopkins. Your husband is being accused of trading in slaves. For three years now, one of the ships of the Spencer & Son Shipping Company has allegedly been taking on slaves and selling them overseas."

"Good God!" Sara gasped, with a horrified look in Sibylla's direction.

"Slander and nonsense!" Sibylla sputtered. "Benjamin has always had difficulties with the *qaid*. I'm certain this is all a plot against him."

Willshire shook his head in doubt. "Apparently, the *qaid* has been having your husband watched for some time and is quite confident in his claim. Please forgive my bluntness, Mrs. Hopkins, but what makes you so certain of your husband's innocence?"

"Because slave trading has been illegal for over thirty years and my husband knows it. He would not violate the law, especially to the detriment of my family's company! And besides, I cannot believe that any of our captains would stoop to such shameful business."

"According to Qaid Hash-Hash, the captain in question is Captain Nathaniel Brown of the *Queen Charlotte*."

Sara got up and solicitously filled her husband's teacup. He gave her a grateful smile.

"There is something more, I can tell," Sibylla said with her heart in her throat. "What are you keeping from me? Mr. Willshire, I beg you to tell me everything you know!"

He cleared his throat. "Earlier this evening, the *qaid* of Mogador interrogated your husband, and His Excellency permitted me to be present. Your husband naturally denied all accusations, but then the governor produced a witness."

"Whom?"

"Samuel Toledano. And, Mrs. Hopkins, his testimony against your husband was severely incriminating."

Sibylla pounded the table with the palm of her hand. "Mightn't it be possible that Toledano is lying to divert attention away from himself?"

"You may be correct." Willshire lowered his head. "Of course, he will try anything to save his own neck. My impression is that he procured the slaves, Captain Brown organized the transport, and your husband was pulling the strings . . ."

"But it's possible that Brown and Toledano are the only guilty parties and are simply using my husband as the scapegoat," Sibylla interjected.

"Perhaps," Willshire replied doubtfully. "But Brown is at sea and the *qaid* cannot arrest him. He cannot touch Toledano because, as *tujjar al-sultan*, he is under the ruler's personal protection. So that leaves only your husband. He is the chief culprit as far as the governor is concerned.

The only thing in your husband's favor is the fact that Hash-Hash has not yet found the revenues of this business."

Sibylla had a lump in her throat. To think that her own husband could be involved in the slave trade!

"Of course, Hash-Hash will do everything to find that money," Willshire continued. "If there is so much as an ounce of truth to the story, it must be a fortune."

Sara Willshire, who had been silently listening to the revelations, moved a little closer to her husband, disgust and horror on her face. Sibylla could well understand. She herself was fighting with all her might not to give credence to the accusations.

"But, Consul, how could it be possible to load slaves in the port of Mogador without attracting attention? The whole thing is absurd!"

Consul Willshire emptied his teacup and sighed. It pained him to be the bearer of such bad news to Mrs. Hopkins, all the more so since he considered the accusations plausible. He was not himself fond of Benjamin. He detested the man's showing off and thought him absolutely capable of something as despicable as trading in slaves. But he respected Sibylla as an honest and incorruptible woman.

And so, he responded with the greatest reluctance. "Toledano claims the slaves were taken aboard at Cape Juby, an abandoned Spanish trading base about one hundred miles south of Agadir. Toledano's *karwan bashi* could conceivably have brought them there straight through the Sahara from Timbuktu."

Sibylla shook her head, bewildered. "And you believe all that? Do you really believe it?"

Willshire raised his shoulders. "To be perfectly honest, I don't know what to believe, Mrs. Hopkins. Your husband has, of course, accused Toledano of fabrication. On the other hand, the overseas sales of slaves are very enticing because of the exorbitant profits. Money like that can lead many an honest man to flout the law."

Sibylla cradled her head in her hands. "Mr. Willshire, what are we going to do to help my husband?"

He hesitated. "If you wish, I can ask Consul General Drummond-Hay in Tangier to address an official note of protest to the sultan."

For a moment, Sibylla thought she had misheard him. "Well, of course you will do that, Consul! But what are you going to do in addition to that?"

Willshire squirmed. "I am very sorry, Mrs. Hopkins, but at this moment, we do not know the whole truth of the matter. The slightest indication of culpability on your husband's part could bring about serious diplomatic disagreements between Great Britain and Morocco."

He rose and Sara followed suit. "Sibylla, perhaps you should take your children and return to London," Sara reflected. "No one there knows about this terrible affair, and you can rest assured that they will not learn of it from us. But here in Mogador, all the foreigners will be affected by your husband's offense."

Sibylla stared at her, shocked that Benjamin had apparently already been found guilty. Consul Willshire bowed slightly. "Goodbye, Mrs. Hopkins. I am truly sorry."

"You are sorry?" Sibylla responded listlessly. "We are English citizens. It is your duty to stand by our side in this country."

He was unable to conceal his discomfort as he looked at her. "Mrs. Hopkins, the *qaid* was eager to see your husband thrown in the dungeon. It was only thanks to my intervention—made at some personal risk—that he was taken to a guarded room. Early tomorrow morning, he will be transferred to the bastion of the Island of Mogador. If you want to see your husband, this is your last opportunity. I am unable to do anything more for you or him at this time. I am sorry."

Dawn was breaking when Sibylla hurried to the harbor. Misty rain blew in her face. She had wrapped herself in a thick woolen shawl, but still, for the first time since she had come to Morocco, Sibylla felt cold. Her head lowered, she rushed along the empty alleyways and through the Bab El Mersa, which the guards had just opened. Fog hung heavy over the water. She could make out the outlines of some anchored ships, and, out on the water, the hazy lights of the fishing boats.

Off to the side, there was a single skiff. The captain stood looking in the direction of the city gate, and the rowers had taken their places. Sibylla sat down on the quay wall and watched. It was high tide, and below her, the waves quietly sloshed against the quay. Above her, seagulls were soaring in the wind and screeching hoarsely. With tears in her eyes, she squinted toward the harbor exit. There lay, at about one mile's distance, a small, craggy island, from which rose a few towers and fortress walls: the Island of Mogador.

The rhythmic sound of boot-shod steps cut through the morning stillness. Sibylla turned around and saw five men coming through the city gate. At the head was a Black Guard captain, Benjamin behind him. He was flanked on the right and the left by soldiers. Another followed. Sibylla jumped up and ran to the small group. The captain immediately drew his saber. "Stay back, Mrs. Hopkins!"

She obediently kept her distance but ran alongside the men. Benjamin looked disheveled and bleary. His frockcoat was rumpled, his pants stained. She was shocked to see that his wrists were chained together.

"Benjamin! Are you all right? What has happened?"

He turned his head and she saw his reddened eyes. "Hasn't Willshire told you?"

"Yes, but I cannot believe that it is true."

"You must help me!" he groaned. "Go to Toledano and force him to recant!"

By now, the group had arrived at the boat. The soldiers shoved Benjamin in and the captain shouted orders to cast off. The oars were plunged into the water and the boat glided swiftly away. Sibylla watched as it disappeared in the morning mist.

Chapter Fourteen

"The master is not at home," the Toledanos' gatekeeper announced to Sibylla, though she was sure she had glimpsed him through the windows of the second floor.

"Please let me in! I must speak with him!" she begged, but he crossed his arms in front of his muscular chest and turned away.

Dejected, she returned home. She wanted nothing more than to lock herself in her bedroom and cry. But there were the concerned and anxious looks of the servants. And her distraught children, who would not leave her side.

"Where's Daddy?" Johnny asked. Tom wanted to know if the soldiers had hurt him.

Sibylla resorted to a white lie. "Daddy has had to go on a trip and the soldiers are going with him. You know that he travels often. But he will come back home."

"And he'll bring us presents," Johnny added with satisfaction. Tom, however, was not so easily comforted. He looked up at his mother with large doubting eyes.

Nadira knocked on the door of the drawing room, where Sibylla was sitting on the divan with the boys. She entered carrying a tray with a bowl of steaming couscous.

"Please take it away again. I'm not hungry," Sibylla said and massaged her aching temples.

Nadira placed the bowl on the table. "You have to eat, my lady. And you must rest. Come, children, there are freshly baked gazelle horns waiting in the kitchen for you."

For Nadira's sake, Sibylla tried a spoonful of couscous. It tasted surprisingly good and she quickly finished the entire bowl. Then she collapsed on the divan. She must have fallen asleep, because a knock at the door shook her from bizarre dreams. The tray was gone, and someone—probably Nadira—had covered her with a blanket.

"Yes?" She quickly sat up and smoothed her hair.

The door opened hesitantly and Firyal appeared. "Monsieur Rouston is downstairs at the gate and wishes to speak with you, my lady."

André! Sibylla's heart began to beat wildly. So news of the events had reached him. How she longed to take refuge in his arms and relive the sweet, carefree moments of a few days ago! But she forced herself not to remember.

"Ask Monsieur Rouston in."

But the young woman did not budge.

"What are you waiting for?" Sibylla asked impatiently.

The servant haltingly came closer. Once she stood in front of Sibylla, she fell to her knees. "Please, my lady," she stammered. "How is the master?"

"How dare you!" Sibylla exploded. But when she saw Firyal's distress, she was ashamed at her lack of self-control. "Your master is being treated decently," she answered in a calmer tone. "That is all I can tell you. Now go and get Monsieur Rouston!"

Firyal hurried away, and after a few moments, André entered. He looked serious. The French consul had informed him of the arrest.

"I can imagine how difficult all this must be for you," he said.

She looked into his honest, sympathetic face and was seized by a crazy idea. "Ride to Abd al-Rahman! The sultan respects you. Tell him that I wish to have an audience with him to clear up this matter!"

"Is that what you truly want?" Her wish to use his relationship with the sultan on Benjamin's behalf took him by surprise, and he did not like it. "If there is anything to the accusations, I cannot help your husband."

But she was not to be deterred. "I know what a great favor I am asking. But I must ask! Benjamin is the father of my children, and he has not yet been proven guilty."

André frowned. Like many others, he thought Benjamin quite capable of being a slave trader. "All right. I'll ride to Marrakesh. But not for him. I'm doing it because I do not wish you to suffer for his mistakes."

"Thank you," she breathed.

Sibylla's courage moved him deeply. He crossed to her, took her in his arms, and kissed her passionately. But her lips stayed lifeless and cold.

"André, no!" she pleaded and freed herself. "I have to take care of my family now—just my family."

He took a deep breath. "I respect your wishes. And so that you know I am serious, I will leave for Marrakesh today. I will be gone for some time. If you should need me, send a messenger and I'll return immediately."

When she did not answer, he lifted her chin with his hand and looked into her eyes. "Promise me."

"Yes," she whispered.

"I shall rely on it."

◆ ◆ ◆

What would happen to herself and her children? Had Benjamin truly traded in slaves or was it all part of a plot?

Several days had passed since André's departure, one week since Benjamin's transfer to the Island of Mogador. Sibylla had tried to visit the *qaid*, but he refused to see her.

She could hear the boys laughing in the courtyard and playing with the wooden horses Benjamin had brought them. They seemed to have accepted Sibylla's explanation that their father was away on a trip.

She sat at the desk in her office, trying to make a list of all the questions she had for Benjamin, but she just could not concentrate. Her thoughts kept wandering back to André. He must have arrived in Marrakesh by now. She wondered if he had spoken with the sultan yet. Had his petition changed anything?

She was torn out of her reverie by Tom's voice, excited and shrill. "Mummy! The soldiers are back!"

Sibylla dashed to the gallery. Just a few yards from her on the landing stood the captain of the Black Guards, accompanied by two guards.

"Mrs. Hopkins, we have orders to search your house. His Excellency believes that your husband hid the money he made from the slave trade here."

Sibylla coolly looked over the giant man. "Not before you show me His Excellency's written order."

Without saying a word, he held out the paper with the governor's seal on it. She briefly considered asking Consul Willshire for help, but she had not seen him since the night of Benjamin's arrest. Nor had Sara inquired after her. Sibylla doubted that they would come to her aid now. She took a deep breath and handed the paper back to the captain. "Do what you must."

It was not until after the *maghrib*, the prayer at sundown, that the three men left. The destruction was shocking, particularly in Benjamin's office. The guards had slit open pillows and sofas, emptied drawers, and moved furniture. They had pushed over cabinets, torn apart books, and pried up floorboards. In the courtyard, they had dug holes around the olive tree and the fishpond and torn the water lilies out of the water. But they had not found a secret hiding place with money. What they had discovered was Benjamin's coffer in one of the closets. The Spencer & Son Shipping Company regularly sent promissory notes that he exchanged for cash at a banker in the Jewish quarter. He used the money to pay suppliers as well as the sultan's customs and tax officials. And he gave some of it to Sibylla, who used it to pay the servants and finance their household expenses. Although she explained all that to the captain of the Black Guards, he still confiscated the coffer. Some time later, he also discovered Sibylla's rosewood box and confiscated that as well.

She protested vehemently. "Put that back! That is not the money you are looking for!"

The captain paid no heed to her and handed both boxes to his soldiers.

A little while later, the nightmare was finally over, and Sibylla was the picture of misery as she sank onto a divan, its horsehair stuffing pouring out.

"These barbarians have left us nothing!" she lamented to Nadira, who had begun at once to clean up the mess. "If all they had done was destroy the furniture, that would be one thing. But how am I going to buy food now? I cannot even give you your pay! If Benjamin had not paid rent for the whole year, we would find ourselves without a roof over our heads!"

The servant put down a cushion she had just picked up off the floor. "I have been saving my pay," she said with dignity. "I always received everything I needed from my masters and rarely spent anything. We will be able to buy food, my lady."

Firyal, who had been in the corner sweeping up shards, dropped her broom and ran out. She soon returned and timidly held out the pair of gold earrings Benjamin had given her.

"Please take these, my lady. You can sell them in the *souk* for a lot of wheat."

Sibylla was touched, but she shook her head. "I thank you both from the bottom of my heart, but I cannot accept your savings or your belongings. I will find another solution."

She furrowed her brow. "I will go to Mrs. Willshire and ask her to lend me some money. I also have my own money, my dowry. It's in a trust, but I will write to my bank in London immediately and have them send me a promissory note."

"I shall have to discuss this with William first." Sara avoided Sibylla's gaze.

The two of them were sitting in Sara's drawing room. On the table between them, on a little lace cloth, stood a vase with flowering orange branches. They were sipping tea and nibbling little raisin pastries. But the external show of peace and harmony could not hide the tension between them.

Sibylla was deeply disappointed, but she swallowed her pride. "I will not need the money for long. As soon as I receive my promissory note from London, you will get it back, of course."

Sara wiped an invisible speck of dust off the polished tabletop. "I wish you would understand, Sibylla, that there is nothing I can do for you. William handles our money. I don't even have a key to the coffer."

Sibylla stopped herself from telling Sara that all she needed to do was explain the circumstances to her husband. It was obvious that the woman she had considered her friend simply did not want to help her. She could no longer conceal her bitterness.

"I understand all too well. You and your husband have already passed judgment. In your eyes, we are swindlers and slave traders."

Sara blushed deeply. "William made a great sacrifice for you," she said defensively. "He immediately wrote to Consul General

Drummond-Hay asking him to write a protest note to the sultan. Do you realize that my husband could get into serious difficulties if the accusations against your husband turn out to be true? And, with all due respect, he is still being held on the island!"

Sibylla stood up. "Please forgive me for inconveniencing you."

Sara also stood, seeming sad and confused. "I am so sorry."

"Good-bye," Sibylla answered frostily and went to the door. "I'll see myself out."

After that, Sibylla and Nadira had rummaged through the house looking for cash.

"Just because the *qaid*'s people didn't find anything doesn't mean there is nothing," said Sibylla at night when they would go from room to room by the light of an oil lamp. She did not want to search during the daytime. By now, Sibylla trusted no one but Nadira, who stood by her side steadfastly and reliably.

She rummaged through the drawers of Benjamin's desk with grim determination. She needed money to cover the most pressing expenses, and so desperately hoped to find some, but, on the other hand, dreaded finding any since that would be proof of her husband's guilt. Her resentment toward Benjamin for subjecting her to this grew with each passing day. She spent hours spinning scenarios of what might have happened. And then she would shake her head over her foolishness. If she wanted to save herself from going mad, she would have to stop brooding and move forward.

Several weeks later, Sibylla sat at her desk trying to compose a letter to her father. It was the end of February and spring was announcing its arrival all over Mogador with delicate herbs and new buds. Laying in front of her on the table, covering the ugly scratch the *qaid*'s guards had made with their scimitars, were two letters with business instructions from her father to Benjamin. Richard still had no idea of the charges against his son-in-law, and Sibylla knew it was high time she enlightened him. But if she told him of the ugly accusation, he would surely order her to return to London with her children—and that was out of the question. She never wanted to live under her father's roof again and be told what was good for her and what was not.

She finally resolved to be as vague as possible. She would write that Benjamin was tied up and she was conducting his affairs for the time being. Of course, her father would have questions, but months would pass before she received his reply and by then, perhaps, this nightmare would be over. At least she would be spared the indignity of having to confess that the foreign families in Mogador had been shunning her since Benjamin's arrest and that she had had to borrow money from her servant, after all, in order to feed the children.

Sibylla heaved a deep sigh and was dipping the quill in the inkwell when there was a knock at the door.

Firyal appeared. "There is a messenger, my lady. He wants to speak with the master."

"He shall have to make do with the mistress," she replied and put the quill aside. "Do you know what he wants?"

The servant nodded eagerly. She was still afraid that Sibylla held her affair with Benjamin against her and worked to fulfill all her duties conscientiously. "He reports that the caravan with the leather that the master bought in Fez has arrived at the Bab Doukkala. There are fifty camels, and he says that the master needs to inspect the merchandise."

Some hours later, Sibylla arrived home exhausted. Only now was she able to relax. She was hardly an expert on the quality of leather. The *karwan bashi*, the camel drivers, and several of the merchants had watched her with suspicion and disdain as she had tried to assert herself. But she had succeeded and, in the end, felt she had even bested the men, who thought themselves so superior.

"Nadira, Firyal!" she called as she entered. "I'm starving! Is there still something in the kitchen for me to eat?"

In the courtyard of the *riad*, she was met by the sight of a familiar Frenchman and her sons. The three had their backs turned to her and were throwing small glass marbles into a hole they'd dug.

"Yes!" screamed Tom, throwing his arms up and jumping in the air. "Mummy! I won! Now Johnny's marbles belong to me! Even the big one with the blue stripes!" He ran to his mother.

Sibylla picked him up and pressed her lips into his soft blond curls. Her eyes met André's. He looked tired. There were lines around his eyes; his clothes and boots were dirty. But his smile was full of warmth. Twenty-one days had passed since his departure and oh, how she had missed him!

"Madame Hopkins! It seems like an eternity since we said good-bye."

She set Tom down and André took her hands. "Much too long."

His dark brown eyes glistened. "How are you?"

She thought of the guards who had confiscated all of her hard-earned savings, of Sara, who had found all sorts of subterfuges to avoid helping her, and of her sons, who asked her every day when their father would be returning, and shrugged. She did not wish to talk about any of those things.

They heard steps behind them and Sibylla quickly withdrew her hands. Nadira was standing at the entrance to the kitchen. "I have taken the liberty of setting the table in the dining room for you and Monsieur Rouston, my lady. The cook has prepared a *tagine* with chickpeas, tomatoes, and onions."

"We have had to make do with simple meals since Benjamin's arrest," Sibylla said apologetically when they were sitting across from each other at the long wooden table.

He had already noticed the slashed dining room chairs, and she'd confessed how the *qaid*'s guards had searched the house for money and taken every last copper *falus*.

"It's delicious," André assured her with his mouth full. "Please forgive my manners, but all I've had today is tea and flatbread."

She nodded and waited for him to finish chewing. "What news do you have from the sultan?"

He folded his napkin and sighed. "The good news is that you are being granted an audience; unfortunately, it will not be until the fall, because the sultan is spending the summer at his palace in Fez."

"And he intends to hold Benjamin and make me wait until then?" Sibylla asked, outraged.

"I am afraid that, at the moment, he is holding all the cards, even if Drummond-Hay has sent a protest note by now. His Majesty told me unequivocally that he is convinced of your husband's guilt. He says that he has incorruptible evidence, and that Christians who flout the law and deal in slaves face execution."

Sibylla was horrified. "He cannot be serious!"

"That is difficult to say at this moment," André replied. "I have known Abd al-Rahman for several years and know that, in contrast to many of his predecessors, he is not a bloodthirsty ruler. But he is facing domestic problems. Many Berber princes are not happy about the presence of foreigners in this country and are urging him to make an example of Benjamin."

"But Benjamin is an Englishman!" Sibylla protested. "I shall write a letter to the queen!"

André scrutinized her with a strange expression. She blushed. "He is the father of my children. They should not grow up in the belief that their father was a criminal and slave trader."

"There is no use in any speculations now. You must be patient until September," André replied after a brief pause. "If all else fails, you might try to buy your husband's freedom. But that is going to be a costly affair. Toledano alleges that Benjamin shipped as many as two to three thousand slaves."

Sibylla looked at him in dismay. "Does Abd al-Rahman really believe that Samuel Toledano has nothing to do with the whole affair? Is he not being called to account at all?"

"Oh yes." André grinned at her. "The word is that he is personally footing the bill to have the Mogador harbor basin dredged. Though not much beyond that is likely. He is much too valuable to the ruler."

"Stop!" She held her hands over her ears. "Is every single person in this country thoroughly corrupt?"

"That seems to be true of your husband in any case," André said before he could stop himself. He was jealous at seeing the woman he loved fighting so fiercely for her untrustworthy husband. Upon seeing Sibylla's face, he added, "Forgive me. That was tactless."

"If only the *qaid* would grant me permission to visit Benjamin!" Sibylla sighed. "There are so many questions I have for him."

She needed information about the shipping business, of course, if she was to take it over. But more important, she needed to hear Benjamin himself deny the terrible accusations. A few days earlier, Tommy had asked her what a slave trader was. Apparently, one of his playmates in the street had called his father that. Her helpless stuttering had told him the expression was less than an accolade and, since then, he had repeatedly come home with torn pants and bloody knees.

"I beat up anyone who says my daddy is a slave trader!" he had told his horrified mother.

Sibylla rested her head in her hands. "Oh, I am so sick of it all! But things must go on somehow. I am handling the shipping company's affairs by myself."

"What do you mean?" André inquired.

She reported that she had accepted a fifty-camel delivery of leather from Fez, verified its quality, arranged for it to be stored in the harbor, and even discussed the formalities of its shipment to London with the harbormaster.

"Sibylla, I am impressed. I had no idea you knew about leather."

"I don't, honestly. But I remembered a few things Benjamin has told me about the qualities of good leather and I somehow managed to pass myself off as an expert. And my husband kept meticulous business records, so I was able to glean some information there."

She smiled at him sadly. There were dark shadows under her eyes. André went to her and drew her into his arms. She laid her head on his shoulder, felt the rough fabric of his jacket against her cheek, and thought about how good it felt to be able to lean on someone for just a moment. He stroked her hair.

"If you want, I'll accompany you to Marrakesh in the fall to help you negotiate with the sultan."

She wrapped her arms around his waist and pressed herself closer to him. "I am already so deeply in your debt. You rode to Marrakesh for me and now you are offering to go again. And yet I know that you have probably long wanted to return to the Chiadma and your life there."

He gently kissed her forehead. "It is settled. I shall see you in the fall. Sibylla, never forget that you are as strong as a lioness!"

Chapter Fifteen

Mogador, April 1840

It was a tranquil day in April and the sun shone warmly on the festivities. More than two hundred people had assembled on the beach. The air buzzed with English, French, Spanish, Danish, Dutch, Italian, and Portuguese. The shrieks and laughter of the children, who were hunting for eggs and sweets behind sand dunes, under rocks, and between clumps of grass, nearly drowned out the sound of the waves rolling onto the beach.

With the *qaid*'s approval, the Christian families of Mogador celebrated Easter together every year. Dressed in their finest clothes, they gathered on the shore in the morning to read the Bible, pray, and sing, and many crew members from ships in the harbor joined them. There were so few Christians in the city that they all celebrated together: Catholics, Lutherans, Calvinists, and Anglicans.

When André jumped off his horse, the service was already over. He threw the reins to one of the Arab boys who had gathered to watch the spectacle, and slowly walked over to the crowd. At times, he stopped to greet acquaintances and exchanged a few words with them, but he was distracted, his gaze wandering from group to group.

I shall see you in the fall, he had told Sibylla.

And yet, here he was again in Mogador, just eight weeks later. A few days earlier, the city's French consul had come to his camp with the Chiadma. He had disturbing news from the north and needed André's help. Berber tribes led by Abd el-Kader were attacking the French military along the border between Algeria and Morocco. They ambushed and shot soldiers, set garrisons on fire, then fled with lightning speed over the border to Morocco and their allies, the Ait Bouyahia Berbers. Their leader, Thabit al-Khattabi, supported Abd el-Kader in driving the French out of Algeria. In return, the Algerian was going to help him in overthrowing Morocco's Sultan Abd al-Rahman, so that al-Khattabi would become ruler.

The consul pleaded with André to ride to Marrakesh and warn the sultan. He was to persuade him to hand over Abd el-Kader to the French in return for this warning and to inform the ruler that his refusal would result in military retaliation in important commercial ports like Tangier and Mogador.

André had agreed to carry out this difficult mission. However, instead of riding to Marrakesh, he had gone first to Mogador. He wanted to warn Sibylla and offer her family the protection of his friends, the Chiadma, in case Mogador was bombarded.

André reached a magnificent red-and-green tent that had been set up near the city wall. Inside, people sat conversing on plush benches, while still others gathered around small round tables. A sumptuous banquet was being set up along the rear wall. Servants arranged tableware, glasses, and porcelain. Others hefted baskets and earthenware vessels filled with food just unloaded from pack donkeys. Spits with roasting lamb turned over several fires burning in front of the tent. André's nose was tickled by the aroma of seasoned meat, which mingled with that of freshly baked bread a servant carried past.

"*¡Felices Pascuas*, Señor Rouston!" A Spanish merchant who had often purchased saffron from him took him by the arm and, before André knew what was happening, the man had cracked a hardboiled egg on his head. "It remains intact! You will have one year of good luck!" the Spaniard shouted and convulsed with laughter. But then he saw the Frenchman's expression. "Why the serious look? Have your saffron seedlings been eaten by mice?"

André forced a smile. "That would be a disaster, indeed, but everything is in order. I am looking for Madame Hopkins. I want to wish her a happy Easter. Have you seen her?"

"Lo siento." The Spaniard shook his head apologetically. "But perhaps she is with my wife somewhere in the tent."

André found the *señora* with a group of five ladies, among whom he recognized Sara Willshire, but he did not see Sibylla.

The French consul's wife, an elegant, capricious woman, leaned over to her friends. "Just look at the unusual visitor who is gracing us with his presence." Her brown eyes scrutinized André's physique approvingly. "A handsome man, don't you think?" she whispered to her Spanish counterpart and the ostrich feathers in her elaborate hairdo bobbed coquettishly.

The Spanish woman looked at her over the top of her fan. "Is it true that he rode to Marrakesh at the request of Señora Hopkins to intercede on behalf of her husband?"

"That is what they say, *oui*." The Frenchwoman nodded. "Do you think that this dedication has anything to do with Madame's beautiful blue eyes?"

"What do you mean?" Sara Willshire interrupted, a touch irritated. But the Frenchwoman merely raised her thinly plucked eyebrows.

"Oh, don't pretend to be so shocked, Senhora Willshire!" the Brazilian consul's wife butted in. "You told us yourself that this Frenchman called on Senhora Hopkins at her house after her husband's arrest. Just imagine—at her house!"

Sara blushed. "Perhaps he was there to inquire about her well-being."

"I'm sure, my dear, I'm sure," the Frenchwoman sneered.

"In any case, it is unseemly to receive a gentleman visitor when one's husband is not at home," the wife of a Dutch merchant piped up as she smoothed her high-necked, dark dress. "But then, this Mrs. Hopkins conducts business with Moorish women. She even dresses like one of them. She is an immoral woman!"

"If a man like Rouston showed an interest in me, I would be an immoral woman as well," the Frenchwoman countered, unimpressed. "Ah, *bonjour*, Monsieur Rouston! *Quel plaisir*!" she called out and extended her gloved hand. "So you have left your secluded mountain home to celebrate Easter with us. Or is there another reason for your visit? A secret love, perhaps?" She winked at him.

André ignored her words and leaned over to kiss her hand. Then he smiled at the group. "I wish you all a happy Easter, ladies. Permit me to remark that you are more beautiful than birds of paradise."

The women smiled, and even the Dutchwoman's mouth twitched a little. Only Sara seemed uncomfortable. The Frenchwoman beckoned a servant carrying a tray. "I am sure you'll drink a cup of tea with us, Monsieur Rouston?" She took one of the white porcelain cups and handed it to him with a charming smile.

To her chagrin, the gesture was answered with a vacant expression. "Have you seen Madame Hopkins?" he asked Sara. "I was sure I would find her with you."

"I'm very sorry, but I don't know where Mrs. Hopkins is. I have not seen her for a very long time."

André looked at her in consternation.

"I doubt she would dare show up here anyway," the Spanish woman remarked snidely.

"But why do you judge Madame Hopkins so harshly, ladies? I am certain that she does not merit your low opinion!"

The Spanish woman said nothing, but the Dutchwoman hissed, "We have those people to thank for the fact that the *qaid* interrogated our husbands as though they were common criminals! He ordered the houses of some merchants searched. And yet Mr. Hopkins is the only foreign slave trader in this town!"

"As far as I know, his guilt has not been proven," André replied sharply.

"He is under suspicion for good reason, I imagine, and that reflects on the entire foreign community in Mogador," the Brazilian woman argued heatedly. "Mr. Hopkins has discredited honorable citizens. I, for one, do not like being associated with swindlers and slave traders!"

André could hardly contain his anger. "Did your 'honorable' husband not make his fortune on the slave market in Salvador da Bahia?"

The Brazilian woman glared at him. "How dare you!"

"If you were a man, I would dare a great deal more," André snapped at her.

"It is to your credit that you are speaking up for us, Monsieur Rouston—but please, leave it be."

Sibylla stood behind him, white-faced. But her back was straight and her chin up. To her right and left were her sons. Tom and Johnny clung to her legs and looked wide-eyed from one woman to the other.

"You're silent, ladies? Go ahead, have no fear! Repeat your accusations in front of me and my children." Sibylla's voice was glacial.

André turned to her. He was desperate to shield her from these witless and self-righteous women. But her look stopped him.

"Should the accusations against my husband turn out to be true—which I do not believe—the fault lies solely with him. Neither my children nor I have even the slightest thing to do with it. Although we are not obliged to justify ourselves to you, if these lies preoccupy you to such an extent, you may come to me in confidence with any questions you have. I shall answer them as best I can." Sibylla looked around. "Well, then?"

Everyone was silent. The Brazilian woman coughed, Sara stared at her hands, and the Spanish woman hid behind her fan. The Dutchwoman looked supercilious, and only the Frenchwoman smiled. The tension between Monsieur Rouston and the Englishwoman interested her far more than any nonsense about slave trading.

"Well, that's settled then," Sibylla continued. "I have one more piece of news for you. As long as my husband is the *qaid*'s prisoner, I am conducting the business affairs of the Spencer & Son Shipping Company in Mogador. Effective immediately, I am responsible for everything, and believe you me: the slave trade is no part of it!" She added somewhat more gently, "Today we are celebrating the feast of our Lord's resurrection and I want to contribute to the annual gathering." She stepped aside and they only now noticed her servant, who had been standing behind her with a large market basket.

"I have baked a traditional English treat. Other countries"—she nodded to the French consul's wife—"may have a more renowned cuisine. But hot cross buns are among my most beloved childhood memories of Easter. Yours too, Sara?"

Sara was tugging at the ruffle on her sleeve and pretended not to hear. Sibylla raised her shoulders. Then she turned to Nadira. "Please give the buns to the ladies and Monsieur Rouston. They must be eaten while they are still warm."

"I have never seen a woman with your courage, Sibylla! You overwhelmed that whole gang of resentful biddies with your wit and your baking."

André had pulled Sibylla behind the tent. Her sons were inside playing with the French consul's little daughter. Here, they could steal a few undisturbed minutes.

Sibylla laughed. She felt liberated and carefree for the first time in weeks. The ordeal with Benjamin was far from over. But tomorrow, she would at last be able to visit him and ask him all the questions that had been weighing so heavily on her mind. Rusa had obtained permission for her.

"This son of a donkey! I am going to teach him some wisdom!" the governor's mother had exclaimed when Sibylla told her the *qaid* had been denying her permission to see her husband for three months.

Sibylla squinted provocatively at André. "Are you out to ruin my reputation or are you back in Mogador so soon because you have missed me?"

André loved the fact that she was flirting with him, yet he had no choice but to ruin her carefree mood. "I would like nothing better than to ruin your reputation in every conceivable way, but unfortunately, the reason for my visit is somewhat grave. War is brewing on the border with Algeria. I have been asked by the French government to travel to Marrakesh with important news for the sultan."

"What kind of news? And why Marrakesh? I thought the sultan was going to be in Fez."

"He has canceled his stay there. The news concerns Abd el-Kader and one of his own insurgent subjects."

"Abd el-Kader? He's the Berber leader who called for the *jihad* in Algeria against the French, is he not?"

"Yes. And he is serious about this. He has joined forces with a Moroccan tribal leader to overthrow the sultan."

"Oh no! But what can that have to do with me?" Sibylla asked.

"The Moroccan Berber leader is sheltering Abd el-Kader. Now my job is to convince Abd al-Rahman to surrender him to France. In return, I am going to reveal to the sultan that the insurgents are planning his overthrow. Should Abd al-Rahman not agree to this deal, the French will begin bombarding Moroccan harbor cities. And you know what that would mean for Mogador."

"War," Sibylla concluded quietly. "Dear Lord!"

They were both silent as Sibylla let André's news sink in. "When do you leave for Marrakesh?"

"First thing tomorrow."

"Please wait one more day. Please! I am finally going to be permitted to visit Benjamin tomorrow. But after that, I shall accompany you to Marrakesh."

"You wish to do what?"

"If what you say is true, I cannot wait until the fall to petition the sultan for Benjamin's release. I must do it now."

"Never! This is absolutely the wrong time!" André was aghast.

"I'll decide what the wrong time is," she snapped at him. "And if you won't take me, I'll ride by myself. Benjamin cannot stay marooned on that island any longer. If war really were to break out, he would need to be with his family."

"But you are completely mad! Can you really believe the sultan is going to give you Benjamin? You told me yourself that the *qaid*'s henchmen took all of your money. Abd al-Rahman is going to want more than a handful of *dirhams* borrowed from a maid for the life of your husband!"

Sibylla smiled mischievously. "There is a simple solution: we buy my husband's freedom with the information about the conspiracy."

The following morning, Sibylla was taken to the Island of Mogador by the same team of rowers who had carried her husband there three months earlier almost to the day. She was nervous and exhausted, having spent the night packing and thinking about her impending visit to the sultan. Now she was focused on her first encounter with Benjamin since his arrest. She had questions about the shipping business: details of merchant meetings, when she needed to consult Toledano, how to deal with the harbormaster and the captains. In addition, she wanted to inform Benjamin that she was now conducting the affairs of the company. And most of all, she needed to hear at long last what he had to say about the accusations of slave trading. This last question had occupied her days and her nights.

At least now she had a little money at her disposal. A promissory note for Benjamin's share of the skins he had purchased in Fez had arrived. As had a promissory note from her dowry, which would last until the end of the year to feed her and her children, to pay the servants, and to repay her debt to Nadira.

Sea spray came over the low side of the boat and splashed on Sibylla's tunic. She wrapped her arms around the basket on her knees and looked back at the shore. Along the sand, pack camels laden with tall loads were moving southward in a long line behind their drivers. Behind them, bathed in sunlight, rose the white walls of Mogador. It was such a peaceful image. She could hardly imagine that war might actually threaten the city soon.

The six men rowed rhythmically past the frigates and brigantines. The Island of Mogador lay before them in the morning mist. The pointy parapets and the tall minaret made the island look like the spiny back of a dragon emerging from the water. High in the air, she saw a falcon, seemingly tiny and almost motionless. Sibylla shaded her eyes and watched as it suddenly swooped down at the island like an arrow.

The thought of her husband made her self-conscious, and she was honest enough to admit that she had not much missed him during his three months of captivity. She had missed André far more.

A few minutes later, the oarsmen slowed and guided the boat through the pointed rock needles protruding from the water to a sandy part of the beach. The commander of the fort and two Black Guards were already awaiting her. The captain helped her disembark.

"Come back after afternoon prayers!" she ordered before the launch cast off again with rapid strokes.

"Assalamu alaikum." She turned to the commander, a bearded, imposing man with a huge scimitar on his belt. He growled something

faintly resembling *"Wa-alaikum salam"* and pointed to her basket. "Unpack!"

She spread clothes, books, newspapers, toiletries, and a package with fresh bread, fruit, and cheese in front of the soldiers. The commander looked bored, but his soldiers fingered Benjamin's clothes with great interest. They confiscated his razor but she was allowed to keep everything else. Next, the soldiers took her to the fortress. Sultan Sidi Mohammed Ben Abdallah had had the first walls built at the end of the last century. His descendant Moulay Abd al-Rahman had expanded it with four cannon-fortified bastions and a mosque. Sibylla noticed that it was teeming with soldiers. If the French did attack Mogador, they would meet with forceful resistance.

She decided not to tell Benjamin about the possible threat of war. She did not want to add to his worries. She wrapped her scarf firmly around her head as the wind here was considerably stronger than on the mainland. Apart from a few windblown thuja trees, the only other flora on the island was junipers, grass, and low-growing lichens bearing tiny yellow and white blossoms. Otherwise, there was nothing but rocks, sand, rabbit holes, and soldiers.

Benjamin's cell was located off the inner courtyard of the western bastion. Sibylla was surprised to find the heavy wooden door open. But then, where was he going to escape to? She stood in front of a small rectangular room. The floor and wall were made of rammed earth, and daylight entered only through the door and a small hole high up on one wall. Sibylla noticed a heavy table with a water jug and an oil lamp. Then she saw Benjamin. He sat on a bed consisting of a simple wooden frame and a straw mattress and was balancing an earthenware bowl of couscous on his knees.

"Hello, Benjamin."

"Sibylla!" He jumped up. The bowl slid off his knees and smashed on the hard floor. Sibylla was horrified to see a mouse flit out from under the bed and greedily fall upon the simple meal. But Benjamin paid it no mind.

"Finally! I was beginning to think you were going to let me rot in here. What is it, can I go? Is the *qaid* letting me go?" He rushed up to her.

"Let me have a look at you!" She almost did not recognize her own husband. He had grown so thin that the soiled suit hung from his shoulders. His cheeks and eyes were sunken. His hair was long and stringy, half his face covered with a matted beard. He smelled unwashed and she immediately began checking for fleas and lice. There was not much left of the Benjamin who used to wear tailor-made suits, silk vests, and diamond-studded cravat pins, who took daily baths and had his hands manicured so that they were softer than a woman's.

"I brought you some things." She placed her basket on the table.

He hastily rummaged through the contents. "Soap? Books? Underwear? Does this mean that I'm staying here? Have you made no attempts to get me released?"

"Well, actually, I've been drinking tea and going on picnics. Unfortunately, the picnics are quite lonely as all my former friends believe that my husband is a slave trader."

He quickly softened his tone. "Don't get upset, I didn't mean it like that."

"I had to let them keep the razor," she continued after a short pause. "But for a few *dirhams*, the commander promised to allow you to use it every morning."

Benjamin reached for the newspapers and scanned the headlines. "Railway shares have risen in England. Just as I predicted! If I weren't stuck here, I would invest. Railways are the future. I can feel it in my bones! But I'm not allowed to take care of any business here and meanwhile there are fifty camel-loads of leather rotting in the *caravanserai*. Spencer & Son is going to go bankrupt in Mogador."

"It is not," Sibylla proudly declared. "I have inspected the leather and had it shipped to England. I have already received the promissory note for our share."

He sized her up. "Are you trying to steal my job?"

"I have preserved your job! The children and I have to eat and the servants need to be paid!" She was painfully disappointed. Why did he not praise her? Still, she forced herself to set aside her bitterness.

"No one in London knows what has happened. All I wrote to Father was that I was filling in for you for a time. But I need your advice, Benjamin. I have many questions."

He placed his hand on her arm. His skin was rough and chapped, his fingernails black. "You are so clean," he said quietly. "So incredibly clean." He shuddered as though he wanted to dispel bad thoughts.

They sat side by side on a piece of grass on the shore. Somewhere behind them on one of the bastions, the commander was shouting orders. One could hear the cannons rattling and squeaking as they were positioned in front of the embrasures. But before them lay the seemingly endless Atlantic Ocean, smooth and silvery, empty but for a few fishing boats.

"Do you know what they're doing up there on the bastion?" Sibylla asked.

Benjamin shook his head. "No idea. But it's been going on for a few weeks. Perhaps they're as bored as I am."

With Sibylla's intervention and *dirhams*, he had been permitted to wash and put on fresh clothes. Sibylla had untangled his matted hair. Except for his beard, he was once again beginning to resemble the man she knew.

"After my first three days here, I tried to escape," he boasted.

Sibylla was horrified. "What? As though we didn't have enough difficulties already!"

He grinned at her sideways. "I jumped in the water and was going to try to swim to one of the English ships that was anchored not too far from here. I'm a good swimmer, or have you forgotten our adventure in the harbor basin in London? Unfortunately, the Negroes came after me in their boat. The commander was fit to be tied. He locked me up for three weeks. Now he lets me out again. But they've been keeping a closer eye on me—and on the boat too."

Sibylla looked at two small emerald-green lizards sunning themselves on the warm earth. "And how is your treatment overall?"

He shrugged. "They leave me alone. We can hardly communicate anyhow. Neither the Moors nor the Negroes speak English, and my Arabic, well, you know how that is."

"And what do you do all day?"

"Every morning, I walk around the island. That takes me two hours. The rest of the day is rather monotonous," he replied vaguely.

He did not want to tell her that his solitude was making him strange, that he carried on quiet conversations with the rabbits, and that he had tried to teach tricks to the mice scurrying through his cell.

"Is Willshire making any effort to free me? I must get off this island, for God's sake!" he suddenly exclaimed. "You have to find out what they're planning to do with me! Last night, I dreamed the sultan was going to behead me!"

"Willshire has sent a letter to Consul General Drummond-Hay in Tangier to ask him to protest your arrest officially," Sibylla tried to reassure him. "But you have to bear up a bit longer. We both know that clocks in the Orient tick differently."

"No! I have to get off this island. Write to your father, to the queen, bribe the *qaid*, but do something!"

"The *qaid* has already helped himself. His people ransacked our house and took everything."

"What?" Benjamin grabbed her arm. "Where did they look? What did they find?"

"Ouch! You're hurting me!" She tried to free herself. "They took your coffer and the money I earned through my trade with the governor's wives."

"That's all?"

"What do you mean? It was everything we had!"

"Yes, of course. I was thinking of the furniture, china, and such," he added hastily.

"Isn't that bad enough? Let go of me! First thing tomorrow morning, I'm riding to Marrakesh to ask Abd al-Rahman to release you. So you see, I'm doing everything I can."

"What? The sultan has agreed to see you?"

"Monsieur Rouston has arranged for an audience. He is going to escort me there and advocate for your release. The sultan trusts him more than any other foreigner in this country."

Benjamin glared at her furiously. "You most certainly are not going to ride to Marrakesh with that slick Frenchman and make a laughingstock of me! I won't allow it."

"I'm afraid you will have to unless you want to stay on this island even longer," she countered.

"I want nothing to do with Rouston," he grumbled. But he expressed no further objections to her plan.

"Will you finally tell me if there is something to the accusations against you?" Sibylla urged. "Did you truly have human beings transported on my father's ships and sold into slavery? You owe me an explanation, Benjamin."

He swallowed hard and turned away. "I can't believe what you're accusing me of," he muttered. "You're no better than the *qaid*."

"But I only want the truth!"

Benjamin turned to Sibylla and fixed his gaze as though he wanted to hypnotize her. "I swear that I could never do anything to harm the Spencer & Son Shipping Company or my family!"

She knitted her brow. "So that means that someone set you up. Was it Captain Brown? Samuel Toledano?"

"How should I know? Perhaps Toledano approached Brown and offered him a lot of money. I can't monitor my captains while the ships are in the harbor. But as soon as I am free, I am going to do everything in my power to expose the guilty party!"

Sibylla let his words sink in. Brown was a sinister-looking character. But so were other captains. Her father was right when he said that the life at sea made a person cruel and solitary.

"I don't know whom or what to believe anymore."

Benjamin squeezed her hand so hard that it hurt. "Think about it, Sibylla! You told me yourself that the *qaid*'s people found no cash that could not be accounted for. What better proof of my innocence is there?"

He moved closer to her and pushed her backward onto the grass. Before she could react, he had rolled on top of her and was squeezing her breasts.

"Benjamin! Stop!" She struggled vehemently.

His face was flushed. "You are my wife," he gasped, trying to fight back.

"The last few years, you've been calling Firyal for this sort of thing. Let me go!"

He rolled off her at last. "You knew?"

"You certainly took no pains to hide it."

He lowered his head and drew imaginary shapes in the grass with his fingers. "Why do you even want to help me? Would you not prefer that I rot on this island?"

She sat up and smoothed her tunic. "I'm doing it for our children, Benjamin—only our children."

Chapter Sixteen

Marrakesh, a few days later

The news that Sibylla Hopkins was riding to Marrakesh in the company of Rouston spread like wildfire among the merchants of Mogador. The men grinned and made suggestive remarks about the fiery Englishwoman, while the women whispered about her scandalous behavior.

Sibylla did not care a whit about the opinion of people who had been shunning her for months. Time was of the essence and so she had left the children in Nadira's care. André had borrowed a fast horse from the French consul's stable for her and they reached Marrakesh after four instead of the usual five days.

The sentries greeted Rouston like an old friend and immediately let them through the main gate. A short time later, Feradge, the head of the eunuchs and the ruler's confidant, appeared. He told them that His Majesty was on a falconry excursion, but was expected back by evening and that he, Feradge, would personally ensure that His Majesty received his guests first thing the next morning.

He put André up in the guest pavilion in the magnificent royal garden, while Sibylla was permitted to stay in the harem quarters.

"Let us meet in front of my guesthouse after morning prayers," André said when they took leave of one another. "Now you must rest. Tomorrow will be a strenuous day."

"*Magnifique!* You are more beautiful than a queen!" he exclaimed when Sibylla showed up the following morning. She was wearing a dress made of royal blue embroidered silk, but without the matching sapphire jewelry, a wedding gift from her father, as those pieces had fallen into the hands of the *qaid's* plundering henchmen. She had dressed English-style for her meeting with the ruler. André believed that Abd al-Rahman would hold her in higher regard if he could see from her attire that she belonged to the English upper classes.

André himself wore the uniform of a major in the Chasseurs d'Afrique and had pinned the medal for his service in the Algerian War on his light blue jacket.

"Abd al-Rahman still thinks of our military as the Grande Armée of Napoleon's time, and as I am appearing before him today as a representative of the French government, I hardly wish to disabuse him of that misconception," he explained somewhat sheepishly to Sibylla, who was looking at him admiringly.

Had the occasion not been so serious, the enchanting garden would have made it romantic indeed. The desert wind rustled in the silver leaves of the olive trees, birds were singing, fountains were burbling, and everywhere there was the scent of roses and mint, verbena, myrtle, and jasmine.

Sibylla took a seat next to André on the low marble bench in front of the guesthouse. "I doubt the sultan is going to value Benjamin's freedom as highly as his own throne," she said with some anxiety.

"We will have to play our cards carefully and pique his curiosity to such a degree that he will be prepared to pay this price for our information."

"I am terribly nervous," she confessed. "I've been telling myself that this audience is no different from bargaining for oranges at the *souk*—and I'm quite good at bargaining, I'll have you know. Only that the merchant is the ruler of Morocco and the oranges are Benjamin's head!"

André grinned. "I like the image of your husband's head as an orange."

"I'm not even sure that Abd al-Rahman is going to like my gift." She looked at the expensive English saddle lying before her in the grass. Benjamin had had it made especially for his flame-colored stallion. Qaid Hash-Hash had confiscated the stallion, of course, but his henchmen had not taken the saddle. Benjamin would not be much pleased to discover that his saddle was now the property of the sultan. But she had had neither the time nor the money for another gift.

André got up and straightened his uniform jacket. "Here comes Feradge. It's time." He extended his hand to Sibylla and helped her up.

"Phew," she groaned. "I had forgotten how tight a bodice is!"

He smiled. "Chin up and shoulders back. And do not forget: I am by your side!"

"His Majesty will receive his guests in the lion's court." Feradge bowed to André and Sibylla. The corpulent man with ebony skin obviously loved resplendence and adornments. His brocaded cloak was embroidered with pearls and gems, and gold rings sparkled on his plump fingers. Sibylla suddenly remembered that she had forgotten to bring a present for the ruler's favorite eunuch, and she could only hope he would not take offense. But Feradge was the epitome of graciousness as he inquired about the well-being of His Majesty's guests and whether there was anything they lacked.

His movements were swift and lithe despite his size. Soon, they arrived at a wall and a large gatehouse made of reddish rammed earth, through which one reached another part of the garden. There were sentries from the Black Guards here too, and they respectfully bowed their heads as the small group hurried past.

They entered a courtyard surrounded by a colonnade and filled with a rectangular water basin. Sibylla noticed how pleasantly the water cooled the heat of the desert. "We are so close to the Sahara, and yet there is so much water here!" she marveled.

"His Imperial Majesty has it channeled here from the Atlas Mountains. In this way, he honors God, who has given the people water and thereby awakened the barren soil," the eunuch explained with great dignity.

They had reached the end of the water basin and were passing an octagonal latticed pavilion. In it lounged a pair of lions watching the visitors with vigilant amber eyes. Sibylla had seen live lions only once before in her life, many years ago in a traveling menagerie of exotic animals in London. As she passed the bars, the male uttered a low warning growl. She looked at the powerful animal with the black-and-yellow mane and the deadly paws, bigger than two men's fists.

"I should not have thought the name 'lion's court' was meant literally!" she whispered to André.

"A reminder of the ruler's power," he replied quietly. "Do not let it intimidate you."

"The audience will take place here," Feradge interrupted.

"Here?" Sibylla said without meaning to.

She had expected an official venue, a throne room with dignitaries and courtiers—certainly not a garden. The eunuch led the guests to the other side of the cage. Silk rugs were spread out on the ground and braziers emitted the scent of fragrant resins. Under a red silk canopy, flanked by two slaves who were fanning him with palm fronds, Sultan Moulay Abd al-Rahman, Imam of all True Believers and Ruler of Morocco, Descendant of the Holy Dynasty of the Alaouites, the last free ruler of Arab North Africa, sat on a divan. He was dressed all in white, with a carefully groomed short salt-and-pepper beard, alert black eyes, and a well-nourished, round face.

The sultan greeted Rouston first. His gaze lingered on the medal of honor. He recognized that André was wearing the uniform of the victors of the Algerian War and understood it to be a show of power.

Sibylla bowed respectfully. "*Assalamu alaikum*. Imperial Majesty, I am deeply moved by your receiving me and Monsieur Rouston. Please allow me to offer you this modest gift."

She turned to André, who placed the saddle at the sultan's feet.

The monarch bowed his head graciously. "*Wa-alaikum salam*, merchant lady. We thank you for the honor of your visit."

He clapped his hands. A slave appeared from the shadows of the colonnade, picked up the saddle, and carried it away. Had Sibylla not already learned that Arabs considered it impolite to pay more attention to the gift than to their guests, she might have feared that he was not pleased with it.

The sultan pointed to another divan opposite his. "Please, my honored guests, take a seat. Please do us the honor of drinking some spiced coffee with us."

Again he clapped his hands. More slaves appeared. One brought bowls with water and towels so the monarch and his guests could rinse their hands. Another brought tiny, delicate porcelain cups. A third served sweetmeats, and a fourth handed His Majesty a coffee mill so that he could grind the freshly roasted beans himself. Then one of the slaves brewed the spiced coffee over one of the coal pans. Feradge stood behind his master's divan and directed the ceremony with tiny gestures.

"Your Arabic is excellent, Mrs. Hopkins," the sultan remarked courteously while he filled the cups.

"Learning the language of a country that has welcomed my family with such kindness is the least I could do," Sibylla replied modestly.

The encounter continued like this for quite some time. Moulay Abd al-Rahman and his guests exchanged pleasantries as though they were at a picnic.

"Now, I am certain that there is a reason for this urgent request for an audience?" the sultan eventually asked.

Although Sibylla was sure that Abd al-Rahman was already familiar with the reason, she calmly answered, "Your governor, Qaid Hash-Hash, has been holding my husband on the Island of Mogador for several months."

The sultan's kindly expression suddenly turned severe. "The merchant Hopkins traded in slaves. We do not permit infidel visitors to our country to engage in this type of business—in agreement with your English queen, as you surely know."

"My husband has been negligent in the respect he has paid you, Your Imperial Majesty," Sibylla conceded. "But he has assured me that he is innocent and has himself fallen victim to a conspiracy. It was likely one of his captains who conducted these odious deals behind his back."

"Do you then accuse us of holding an innocent man captive? We have it on good authority that your husband shipped slaves from our coast to the Caribbean!"

Sibylla decided to drop the presumption of innocence. She lowered her head in supplication. "As the mother of two small sons, I throw myself at your feet, honorable monarch, and ask for mercy for my husband. You are renowned as a wise and magnanimous ruler. Please do not deny a mother's plea!"

Abd al-Rahman's face twitched. He motioned to Feradge, who leaned over him, and a rapidly whispered exchange arose.

"Your husband has severely damaged our reputation in the world. This kind of offense can be absolved only with some kind of compensation," Abd al-Rahman finally pronounced.

There it was: the demand for money Sibylla had been dreading, for she still had little. "I suspect I know which captain is responsible for these trades, and I will be personally responsible for seeing to it that he receives his proper punishment in England. Not the slightest blemish will remain on Your Imperial Majesty's honor."

"That will not suffice," Abd al-Rahman replied coolly.

André took this opportunity to intervene. "Perhaps it will suffice if we bring news about Abd el-Kader, the Algerian rebel—and your own subject, Thabit al-Khattabi. The two of them have made a pact that is not likely to please Your Majesty."

Abd al-Rahman froze. "What about al-Khattabi?"

"This information is worth Benjamin Hopkins's freedom," André replied. "And not only that. In exchange for this information, I ask that you hand over Abd el-Kader, who is hiding in the Rif Mountains and whom you are protecting."

Sibylla held her breath as she watched the two men size each other up. The sultan's black eyes glowed, but André did not seem to fear him. Finally, Abd al-Rahman clapped his hands, and when a slave appeared, he rapidly whispered a command to him.

"The merchant will be released," the sovereign declared. "Our scribe will give Mrs. Hopkins an official order for the *qaid*. Abd el-Kader's handover depends on the information you have, Rouston, so speak!"

Abd al-Rahman's demeanor remained tense but steady while André laid out the conspiracy that Abd el-Kader and Thabit al-Khattabi had hatched. Sibylla was on pins and needles. Even the lions paced in their cage and uttered menacing growls.

When André was finished, the sultan pounded the divan with his fist. "May God curse the evildoers! Oh, the vipers we have nurtured in our bosom!"

He swung around to the eunuch, who flinched. "Why did we not know about this? Why do we pay a fortune for informants only to learn about treason from a Frenchman?"

"Your Imperial Majesty," Feradge stammered, "I shall initiate an investigation . . ."

"Bring us al-Khattabi! We shall flog him personally, quarter him, and feed his stinking carcass to the lions!" the sultan raged. "What happens to traitors in your country, Mrs. Hopkins? Tell us so we may do the same to this hyena al-Khattabi!"

"Well, Your Imperial Majesty, I th-think that high treason is punishable by death in England as well," Sibylla stammered. "Not in a lion's den, however." She warily looked over at the formidable predators, which were baring their long, sharp fangs.

The sultan hesitated. Sibylla could have sworn that the corners of his mouth twitched in amusement. Then he turned to André. "Your information is worth its price. However, we cannot hand over Abd el-Kader to your government. Though an Algerian, he has many friends in this country and they would clamor for revenge."

"Your Majesty is making a grave error," urged André. "The French government wants Abd el-Kader at all costs."

The sultan reached for a silver tray with candied dates and offered them to Sibylla and André. "Tell the French: it is not the amount of time spent on the hunt, but the kind of animal killed. Abd el-Kader will be this animal at the right time." He placed a date in his mouth and chewed it with relish.

At that moment, a slave once again darted from the colonnade and gave Feradge a small piece of rolled-up parchment.

"Your Imperial Majesty! A carrier pigeon just delivered news of great importance from the north of the country." He handed the sultan the parchment.

Abd al-Rahman read the contents carefully before rolling the parchment up and saying to André, "Abd el-Kader, together with the tribes of our province of Oran, to which the traitor al-Khattabi belongs, has launched renewed attacks in Algeria. The French navy has bombarded Tangier in retaliation."

Sibylla was shocked. Their visit was too late! Would the sultan still release Benjamin? André too seemed unnerved. "Your Imperial Majesty, if you wish, I will personally intercede on your behalf with the French consul general."

Abd al-Rahman raised his right hand. "Your offer comes too late for Tangier, Monsieur Rouston. But, Mrs. Hopkins, you need not worry. A ruler from the house of the Alaouites does not go back on his word. Your husband will be released. But mark my words: it is not an innocent man who is being freed!"

"Are you in such a rush because you cannot wait to be reunited with your husband?" André inquired querulously as he tightened the saddle girth on his horse.

"My children have been without their mother for a week. I should think that that is sufficient reason to rush," Sibylla replied sharply. "I wish to reach Mogador tonight."

"Vos desirs sont des ordres, madame!" André stashed the leftovers of their midday meal in a saddlebag, mounted his brown mare, and galloped away. Sibylla had trouble keeping up as he spurred his horse more and more, driven by rage and jealousy. Although he had told himself a hundred times that it was not Sibylla's fault, he nonetheless let her feel the brunt of his bad mood.

Ever since they had left Marrakesh three days earlier, he had been asking himself why he'd agreed to such an absurd act of heroism to save his rival. It must have been his desire to impress Sibylla with his diplomatic *savoir-faire* and his influence with the sultan. A tiny part of him had even hoped that, during these few days and nights, he might be allowed to hold her in his arms and to love her. And yet she had not encouraged him in any way, which hurt him even though he told himself a hundred times that it was wrong to expect such recompense for his support.

"I ought to have let that fellow rot on the island," he growled under his breath and pressed his heels into his mare's flanks.

"André, wait! I think my horse is lame!"

He spun around to investigate.

"The right front leg feels hot. Probably a strained tendon," he concluded after dismounting and checking the horse. "Dismount and get on my horse. I am going to lead yours. Fortunately, we're almost there."

Sibylla slid out of the saddle. "I can lead my horse myself!"

"You cannot seriously think that I am going to ride while you walk next to me! Now get on my horse, *zut alors*!"

"I understand French curses quite well, and I am not going to take orders, not even from you!" she hissed.

They stared at each other furiously for a few seconds before breaking into laughter. He leaned forward and cupped his hands to help her mount his mare more easily.

"*Excuse moi!* My behavior has been atrocious."

"I'm not going to disagree." She sighed. "Without your help, the sultan would never have agreed to release Benjamin, and I am aware of how difficult that must have been for you. Benjamin is my husband only on paper at this point. Still, we are bound in the eyes of God and the law, and it is almost impossible to dissolve that union."

André swallowed hard. She was right. A woman like Sibylla, coming from an affluent family, might be able to obtain a divorce after long and costly litigation. But she would lose her good name and almost certainly her children as a result. And what right did he have to expect her to make such a sacrifice?

"Oh, I haven't yet told you about Abd al-Rahman's gift to me," he said to distract himself from his despondency. "On the evening before our departure, he summoned me and said that I could have one wish fulfilled in return for saving him from the conspiracy."

"That sounds like a fairy tale!" she exclaimed. "What was your wish?"

He absentmindedly stroked the horse's nose. "A piece of land for me to work and my own house in which to live. That has been my most ardent wish ever since I was old enough to understand that my eldest brother would inherit the farm and the rest of us would have nothing." He laughed. "I cannot deny that I am the son of a farmer."

"Did he fulfill your wish? Abd al-Rahman has never permitted a foreigner to own land in his country."

"Now he has!" André disagreed proudly. "There is a compound with a large pleasure garden approximately a day's journey southwest of Mogador, where the Oued Zeltene flows into the Oued Igrounzar. Abd al-Rahman often spent his weekends there when he was a young man and *qaid* of Mogador, but he hasn't gone there since his ascension to the throne. It must be rather overgrown and dilapidated."

"But now you are the new owner and your dreams are fulfilled. How wonderful, André!"

He was moved that she was genuinely happy for him, and disconsolate at the same time. "My dreams will not be fulfilled until you live there with me."

Sibylla lowered her gaze. "Do you remember what you said to me in the Portuguese church?"

He smiled sadly. "That we must leave our future up to fate."

She nodded and her eyes shone with her love for him. "Let us put our hope in that, André, *inshallah*, God willing, even if we cannot foresee our future."

Chapter Seventeen

The closer they came to Mogador, the more humid the air grew. When they reached the city in the early afternoon, the outlines of the walls and the buildings were blurred by the low veils of mist, lending an eerie atmosphere to the place.

"Where are the caravans?" André wondered as they rode across the square in front of the city gate. Normally, at least a hundred camels loitered here, but today the place was empty. Apart from the sound of their own horses' hooves and the wind driving dust clouds across the vast square, all was eerily still.

"The city gate is closed!" Sibylla cried. "And sundown is at least another two hours away!"

André studied the bastions. "Strange. Wait here, I shall survey the situation." He threw his reins to Sibylla, went to the locked gate, and hit it with the butt of his rifle. "Hello! Open up!"

The muffled sound of boot steps came from inside. Next, gun barrels appeared out of the narrow slits directly above him.

"Watch out!" Sibylla screamed.

He took a few steps back, placed his hands around his mouth, and bellowed, "Open the gate!"

"Who goes there?" a voice barked back.

"Residents of this city!" André answered and gave their names. The gun barrels disappeared, then the locks and bolts were pushed aside and the gate was opened just enough for Sibylla and André and their horses to fit through. Several soldiers and the captain of the Black Guards—the one who had conducted the search of her house—were waiting for them. The men had their muskets trained on the pair.

"Dismount!" the captain ordered Sibylla.

She obeyed, utterly confounded. The soldiers took the reins, but André quickly stopped them. "Don't touch these horses!" He turned to the captain. "Why are we being received like criminals?"

The captain's expression grew even darker. "The horses are confiscated. Now come!"

"I wish to speak with the *qaid*!" André placed his hand on his weapon. At once, the soldiers surrounded him. Reluctantly, André relinquished his weapon and grumbled, "*Gare a toi*, if there isn't a very good reason for this."

Sibylla anxiously looked around. "I have to go home! I must know how my children are." One of the soldiers shoved the barrel of his gun under her nose and she recoiled.

"You come!" the captain repeated threateningly.

She instinctively pressed herself against André. "What on earth happened while we were gone?"

Sibylla hardly recognized the cosmopolitan trading city as the guards marched them through Mogador. The houses appeared closed and forbidding, the people hostile. Sibylla saw no foreigners at all, but there were many locals coming toward them from the *souk*. She recoiled when an old man spat on the ground at their feet. Another uttered ugly curses and clenched his fists, and the women pulled their veils down farther and made the sign to avert the evil eye. She also noticed the soldiers' demeanor. In all the years she had lived there, Sibylla had never seen them so battle-ready. It seemed as though the city was preparing itself for a siege. Whole companies armed to the teeth marched past. Artillery and donkey carts with cannonballs were being transported in the direction of the harbor bastions. Slaves rolled barrels behind them.

"Those must contain gunpowder," André whispered.

"Do you think that now the French will bombard Mogador too?" Sibylla whispered back.

"Possibly."

"*Uskut, faransawi!* Be silent!" One of the soldiers dug the barrel of his gun into André's ribs.

Sibylla assumed that they were being taken to the *qasbah*, but the soldiers turned down a dead-end alleyway behind the western bastion.

"What are we doing here?" she exclaimed when she recognized the place.

"Uskuti!" the captain barked.

They had stopped before André's secret Portuguese church. Sibylla could hardly believe her eyes: the old door with the rusty hinges was being guarded by several heavily armed guards.

"Inside!" Two soldiers shoved them through the door, letting it crash shut behind them.

There was fearful muttering in the interior. Sibylla smelled the odor of many people, sweat, vomit, excrement. She tried not to gag and squinted in the dim light. Men, women, and children were cowering close together. All the foreigners of Mogador were being held prisoner in this small church. Sibylla recognized her neighbors, the Willshires and the de Silvas, and all the other consuls and merchants and their wives.

"Mais ce n'est pas possible!" André muttered.

Sibylla scanned the crowd until she spotted Nadira, sitting on the edge under the clock tower, with Firyal close to her. Tom and Johnny were with them.

"Mummy!" The boys struggled to free themselves from the servants' arms. Sibylla uttered a cry and ran to them.

"We've been held here since the soldiers came and pulled us out of our beds at dawn three days ago," Consul Willshire told her as the excitement over the new arrivals died down. "We don't know why. I have demanded an explanation from the *qaid*, but to no avail. They don't let us out, but they leave us in peace. We get water and something to eat twice a day—"

"If you refer to that slop as food!" the French consul's wife objected. "Many children are suffering from stomachaches and diarrhea!"

"And none of us has ever done anything to harm a Moor!" a Portuguese merchant said indignantly.

"Perhaps we all have to atone for the deeds of the slave trader," a woman said and pointed accusingly to Sibylla. Hostile murmurs became louder.

André immediately stepped in front of her and her children. "The sultan himself has ordered the release of Mr. Hopkins. So he is innocent!"

"Can you prove that?" Consul Willshire asked.

Sibylla pulled out the scroll, which she had worn under her tunic this whole time, unfurled it, and held it up so that all could see the sultan's seal. Again the murmurs grew, some in doubt, some in agreement.

André raised his voice again. "Friends, I believe I know why we are here." He briefly explained about Abd el-Kader, the fighting along the Algerian border, and the retaliatory actions of the French. "When we left Marrakesh, the sultan received news that Tangier had been bombarded by the French navy. Everything in Mogador indicates that this city is also facing the threat of bombardment. I assume that we are being held as hostages."

His last words caused an uproar. Several of the men wanted to subdue the guards and flee, while others feared being used as human shields. Still others swore that their imprisonment would have diplomatic consequences for the sultan and his *qaid*. Suddenly, a door flew open and guards stormed into the church interior, screamed, and fired into the air. Sibylla threw herself over her children. Sara Willshire went deathly pale and moved her lips in silent prayer. Firyal wailed and closed her eyes. But the soldiers vanished just as quickly as they had appeared.

"So we owe this treatment to the French!" an English merchant cried out in a voice filled with hate. People muttered their agreement.

André raised his arms. "I do not believe that anyone will harm us. Abd al-Rahman does not wish to risk war with all the European powers. We have about one more hour of daylight. I am going to climb the clock tower. There are almost certainly no guards there, so I shall be able to have a look around."

A little brown owl flew from its nest as André climbed the dilapidated tower.

"This will bring ill luck," Firyal whispered and buried her face in her hands. But no one was listening to her. Two hundred people had their eyes glued to the cracked walls of the clock tower. What would Monsieur Rouston see up there? What news would he bring? What would happen to them all if he was discovered?

Sibylla thought of the enchanted afternoon they had spent in this place. Was it really only three months since they had lain right here in each other's arms, kissed for hours, and talked about their lives, oblivious to the world and happy?

"Mummy!" Tom had climbed out of Nadira's lap and was clinging to her. "Where is Daddy? Did the soldiers take him too?"

She stroked his soft curls. "Daddy is going to be with us soon, darling."

"Really?" He beamed at her.

Sand and small stones rained down from the clock tower as André carefully descended.

"I saw some ships' masts," he announced as soon as he had safely reached the ground. "They were just visible through the fog—twelve, maybe fifteen. They are French, I saw the flag. There is also what looks like an English frigate, although it was difficult to make out the flag in the fog. Perhaps it is an observation vessel, or perhaps they came to take the British citizens out of Mogador and the *qaid* stopped them."

The room was silent. Tears streamed down Sara Willshire's face.

"Might those ships not be merchant vessels?" her husband finally asked.

André shook his head. "No. Except for the English one, they all had their battle flags hoisted. I recognized the pennant of the commander in chief. It is the Prince de Joinville, who served in the Algerian War. As soon as the fog lifts, Mogador will be bombarded."

Twenty-six hours later, when the blazing sun stood high above the churning gray ocean, the cannons finally fell silent. The *qaid* had surrendered his city after the Island of Mogador was taken by five hundred French soldiers.

André stood with the *qaid* on the roof of the governor's palace and looked through a telescope at the British frigate *Warspite*, anchored among the French warships in the harbor entrance. Several longboats full of people bobbed like nutshells around it in the waves.

After the cease-fire, French soldiers had crossed over and freed the prisoners in the Portuguese church, which fortunately had avoided a direct hit. Now they were being safely taken to the *Warspite*. André was the only foreigner to remain in the city. He had learned from one of the French commander in chief's adjutants that the victors would take Moroccan officers and soldiers hostage until the sultan had agreed to all their demands for the surrender of Abd el-Kader. André had offered his services as translator and mediator.

His eyes wandered from the longboats to the *Warspite*, where the sailors were helping the men, women, and children to climb the swaying jack ladder. But try as he might, he could not make out Sibylla, the children, or her two servants. She had wanted to go to her house to see what damage, if any, the cannons had done, but André had urged her to go with the others to the *Warspite*.

"You'll be safer on the ship," he'd told her, not mentioning that he feared looting and retaliatory attacks on foreigners.

Now, the *qaid* watched as French soldiers emptied barrels full of gunpowder into the water. "The French soldiers have defiled the Blue Pearl of the Atlantic and now they are plundering her!" he moaned. Others loaded captured guns and flags onto longboats and pushed artillery along the quay to show to the admiring crowds in Paris later on.

"The Prince de Joinville will acknowledge that you did not harm the foreign hostages, Your Excellency. Furthermore, I am convinced that the government of France has no intention of humiliating His Imperial Majesty the Sultan," André said, trying to mollify the governor.

Hash-Hash snorted contemptuously. "Do you really believe that, Rouston? The British, French, Spaniards, and other European powers have been struggling for the greatest possible influence in Morocco for years. This morning, a carrier pigeon from the north delivered the news that Tangier too has surrendered. After such a victory, you French are going to dictate your demands and it is only a matter of time until you have subjugated proud Morocco just as you did Algeria!"

"Algeria was subjugated by the Ottomans in the sixteenth century."

"The Ottomans are our brothers. But it means profound humiliation for the children of God to be under the rule of infidels!" shouted the *qaid*.

André chose not to reply and pointed his telescope at the island. Frenchmen were taking the surviving Moroccan soldiers to their ships in rowboats. He saw a number of corpses floating in the water. The Prince de Joinville's adjutant had reported that the Moroccan losses were considerable while the French had hardly any casualties. This did not surprise André. He knew that the Moroccans had very bad weapons and little training.

The wind carried the acrid stench of death and fire. He peered at the western bastion, where Sibylla had told him Benjamin was being held. Dense smoke still wafted from the area hours after the cannonade. Charred ruins rose out of the smoke. The French must have firebombed the island.

"The prisoner Hopkins was being held in the western bastion," he said to Hash-Hash. "His Imperial Majesty has ordered his release. Do you think that he has survived?"

The *qaid* took the telescope from André and looked through it. "That would be a miracle, Rouston. You French have ravaged that island like hungry wolves!"

Sibylla stood at the bow of the *Warspite* and stared at the smoldering remains of the island fortifications. The deck was crowded with exhausted men, women, and children. The crew fed them and the ship's doctor examined them.

"You wanted to speak to me, Mrs. Hopkins?" Captain Wallis bowed politely.

She turned around with a smile. "Thank you for taking the time, Captain! I have an enormous request: Do you think you could find out if my husband is among the survivors on the island? He was in the western bastion at the time of the bombardment." She dispensed with any explanation.

The captain nodded solicitously. "I will dispatch an officer to the *Suffren* at once and obtain information from the French staff of command. Do not despair, Mrs. Hopkins, we will soon know more. In the meantime, may I have a cup of tea brought to you? And if I may say so, the battlefield on the island is no sight for a lady." He bowed and missed Sibylla's grimace of irritation.

Two hours later, he returned, accompanied by a French naval officer. "May I present Lieutenant de Maillard, Mrs. Hopkins. He is the personal adjutant to Commander in Chief Joinville."

She greeted him and asked, "Do you have news of my husband, Lieutenant? Is he on one of your ships?"

The young officer bowed. "I fear, madame, I'm not bearing good news. Your husband is not on any of our fifteen ships. He was neither among the prisoners of war nor any of the casualties."

"So he is missing?"

"You might say so, madame," Lieutenant de Maillard replied uneasily. "The fortifications on the island were utterly destroyed. The western bastion, where your husband was being held, is completely gutted . . ." He swallowed hard. "I am afraid, madame, you must prepare yourself for the worst."

"That he is dead," Sibylla whispered.

The captain and the officer both stepped forward to catch her should she collapse, but she raised her hand to stop them.

"Thank you, gentlemen, I shall manage." She looked again at the smoldering ruins and back to the two men. "Is the destruction really so devastating? Could he not have survived somehow? Be buried under the rubble?"

De Maillard shook his head regretfully. "I am very sorry, madame, but it is very unlikely."

"Unlikely or impossible? Please, Lieutenant, tell me the truth!"

The young officer helplessly glanced over to the captain, who shrugged his shoulders. "The western bastion was bombarded and was fully engulfed in flames. Even the iron mountings and artillery pieces melted in the heat. No one there could possibly have survived. We found only a few charred bones in the ashes."

"Good God!" Sibylla put her hand over her mouth.

"My sincerest sympathy, madame." Once more, the young officer bowed. Then, upon a signal from the captain, he withdrew.

Wallis motioned a sailor to get a chair and compelled a reluctant Sibylla to sit. "Mrs. Hopkins, the *Warspite* is going to sail for England in a few days' time. I am sure you will want to return home to your family."

Sibylla numbly shook her head. "Right now, I wish to speak with my sons. Thank you for your trouble, Captain."

She got up and went to look for Tom and Johnny. They were standing at the railing with Nadira and Firyal and were engaged in a spitting contest. When they spotted their mother, they came running to her. She took them by the hand and led them to a quiet corner.

"What are we doing, Mummy?" Johnny looked around curiously.

Sibylla squatted down and embraced first him and then his brother. "Thomas, Jonathan, you must be very brave, big boys now!"

Island of Mogador, one week later

"Mummy, it smells funny!" squawked Johnny. He was standing next to his mother in front of the ruins of the western bastion and holding his nose.

His brother asked with great concern, "Are you crying, Mummy?"

She forced herself to smile. "No, Tom, dear, it's just that the strong smell is burning my eyes."

Tom, satisfied with that answer, leaned against his mother. His brother, however, whined. "Too dirty here, Mummy. I want to go home."

"The soldiers have said that we can go home today," Sibylla consoled him. "You two run along to Nadira and Firyal. I'll be there in a minute."

Her sons ran away, laughing. They seemed so unaffected by their father's death. Apparently, they were still too young to understand.

"The angels carried him off to heaven," she had told the boys.

They had been intrigued by the idea. Johnny had asked if the angels would lend his father a pair of wings or if he would grow his own. They still failed to grasp the finality of death, even though Sibylla had taken them with her to the western bastion so that they could all recite the "Our Father" for Benjamin together.

They had been camping on the island for six days. Just as the sailors were lowering the longboats into the water to take the foreigners back to the mainland, a sloop from the *Suffren* had arrived and they had been told that Haha Berbers had invaded Mogador and were looting the city.

Since the *Warspite* was not equipped to accommodate so many additional people, the foreigners were staying in an improvised camp with tents made from sails and blankets. But a few hours ago Commander in Chief Joinville had announced that the Berbers had retreated, driven out with the help of his soldiers.

Even more than a week after the bombardment, the destroyed western bastion still emitted a pungent stench. Sibylla coughed and held a handkerchief over her nose.

Maybe I can find some sign of Benjamin after all, she thought, as she held up her hems and stepped through the cold ruins. *A button, a seal, something.* It was difficult to deal with Benjamin's death when there was no body for her to bury. She hesitated when she discovered a small object under a charred beam. But once she had removed the soot, she had to admit the deformed lump of metal could just as easily have come from a door hinge as a button from Benjamin's jacket.

I was too late, Sibylla thought with a heavy heart. If she had ridden to Marrakesh just one week earlier, her husband would still be alive! Now she had to reconcile herself to the fact that he had died an excruciating death.

"The boats are ready. We are going to cross to the mainland."

Surprised, Sibylla turned around. Sara Willshire was standing behind her, looking with horror at the ruins.

"Thank you." Sibylla wanted to walk past her, but Sara held her back.

"What a terrible misfortune!" she whispered. "I . . . we all have done you an injustice. I am so sorry!"

Sibylla looked into Sara's eyes and thought of the long months when the support she had so desperately needed had been denied her. She did not want to be bitter. After all, they had all endured hardship now. But she simply could not forget how the people she had considered friends had let her down.

"As indeed you should be," she replied coolly. "You and your husband abandoned me in my hour of need. There is nothing more to say."

Sara broke down sobbing as Sibylla walked away.

Chapter Eighteen

"God be praised, my lady, you have returned!" Hamid's cries had alerted the cook and the other servants. They all came running, and they also thanked God for returning their mistress safe and sound.

Sibylla greeted her servants warmly. "What a relief to see that you are all well! How did you fare during the attack? Were you at home the whole time?"

"When the French attacked, we were here, my lady, but when the Haha Berbers came, we hid in the cemetery outside the city. The Haha avoid the cemetery because they are the sons of oxen and are afraid of the *djinns*," Hamid proclaimed, clearly proud of having thought to hide everyone among the graves.

"Oh, how good it feels to be back home!" Sibylla sighed.

"And the master?" inquired Hamid.

She shook her head and told them Benjamin had been killed during the bombardment of the island.

The gatekeeper immediately began to wail loudly and tear his hair. "*Inna lillahi wa inna ilaihi rajiun* . . . we belong to God and to him we return . . ."

"We should be grateful that we are still alive and that the house was not damaged by the cannons," Sibylla said, trying to console him.

But at that, the cook threw his hands in the air. "God protected the house from the cannons, but not from the Haha. They destroyed everything! Oh, what a disaster, my lady!"

It soon became apparent that the house had not entirely been spared from the cannonballs. One had landed in the courtyard and hit Benjamin's sundial. As Sibylla checked the damage, she discovered that the base had lifted a little, so it was now crooked. The bronze globe with the serpents' heads was undamaged, but the Union Jack lay next to it, burned and shredded. Benjamin's exotic carp were missing from the pond.

"The Haha stabbed them with their bayonets," Hamid said glumly.

"And fried them," added the cook.

The inside of the house looked as though a whirlwind had swept through. Furniture was broken, books were ripped up, clothing was torn, and toys were destroyed. The Haha had stolen everything of value. Except for the half-empty bottle of whisky in his desk, they had even broken all the bottles in Benjamin's hoard of alcohol.

"These louts have caused more havoc than the *qaid*'s henchmen," Sibylla remarked grimly.

Still, she rolled up her sleeves and, with the help of Nadira, Firyal, and Hamid, began to clean. The cook disappeared in the kitchen to prepare supper with the paltry remnants the Berbers had overlooked. Sibylla's sons had found their marbles and were playing in the courtyard.

"Mummy! Johnny threw my prettiest marble in the hole by Daddy's sundial and it's gone!" Tom stood in the doorway of Sibylla's room and wiped his tears.

"Can I not leave you two alone for half an hour?" Sibylla was kneeling in her room surrounded by piles of books. She was placing those that had survived the Hahas' destructive frenzy on the only unbroken shelf and the damaged ones in a box—not to throw away, but to have rebound.

"It's my very favorite!"

Sibylla sighed and followed her son to the courtyard. Johnny was lying on his stomach and peering into the hole left by the cannon. "It fell in," he explained sadly.

"Let me have a look, darling."

She squatted down next to him and looked into the hole. The bricks Benjamin had used for the base were mostly destroyed and the pedestal of the sundial had been lifted out of the foundation. Sibylla sighed. She had no choice but to lie on her stomach and try to fish the marble out. She reached her arm in blindly, turning over stones and digging in the earth—without success. Just as she was about to give up, she felt a hollow under the base. Several bricks had been broken here as well. She carefully felt her way into the opening and finally touched something cool, smooth, and soft: linen. It was a sack about the size of a child's head, with something jangling inside when she pulled on it. She found the cord, opened the sack, and let her hand glide inside.

Coins, she thought, stupefied. She grasped one and carefully withdrew her arm.

"Do you have the marble, Mummy?" Tom was hopping from one foot to the other.

"No, but . . ." She opened her fist and held her breath.

"What's that, Mummy?" Tom asked.

Johnny leaned over and declared with a frown, "That's not Tom's marble."

Sibylla stared at the yellow shimmering coin on her palm. She carefully brushed away some dirt although she was already sure it was a British sovereign, an extremely valuable coin with a high gold content.

But how did a British gold sovereign get under Benjamin's sundial? As she turned the coin over between two fingers, she tried to make sense of her discovery. The coin could not have belonged to Mr. Fisher, the previous resident, because the date on the coin was 1839, meaning it was new. It must have belonged to Benjamin, just like the others in the sack. But why was it under his sundial?

Because he did not want anyone to know about it.

She got down on the ground again and explored the hole more extensively. It was about three hands high, an arm's length wide, and a yard deep. The entire space was filled with similarly stuffed sacks.

Now Sibylla understood why her husband had been so nervous upon hearing of the *qaid*'s search. Why he had insisted on knowing exactly where the henchmen had looked and how much money they had found. She now understood the reason behind his prodigality—Benjamin had become richer than he had ever dared hope and he had wanted all the world to see, even as he knew he needed to hide it. And at the same time, he had lied to and betrayed his wife mercilessly, relentlessly, to the very end. She had fought for his life and mourned his death, and he had deceived her.

When night had fallen, Sibylla returned, stealthily, like a thief in her own house.

She pulled so many sacks out of the hole that it took a large basket and several trips to carry them to her bedroom from the courtyard.

She also found a leather portfolio—stained from the soil—which contained detailed accounts of Benjamin's appalling transactions. Sibylla learned not only how many slave journeys the *Queen Charlotte* had undertaken, but also how many Africans were on board each time, how many died at sea, how much her husband had paid for their provisions, who had collected bribes, and lastly, in which Caribbean ports Captain Brown had sold the slaves.

Locked in her room, by the flickering light of an oil lamp and with growing disgust, Sibylla read these accounts of horror. It was difficult to believe that, in the last three years, her own husband, the father of her children, had sold around two thousand human beings into slavery. Had she known him so little, or had he been a different person before greed changed him?

Her hands shook as she began to count the money. There were precisely 16,625 British gold sovereigns, an incredible fortune, amassed through inconceivable misery. She contemplated the floor of her bedroom, covered with little towers of coins, and for the first time, felt relief that Benjamin was dead. Yet his fate did not absolve her of the decision of what to do next.

She anxiously listened for sounds in the house, but all she heard was the sound of her own breath. She did not want this blood-drenched money. And now that she had it, they were all in grave danger. The *qaid* would have her arrested, perhaps tortured. In England, she would be held to account in court for Benjamin's misdeeds. The scandalous trial would do untold damage to the Spencer & Son Shipping Company and forever cast a pall over her sons' lives. Not to mention the many people who would happily commit murder to get their hands on such a treasure!

Sibylla's head hurt. She remembered the half-empty bottle of whisky in Benjamin's desk. She had never tasted whisky. The strongest beverage a lady was permitted to drink was a little glass of port, but at this moment she did not care. She urgently needed something to calm her nerves.

A little while later, she was back in her bedroom. "No one!" she swore as she held the list of Benjamin's accounts over the flame of the candle and watched it turn to ash. "No one is ever going to find out about this!"

At dawn, Sibylla stood on the shore, far behind the harbor, where there were only gently undulating dunes overgrown with grass. It was still dark over the ocean. She listened to the soft splashing of the water and watched the fishing boats returning from their nightly sardine catch, their lights swaying gently on the waves. She'd had to get out of the house, where everything reminded her of Benjamin and the horror he'd wrought. The beach felt soothing, safe.

"Allahu akbar!" The *muezzin*'s ceremonious call to prayer broke the silence. A thin strip of light over the city announced the day.

Sibylla put her head back and breathed in the fresh salty air. *I should throw the money into the sea*, she thought, and suddenly felt an irrepressible urge to laugh. She well and truly had the exciting life she had always wished for as a young girl in London. How naive that girl had been.

She definitely did not want to use Benjamin's gold treasure for herself, but she did not want to sink it in the Atlantic either. For the time being, the money was hidden under some floorboards in her bedroom that the Haha had pried up. She had pushed her bed over it. Not as good a hiding place as Benjamin's, but the best she could manage on short notice.

The *muezzin* had finished his call and daylight was breaking fast. The ocean changed from gray to blue. She thought she could make out the whitecaps of the waves and the outlines of the fishing boats, which extinguished their lights one by one. Movement in the corner of her eye told her she was no longer alone. She turned her head. André! She had not seen him since she had been taken to the *Warspite* with her children. She had assumed he was no longer in town.

She ran toward him, flung her arms around his neck, and kissed him with abandon. Any passerby could have seen them, but after a few glasses of whisky and the discovery of Benjamin's dirty money, that hardly seemed to matter.

"André! Thank God! How did you know I was here?"

He freed himself somewhat breathlessly. "I slept on the beach because the French consulate has been destroyed. You, my dear Sibylla, reek of alcohol, if you will permit me to say so. And you also look as though you've been working a field!"

She glanced down at her soiled kaftan and her dirty fingernails and laughed. "Well, not exactly a field, but you're close."

He looked at her somewhat confused. "Have you had any news about your husband?"

She stopped laughing. "Dead. Burned to death. There is not a stone left of the western bastion, where his cell was."

"I'm very sorry," he said, looking aggrieved.

She stared at him with determination. "I don't want your pity, André. Benjamin is dead, but I am alive. And I swear to you: today is the beginning of a new life for me!"

He took her hand and they walked along the water's edge, farther and farther away from the city, silent and content to be together. The air was still cool, but the sun warmed it more and more as it rose. Rabbits scampered across the sand and storks circled in the sky.

Sibylla gripped André's hand and led him to the dunes, where it was warm and protected from the wind.

"What are you doing?" he asked.

She looked at him. "Show me how it really is when a man and a woman love each other."

He thought he had misheard her, but then she slid off her leather slippers. When she was about to pull her tunic over her head, he stopped her. "Wait!" He cleared his throat. "I want to do that."

He took off his jacket and laid it on the sand. Then he sat down and pulled Sibylla next to him. He took her face in his hands and kissed her. Her forehead and blonde eyebrows, her eyelids, the freckles that the sun sprinkled on the tip of her nose, and her soft, moist mouth. He slipped his hand under her clothing, stroked her delicate skin, and felt the curves of her body. He pulled the tunic over her head and smiled when he felt her getting goose bumps. Then he leaned over and kissed her nipples. He helped her get out of the wide *chalwars*. He saw her naked for the first time, and the sight of her slim figure, her small breasts, her softly curved Venus mound aroused him.

Sibylla blushed. Uncertain whether she was pleasing to him, she pulled up her legs and wrapped her arms around her knees. He let her be as he himself undressed. She watched him intently and thought about how strange it was that she and Benjamin had never seen each other naked even though they had been married for over four years and had two children together.

"Are you all right?" André inquired.

She nodded. He took her in his arms and she allowed herself to be rolled onto her back while he pressed his body against hers. His body completely covered hers, making her feel safe and protected. While they kissed again, her hands slid from his shoulders to his buttocks, then down his arms to his fingertips. He felt completely different from Benjamin—broader, stronger. She had only ever felt her husband through his nightshirt, but that was enough to know that he had a narrow body with no muscles. But here with André, she could feel his strength and the firm, smooth flesh under his soft skin.

Yes, thought Sibylla, *what we are doing here is right. Right and good.*

The sun had moved over the buildings of Mogador and was quickly warming the sand on which they lay. Sibylla was nestled closely to André and said sleepily, "Now I have really felt what it's like to be loved."

He kissed her hair. "*Je t'aime*, Sibylla. I am glad that I can finally tell you that."

She lifted her head out of the crook of his arm and looked at him. "I want to ask you something, André."

"Yes?"

She thought about Benjamin's gold in its makeshift hiding place. "What would you do if you unexpectedly received something very valuable that you cannot and would not keep?"

Worried, he answered, "I do hope that you aren't referring to us and to the feeling we have for each other."

"Certainly not."

"What, then?"

She hesitated. "Something that Benjamin has left me."

He frowned as he thought. "If you don't want to keep it, give it to someone who needs it."

She reflected and smiled. "Why not? No, truly, that sounds very sensible."

A short while later, she carefully extricated herself from his arms. "I have to go. The Haha have turned our house upside down. There is a lot of work waiting for me."

André reached for his jacket. "I'm leaving Mogador today. The *qaid* no longer needs me and, quite honestly, I can hardly wait to see the land the sultan has given me." He tied the sash of his tunic. "Do you want to come? Perhaps you'll like it so much you'll want to stay—with your sons, of course."

Sibylla blushed. "If you don't mind, I'm going to remain here in Mogador for the time being. I have to figure out how to proceed without Benjamin. I could imagine myself taking over the business for Spencer & Son permanently—if I can convince my father, that is."

André bent over to tie his boots, trying to hide his disappointment. "I'll ride alone then. I don't have any idea how much work awaits me, but I would like to visit you now and again."

She beamed at him. "That would be wonderful!"

Qasr el Bahia in the Atlas Mountains, May 1840

André slid out of his saddle, kneeled on the ground, and picked up a clump of soil and crumbled it. Was this soil suitable for his great dream of growing saffron? He let the soil run through his fingers.

Sultan Moulay Abd al-Rahman's present lay on a plateau a quarter mile above sea level in the foothills of the Atlas Mountains. At this altitude, the little sand-colored bulbs of the *Crocus sativus* received sufficient warmth without being parched by the desert heat. At the same time, it was not so high that the valuable bulbs would freeze in the cold earth during winter. The air and the chalky ground stored enough moisture, although the region was dry and deficient in rain. Irrigation was also provided. The sultan's architects had installed the same underground *rhetaras* as on the caravan route to Marrakesh and thereby irrigated the magnificent pleasure garden that had flourished here at one time. He would build low protective walls out of quarry stones to prevent the thin layer of soil from being blown away by the wind. André got up, placed one foot in the stirrup, and mounted his mare.

I shall do this, he thought as his gaze wandered over the area and he felt a deep sense of contentment.

He had been filled with pride a week before, when he rode through the gate of the impressive four-part complex that was half palace, half fortress. The sultan had named this property Qasr el Bahia, the Palace of Beauty, and André immediately understood why.

It had taken him almost a whole day ride's from Mogador on the rocky, winding path along the riverbed of the Oued Igrounzar, first east and then south, until he had found the tributary of the Oued Zeltene and first seen the property from afar. Its majestic walls were painted red-golden by the evening sun and the cedar forest on the hills behind it almost black with the coming night. All of it—the mud-and-stone fortification walls, the stables, storage buildings, and farm buildings—reminded him of a Chiadma *tighremt*: a closed-off compound that could be easily defended against enemies. In the residential buildings, however, he found the colorful opulence of Moorish architecture.

Although a closer look revealed that the erstwhile splendor of the Palace of Beauty had faded, this did not dampen his enthusiasm. The wind, heat, and cold had taken their toll on the walls, the two-winged cedar gate hung crookedly from its hinges, and wild animals had taken up residence in the buildings. When André entered the stables, he disturbed a family of jackals. Swallows and sparrows nested in the rafters, and wild pigeons filled the two towers to the right and left of the gate.

Upon entering the rooms of the former lord and his court, he discovered mice living in the torn upholstery of cushions and sofas. In one room, he stumbled over a fallen chandelier and, in another, moth-eaten rugs. Floor tiles were broken and the roof had holes in several places. There was much work to be done, but his Chiadma friends would surely help him.

André was completely alone here and grateful for the solitude. He made himself a bed in the stable next to his horse and awoke in the middle of the night when a predatory animal slunk around outside, growling and hissing. Yet he was not frightened. He was happy and full of plans for the future.

The following morning, he saddled his mare and explored the grounds. Bees buzzed among the poppies and thistles. There were wild roses and sprawling bougainvillea. He even discovered an olive grove and the remnants of water basins. Standing in the center of the courtyard was the emblem of Qasr el Bahia, a magnificent Atlas cedar tree. He planned to build terraced fields to ensure his saffron crocuses would get ample sun. In between, he would plant pomegranate trees. The juice of their fruit was in great demand by rug makers as a dye. And he would plant a new flower garden. Or better yet, he would ask Sibylla to do that, so that she could see that Qasr el Bahia was her home as well.

When he returned to the residential buildings around noon, he encountered two thin, ragged shepherd boys eyeing him suspiciously. The bigger one, who had a conspicuous port-wine stain across his face, stared at him with hostility and squeezed a rock in his hand. However, when André shifted his gun to the front of his saddle, the boy dropped his rock. André greeted them, first in Arabic, and, when they did not respond, in Tachelhit, a Berber language spoken mainly in the south of Mogador. Now the one with the port-wine stain replied that they belonged to the Ait Zelten, a clan belonging to the Haha tribe.

André thought it wise to explain the ownership situation right away. "His Imperial Majesty Moulay Abd al-Rahman, the ruler of this country, has given me Qasr el Bahia as a gift. Go and tell your sheikh that Qasr el Bahia now belongs to André Rouston, and also tell him that I look forward to smoking *shisha* with him."

"This land always belonged to our people until the sultan stole it from us. He has no right to give it away!" the boy explained angrily.

The little one chimed in. "Where are our goats going to graze now?"

André pointed to the entire area around them. "There is plenty of land around this estate. And anyway, I'll need some skilled hands to help me rebuild. With the money I pay, your sheikh will be able to buy feed as well as comestibles."

"The Ait Zelten are no accursed slaves!" The older one spat on the ground in front of André. He motioned to the younger one and the two of them and their herd went on their way.

Mogador, June 1840

Shortly before dinner, Sibylla was sitting at the table in her drawing room. She wanted to write a letter to her father, but her mind kept returning to her meeting with Qaid Hash-Hash that afternoon. He had deigned to speak with her only after she had had him informed that she was in possession of something for which he was searching. Of course, he had known what it was and had flown into a terrible rage when she had refused to divulge Benjamin's hiding place for his treasure. But she had shocked and subdued him with her proposal that the entire amount be used to rebuild Mogador with only one stipulation: that he proclaim to the whole city that Benjamin Hopkins had always been a respectable businessman and never involved in the slave trade.

"Why did you not just keep the money, Mrs. Hopkins?" he wanted to know when she was leaving.

"Because I wish to give it to someone who really needs it," she said, thinking of André. She added, "And no one needs it more than the citizens of Mogador."

How grand, she thought triumphantly, to see such respect on the governor's face!

Sibylla dipped her quill in the inkwell and returned to the letter. She wanted to inform her parents about the bombardment of Mogador and tell them that Benjamin was killed as a result. She also wanted to suggest to her father that she continue managing Spencer & Son's business in Mogador permanently. She would not, however, mention the slaves or the money under the sundial.

There was a knock at the door.

"Yes," Sibylla called.

Nadira entered. "The captain of the *Queen Charlotte* is here, my lady. He insisted on seeing the master. I told him that the master was dead. And so he wants to speak with you."

"Where is he?" Sibylla shot out of her chair. Brown! At last! For months she had waited to confront him.

"I have shown him into the master's old office."

"Thank you, Nadira." She ran along the gallery. But when she reached the door to Benjamin's office, she stopped dead in her tracks. The red-haired, bearded man inside might have been wearing the uniform of a captain for the Spencer & Son Shipping Company, but he was definitely not Nathaniel Brown.

When the stranger beheld Sibylla, he quickly removed his bicorne and bowed awkwardly. "My sincerest sympathy, Mrs. Hopkins, for the death of your husband. My name is William Comstock, and I'm helmsman and temporary captain of the *Queen Charlotte*."

Sibylla motioned to the divan and sat on a chair. "Why temporary captain? What has happened to Brown?"

"Dead, Mrs. Hopkins. Killed in a mutiny."

She was horrified. Mutiny was a serious crime, punishable by hanging. "Tell me," she demanded.

Comstock reported that they had been on the open seas when some of the crew had mutinied. Brown, all the officers, and the first mate, who had tried to overpower the leader, were murdered. But then a quarrel had broken out among the mutineers and the leader had had several of his cronies hanged on the mainmast.

"That was good for us loyalists, Mrs. Hopkins, 'cause then it was easier to kill the leader and those other criminals. And now we are here, because we had got off course quite a bit and Mogador was the nearest port."

Sibylla needed a moment to recover from the shock. The only good that had come out of the mutiny was that the contemptible Nathaniel Brown had descended into hell!

She crossed her arms and looked at Comstock. "You have acted bravely, Comstock, but there is something I must ask. How was it possible to transport so many slaves on the *Queen Charlotte* without my father's knowledge?"

The man grew pale. "I don't understand, madam . . . what do you mean?"

"Don't play me for a fool! I know that the *Queen Charlotte* secretly transported slaves and not just one time." She swallowed before continuing. "And I also know how my husband figured into it. So, out with it!"

Comstock cleared his throat. "The *Queen* only got loaded to half capacity in Mogador. When she left, she didn't set course for America, but south to Cape Juby. That's where we took on the blacks and then sold them in the Caribbean. In the logbook, we said there was storms, calm, fog, and the like to explain the delays."

"And the whole crew participated?" Sibylla asked, repulsed.

"The officers were bribed, and Brown told the ordinary sailors he would throw them into the ocean if they didn't cooperate. It's some of them that mutinied. They wanted their cut."

"And what about you, Comstock? Did you receive your cut?"

He hung his head. "I swear to God, I wouldn't have taken a shilling but for my wife. She was so ill, and them doctors is such cutthroats."

She bit her lower lip and pondered his words. Finally, she said, "At least you are being honest now. And you proved your loyalty to the company during the mutiny. For that reason, I will not say another word about this contemptible slave trade—on condition that, from now on, you are a reliable and loyal employee of Spencer & Son." She scrutinized Comstock.

He jumped out of his seat and bowed low. "Thank you, Mrs. Hopkins! That's really very generous of you, Mrs. Hopkins!"

"Very well then." Sibylla got up and accompanied him to the door. "Sail home to London and brief my father on the events, but leave my husband's name out of it."

Chapter Nineteen

Qasr el Bahia, end of June 1840

"You have company, André!" Udad bin Aziki, sheikh of the Chiadma Berber, shaded his eyes and squinted to the east.

"Who could it be?" André wiped the sweat off his brow with the back of his hand.

It was almost noon and the sun was bearing down relentlessly on the flat roof of the left watchtower of Qasr el Bahia. He and Udad's sons had been busy since early that morning covering the holes in the roof with palm fronds. They were using a thick mixture of clay, sand, straw, and dung that bin Aziki had put together. Once the mud had dried, it would keep the interior of the watchtower cool despite the sun's heat, and conversely, warm, by holding in the accumulated heat.

"I see only a dust cloud," Aziki reported. "It's not very fast, but it's big."

"I don't think it's the Ait Zelten," said André, also watching the cloud. "But we should lock the gate just in case."

Ever since André had settled at Qasr el Bahia, Ait Zelten men had been skulking around the premises. While they never came close, they followed the activity there with both suspicion and curiosity. Their sheikh had never paid André a visit, but his men were still letting their herds graze on his land. Winter and spring had been very dry, so that the low pastures already did not provide enough nourishment for the herds. Since André knew the Berbers depended on whatever the barren land gave them and that, aside from their horses, their goats and sheep were their most prized possessions, he left them in peace in the hopes that the sheikh would later remember his generosity.

After closing the heavy gate and locking it with a crossbeam from the inside, he climbed back up the watchtower.

"By the beard of the Prophet!" bin Aziki muttered when he recognized the first riders. "Is this a procession?"

André squinted and hesitated. "The first rider is the sultan's personal eunuch. It's safe to open the gate again. We have nothing to fear from Feradge."

Half an hour later, horses, mules, camels, donkeys, and people filled the interior courtyard of Qasr el Bahia. Feradge dismounted and greeted André. His face glistened with perspiration; his brocade robe was covered in dust. Still, he radiated all the solemnity of a master of ceremonies. He explained that His Most Holy Majesty Sultan Moulay Abd al-Rahman had sent his best mosaicist, blacksmiths, gardeners, carpenters, and lime-and-mud plasterers to help the Frenchman. Rouston was to dispose of them as he saw fit.

"I also bring another gift," Feradge continued. "His Imperial Majesty thanks you for advocating for the interests of Morocco after your compatriots dictated their demands following the ignominious bombardment of Mogador and Tangier."

The eunuch whispered a command to a waiting boy, who ran off and soon returned with an adult slave holding a camel's reins. It was wearing a silver-studded bridle and a blanket adorned with tassels and fringes, and carried a palanquin that was closed off on all sides by curtains. An older black woman wearing a striped turban and a cotton dress followed behind.

"What the devil . . ." André mumbled as the camel slowly kneeled.

Feradge stepped close to the animal, opened the door of the palanquin, and solemnly declared, "A gift for you, Monsieur Rouston!"

A hand appeared, small and narrow like that of a child, only gloved in silk and adorned with precious rings. Feradge grasped it gingerly and a small veiled figure slid out of the palanquin. The wind gently blew her silk veils—rose and gold, orange and deep red, they seemed to change color like the desert sands throughout the day. Gold wrist and ankle bangles jingled softly and André caught a glimpse of tiny pearl-studded slippers. He was almost paralyzed when she turned around and scrutinized him with kohl-rimmed eyes crested with long curved lashes and, above them, arched eyebrows like butterfly wings. She studied first his face, then his figure, and he noticed the interest he aroused in her before she gracefully pulled the veil over her face and turned away once more.

Feradge looked pleased with the Frenchman's dazed reaction. "His Imperial Majesty knows how lonely the Palace of Beauty is without women and children, and so, he sends you a flower from his garden: Aynur El Glaoua. Her father is the chief of the Glaoua Berbers. He had her educated at his court."

André had perspiration running down his back and the midday sun had nothing to do with it. Out of the corner of his eye, he could see his friend Udad bin Aziki, whose expression did not betray his thoughts, but the man's sons grinned and smirked. The young Berber woman stood just a few feet away. Her fluttering veils traced the silhouette of a delicate feminine body. Against his will, André felt a tingling sensation in his loins and forced himself to look away.

The Berber woman summoned the older woman with a tiny movement of her hand and whispered something to her. The servant nodded and said to André, "El Sayyida Aynur wants to know where the harem quarters are. She wishes to retire."

He fought the urge to laugh out loud. "There is no harem here, and I do not intend to create one."

"Then have some other rooms prepared for me!" He was startled to hear her voice, which was melodious and soft, yet determined and surprisingly powerful. She stalked away with her veils flowing as though she owned Qasr el Bahia, and he just watched her go, unable to utter a single word.

It was only after she had disappeared inside the house that he found his voice. "Take her away!" he snapped at Feradge. "I don't want her here!"

The eunuch wrung his bejeweled hands. "That would be a disaster, *Sayyid*! You may not refuse a gift—or do you wish to insult His Imperial Majesty?"

"It's not possible, Feradge, please try to understand!" André threw up his hands in exasperation. The whole thing was a colossal disaster! How could he go to Sibylla and say, "Dearest, you don't mind that the sultan has placed a seductive harem girl in my bed, do you?" Qasr el Bahia was the paradise he wanted to share with Sibylla and only Sibylla!

Feradge too was frantic. "What do you not like about her, *Sayyid*? She has the figure of a gazelle. You will not find a single blemish on her skin. Her hair is soft as silk, her teeth are like a string of pearls, her mouth is sweeter than honey, and I swear by God and on my life that she is a virgin. Not even the sultan has broken this rosebud!"

"Well, I won't break it either, because I'm sending her home today!" André cried out angrily.

Feradge tore the turban from his head and pulled his curly hair. "Do you not understand, sir, that you cannot send her back? She would be dishonored; His Imperial Majesty would have her killed!"

"Merde! Putain bordel de merde!" André clenched his fists. Even uttering the worst curses, he knew, did not change the fact that he was caught in a terrible trap. "Is there no solution?" he implored the eunuch.

Feradge sighed deeply. "I am going to be entirely honest with you, Monsieur Rouston, even if His Imperial Majesty throws me to his lions for this . . . Aynur is without a doubt one of the most beautiful roses in the sultan's garden. But every rose has thorns and Aynur's are particularly sharp." He looked in the direction in which the young Berber woman had disappeared, and continued. "Aynur's father is wealthier than the sultan. From his fortress, Aghmat, he controls the only caravan route from the Sahara to Marrakesh. His Imperial Majesty the sultan—may God grant him a long life—knows that the Glaoua sheikh craves power. That is why he forced him to educate Aynur and her siblings at his court. As long as the sultan has his children, the Glaoua will not instigate an uprising. But Aynur has become very burdensome because she is as unpliable as a cork oak and refused the sultan when he wanted to possess her. If you send her back, he will kill her."

A sharp pain throbbed behind André's forehead. He felt as though the ground underneath him were opening up and swallowing the very thing of which he had been dreaming: a life with Sibylla at Qasr el Bahia.

Feradge looked at him with pity. "Keep her here for a while," he counseled softly. "And if you still don't want to keep her, send her not to the sultan but to her family."

At the beginning of August, André was standing on one of the newly planted fields, surveying his land. On the southern slope, several terraced areas were still untilled. He would wait until the following spring to plant orange trees there. But soon he would be able to plant the saffron crocus bulbs his friend Udad bin Aziki was sending to him.

First thing the following morning, the sultan's workmen would leave Qasr el Bahia. Only one gardener, a cook, and a stable boy would remain. With the help of the sultan's workmen, André had transformed Abd al-Rahman's dilapidated and overgrown weekend palace into a halfway-livable property. True, there was still much to be done, but the roofs were newly covered, the stables repaired, broken door and window hinges fixed, broken wall tiles and floor mosaics replaced, and the hearths cleaned.

They had toiled from dawn till dusk for six weeks. Six weeks without Sibylla. André could hardly wait to see her again. Early tomorrow, he would ride to Mogador at last, and by afternoon, he would hold her in his arms.

"You wished to speak to me?" The Berber girl's servant stood behind him.

He cleared his throat. He had assiduously avoided his "gift" for the last six weeks. Aynur had withdrawn with her servant to the former harem quarters, where he had not set foot even once. At the very beginning, he had asked Feradge if the two women had everything they needed and when the eunuch had nodded sadly, he had banished Aynur from his thoughts.

"Pack your mistress's belongings. You are both leaving Qasr el Bahia tomorrow morning. You are returning to Aghmat. Sheikh Udad bin Aziki of the Chiadma Berbers will accompany you."

"But, *Sayyid*—" The old woman looked at him with fear.

"Go! Tell your mistress to get ready!"

"Very well, master." She scurried away.

"You cannot return to Aghmat, *Sayyida*! You know your father will punish you!" Tamra, Aynur's servant, anxiously paced the floor of the small room in which the two women had slept these last six weeks.

"But what am I to do?" Aynur stood at the window and stared into the inner courtyard, then pushed away from the windowsill, making her bangles jingle. "He does not want me. He has not looked at me even once!"

She had been seven years old when her father sent her to the sultan's harem in Marrakesh.

"My little flower, you are more beautiful than the full moon when it rises over the top of the Atlas Mountains," he had told her. "Make sure that your beauty catches the sultan's eye. Then he will follow you like a little dog follows its mistress, and he will do whatever you wish—for the benefit of our family."

During the following ten years, Aynur had received a thorough education. She could recite poems by Al-Jahiz, as well as the fables of Ibn Al-Muqaffa and the erotic verses of the Persian poet Hafez. She played the lute and sang. She was fleet-footed as she danced to the flute and the *riq*. She could prepare traditional spiced coffee and serve it gracefully, and it was while doing so that she finally caught the ruler's attention. Just as her father had predicted, the sultan was enchanted. That very evening, she was bathed, made up, bedecked with jewels and pearls, and sent to Abd al-Rahman's bedroom, smelling of precious oils. As soon as he started to touch her, she had hidden behind the bed like a frightened kitten and, when he had yanked her onto the cushions and pawed her with his greedy fingers, she had fought him with all her might.

After this unsuccessful night, she had been ostracized at court. All the women of the harem, from the favorite concubine to the lowliest of slaves, had laughed at her. Abd al-Rahman had issued an order prohibiting her from ever coming into his sight again. Her family, fearing that the entire clan had now fallen from the ruler's favor, shunned her.

The foreigner, her new lord, represented her last chance. This man was no longer very young either, but he was handsome and well built. He appealed to her. But even more appealing was the idea of becoming the mistress of Qasr el Bahia.

"He has not even looked at me," she repeated, perplexed. "And I don't have crooked teeth or warts on my face, and I am a virgin!"

"There must be another woman who has captured his heart," Tamra explained. "We have to make him forget this woman. There is no other way for you." She studied Aynur. "Where are you in your menstrual cycle?"

Aynur did a quick calculation. "The moon is full in two weeks. That is when it begins again."

"That means you are now ready for his seed!" the servant said with excitement. "You must lure him into your bed this evening. Remember: you have this one night to save your life!"

Aynur lit up as Tamra's words sank in.

"Go to the foreigner and tell him I want to prepare a farewell dinner for him." Aynur ran to a chest of drawers on which stood a small carved wooden box. She opened it, took out a pea-sized ball covered in gold leaf, and held it between her thumb and forefinger. "I will season his food with the nectar of paradise. And then I will tear the other woman out of his heart."

Tamra nodded ceremoniously. "*Inshallah*. Let it be so."

"Please, my lord, taste this!" Aynur kneeled gracefully on the floor before André and offered him a silver tray.

He propped himself up on the cushions and looked at the appetizing morsels. "Stop calling me that. I am neither your lord nor your master. What is this?"

The aroma was enticing. He had accepted Aynur's invitation out of guilt. After all, he had hardly been very accommodating since her arrival at Qasr el Bahia. He had ignored her and, tomorrow, he would send her away like a misdelivered package. Dining with her this evening was the least he could do. But if he was truly honest with himself, he was also curious to find out who the veiled little person with the mysterious dark eyes really was.

Her servant had come to fetch him when the sun began to disappear behind the top of the Atlas Mountains. Since then, he had been lying on a mountain of cushions in a small room. Aynur floated like a shadow in the almost-dark room lit with an oil lamp and served him one temptation after another. Her arm and ankle bracelets jingled softly in harmony with her caressing voice as she offered him the little mouthfuls, each one a new surprise for his palate. He had long forgotten his resolution to stay only a short while. He sprawled lazily on the cushions and his thoughts were as blurred as if he'd had many glasses of red wine. At one point, the thought crossed his mind that she might have drugged his food. After each successive bite, he felt more relaxed and content.

He watched as Aynur balanced the tray on her knees. Her round breasts were visible through the gossamer garment. Was he mistaken or had she colored her nipples?

"It is steamed quince, stuffed with couscous. They should really contain lamb as well, but since you do not own any livestock yet . . ." With a little smile, she took one of the round, stuffed fruits and placed it between his lips.

"*Mon* Dieu, that's spicy!"

She smiled mischievously. "Chili. The spicier it is, the happier it makes you. But wait! Some sweet tea will counteract the spiciness."

She placed the tray on the floor and clapped her hands. Tamra rushed in and handed her mistress a glass of lukewarm tea. André saw the two women exchanged a quick glance. When Aynur was about to hand him the glass, he shook his head.

"Come on, tell me. What are you two up to?"

She opened her dark-rimmed eyes wide. "Are you not happy, my lord? Do you not like it? Drink some tea. It will do you good." She leaned forward to hand him the glass. He smelled her intoxicating scent of roses, vanilla, and ambergris and had to force himself not to stare at her breasts, with their large, dark nipples. He hastily gulped the tea.

When Aynur extended one hand to take the glass, he grasped her small wrist and turned it around.

"What did you do here? It looks pretty."

She looked at the artful ornaments that Tamra had drawn with henna on her palms and whispered, "It is *mehndi*. A bride uses it to adorn herself before her wedding night." The spirals spun before André's eyes. He let go of her hand and fell back on the cushions. "How old are you, Aynur?"

"Seventeen," she replied shyly. Seventeen and still a virgin, a disgrace! She feared the Frenchman would reject her because she was so old, but to her surprise, Rouston mumbled, "You're much too young for me, child. You could be my daughter."

She regarded the chiseled masculine contours of his face, his skin, which shimmered like gold in the light of the oil lamp, his curly black hair, and his eyes, drowsy from the effects of the opium she and Tamra had mixed into his food. The feelings she had for him were not at all like those of a daughter for her father. She rose lithely. "Do you want me to dance for you, Monsieur Rouston?"

He wiped his forehead with the back of his hand and began to laugh uncontrollably. Sibylla appeared in his mind's eye. She was the woman he loved, and not this little seventeen-year-old siren.

"Don't dance for me, Aynur," he protested with a heavy tongue. "Go to sleep! Leave me alone!"

But already he heard the melodious sounds of the *al rababa* coming from behind the screen, accompanied by Tamra's voice, deep and raspy. Aynur moved toward André. Her arms moved like snakes, her breasts bobbed, and her hips swayed to the music. He watched with fascination as the tips of her hair swept along the floor as she bent back her supple and immaculate body.

At this moment, he was anything but lethargic and dazed. All of his senses were keen. Tamra had now put the *al rababa* aside and was beating the *darbouka*, still hidden behind the screen. Despite the thud of the drum, he could hear Aynur's feet, beating the ground to the rhythm. Her breath reverberated in his head. Her scent filled the room and aroused his desire, unexpectedly and overwhelmingly. The silver threads of her tunic flashed like shooting stars, and the notion that she might have colored not only her nipples with henna but also the triangle between her thighs aroused him.

Thoughts of Sibylla dissolved into nothingness. When Aynur danced directly in front of him, he reached for her. She dodged with such speed that his hand grasped only her tunic. The thin material tore and fluttered to the floor. Now all she was wearing was silk harem pants. The flickering light glittered on her shoulders, her breasts, and her stomach.

"Come here!" he commanded hoarsely.

"Of course, my master." She slowly sank to her knees before him, placed one hand on his trousers, opened them, and clasped his hard member.

He sat up with a groan, but she placed her other hand on his chest and pressed him back onto the cushions.

"Are you comfortable, my master?" she asked softly. "Yes? Then stay as you are. I will take care of everything." She leaned over his lap.

Late the following day, André staggered across the courtyard. Qasr el Bahia was deserted and quiet except for a few doves cooing on the rooftops.

"*Salam*, master." The stable boy was hauling a bucket of water.

André suppressed a groan. At the slightest movement, his head felt ready to burst. Overwhelmed with nausea, he could not remember his stable boy's name.

"You!" He beckoned the boy. "Come here!"

The boy shyly obeyed. André took the bucket and poured its contents over his head in one motion. The water was ice cold. He gasped for air, but at least he felt more awake now.

"Where is Feradge?" he asked the stable boy. "Where are the Chiadma and the workers?"

"The caravan with the workers and the sultan's eunuch left for Marrakesh at the break of dawn, and the Chiadma have returned to their tribe. The sheikh said that you would keep Aynur. If not, he said you should send for him," the boy reported.

André stared at him. His memories of the previous night ended with the moment he had entered the room where Aynur was awaiting him with the farewell meal. Everything after that was shrouded in blackness, but he did not have a good feeling. He squinted at the sky, felt a sharp pain behind his eyes, and quickly lowered his head again. "What time is it?"

The stable boy also looked up. "The sun will set in two hours, master."

André groaned once more. What had Aynur and Tamra done to him? And where were they now? He would confront them, both of them! But first he needed some strong tea. Maybe he would also manage to eat some dry flatbread. He was about to return to the house when he heard horses' hooves and turned around painfully. Two riders were trotting through the gate. Two women.

"Hello, André! Your directions were excellent. We had no trouble finding Qasr el Bahia."

He was stunned. "Sibylla, what are you doing here?"

"For not having seen me for six weeks, you don't seem particularly pleased that I am here!" She turned toward her companion. "Perhaps my idea of visiting Monsieur Rouston was not such a good one after all, Nadira."

"*Mais oui!* Of course it was!" André hurriedly replied. But his head throbbed.

Sibylla looked him over. "You look ill. I'll make you some tea and some good strong broth." She was about to dismount but suddenly froze.

He slowly turned around. There was Aynur, young and beautiful like the rising sun, wearing a pearl-studded garment with a thin red veil over her black hair. Her brown eyes flitted back and forth between Sibylla and André.

"Who is that, dearest?" Aynur asked softly. "Is she your other wife? Or just a concubine?"

The pain in André's head suddenly became like a thunderbolt. He looked at Sibylla and tried to remember the previous night, vainly searching for words.

She scrutinized him icily. "Now I see what has kept you from visiting me! Come, Nadira, we don't want to intrude any longer." She pulled her horse around and galloped away through the gate.

"You surely know it yourself, don't you, my lady?" Nadira said three days after their return from Qasr el Bahia. "You are expecting another child."

Sibylla, who was sitting at her desk brooding over Benjamin's list of suppliers, placed her head in her hands. "I have tried to tell myself that it was only an upset stomach."

Since Benjamin's death, she had been so busy ordering her life anew. She had attributed the intense fatigue, the need to sleep all day, and the queasiness to all the work she had taken on, or at least to the heartache over André. He had been such a bitter disappointment. For the first time in her life, she had opened up to a man, given herself to him with body and soul. And while she was still flushed with happiness, he had wasted no time in taking another woman into his bed!

"I wished for another child," she said quietly. "But now . . . I feel absolutely nothing."

Nadira carefully placed the tea tray on Sibylla's desk. "A new life is always a gift, my lady." She pushed a steaming glass toward her. "Will you tell Monsieur Rouston, my lady?"

Sibylla looked at her, aghast. "You know that the child is his?"

Nadira lowered her head. "I do, my lady."

"Who else knows, apart from you?"

"The other servants don't suspect. They don't even know that you are pregnant."

"But you noticed."

"It is my job, my lady!" Nadira sounded hurt. "Of course, I noticed the symptoms. And after we went to see Monsieur Rouston, I understood."

Sibylla found herself smiling against her will. "I am so grateful to have you with me." She grew serious once more. "We share a secret now, Nadira. No one apart from us must know it, do you hear? No one! As far as other people are concerned, even my family, Mr. Hopkins is the father of this child. Can I trust you, Nadira?"

The servant's face seemed carved in stone. "My lips are sealed, my lady."

Once Sibylla was by herself again, she devoted herself to the papers on her desk. For the first time since her return from Qasr el Bahia, she felt her despair subsiding. It felt good to confide in Nadira. Now life would go on. She would forget André!

She was again engrossed in Benjamin's lists when loud voices came from the street in front of the house.

Sibylla banged the desk with the palm of her hand. Was there no peace for her? She angrily pushed back her chair and rushed out of the room. As she neared the door, she heard André's voice. "Why will you not let me in? What is this nonsense? Open the door!"

"I am sorry, sir. But I am not allowed," was the gatekeeper's reply. "My mistress has forbidden it."

He was about to close the hatch, but André prevented him. "The hell you will!" he panted. "Let me see her unless you want the whole street to know that I am here!"

The nerve of this man! First, he stole her heart, then trampled on it, and now he even had the effrontery to show up and harass her! Sibylla stepped in front of Hamid and looked through the door hatch, straight into André's face. He looked awful, unshaven, and pale.

"Sibylla!" he wailed. "Let me in, my love! I must speak with you."

He looked so utterly devastated that it almost broke her heart. But then the images of Qasr el Bahia reappeared in her mind, how he had stood in the courtyard, burning with guilt. And the terrible moment when she realized he had just left the arms of another woman. And that child, who did not even deserve to be called a woman yet, had insulted Sibylla, fully cognizant of her youth and beauty, while André had stood by and done nothing!

"I don't want to talk to you or see you ever again!" she hissed. "Why don't you go back to your . . . your . . ." She wanted to say "Berber slut." But she held her tongue and slammed the hatch in his face.

Part Two

The Red Gold of the Maghreb

1859 to 1862

He who has never hunted, never loved, never sought out the fragrance of a flower, and never quivered at the sound of music, is not a human being but a donkey.

—Arab proverb

Chapter Twenty

London, October 1859

Big Ben gloomily rung seven times. Rain fell from the evening sky and drummed on the wet leaves covering the sidewalk on the southeast side of Hyde Park.

Directly across Piccadilly Street was Spencer House, the impressive three-storied villa in which Oscar Spencer, owner of the Spencer & Son Shipping Company, resided with his family. A landau pulled up. Footmen with opened umbrellas ran to the carriage door to lead the guests through the majestic portal to the warmth inside, while the coachman guided the carriage to the end of the long line parked along the curb.

The second-floor ballroom's four-paned windows were brightly lit. Gentlemen dressed festively in dark evening attire already filled the room. Ladies in gauzy ball gowns fluttered about like birds, their jewels glistening in the light of crystal chandeliers and reflecting off the gilt mirrors. The orchestra played waltzes and liveried servants bore champagne.

Oscar Spencer stood with a group of guests by the window. In a jovial mood, he beckoned one of the servants and everyone took a glass.

"Before this party in honor of your success begins, I would like to toast you privately, my dear nephew," he said ceremoniously and raised his glass. "Thomas, as of today, you are a fully qualified doctor! May your skills always contribute to the well-being of humanity!"

The tall young man in the black academic gown bowed his head in gratitude, the tassel on his mortarboard falling into his face. His brother, John, just as tall and blond as he, playfully pulled on it. "Just don't get a swelled head!"

"I shall see to that," another man interjected. He was about the same age as the brothers and had a slender, athletic build. His bronze skin, the short black beard on his cheeks and chin, and the gray turban he wore identified him as an Arab.

Thomas grinned. "I don't doubt it, bin Abdul. I am looking forward to practicing medicine with you in Mogador."

Sabri bin Abdul and Thomas Hopkins had been best friends ever since the first time they flew a kite on the beach together. Later, they had both studied medicine, Tom in London and Sabri at the famed University of Al Quaraouiyine in Fez. The last two years, they had interned together at Charing Cross Hospital. Now they planned to return to Mogador along with John, who had come to London to learn the shipping and overseas merchant business from his uncle Oscar—after years, of course, of watching his mother.

"I believe we can take our seats." The young woman next to John placed her hand on his arm.

John had met Victoria Rhodes at the newly opened National Portrait Gallery three years before. They had run into each other at the controversial Chandos portrait of William Shakespeare, and John had quickly realized that she was the kind of wife he was looking for.

With her pale complexion and ash-blonde hair, Victoria was hardly an exceptional beauty, but she was educated and knew how to perform her social duties. In addition, her family owned a large ironworks in Cardiff, which John regarded as part of her dowry. Steel was the building material of the future, particularly in shipping, and he had been badgering his uncle for some time to modernize the company's fleet with state-of-the-art steamships.

Forty people were seated at the long table. It was festively decorated with flower arrangements and silver candlesticks, sparkling crystal, Royal Worcester porcelain, and the magical creations of Oscar's French chef. The room was filled with the sound of laughter and quiet conversations. Now and then, one of the gentlemen rose to propose a toast to the newly minted Dr. Hopkins.

"I wish your grandfather could have lived to see this day! He has been gone for a year already, but, oh, how proud he would have been of the first scholar in the Spencer family!" sighed Mary as she fingered the necklace containing a lock of Richard's hair, the only jewelry she wore with her widow's attire.

"I too am the first scholar in the Hopkins family," John gently corrected his stepgrandmother. He thought of his mother and little sister living far away in Mogador.

Mary smiled. "Of course," she said. "Poor Sibylla has had a difficult time of it, so far away from England, without a husband's help, and without you two these five years! I'm sure she's beside herself with joy, knowing that you will be back with her in Mogador for Christmas."

"Is it not unbelievable how quickly time has flown?" Oscar interjected. "I can still remember as though it were yesterday when you arrived in London—immature young lads, seventeen and eighteen years old. You shall do the company proud, John, when you become my new business partner in Mogador!"

John laughed. "Well, I'll support Mother initially. I doubt she'll just hand over management of the company to me right away. She enjoys the work far too much."

Oscar shook his head. "My sister has always been a little strange in that regard. Benjamin, God rest his soul, was right when he used to say that she was a bluestocking. No doubt there is a suffragette hiding in her."

"You can't be serious, Oscar!" Mary exclaimed.

"I most certainly am, Mother. If Sibylla lived in London, she would be in the street agitating for women's suffrage, just like that horrible Mrs. Bodichon. Ah, here comes our *filet de sole*. Wonderful!" He nodded approvingly as the servant placed the dish in front of him.

Mary leaned over to John and quietly said, "Is it true that your mother wears trousers like a man?"

John bit his lips so as not to laugh out loud. "Who would say anything like that? She often wears the traditional clothes of Arab women, which includes wide pants. But these pants are made of colorful silk, embroidered with silver and gold threads. Do you know men who wear embroidered silk trousers? I don't."

"I suppose I must have misunderstood," a blushing Mary mumbled.

Thomas took his glass and stood up. "I would like to propose a toast to an extraordinary woman: our mother. It was her determination, her strength as a businesswoman, and, not least, her love that allowed John and me to enjoy a carefree childhood despite our father's untimely death. To Sibylla Hopkins!"

"And to our little sister, Emily!" John added. "We look forward to being reunited with them soon!"

Once the guests at the table had clinked glasses, Oscar turned to the young Arab sitting opposite Thomas. "Well, Dr. bin Abdul, after having lived here for two years, how do you like our Western cuisine?"

The young man smiled wryly. "If you are asking my opinion of English cuisine, I would prefer to reserve judgment. Your French chef, however, has demonstrated once again that his skills are unsurpassed."

"What sort of work do you expect to do as a physician in Mogador?" Oscar's wife inquired.

"Well, the same as here, I imagine," Sabri replied. "Since it is the community of expatriates that is employing me, I will be tending primarily to their needs. And if there is time, my friend Dr. Thomas Hopkins and I will devote ourselves to the fight against cholera and typhus, which wreak havoc in Mogador just as they do in our slums here."

It was Sibylla who had convinced the community of foreigners to hire Thomas. He would be Mogador's first European physician and primarily tend to the medical needs of the expatriate merchants.

"How do you intend to fight these epidemics?" a clergyman in a black suit and stiff white collar wanted to know.

"By sticking to the advice of the goddess Hygeia," Thomas replied. "I am convinced that many epidemics can be prevented by means of consistent measures such as clean drinking water and adequate ventilation of living spaces. Don't you agree, bin Abdul?" He looked over at Sabri, who was nodding emphatically.

While the reverend contemplated Thomas's words with a furrowed brow, the Hopkinses' nanny entered the room. She was leading fourteen-month-old Charlotte by the hand and carried Charlotte's twin brother, Selwyn, in her other arm. John and Victoria suddenly became serious. Charlotte was sturdy and lively, but her brother was delicate, almost frail. London's cold, damp climate and polluted air did not agree with him, and he suffered from asthma. Thomas had been urging John and Victoria to return to Mogador with him for some time. He believed the little boy would improve only in the dry warmth and curative sea air of Morocco.

John leaned down to his daughter. "Well, my little one, have you come to say good night to me?"

Charlotte beamed at him and he gave her a kiss. Then he turned to his son. Victoria had taken him from the nanny. Looking pale and tired, little Selwyn snuggled in his mother's arms.

The nanny said quietly, "He coughed an awful lot again today. I have had damp cloths hung around his bed, as Dr. Hopkins ordered, to facilitate his breathing."

Victoria observed Thomas, who was looking at the little boy with great concern. When he had first mentioned that the climate in Mogador would do Selwyn good, she had hoped that John would nonetheless stay in England with her and the children. Morocco was an uncivilized, heathen country, and several weeks' journey away! But by now, Selwyn's condition had worsened so much that they had no choice but to move. And John wanted to return to the city he regarded as his true home. Victoria brushed aside her own misgivings and kissed Selwyn's ash-blond curls. "You'll feel better in Mogador, darling. You're going to turn into a strong, healthy boy."

Mogador, December 1859

There was a smell of leather and tanning agents in the Spencer & Son Shipping Company's warehouse at the Mogador harbor, and a light draft coming through the windows, keeping the air sufficiently dry and cool. The skins ready for shipment lay on duckboards. The piles of leather had been covered with protective blankets.

Sibylla pulled back the blanket, had her clerk, Aladdin, hand her the oil lamp, and held it directly above the top layer.

"No stains, no mold, very good," she muttered and stroked the soft surface with her other hand.

The quality could be affected not only by stains and mold but by irregularities as well. She held the skin up against the light coming through the open door and examined it with a frown. The light shone through in some places. After several years of drought, even by Morocco's standards, the leather of malnourished animals left much to be desired in terms of pliability and thickness, despite the best efforts of the tanners in Fez. Sibylla knew that.

"So, let's start counting then." She slowly went down the pile with her index finger while her clerk patiently waited with pen and clipboard.

"Three hundred and fifty pieces for Champion & Wilton, London," she said over her shoulder.

Not one sack of grain, not one piece of leather, not a single ostrich feather was allowed to leave the country unless one of the *qaid's simsars* had inspected the merchant's export list. He would then calculate the export tariff and taxes—a reliable source of revenue for the governors, who were always short of cash.

"Yes, Mrs. Hopkins." The young man nodded and made a note.

Ten years earlier, after a cruel drought that had dried the grain on the culm, little Aladdin had dragged himself to Mogador, his little brother on his back. The old and the sick had starved to death in the villages, and those who still had enough strength streamed to the cities in search of work and bread.

Sibylla had found the exhausted children in front of her warehouse and taken them to her home. She had given Aladdin and his brother food and a roof over their heads. At the school she'd had built, they had learned reading, writing, and arithmetic. Now they were earning their living as clerks for the *Engliziya*.

She had insisted that the new school accept boys and girls, foreign and Moroccan children. Until then, only the Arab *zaouia* and Jewish *yeshiva* had educated the children of Mogador. The foreigners had educated their children themselves and later sent them to boarding schools back home. That was no longer necessary, and Sibylla's standing had risen significantly, although there were still those who refused to let their children mingle with children of other religions or nationalities.

Sibylla continued with the next stack, counted, and told her clerk, "Two hundred and fifty skins for Tricker Shoes of London . . ."

"*Bonjour*, madame!"

The silhouette of a man wearing riding attire and sturdy boots was visible in the frame of the open warehouse door.

She straightened up, smoothed her hair, and replied a little stiffly, "Hello, André. I take it the saffron harvest is in."

He took a few steps closer and kissed her on both cheeks. She smelled sunshine, earth, and horse on him, the smell he always brought from Qasr el Bahia. She quickly took a step backward. "Please! You know I don't care for that French custom."

Although they had been speaking with each other again for some time, Sibylla insisted on keeping their association strictly businesslike.

He smiled. "Do you expect me to greet a lady by shaking her hand as though she were a man? And yes, I did bring the spice of the gods. One kilo just for the Spencer & Son Shipping Company." He patted the saddlebag that hung from his right shoulder along with his gun.

He was still as flexible as a young man, his figure was strong, and his shoulders were straight. But his skin, weathered by wind and sun, as well as the gray streaks in his hair and the wrinkles around his eyes, betrayed the fact that he was in the second half of his life.

Sibylla raised her eyebrows. "Only one kilo? What a pity! You could make far more money if you used your land exclusively for saffron. I could easily sell this quantity many times over because of its quality."

Sibylla simply could not understand why André, with such ideal land for growing saffron, wasted half on oranges trees, dates, grains, and vegetables. And he never sold the entire crop but always held some of it back—his rainy day fund, he claimed.

"Do you know how many hands I need to harvest all my saffron?" he countered. "I have tried to hire more Ait Zelten, but many of them don't like working for foreigners. Your business is diversified too, madame."

In addition to leather and saffron, Sibylla exported grain, ostrich feathers, gum arabic, sheep's wool, and cork, which originated in the oak forests north of Marrakesh. She also developed strong relationships with her suppliers, and they'd remained loyal to her even when the sultan opened the larger and more navigable port of Casablanca for international trade a few years ago.

Sibylla adjusted her shawl. "We'd best go into my office so you can show me the saffron. I don't have all day."

André made a mock bow. "*À vos ordres*, madame."

As he followed her up the stairs leading to the second floor, he studied her tall, slender figure and thought how, over all these years, she had remained a remarkable woman, radiating self-assurance and wisdom. He looked at the skin on her neck, still delicate. Her formerly golden hair was a shiny white blonde now, and the soft curls at her neck were held together with a beaded clip. As usual, she was wearing traditional clothes: *chalwars* and a kaftan of precious silk and embroidered with small blossoms. Apart from her daughter, Emily, she was the only foreigner who dressed like an Arab woman, but by now that was no longer the subject of gossip.

People in Mogador had long become accustomed to the fact that Sibylla Hopkins was her own woman. She was seen as aloof and wayward, closer to the women of the governor's harem than the foreign ladies. Some admired her for the way that, years before, she had fought the sultan for her husband's life. Others praised her for generously funding the city's reconstruction. The indomitable Qaid Hash-Hash had even praised her benefaction publicly at the opening of the first water-supply system she had donated.

Hash-Hash had since died, but Sibylla maintained good relations with his son and successor, Samir, who was nicknamed el Tawfiq, "he who is favored by fortune." She had been in business with Samir's mother, Wahida, and Hash-Hash's first wife, Lalla Jasira, for many years. André knew from Sibylla that she had helped Wahida and the childless Lalla Jasira to push through Samir's succession against the sons of Hash-Hash's other wives. To express their thanks, the two saw to it that the women could continue trading without interference. It was around that time that the Arabs began calling Sibylla "the Lioness of Mogador."

She still made André's heart beat faster, for she was a woman like no other. He would not forgive himself until the day he died for having been so stupid as to forfeit her love.

He remembered how happy he had been when they faced each other alone again for the first time since the disaster with Aynur five years before. During those intervening years, he had tried knocking on her door many times, but in vain. He had written her letters she had never answered. He had come to see her in her newly built office in the warehouse, and she refused him entrance. If by chance they met in town, she had ignored him. It was only the saffron trade that had finally brought them closer.

Now, they stood in Sibylla's office. "Please see to it that I am not disturbed for the next hour," she told Aladdin's brother before closing the door.

She turned to André and her smile made her face seem less severe. "With you, at least I know I'm not getting marigolds or safflowers."

He hung his gun over the back of a chair, took his saddlebag off his shoulder, and pulled out a linen sack. "If you had bought from me back then rather than from those scoundrels from the High Atlas, that wouldn't have happened. But you had to learn the hard way."

While he loosened the cord, Sibylla spread a cloth on the desk. André carefully emptied the contents of the sack, plucked a few of the delicate red-gold threads, and held them up to Sibylla's nose. She took a deep breath with her eyes closed, and he could tell by her expression that she was satisfied.

When, after several years of experimenting, he had finally succeeded in harvesting saffron of the highest quality, he could think of only one person to whom he would offer the spice. With a sample in his suitcase, he had ambushed Sibylla as she was leaving her office at the harbor one cool evening just before Christmas. She had been paralyzed by fear when he had suddenly blocked her path and had shouted at him, "Leave me alone, André! Just go away and leave me alone once and for all!"

Her bitter words had hurt deeply, though he knew he deserved them. "I would fall on my knees and beg for your forgiveness if I didn't know that it would have no effect. So I have brought along something that perhaps will help you to forgive."

"There are some things that are simply too grave as to be forgiven!" she had hissed at him and tried to push her way past.

But again he had blocked her way. "At least take a look! If you don't want it, I won't trouble you again. I promise, Sibylla. I shall leave you alone forever."

She had acquiesced and taken André to her office, where they had stood at her desk as they were standing today. He had shown her his saffron and explained what a large quantity of bulbs he'd had to plant to reap one single kilo. The precious threads could be harvested only on the first day of the bloom, early in the morning before they were burned by the sun. He had instantly noticed the interest with which Sibylla was listening to him and, when she inquired about the price, he knew that he had won.

"What do you think of this year's crop?" he asked now in anticipation.

She opened her eyes. "Aromatic, somewhat bitter, with a trace of honey. Very good! But I would not have expected anything less from you. As agreed, here is one hundred pounds sterling."

"What's the rush?" André pushed the cloth with the saffron aside and leaned toward her gently. "Why don't you tell me how you are? After all, we've not seen each other for almost a year."

Sibylla was silent. The single deep wrinkle that had appeared on her forehead back when he'd hurt her so unspeakably deepened.

"Have you made preparations for Christmas?" he ventured.

She nodded and her face brightened a bit. "This year I am celebrating in a grand way. Thomas and John are coming home. I expect them any day now. John is bringing his family: his wife Victoria and the twins. I've been a grandmother for a year, André, and haven't seen my grandchildren yet, can you imagine?" Now she was radiant.

"No, quite honestly, I cannot fathom that you are a grandmother, Sibylla. Not if I compare you with my old *mémé*, sitting by the fire in the wintertime, knitting socks with her arthritic hands. I believe your daughter-in-law is going to be quite surprised, and quite taken with her remarkable mother-in-law."

"You're flattering me, André Rouston. Victoria is a Londoner. She will surely find me backward and out of touch."

"Never!"

He was delighted to see her blush and added, "Incidentally, I just saw Emily at the harbor. She was sketching the fishermen. I must say, your daughter is growing ever more beautiful. Can she really be eighteen already?"

Sibylla's smile vanished. "What about this saffron? Do you accept my offer?"

André tried not to sigh. He had so many questions he wanted to ask about Emily. But every time he tried, Sibylla shut down.

Chapter Twenty-One

Emily Hopkins sat on the quay wall, chewing on a dried date and looking at the warehouse from which André Rouston had just come. She really liked Monsieur Rouston. He always inquired how she was and always brought her a little gift. Today, it was dates from his estate.

When she was younger, Emily had sometimes pretended that Monsieur Rouston was her father. She knew next to nothing about her real father, Benjamin Hopkins, other than that he had been killed before she was born. Her mother did not like to talk about him. But Firyal had told her that he had been a gentleman and had died a hero.

"El Sayyid Hopkins was very handsome," she had said reverently. "It was my duty to take care of his suits. He had very elegant suits from England, not like the tunics that Arab men wear. He was also taller than Arab men and did not have such coarse hair. The master's hair was like gold."

Unfortunately, Emily's mother had caught Firyal waxing lyrical about her master and sent her to the kitchen at once. After that, Firyal had never mentioned Benjamin again.

The other servant, Nadira, never mentioned him either. "The mistress does not wish for us to talk about the deceased master," she had explained to Emily. "It causes her pain."

Once, Emily observed to her mother that she and Monsieur Rouston had the same dark, curly hair. But her mother had reacted so angrily that Emily had never mentioned Rouston to her again.

She picked up another date and looked over at the fisherman, squatting in his small boat and repairing his net, undisturbed by the rocking of his boat. He had spread the coiled net out on his lap and was carefully checking for tears in the meshwork.

Emily took her charcoal and began to draw. She started with the broad strokes before getting down to details. She sketched the fisherman's weathered features, which told of his hard life at sea as well as the concentration with which he worked. She drew his bent back, his crooked fingers that stitched up holes with a wooden needle.

Ever since Emily could remember, she had been passionate about drawing. She had scribbled in her fairy-tale books, on the whitewashed walls of her room, and later on at school, she had drawn figures and landscapes on her slate instead of numerals and letters. Her teacher had been extremely angry upon discovering his portrait with an unflattering bulbous nose in Emily's arithmetic book, but later, she and her mother had laughed about it. After that, Sibylla had ordered colored pencils and drawing paper from England, as well as a book that taught Emily to develop drawings of people and animals from geometric figures, how to show perspective and adjust proportions.

Yet this was a learned technique. The expressiveness with which she drew had never been taught to her. Monsieur Rouston had once remarked that she expressed the soul of her subjects. And for her fifteenth birthday, he had given her an easel, canvases, brushes, and paint.

Emily especially liked to draw at the harbor or in the *souk*, wherever there was a lot of activity. Many of Mogador's inhabitants knew her and were happy to have her draw their portraits, while others did not like it, as representative drawing was considered a sin against God, the sole creator of everything.

But the fisherman by the quay wall did not mind. Every now and then he smiled at Emily. She sketched the folds of his kaftan with very few lines and smudged them with her thumb to show shadows. When the drawing was finished, she scribbled her name and the date at the bottom and placed it in a leather portfolio. Then she propped herself up with her hands on the rough stone wall, leaned back, and enjoyed the warmth of the sun on her skin and the wind in her curly hair.

In three months, she would turn nineteen, and she knew it was about time for her to figure out what to do with her life. Most of her peers from school had traveled to Europe to be introduced into society and meet suitable husbands. Some had written her to tell her that they were engaged. John's wife, Victoria, was only one year older than Emily and already a mother! But Emily felt no longing for marriage or motherhood and was grateful that her own mother did not press her. Her greatest desire was to attend an art academy in Europe to study painting and perhaps even learn about the new art of photography.

She had shared this wish with her mother not long ago. "Why not?" Sibylla had answered, much to her Emily's delight. "But it's impossible just now. You cannot travel to Europe by yourself and I cannot abandon the business here. Once your brothers return from Europe and John can take over some of the business, we'll talk about it again."

Now that Thomas and John were about to return from England, Emily passionately hoped her mother would keep her promise.

A shadow fell on her face. She opened her eyes and recognized Mr. Philipps, the harbormaster, standing next to her.

"Good morning, Miss Hopkins. I have received word that the *Urania* is coming through the port entrance. If I am not mistaken, that's good news." He winked at her congenially.

Emily jumped up. "Tom and John are back! I must tell Mother right away! Thank you, Mr. Philipps!"

"It's unimaginable that Emperor Nero had saffron strewn on the streets of Rome for his triumphal procession," André remarked and ran his fingers through the tiny dried pistils. Just a few weeks before, they had still been embedded in the heart of the small crocus plants that had created a thick carpet of lilac blossoms. Soon they would tickle fastidious taste buds in dining rooms and restaurants all over the world.

"With the quantities that would entail, I suspect that he resorted to marigolds and the like," Sibylla replied dryly. She unlocked the wooden cabinets, took out two round earthenware vessels and a scale, and placed everything on her desk. After weighing the saffron, she filled the two pots with it, returned them to the cabinet, and checked that the padlock was locked.

"May I offer you a cup of tea?"

"Avec plaisir." André was delighted.

"How has business been this year?" he inquired, after Aladdin's brother had placed the steaming glasses on Sibylla's small table.

"Please, take a seat." She pointed to the low table with some chairs in the corner of the room. "To be honest, this year has been patchy. On balance, Spencer & Son has not suffered any losses, but the years of drought have definitely impacted the local leather, our main export."

He grinned. "Businessmen always complain. I am sure that your brother in London will still be pleased. He knows that no one is better equipped to handle the Morocco trade than you."

"You know, I believe you are right," she said, flattered.

"Of course I'm right. If he weren't pleased, he would have sent someone else to Mogador."

Sibylla took a sip of tea. "Luxury items are what sells best these days. Qaid Samir's wives do the most exquisite embroideries for me." He could hear the enthusiasm in her voice. "The fashion-conscious ladies in Europe can't get enough of handkerchiefs, shawls, and cushions embroidered by dainty hands in an exotic Oriental harem. I'm negotiating at the moment with embroiderers in Fez and Marrakesh because the demand is so great. Unfortunately, I am in competition with the merchants of Casablanca and, since the harbor there is larger and more modern, I don't fare very well. Sultan Sidi Mohammed ignores all my contributions to the expansion of the harbor here."

After ruling Morocco for thirty-seven years, Moulay Abd al-Rahman had died that August, and his son, Sidi Mohammed IV, had succeeded him. The new ruler was already a mature man of fifty-seven years and had inherited an onerous task. His country was deeply in debt, and the populace was discontented and ready to revolt after several crop failures and a devastating cholera epidemic. At the same time, France, England, and, most recently, Prussia were competing for the greatest possible influence in his country. Their consuls in Mogador and Tangier were saying quite openly that it was only a matter of time before one of three countries incorporated Morocco into its colonial empire.

Sibylla finished her tea and rose. "How long will you be in Mogador?"

"One week. I have been given a terribly long shopping list. I'm probably going to need a pack donkey to get everything home."

He noticed too late how Sibylla's cheeks flushed, and he could have kicked himself. He knew any mention of his family in Qasr el Bahia could endanger their tenuous truce.

Sibylla stiffly looked at the floor and declared, "I have to go to the warehouse anyway. If I don't get the numbers to the *qaid*'s *simsar*, I won't be able to ship my leather tomorrow. Good-bye, André. I wish you a merry Christmas."

He wanted to thank her, but all he saw was her back.

As Sibylla stormed down the stairs, she asked herself if she would ever be able to forgive him for deceiving her with Aynur.

There was one moment when she had been ready to do so—when she first held her newborn daughter, a tiny bundle with her father's dark curls. But a few weeks later, Nadira had reported the gossip from the *souk* that André's wife had given birth to a baby girl in Qasr el Bahia, a mere six weeks after Emily's birth. Sibylla felt more betrayed than ever. Had André not implored her to examine his saffron five years later, she would not be speaking to him to this day.

Sibylla was about to open the door to the warehouse when Emily burst in. "The *Urania* is here, Mother! Tom and John are back!"

André, who had followed Sibylla, could not take his eyes off Emily. The lovely young woman had an unusual beauty. She wore her long black hair down, with a colorful scarf to keep it off her face. Her eyes were a deep, almost lilac blue. Like her mother, she favored Arab clothing, but hers was colorful and bright. From afar, she might have been taken for a Berber girl if not for her height.

André had been fond of her ever since he had first seen her, a cheerful five-year-old, who had trustfully taken his hand and shown him her toys. He felt for her the same strong love as for his four children with Aynur. Yet Emily was Benjamin Hopkins's daughter, at least according to Sibylla. Of course, André could count and knew that pregnancy lasts nine months and not almost eleven. Years ago, he had cautiously attempted to speak to Sibylla about Emily's parentage. She had practically turned to a pillar of salt and threatened that he would never see Emily again if he ever put ideas in her head. But as Emily grew older, it became painfully obvious that she was his child. André longed to have the truth come to light, but he did not wish to discredit Sibylla nor ruin Emily's future with a scandal. So he told himself that, at least on paper, Benjamin Hopkins was the best possible father for Emily.

Sibylla interrupted his musings. "Excuse me, André, if I say good-bye now, but I want to welcome my family."

He nodded politely. "Of course, it's been far too long since you've seen them. Please give them my best regards. *Joyeux Noël à toute la famille.*"

"That's your mother?" Victoria whispered incredulously. She sat next to her husband on a slimy plank on the small boat that was ferrying them from the *Urania* to shore.

"I haven't seen my mother for five years but yes, I am fairly confident that's her," John replied dryly. "And next to her, that's my sister, Emily. The older man in the black kaftan is the harbormaster, Mr. Philipps. The donkeys for us to ride home on and porters for our baggage are ready." He looked over at the three donkeys waiting in the background with their drivers.

"Donkeys?" Victoria cried in dismay. "You can't be serious! Does your mother not have a carriage?"

John convulsed in laughter. "A carriage would be of no use here! The alleyways in the *medina* are much too narrow. And besides, the streets here are very bad, and we would have a broken axle after just a hundred yards. No, dear Victoria, in town we usually go on foot, and to cover distances, donkeys. You'll get used to it!"

While Victoria was busy recovering from this information, she studied her mother-in-law and sister-in-law. They were certainly not dressed like Victoria, who was wearing a dress with a bodice and loose crinoline as well as a fashionable hat with feathers. They were each wearing—what was that anyhow?—a nightgown with trousers? And no hats. Her mother-in-law wore only a shawl loosely covering her hair, and Emily had a colorful scarf that held back her wild curls. With her hair blowing in the wind, she resembled—Victoria searched for a kinder expression—a Gypsy. It was unfathomable that these two women belonged to one of England's most respected merchant families. *Mother isn't going to believe it when I write to her*, Victoria thought, shaking her head.

Before she had even set foot on Moroccan soil, she was already feeling alienated. The strange-looking Arabs with their black eyes and their scruffy beards. The half-naked slaves rowing their boat. A shocking sight! She nervously eyed the bare torsos of these men, whose pitch-black skin glistened with perspiration. She was embarrassed even to see her own husband exposed in such a way, but complete strangers . . .

The boat pulled up to the quay wall with a little jerk.

"Here we are!" John extended a hand to help her out. Next, he took Charlotte on his arm while the nanny carried Selwyn. Thomas and Sabri were last to disembark.

Sibylla hurried to them with a radiant smile. However, as Victoria reached out to greet her mother-in-law, she found her words drowned out by hideous cries of lament. Horrified, she covered her ears. Yet no one but she and the nanny seemed upset. She watched as the donkey drivers and porters rolled out small carpets. They picked up some dirt from the ground and rubbed it over their faces and arms as though they were bathing and then kneeled on their rugs, foreheads on the ground, mumbling to themselves. A few minutes later, the Moors rose, rolled up their rugs, and began loading trunks and baskets as though nothing had happened.

Victoria wondered what bizarre kind of conspiracy she had just witnessed.

"Do not worry, dear girl. The men were complying with the *muezzin's* call to midday prayers. Arabs pray to their god five times a day. They fulfill this duty seriously and solemnly," explained Sibylla, who had been watching her.

Victoria stared at her and Sibylla continued, "You'll soon get used to the local customs." She embraced her daughter-in-law. "So, you are John's wife. I am so glad to meet you at last and to be a second mother to you from now on! Did you have a pleasant crossing? I remember well how cramped and uncomfortable it was to be on a ship!"

"To be honest, the journey was a nightmare. The North Sea was so rough that I feared we might be shipwrecked," Victoria reported.

Sibylla nodded empathetically. Then she turned to the two little children. "And you are my grandchildren! Do you want to say hello to your grandmother?"

Charlotte looked at her with curiosity. Selwyn, however, hid his face on his nanny's shoulder. Sibylla stroked his little head.

"You don't have to be afraid of me, little man. Look at the big stork's nest over there. You don't have anything like that in London." She pointed to the *qasbah* tower. The little boy hesitantly looked before a coughing fit racked his body.

"There, there now. That's still the filthy London air in your lungs. Not to worry, the climate here will soon make you well." Sibylla took Selwyn from his nanny's arms and patted his back.

Victoria watched in amazement how her son trustfully snuggled up against Sibylla. "He's usually so reserved with strangers."

"Oh, but we're not strangers. We're getting along quite well already, wouldn't you say, Selwyn?" Sibylla kissed the little one again and handed him back to his nanny.

"Hello, Mother. Do you finally have time for your son?" John jested. The twenty-two-year-old resembled his father so much that, for a few perplexing seconds, Sibylla felt herself transported to the days when Benjamin had courted her. With tears in her eyes, she took her younger son into her arms. "I am so happy! Now we shall be able to celebrate Christmas together."

Thomas and Sabri stood next to each other on the quay. "You're not praying, my friend?" Thomas asked.

"God does not have a religion as far as I'm concerned," the young man replied. "I often speak to Him, but not always when the Koran prescribes."

"Your father would not be pleased to hear that," Thomas remarked. Sabri's father, Abdul bin Ibrahim, was the headmaster of the *zaouia* of Mogador. He had even made the pilgrimage to Mecca and was thus allowed to call himself *haji*. He was one of the most highly regarded men in the city.

"I am a son of two worlds," Sabri explained. "As you know, my mother was a member of the Christian Orthodox churches of her country. When she became my father's second wife, she converted to the faith of the Prophet."

Sabri's mother, Almaz, came from Abyssinia. His father had bought her in a slave market near Mecca and brought her back to Mogador. When she gave birth to Sabri, Haji Abdul's only son, he took her as his second wife.

Thomas patted his friend on the back. "Here comes my mother."

When Sabri smiled and turned his head, he saw not Sibylla but Emily. He had not seen her since he left for Fez to study Arab medicine, and he hardly recognized her. The skinny little girl with the long arms and legs had become a woman. She returned his gaze for a moment, then quickly looked down. She blushed slightly and threw her hair back with a graceful motion. Her earrings caught a ray of sunlight, and Sabri noticed that they were the same unusual color as her eyes. He desperately wanted her to look at him again with those amethyst blue eyes and, just as this wish passed through his mind, she did so with a mischievous smile. He admired the little dimples in the corners of her mouth.

"Dr. bin Abdul. How nice that you have returned to Mogador," Sibylla said.

He grudgingly took his eyes off Emily and bowed before his friend's mother. "*Assalamu alaikum*, Mrs. Hopkins."

He watched as Emily greeted her brothers. She seemed so full of life. Just looking at her filled Sabri with joy. After she had embraced Victoria, she finally turned to him. "*Assalamu alaikum*, Dr. bin Abdul."

He bowed. "Miss Hopkins, is it really you—little Emily?"

"I'm really not little anymore, Dr. bin Abdul," she replied impishly.

He nodded earnestly. "Indeed, Miss Hopkins! You have become a young lady and more beautiful than all the stars in the sky."

Suddenly shy and speechless, she stared at Sabri as though hypnotized.

No part of this exchange was lost on Sibylla. Sabri was an honorable young man, but what would it mean to Sabri and Emily if they fell in love? A Muslim and a Christian. What would it mean for Emily if they desired a shared future? Would she have to convert to Islam? Or perhaps even lead a life as a low-ranking concubine?

Sibylla had raised Emily to be an independent young woman. She certainly did not want her hidden away in a harem. She placed a protective arm around Emily. "It's time we went home, dear. *Ma'assalama*, Dr. bin Abdul. Please pay my respects to your honorable parents."

"*Ma'assalama.*" Sabri bowed.

Emily took one last look at him. Without realizing, she let out a soft sigh.

Chapter Twenty-Two

Mogador, July 1860

"We'll never find a new nanny for Charlotte and Selwyn. No one wants to come here, no matter how much we pay!"

Victoria stormed into John's study and threw a letter on his desk. Her husband looked up from his paperwork with annoyance.

"Here you have it: Grandmother Mary writes that twenty governesses with outstanding references answered her ad, but when they heard the position was going to be in an African country, they all withdrew!"

John needed to prepare for an important meeting with the harbormaster, the governor, and Consul Willshire, and did not wish to be disturbed. He was well aware that Victoria was unhappy in Mogador, but told himself it was because she had not yet settled in. Ever since the twins' governess had impulsively resigned and returned to England, Victoria had become upset at the slightest provocation.

"Please calm down," he bade her in as controlled a voice as possible. "Nadira is doing an excellent job of taking care of the children. And my mother is supporting you as best she can."

"You might not mind that our children are being raised by a Negress," Victoria hissed. "But do you also want her to turn them into Moors? This morning, I caught her showing Charlotte how people in this country pray! I want an English nanny, John, one who knows manners and who raises our children properly!"

"Now you're exaggerating. Nadira raised me and my brother, and did we turn into Arabs?"

"She's teaching the children godless, heathen behavior!"

"That is an absolute exaggeration!" He would have liked to throw his stepgrandmother's letter, which had caused such a fuss, into the wastepaper basket, but instead he set it aside with seeming indifference, gathered his papers, and placed them in a leather portfolio. "I have no time to discuss this at the moment, dear. I have an important meeting to attend." It was still two hours until the meeting, but he would prepare in the company office at the harbor, where he could work in peace.

With a hiccupping sob, Victoria sank onto the sofa along the wall. "You never have time for me, never listen to my concerns. Sometimes I have the feeling that we don't matter to you!"

John took a deep breath. He hated these constant arguments with his wife. In England, she had been much more sensible. Here, he sometimes had the feeling that he was married to a stranger, and he had no idea how to handle her moods. His mother had explained to him that Victoria was suffering from homesickness and that he should be patient and understanding. But they had been living in Morocco for seven months now, and he felt she had been homesick long enough.

"Did you know that Nadira is the real reason the nanny left?" Victoria lamented. "That woman was constantly meddling in her child-rearing methods—just imagine, an African who grew up in a straw hut giving advice to a trained English governess, and you did nothing about it! I well understand why she went back to London, and I envy her!"

"My wife envies her servants! Why, I ask myself? Because they take orders all day long?" John replied sarcastically. He pointedly took out his pocket watch and looked at it.

Victoria stared at him in disbelief for a moment and then buried her face in her hands. John heard her stifled sobs, saw her shoulders trembling. She had become thin, and the misery of having to live in Mogador was written all over her.

"It's easy for you," his mother had said. "You were born and raised here. Mogador is your home. Your wife comes from another world. She made a big sacrifice for you and Selwyn in leaving everything that was dear and familiar to her. Never forget that!"

John hesitated. Then he placed his portfolio on the desk, sat next to Victoria on the couch, and clumsily stroked her back. He himself would not have traded his life here for huge, loud, damp London for anything in the world.

Victoria rested her head against his shoulder. "Oh, John! I am so sorry that I lost my temper again. It's just that I feel so alone here. I imagined Mogador would be completely different."

"How, dear?" John asked although he had already heard the answer a dozen times. Victoria felt like a prisoner in tiny Mogador. Excursions were not an option because of the recent ambushes on travelers by bands of robbers driven from their villages by hunger. Life inside the city walls was safe but boring and monotonous. There were no diversions, no theater, no exhibits, no sporting events. The house in which they lived was old-fashioned and small compared to Victoria's villa in elegant Mayfair. There was no gas lighting, the rooms were cramped, and the servants did not follow her directions because they considered her mother-in-law their only mistress. Sibylla had assigned Firyal as her chambermaid, but the woman did not even know how to tie a bodice correctly.

And besides, Victoria was afraid of Firyal's dark, inscrutable face and, ever since an Arab merchant had charged her triple the usual price because she did not know that she was expected to bargain, she was convinced they were all crooks.

"The streets are so filthy!" Victoria wailed. "There are beggars in front of every home and they try to latch onto you. I have never seen so many disfigured and crippled people. Oh, it's simply horrible!"

"There are plenty of disfigured and crippled people in the East End as well, as my brother will confirm," John tried, but she stubbornly shook her head.

"Such wretched conditions just don't exist in England. We have clinics, orphanages, and relief organizations. I myself was on the committee of the Home for Orphaned Daughters of Soldiers."

John took Victoria's hands in his own. "Now look at me for a moment, dear. Don't you think that in all your woe you have forgotten something very important? Have you not noticed how much better Selwyn is? He hasn't coughed in months. I believe his lungs have been healed here. Is that worth nothing to you?"

"Of course!" she professed. "Selwyn's health is the only thing that makes life bearable for me here."

John again pulled out his pocket watch. "I'm sorry, dear, but I really must go now. I'm already late."

She gave a resigned nod. "What is your meeting about?"

"The harbor basin, yet again. Consul Willshire and I want to persuade the *qaid* to expand it so that steamships might finally come to Mogador."

"Steamships? Are the shipping companies really going to stop using sailing ships?"

"No, but I'm convinced that steamships shall replace them eventually. Even now, there are steam-powered ships traveling between Europe and America. There is no stopping this development. The future of all of us here in Mogador depends on our being prepared for the future." He kissed Victoria on the head and got up. "I'll see you this evening, darling."

"Good-bye, and, John—"

"Yes?" He turned around, his hand already on the door handle.

"I'm staying here not just for Selwyn's sake, but also for yours."

"Really, dear? You are so good to me." He waved absentmindedly. Seconds later, the door was closed.

Victoria followed him with her eyes, a crooked smile plastered on her face. The ticking of the grandfather clock she had brought from England was more audible in the stillness. It was almost twelve o'clock. This afternoon, her neighbor Sara Willshire was hosting her weekly ladies' tea for wives of expatriate merchants and consuls. Her mother-in-law never attended these get-togethers, which, according to her, were no more than a pretext for exchanging the latest gossip. If Sibylla did go to tea, it was in the harem with the *qaid*'s wives and, even then, she managed to do business. She had repeatedly invited Victoria along, but she had steadfastly refused. It was bad enough that the cook, the gate-keeper, and the gardener in this house were all Arabs, but to socialize with them was really going too far.

She could hear Charlotte's and Selwyn's muffled laughter through the closed door. Victoria felt a longing to be with the children. *I shall take them to the beach*, she decided. They could hunt for shells there.

The *muezzin*'s midday call to prayer blared from the nearby mosque. Victoria would never have thought she would miss the ringing of church bells so much.

Charlotte was sitting on a blanket on the ground next to Nadira. The sun created magical little sparkles in her blonde curls. She was rocking her doll in her arms, trilling a little song with her squeaky voice. She beamed with happiness when she saw her mother.

Victoria kissed her and looked around for Selwyn. He was sitting on the swing that John had hung from a solid branch on the gnarly old olive tree. Sibylla was gently pushing him and he squealed with pleasure. Gone was the pale, coughing little boy. Selwyn had grown, his cheeks were round and rosy, and he was stronger and more self-assured with each passing day.

Although Victoria knew well that she ought to be happy that her little boy was thriving, she was jealous. Why did her son smile so at Sibylla and not her, his mother?

She pulled him from the swing more roughly than she had intended, and he promptly began to cry.

"No!" he squealed and kicked furiously.

Tears flooded Victoria's eyes and all her disappointment erupted in Sibylla's direction. "Why do you have to push him so high? He could have fallen off and hurt himself!"

"I'll see that that doesn't happen," Sibylla answered calmly. "Let him have his fun."

"Don't tell me what's right or wrong for my children!" Victoria held Selwyn even more tightly. But he pressed both his fists against her shoulders, leaned back, and bawled so loudly that she had no choice but to put him down. He ran to Sibylla and buried his face in her legs.

"Just look at him!" Victoria screamed. "You have stolen him from me!" She ran into the house, sobbing.

Maristan was written in beautiful Arabic calligraphy and *Hospital* underneath in English over the entrance to the two-story *riad*. Drs. Thomas Hopkins and Sabri bin Abdul's practice was located behind the mosque in the same neighborhood as the *zaouia*. The hospital had stood here since the city's founding, but the building had been vacant and run-down for years until Thomas and Sabri brought it back to life.

Emily stepped through the door and was pleased to see the freshly painted white walls and the newly glazed tiles on the roof. The interior courtyard was paved, the fountain was splashing, and several palms provided shade. A colonnade ringed the courtyard. Benches had been set up for the patients on opposite sides. Thomas's patients, the expatriates, usually waited on the left, but his clinic hours were past right now. On the right, there was a throng of people. Old and young, men and women, children and crying infants were sitting on the benches or the floor. They were barefoot and draped in filthy rags. They had stringy hair and many of the men had matted beards. Emily saw open wounds and festering sores. Some people were missing an arm or a leg. A withered old man was drinking thirstily from the fountain while a one-eyed man draped in a tattered blanket used the water to clean his hands and feet in preparation for seeing the doctor.

"Assalamu alaikum!" Emily said.

The patients knew her and waived congenially. Most of them came every Friday afternoon, when Hakim bin Abdul saw poor patients free of charge.

Instantly, a dozen scrawny children encircled her. She took a stack of freshly baked flatbread from her basket and passed it around.

"Enjoy!" she called out and ran up the stairs, elated at the prospect of seeing Sabri. The second floor was where Thomas and Sabri had set up one treatment room each, as well as a small ward. Thomas's living quarters were on the third floor. Some of the rooms were still empty, but the two friends were planning a European-style operating room.

Emily walked over to the door with the Arabic for the word "Surgery." An old woman draped in black sat on a bench in front and gave her a broad, toothless smile.

"*Assalamu alaikum*, Fatma," Emily said. "Are you feeling better?" The old woman had been suffering from painful plantar warts that Sabri had excised.

Fatma lifted her cloak and proudly showed off her bandaged foot. "The young *hakim* is a good doctor. His knife did more to get rid of the pain in my foot than Sidi Hicham's prayers."

Sidi Hicham belonged to the Regraga Brotherhood, a mystical order, who were believed to have healing and sometimes even magical powers. Many of Mogador's inhabitants had greater faith in Sidi

Hicham's songs and prayers than in the medicines and salves of a *hakim* who had studied among infidels.

"Dr. bin Abdul will be very happy that you are doing better." Emily knocked on the door.

Fatma winked shrewdly. "Yes, Miss Emily. But he will be even happier to see you!"

Emily blushed. She quickly opened the door and entered. Sabri's office had plain whitewashed walls and was sparsely furnished. On a rack, there were medicine bottles as well as baskets with scalpels, scissors, glass syringes, and bandages. One whole shelf was reserved for medical reference books, beginning with the five-volume *Canon of Medicine* by Ibn Sina, the greatest physician of Eastern medicine, and continuing with Hippocrates and Paracelsus, then onward to books about modern nursing, wound care, and obstetrics, which Sabri had brought back with him from England. Under a small window on the front wall stood a washstand with a water jug, soap, and a stack of towels. A small desk with a few chairs sat in the middle of the room. When Emily entered, Sabri was sitting at the desk, working on something. On the wall behind him hung his English diploma, next to a photograph of him and Thomas in white coats standing in front of Charing Cross Hospital in London.

"*Assalamu alaikum*, Miss Hopkins! How are you?"

"*Wa-alaikum salam*, Dr. bin Abdul!" She grinned and placed her basket on the table in front of him. "I hope you are hungry. Our cook has prepared stuffed eggplant with harissa. And for dessert, I have brought you fresh figs."

"Wonderful!" He smiled at her and pushed his work aside. His dark eyes flashed behind the round glasses he wore for reading or when treating his patients. He was dressed in the traditional Eastern physician's garb: white pants and a long white shirt with a black vest and a turban on his head.

Emily spread a napkin on the table and placed tableware and silverware on it. She was about to remove the wrapped *tagine* when he preempted her. "Let me do this, Miss Hopkins!"

"Oh, thank you. But be careful, it's very hot."

His arm brushed against her shoulder when he moved forward. She relished the brief touch and leaned against him a little more. He turned his head and smiled. "I hope you'll be joining me, Miss Hopkins?"

"I already had lunch with Mother. Had I known you would invite me, I would have waited, of course, but . . ." She hesitated and began rummaging in the basket. ". . . I have brought you something else, Doctor." She held out a rolled-up piece of paper.

He unfurled it and looked silently for a long time.

Emily waited nervously for a reaction to her sketch of him treating patients in the *maristan*'s courtyard. "Do you not like it? Is it not good?"

"Oh yes." Sabir nodded slowly. "It is very good. And I didn't even notice when you did it. What do you think, should I hang it next to the diploma?" He held the drawing up against the wall.

"It looks quite nice there," she replied happily.

He cleared his throat. "Would you mind calling me Sabri? Of course, only when there is no one else around."

She beamed. "Not at all, Dr. bin—I mean Sabri! But then you have to call me Emily."

"If we were in London, I would invite you out to a fancy dinner to thank you for this picture," he said, and his voice sounded a little hoarse.

"I would very much like to accompany you, Sabri," Emily said softly.

Encouraged, he continued, "There may not be any such restaurants here, but what would you say if I—"

"Do I have to wait until my food is cold before I may eat?" Thomas stuck his head around the door. "Fatma told me you were here."

"Thomas! I was just coming to see you! But Dr. bin Abdul is about to see patients. That's why I came to see him first. Besides, I wanted to ask him if he minded if I drew his patients, isn't that right, Doctor?"

Emily turned to Sabri and winked at him. Thomas raised his eyebrows in surprise.

"Are you practicing for London, Emily?" he asked. Turning to Sabri, he said, "Has she told you yet that she's been accepted at the Royal Academy of Arts? She's starting this fall."

"I didn't know. Congratulations, Miss Hopkins."

"Thank you." Emily sounded dejected. She had been so proud when the letter had arrived. Now, her heart grew heavy at the thought of being away from Sabri. "Good-bye, Dr. bin Abdul."

Thomas's office looked much like Sabri's, only that next to his diploma hung a photograph of him, wearing his academic gown and mortarboard, surrounded by his London relatives. The first thing visitors would inevitably see was John's graduation present to his brother: a human skeleton bought from Charing Cross Hospital. As a special jest, John had dressed it in one of his old suits before he surprised Thomas with it. Now the skeleton stood in the corner of Thomas's office, without the suit but with Thomas's hat on its skull, much to the delight of the younger patients.

"You're coming to see us more often these days," Thomas remarked as he closed the door behind him.

"I'm interested in medicine, that's all."

He shook his head. "You have never before in your life been interested in science. I can tell when you're fibbing, little sister."

"Have you never thought that you might be wrong?"

Instead of answering, Thomas took Emily's wrist. "Your pulse is racing," he pronounced after a few seconds. "And you're flushed. These symptoms indicate the serious and dangerous disease of being in love. I strongly suspect, dear Emily, that you caught this disease thanks to my friend bin Abdul."

"You're imagining things!" She turned away from him and busied herself with the food basket.

"Does Mother know?"

"No! And besides, there's nothing for her to know."

He sighed. It was not that he begrudged his sister and his best friend their happiness, but such a relationship was hopeless, simply impossible. He placed his arm around Emily.

"You are a grown woman and so I can speak honestly with you. End this infatuation now. Sabri will never requite it."

"How do you know?" She tried to free herself, but Thomas held on tight.

"Sabri's parents chose a wife for him when he was still a child, and you know as well as I that these agreements cannot be broken."

"You're just saying that," she responded feebly. "You want to annoy me." After all, Sabri had been on the verge of asking her for a rendezvous when Thomas had butted in. That had not just been her imagination.

Thomas pulled his sister closer. "Do you really think I would be so cruel? You know that Sabri owes his parents respect and obedience. If he had feelings for you, he would be putting you before those obligations."

Emily sank into the nearest chair. Just a few minutes before, she had been so happy, and now she was crestfallen.

"You're going to be leaving for England soon," she heard Thomas say. "You are going to become acquainted with the country of our parents and study art. It's what you've always wanted."

She did not answer. There were tears in her eyes.

"I'm sure things will look different with a little distance between you," Thomas said, trying to console her. "You're going to meet many interesting people in London and forget your heartache. And surely another nice young man will win your heart."

"Oh, what do you know! The only thing you have ever loved is your work!" Emily ran out of the room and slammed the door in her wake.

Chapter Twenty-Three

The atmosphere on the roof of the British consulate was peaceful and relaxed. Sunlight was shining through the straw sunshades and falling in golden patches on the floor. The air smelled of sea salt and freshly baked raisin buns. Sara Willshire's guests sat on wicker chairs placed around two folding tables. Behind each of them stood a Negro girl who fanned the ladies with palm fronds. Sara Willshire opened to the first page of Wilkie Collins's novel *The Woman in White* and began to read in a clear voice. Victoria picked up her teacup and, when she sniffed the bergamot aroma with her eyes closed, was transported back to England for a few bittersweet moments.

"I'm making my opening bid," she heard the French consul's wife say at the next table. She was playing bridge with her daughter and two merchants' wives from England and Portugal. Victoria, the Italian consul's wife, and a young recent arrival from Hamburg had all brought their embroidery.

Victoria felt comfortable here, in the company of women like her. These women thought like she did, dressed like she did, and spoke in languages she understood. Unfortunately, these gatherings only lasted a few hours. They were the highlights of her otherwise dreary and monotonous life.

Victoria reluctantly opened her eyes again and caught a glimpse of one of the servant girls stifling a bored yawn while another made faces at the two green parrots sitting on a perch in the corner.

Why must my mother-in-law be so unlike these women? she wondered. *How can an Englishwoman prefer the company of Arabs to this refined social gathering?*

Her sister-in-law Emily was no better. She was actually an even greater disappointment than Sibylla. Victoria had imagined that she and Emily, who was almost her age, would become friends. But she had soon been disabused of that notion. She could not deny that Emily was always very pleasant to her, but the two of them were entirely different. Once, Victoria had tried to tell Emily about London. She had described the National Portrait Gallery, where she and John had first met, talked about the opera in Covent Garden, the elegant shops, department stores, and shopping arcades between Knightsbridge and Piccadilly. But Emily had not understood anything. She had actually said that it all sounded much like a *souk*!

"I believe that our dear Signora Hopkins is miles away from us right now!" The amused voice of the Italian consul's wife jolted Victoria out of her thoughts. She quickly bent over her embroidery and pretended to examine the pattern.

"Will you not tell us what has you so preoccupied?" The Italian woman smiled amiably.

Victoria, not wanting to admit her dismay with her sister-in-law, replied, "I was just wondering why my mother-in-law never accompanies me here. I had so hoped that she would do so today, but she once again turned me down."

Sara lowered her book. "Mrs. Hopkins usually has more important things to do than take part in our harmless pleasures."

Victoria was surprised. This irritated tone of voice did not suit the gentle wife of the British consul!

The French consul's wife tapped her cards on the table and declared, "I can understand Madame Hopkins. *Franchement*, ladies, our little rendezvous are dreadfully quiet. We embroider doilies nobody needs and play cards to make the time pass!"

"You are welcome to spend your time elsewhere if you find my house boring!" Sara said indignantly.

"*Mille regrets*, Madame Willshire! That was extremely rude of me," the Frenchwoman said, trying to placate her. "But is not every day the same as any other in Mogador? Do we not all sometimes wish that we were far away from here? Madame Hopkins spends her time doing something useful, and I confess that I sometimes envy her. Although personally, I would wish for less work and more amusement . . ."

"It seems Madame Hopkins prefers Moors," the woman's daughter remarked caustically.

"She speaks Arabic?" The Prussian merchant's wife was astonished.

"*Bien sûr*, and fluently. There are those who say that her years in Mogador have turned Madame Hopkins into a Moor herself, but I don't see it that way," the Frenchwoman replied.

"How do you see it, then?" Sara inquired with a sour expression.

"Well, that she is more respected among the Moors than any other foreigner here. They have not forgotten how much she helped the city after the unfortunate *affrontement* with my country."

"My husband says that she just did it to make people forget her own disgrace," the Portuguese woman added while staring straight at Victoria.

Victoria looked at her in shock and remained silent.

"What good are these old stories? It is nothing more than stupid gossip," the Italian lady objected.

"I would hardly describe it as gossip," Sara said snidely.

Victoria could no longer hold back. "What stories?"

"Oh, there is a very interesting secret your mother-in-law is keeping," Sara said. "Of course, no one speaks about it openly, but anyone who can use his eyes and do arithmetic . . ."

"What do you mean?" the young Prussian woman now wanted to know.

Sara leaned forward in her chair. "My dear, have you never noticed that Emily looks nothing like the rest of the family?"

"She probably resembles her father," Victoria ventured.

"Exactly, she resembles her father. Benjamin Hopkins, however, was blond. But Emily's hair . . ."

". . . is black," Victoria completed in a toneless voice.

Sara smiled with extreme satisfaction. "By the way, Victoria, have you met Monsieur Rouston? The Frenchman who sells his saffron to your mother-in-law?"

Both Victoria and Emily were quiet and withdrawn over dinner. Emily poked at her food unhappily and wished that she and Sabri could run away to a place where no one knew them and no one could tell them whom to love.

Victoria's mind was racing too. Should she give any credence to the outrageous claims made by Mrs. Willshire and the other ladies? Was her mother-in-law really carrying on a scandalous affair with André Rouston? She had met Rouston just once at the *souk* with Sibylla. He was a charming, good-looking man. But she had not noticed her mother-in-law affected by his charm. Quite the contrary, her demeanor had been cool and distant.

She looked at Emily surreptitiously. Like the Frenchman, she had dark hair and a brownish complexion. Her slightly curved nose was also reminiscent of his. The longer Victoria thought about it, the more likely it seemed that André Rouston, and not Benjamin Hopkins, was Emily's father.

She flinched when John touched her hand. "A penny for your thoughts, Victoria. I think you weren't listening. Mother is planning to transfer sole responsibility for the business here to me when she goes to London with Emily in the fall. Isn't that wonderful?"

Victoria feigned enthusiasm, but her thoughts quickly returned to Sara Willshire's revelations. She pursed her lips in disgust. What kind of family had she married into?

At the end of September, Sibylla and Emily had packed their trunks for their journey to England and the whole family gathered for a farewell dinner. After Sibylla had risen from the table, Thomas and John withdrew to John's office to smoke a cigar, a stylish new habit they had acquired in London.

Sibylla, Victoria, and Emily went to the drawing room, where Firyal served tea, candied almonds, and lemon peel dipped in rose syrup. Aromatic smoke wafted from the scented quartz in the coal pans. But the atmosphere in the room was uncomfortable. Sibylla looked furtively at her daughter. Emily had taken one of the embroidered cushions from the sofa and was hugging it. She seemed distant, as she had so often in recent days. She did not even seem to enjoy drawing anymore. Perhaps she was nervous about the upcoming trip to faraway London. Or did some secret sadness gnaw at her? Whenever Sibylla asked, Emily claimed nothing was wrong.

Victoria was sitting on another sofa, staring into space. Like Emily, she seemed unhappy and withdrawn. Sibylla so wished to have a warmer relationship with her son's wife, but no matter how she tried, Victoria was unresponsive. Nor did she seek out the company of Emily, who should have been her friend. Sibylla stifled a sigh. Instead of laughter, her home was filled with sadness and ill humor.

The conversation dragged terribly, Emily and Victoria speaking only when Sibylla addressed them and, even then, their answers were monosyllabic. So when Thomas and John at last came back from smoking their cigars, Sibylla smiled with relief.

John, her hands-on younger son, was always full of drive, and immediately launched into his favorite subject: the advantages of steamboats over tall ships.

Sibylla was of a different opinion. Her chief concern was the horrendous cost involved in the development and construction of coal-powered steel ships, and in no time, mother and son were absorbed in a lively debate.

Thomas stood by the fireplace, sipped his steaming tea, and looked over at Emily. Ever since he had told her that Sabri's parents had long ago chosen a bride for their son, she had not been the same, and he often asked himself if it might have been better to keep the information to himself. Her little infatuation with Sabri would likely have ended anyway once she left for London. He sat down on the sofa and gave her a friendly nudge. "I thought you were looking forward to London, but you are as gloomy as can be."

Emily merely shrugged. She'd been thinking about how she had nearly collided with Sabri outside the *hamum* today. When he asked why she no longer visited him at the office, she had run away like a silly child.

John's impatient voice rang through the drawing room. "Believe me, Mother, if we invest now, we will be light-years ahead of all our competitors. Trust me! Why did you have me educated in London for all those years if I am not allowed to implement my knowledge now?"

"Why don't you write to Father and ask him for support?" Victoria asked. "My family's steelworks will surely help keep the costs tolerable."

But John impatiently waved her off. "You don't understand these things, Victoria. I have already written to your father and asked him for advice. Incidentally, Mother, he feels that the steamboat business is going to be very profitable. We would be faster than the competition with steamships made of steel, we would have more cargo space, and would make more money than other shipping companies."

Sibylla poured herself a fresh cup of tea. "Even if you're right, the harbor here in Mogador is too small for steamships."

"That's why I'm so keen for the *qaid* to expand the harbor," replied her son.

"John." Victoria's voice sounded brittle, on the verge of breaking. "Please do not dismiss me so."

He turned around in surprise. "What? Why, darling, what's the matter?"

"You really want to know? If you weren't only concerned about your business, you might have noticed that you have neglected me for months!" Her voice grew louder with every word. But before John could come up with an answer, the door was opened and Nadira entered with the twins. Charlotte had her favorite doll in her arm.

"Say good night to your parents!" Nadira gave them both a little pat on the bottom.

Victoria's expression relaxed for a moment. Only, instead of running to her, the children turned toward Sibylla. Nadira quickly took their hands and led them to Victoria, who was stiff with rage.

"Go!" she hissed at the toddlers. "Go to your grandmother! That's who you want anyway!"

She grabbed Charlotte, who had a look of utter confusion, by the arm and gave her a little shove. The little girl stumbled, her doll fell from her hand, and the porcelain head shattered as it hit the floor.

"Victoria!" John exploded. "Have you gone completely mad?"

Charlotte began to wail. Sibylla rushed over and picked her up. The little girl sobbed into her shoulder.

Victoria suddenly felt very hot. Her heart was beating wildly under her tight bodice. She had not wanted to be rough with her children! At the same time, frustration with her husband and mother-in-law spilled over into rage.

"How dare you reproach me?" she shouted at John. "Don't you see what's happening here? Your mother is trying to steal my children from me!"

"Victoria, I would never do anything of the kind." Sibylla tried to assuage her. She handed Charlotte to Nadira, who hustled the children out of the room. "I was only trying to help. We . . ." Sibylla gestured to all those present. ". . . are a family."

"A scandalous family!" Victoria said before she could stop herself.

"Victoria, I can't believe this!" John intervened.

Thomas, who was as dumbstruck as Emily, said loudly, "Now you owe everyone an explanation."

"Victoria didn't mean anything by it," Sibylla quickly assured him. She was pale and clutching the handle of her teacup so fiercely that her knuckles had turned white.

Victoria scrutinized her with a feeling of triumph. Time for Thomas, John, and Emily to learn what kind of woman their mother really was!

"Don't the three of you know what everyone in Mogador is saying?" She turned to the siblings with vehemence. "Well, I do. Respectable people, whose word is their bond, have told me the truth. I am talking about your mother and, Emily, of your father."

"Let the dead rest in peace," Sibylla countered.

But there was no stopping Victoria. "Oh, I am not speaking of Mr. Hopkins, but of the Frenchman, André Rouston. He is Emily's father, is he not?"

The room was filled incredulous silence.

"Who makes such allegations?" Sibylla finally inquired in a strained voice.

"The wife of Consul Willshire! But it was obvious that this scandal was very old news indeed for all the ladies assembled," Victoria declared with her head high.

John seized his wife's wrist and pulled her up from the sofa. "How dare you!"

"Leave her!" Emily's voice was shaking. "I want to know everything, Victoria!"

Sibylla stood up. "You ought to go to bed, Emily. It's late. We're all tired."

"Please don't treat me like a child! I want to know the truth, either from her"—she looked at Victoria—"or from you."

"It is not a good idea," Sibylla replied. Her expression was like stone.

Thomas piped up. "Victoria has made a grave accusation against you, Mother, and thus against our entire family. We have a right to know the truth, especially Emily."

Sibylla closed her eyes. She would never have dreamed that her past would catch up with her after all these years. Especially not through the instrument of her daughter-in-law. All of a sudden, the past was present again. The agonizing pain when she discovered that André had betrayed her with the Berber woman, the fright when she discovered that she was expecting his child, and the bitter disappointment of seeing her happy future with the man she had loved so dearly slip away.

Victoria could feel her pulse in her throat. She regretted causing such an uproar, but she could not take back her words now, and who was to say, it might even be better to have the truth finally come out. Maybe John would be so disappointed in his mother that he would leave Mogador and they could all return to London at once. The very thought almost brought her to tears. And anyway, Selwyn's lungs were healed by now. There was nothing keeping them in this horrid country! She eyed John carefully, but the look he gave her was so angry that she quickly lowered her gaze.

Sibylla was beside herself, but had no choice but to confess the truth to her daughter and her sons. She looked at her children one by one. "What Victoria has said is true, Emily. André Rouston is your father."

For a few seconds, everyone was paralyzed by shock. Emily gasped.

"This is not how I wanted you to find out," Sibylla added faintly.

"I rather think you didn't want me to find out at all!" Emily's animosity cut Sibylla to the quick.

"I so wanted you to have a happy and carefree childhood. I did not want the stigma of illegitimacy to cast a pall over your life. Benjamin had just died, I was alone and had no idea what would happen next. In that moment, Rouston offered me support and stability. I was convinced that we would have a future together, but unfortunately . . ." She choked on her words. "But things turned out differently. Believe me, Emily, I kept silent only to spare you this heartache."

Emily got up. "All my life, you have told me that my father was dead. I will never forgive you for lying!"

Chapter Twenty-Four

Mogador and Qasr el Bahia, December 1860

André stopped in front of the door to Sibylla's office and closed his eyes. He had not felt this happy, almost elated, for quite some time. He took a deep breath, then opened his eyes and knocked on the door.

"Come in!"

Sibylla was standing by the window and looking down over the harbor. Her clerk stood behind a high desk, pen in hand, looking at her expectantly.

"We hope that the shipment meets your expectations and we look forward to a long and successful collaboration with you. Yours sincerely, etc.," she dictated. "That's all for now, Aladdin. Leave the letter here so that I can sign it."

"Very well, Mrs. Hopkins," the clerk said as he left the office.

Sibylla turned. "Hello, André. I've been expecting you. Did you bring me more saffron?"

The sight of her evoked in him the familiar feelings of pain, tenderness, and admiration. The sunlight sparkled in her white-blonde hair and was refracted in her tiny diamond earrings. Her straight shoulders and back radiated authority, but he also took note of the worry lines around her eyes.

"As I do every December." He placed his saddlebag on the desk and took out the linen sack. Then he looked up with concern. "You don't look well."

"Why, aren't you gracious! Is that what you call the famous French charm?" Sibylla opened the sack and poured out some of the saffron. But she did not inspect the quality of the pistils with her customary diligence.

"I could probably foist a sack of marigolds on you today," André remarked with a smile.

"I wouldn't bet on it." She unlocked the cabinet in which she stored the saffron until it was shipped. They could hear muffled shouts, the clatter of crates, the squeaking of a winch, and a door being slammed shut in the warehouse below.

He took the earthenware vessels from her and placed them on the tabletop. "I just ran into Emily."

The young woman had been lying in wait for him. She knew that he would be coming to Mogador around this time and had instructed a beggar sitting at the Bab Doukkala to inform her as soon as Monsieur Rouston rode by. He had only just dismounted from his horse in front of the French consulate when she had appeared in such a state of agitation that for a moment he had feared something had happened to Sibylla. He had been completely unprepared for what Emily did say.

Sibylla fetched the scale from the cabinet and slammed it on the table. "We should be discussing the quality of your crop and not my family."

"Sibylla." André gently placed his hand on her arm. "Emily told me what happened. Don't you think that twenty years is long enough to live with a lie?"

"How dare you?" She jerked her arm back.

"I can imagine how painful this must all be for you, but I am glad Emily finally knows I am her father."

Sibylla's face twitched. For a brief moment, he expected her to throw him out along with his saffron. However, she only noted, very softly, "I expect you have known for some time."

He thought back to that day when he had first met five-year-old Emily. He was standing on the city wall, looking out at the ocean and allowing his thoughts to drift like clouds across the sky when he caught sight of them: Nadira and Sibylla on the beach, playing with a little girl. The first thought that flashed into his mind was that that girl with the black curls could not possibly be Hopkins's child.

He had asked around in town and been relieved beyond measure to discover that Sibylla had never remarried, that she lived alone with her children and was running her father's shipping business. But he simply could not stop thinking about the child. A short while later, he had been successful in reestablishing his contact with Sibylla by way of his saffron and managed to meet the little one. Over the years, the certainty that he was Emily's father had only grown stronger.

"You would never have told me, would you?" he asked gently.

She covered her eyes with her hand and said nothing. When he stepped closer and touched her shoulder, she flinched.

"What did you expect me to do?" she asked angrily. "You preferred your life with Aynur to a life with me. She bore you a daughter mere weeks after Emily was born!"

"I would have preferred a life with you, Sibylla . . ." He stopped. Aynur had lured him into her arms with a ruse back then. But later, he had understood her reasons, and she had become a good companion for him. He did not wish to speak ill of her. "Emily has asked if she might stay with me at Qasr el Bahia for the time being. I told her that she may."

She spun around. "That is out of the question! I won't allow it."

"This is Emily's decision. You must respect it."

"Never!" Sibylla felt deeply wounded—by Emily, who had turned her back on her, and by André, who was helping her do so.

"You have withheld the truth from me for twenty years and denied me the opportunity to be a father to Emily. But now that she really needs a father, I must be one for her!"

"Do you believe that I would surrender Emily to your . . ." Sibylla could not bring herself to say the word "wife." "To Aynur?! She will refuse to accept her because she's my daughter. She will attempt to harm her, she will—"

"Please calm down, Sibylla! First of all, Aynur will do nothing of the sort. Secondly, I will be there as well. And thirdly, it is Emily's wish."

"But she is still a child and has no idea!" Sibylla protested.

André gingerly wrapped his arms around her and pulled her close. For a few seconds, all they heard was the distant breaking of the surf and the sounds of the harbor until Sibylla burst out, "Oh, that Sara Willshire, I could kill her! She has turned my whole family against me! Emily has thrown away her chance to study at the Royal Academy of Arts, and now she hardly speaks to me at all. The minute I say something, she leaves the room."

"Give her time. The news has been a shock."

"Easy for you to say. You're not the one she's treating like a criminal."

Sibylla haltingly told André that Emily wasn't the only one angry with her. Thomas was resentful that she had not confided in him and

John felt personally disgraced. "And to think that all our acquaintances knew," he had fretted. "What a fool the other traders must think me!"

And Victoria, the instigator, stayed hidden in her room. Whenever Sibylla crossed paths with her in the house, the young woman quickly hurried away.

Sibylla looked into André's eyes. "Victoria is ashamed, but she still has not asked for my forgiveness. To be perfectly frank, I'm not ready to give it yet. You must be upset with me as well."

"*Mon* Dieu, no! What else could you have done? I was the one who made a grave mistake. I betrayed your feelings. And mine." He drew a deep breath. "You wanted to protect Emily, as did I. So I said nothing for all these years, even though it wasn't always easy."

"I fear that Emily will be called a bastard if you publicly acknowledge her as your daughter. I couldn't bear that, André."

"Anyone who even thinks about uttering that word will have me to deal with," André replied. "That's another reason for Emily to go with me to Qasr el Bahia. People will gossip, but soon they tire of it and accept that I am Emily's father."

Sibylla leaned against him. "Had I known how you felt, many things would have turned out differently." She sighed softly.

"Would you have forgiven me?" he asked earnestly.

She said nothing, but permitted him to stroke her hair.

One week later, Sibylla and Emily left the city at daybreak, riding through the Bab El Mersa and headed in a southeastern direction to the mouth of the Oued Igrounzar river, where André was waiting for them. He had left through a different gate to avoid attracting attention. After a brief greeting, he rode off with Emily and a pack donkey carrying his purchases from the *souk*. Sibylla stayed behind. Before the riders disappeared behind a bend, André turned around to wave. Sibylla squinted, not because of the rising sun but the tears stinging her eyes. At last, she slowly rode back to town. Emily had not turned and she had not bade her farewell.

"We'll be there soon."

Emily shot up in her saddle. André smiled. "You're not accustomed to riding all day, are you? It won't be long now before we reach the Oued Zeltene tributary and, from there, we'll be home in half an hour."

Home, Emily mused. *Mogador has always been my home until now.* "It's getting dark," she said. "What if we get lost?"

"Don't worry. There is a full moon and I know every rock around. I could find my way from here blindfolded. Look, the evening star has risen."

Emily looked up into the lavender sky and saw a single bright star over the jagged mountaintops.

It had been a pleasant day for riding. At one point, a light rain had fallen, leaving the air mild and soft like balsam. Next to them, the Oued Igrounzar gurgled over the rocks. They heard some rustling in the shrubs and a nocturnal bird called out from a jujube tree. Emily's horse snorted. She patted it on the neck and listened to the rhythmic *clip clop* of the hooves on the hard soil. Her heart beat faster as she thought about the people at Qasr el Bahia, her father's family, who were now her family.

"Father?" It was difficult for her to address the man who had so long been "Monsieur Rouston."

"Yes, *ma petite*?" He turned to her in his saddle.

"Does your family know about me?"

During their journey, André had told Emily about his family, that his wife, Aynur, was a Berber from the Glaoua tribe and that they had four children. The eldest was almost as old as Emily and was named Malika. Her name meant "angel" in Arabic, but André insisted that there was nothing angelic about her and that she was full of mischief. His three sons, Frédéric, Christian, and André, who was called André

Jr., had been given names from their father's country according to Aynur's wishes. They were seventeen, fourteen, and ten years of age. There had also been two other girls who had died in infancy.

André considered his answer carefully since he did not want Emily to misunderstand. "My family does not know about you," he eventually admitted. "But that is only because, until just a few days ago, I could not be sure you were my daughter."

"I simply can't believe that Mother lied to us for so many years!" Emily said.

He looked at her very seriously. "She had your well-being in mind. You must not judge her so."

By now, it was almost completely dark. The bright moon was huge and seemed close enough to touch. The wind carried the scent of cedar down from the Atlas. Emily thought she could see shadows scurrying through the thicket. An owl silently glided directly over their heads and her horse reared back.

"You don't suppose there could be robbers here, do you?" she inquired apprehensively once she had calmed the horse down. The traders from Mogador relied on heavily armed mercenaries from the sultan's Black Guards to protect their caravans. But Emily and André had no such protection.

"There are no robbers here. We're too far from the caravan route," André reassured her. "And I get along well with the Ait Zelten that live here. In fact, many of them work on my estate."

During his early years at Qasr el Bahia, the Ait Zelten had not been disposed kindly toward him. The shepherds had driven their flocks across his fields, their goats and sheep grazing on his barley and trampling the saffron crocuses. At night, the people had stolen the fruit off his trees and tried to break into his stables and storerooms. It was not until his friend Udad bin Aziki had arrived with two dozen well-armed Chiadma that the Ait Zelten had conceded defeat and their sheikh had accepted the foreigner.

They had become good neighbors over the years. During times of drought and famine, when they lost the greater part of their crop, André shared his food reserves with them. In return, they helped out in the fields and on the farm. A handful of young men objected to the unholy friendship with the infidel, but as long as the sheikh and the rest of the tribe stood by André, they were powerless to do anything about it.

Emily listened intently. The rushing of the water seemed louder than before. "Have we reached the Oued Zeltene?"

Her father nodded. "Qasr el Bahia is directly in front of us."

She followed his extended arm and beheld the elevated estate. A gigantic, angular building with two massive towers arose dark and majestic before her. Tiny stars sparkled above it in the infinite blue-velvet sky. Suddenly, lights began to glow in one of the two towers, swung several times from right to left, and disappeared. André turned to his daughter. "Those are flare signals. They have heard us arrive."

Soon after, the lights appeared again, dancing through the darkness in the direction of the two riders. Deliberately placing one hoof in front of the other, the horses and the pack donkey climbed toward them. Water could be heard running underneath them in the *rhetaras* leading to the terraced fields on either side of the narrow path. In the pale light of the moon, Emily could make out the round-edged stone walls bordering the fields in which one could still see the headless stalks of harvested saffron plants. In between, about a horse's length apart, were rows of pomegranate trees, the branches of which looked like thin little black arms reaching upward.

Emily heard the torchbearers calling out to them. She was about to meet her new family.

"Will your wife welcome me, Father?" she asked him, her heart in her throat.

André hesitated. He had been preoccupied with this question ever since Emily had told him that she wanted to live with him. He feared that Aynur would not exactly welcome Emily with open arms, but he did not want his daughter to know that.

Aynur was jealous. She did not like it when he went to Mogador. Whenever he returned, she would be distant and unapproachable, making him court her anew and prove that he loved her and not the *Engliziya* to whom he sold his saffron.

What would happen when he rode into the courtyard with his and Sibylla's daughter? He would protect Emily and make it clear to Aynur that she must respect this child of his as well, but it would not be easy.

"My life has taught me not to make grand plans. Most of the time, fate decides," he said as airily as possible.

"So you'll let fate decide how I am received?"

"Not entirely, because I am by your side." He reached out and touched her shoulder. "*Inshallah*, my daughter."

"*Inshallah*, Father," she muttered without much conviction.

"Baba?" The voice of a young man came through the darkness. "Who are you talking to?"

The torchbearers were approaching. Emily looked expectantly at the dark-haired young man who came jumping down the hill with the agility of a mountain goat. One of André's sons, probably Frédéric. He was followed by two farmhands, also bearing torches. Emily tightened her grip on the reins. In Mogador, she had asserted herself against two older brothers. She would have to do that and more with three younger brothers, one sister, and their mother!

Aynur narrowed her eyes in disbelief when she saw Emily ride into the courtyard behind André. Had her husband brought back a wife from Mogador?

She had been dreading this for a long time. Although her face was still smooth and her body still slender and lithe after six pregnancies, she was no longer young at the age of thirty-seven. But she had not become pregnant in the two years since the tiny newborn body of her youngest daughter, Thiyya, had been laid to rest next to her sister, Izza. Perhaps her husband did want more children, even though he assured her time and again that he had enough.

But did he have to humiliate her with a wife young enough to be his daughter? The stranger was beautiful, supple like a young cedar tree and with regal bearing. She could not be Berber because she wore neither traditional clothing nor bore tribal tattoos on her forehead and cheeks. And an Arab woman would wear a veil. She had to be a foreigner.

Another foreigner! Jealousy flared inside Aynur. She would have liked to yank the strange woman off her horse and press her face in the dust. Wherever the creature came from, she would learn not to intrude into Aynur's home!

"Frédéric!" She took her eldest by the shirt and pulled him closer. "Who is the guest that Baba has brought?" she hissed in her native Glaoua language.

The dancing torchlight lent him an insolent, rakish look. "He said he'll introduce her at dinner. But she's pretty, isn't she, Imma? Perhaps she'll become my bride."

Aynur playfully punched her eldest, secretly relieved by a possibility she had not considered. "Don't stand around and talk all night! Go and help your brothers unload the donkey."

André jumped off his horse and threw the reins to a stable boy. Then he helped the young woman dismount. Aynur watched him hold the stirrup steady with one hand and extend the other. The young woman smiled nervously, slid out of the saddle, and stood close to André.

Aynur grasped the locket with her children's hair that she wore on a silver chain around her neck. Then she resolutely lifted her chin.

Chapter Twenty-Five

Emily sat next to her father on one of the two sofas in the dining room and tried to look as confident as possible. She was glad that a flat cedarwood table separated her and Aynur, since the lady of the house had given her a cool reception indeed. Now she sat enthroned on the opposite side of the table, demonstrably surrounded by her sons. Cowering on a chair in a corner was a frightening figure: a very old Negro woman, her talon-like fingers clutching the armrests and her gaze unremittingly fixed on Emily. André had introduced her as Tamra, Aynur's servant. Still, Emily felt uneasy at the sight of the almost-bald old woman, who continually made disagreeable grunting sounds.

The dining room was not furnished in the European style like her home in Mogador. This one had low sofas with colorful throws. A wool rug covered the blue, green, and red floor tiles, bowls of fragrant dried flowers filled in the alcoves, and iron chandeliers threw flickering shapes on the whitewashed walls. The arched windows were large, with elegant colored panes that dated back to the previous owner, the late Sultan Moulay Abd al-Rahman.

The hearth gave off cracking sounds, the old woman in her chair went on mumbling to herself, but everything else was shrouded in explosive silence. Aynur sat very straight on the sofa. With her embroidered blouse, her wide, colorful skirt, and her opulent silver jewelry, she reminded Emily of a pretty doll, if not for her tight lips and the hostility in her brown eyes.

However, Emily was determined not to be intimidated. If she had succeeded in standing up to her own formidable mother, she could surely do the same with this woman.

The door was opened and Emily's half sister, Malika, entered, followed by two servants. The women brought platters with steaming couscous, fresh flatbread, and tureens from which emanated the tempting aromas of mint, honey, and lemon.

Malika was a younger version of her mother, so small and dainty that Emily felt like a giant. Her skin glistened and her shiny pitch-black hair reached down to her hips. Whenever she moved, the silver bangles she wore on both wrists jingled. Like her mother, she was dressed in a tunic, a wide calf-length skirt, and boots made of soft leather. She reminded Emily of the dancer in the music box her stepgrandmother Mary had sent her from England years ago.

Malika daintily placed the heavy platter on the table and threw an inquisitive glance at Emily with her gorgeous kohl-rimmed eyes. Emily found herself hoping that they would be not only sisters but also friends.

At a nod from Aynur, the servants left the room. André placed his arm around Emily's shoulder and cleared his throat.

"My dear family, I'm sure you're asking yourselves who our guest is."

"I hope it is the wife you have chosen for me," Frédéric said impertinently.

Emily blushed, Aynur hissed something to her son, and André merely shook his head and laughed. "I'm afraid I have to disappoint you, son, but I am still expecting that you will choose your own bride." He looked at Aynur and paused for a long moment. "This young woman is Emily. I have known her for a long time, but it was only a few days ago that I discovered that she is my daughter. From now on, Qasr el Bahia will be her home as much as it is yours."

The room was so still that one could have heard a pin drop. Then the old woman in her corner uttered a whistling sound as though exhaling all her breath.

Emily looked uncertainly at Aynur, who had her hand before her mouth. Her face revealed surprise and pain, but also relief. At least she no longer looked hostile, and Emily felt her confidence return.

Malika was the first to rise. She walked to Emily with her arms wide and kissed her. "*Asselama outletsma*, welcome, Sister!" she quietly said in her Berber language before switching to Arabic. "I have always wanted a sister."

The brothers too gathered around their new family member. Christian was a little shy, Frédéric announced grandiloquently that he would be able to show off two beautiful sisters at the next tribal meeting, and the little one shyly touched Emily's curls.

Tamra's head wobbled and she grunted something, but Emily couldn't discern whether it was a greeting or curse.

Now Aynur got up, went to Emily, and embraced her formally. "Welcome to Qasr el Bahia, my husband's daughter. His guests are also my guests."

Only much later on that night, when they were alone in their bedroom, did Aynur tell her husband what she felt in her heart of hearts.

"So the *Engliziya* got herself pregnant by you. I have known there would be misfortune ever since Tamra read the bones of a dove for me!" She turned her back to André, but observed him carefully in her silver mirror while massaging argan oil into her hair.

André was sitting on the edge of the bed, taking off his boots. He grimaced at her words and angrily threw his boots in the space between two carved trunks. "Will you never stop believing that old witch's nonsense? And another thing: I'll thank Tamra and you not to characterize Emily as a misfortune ever again, is that clear?"

He longed for peace and quiet and, after a week's absence, to hold Aynur in his arms again. She looked sensual and seductive in her flowing, floor-length silk shirt. The flickering lamplight outlined her figure in shadow and made her bronze skin shimmer. When she shook out her long black hair, making its ends brush against the curves of her bottom, he became aware of his growing desire.

"Come here," he whispered to her. "I've had an exhausting day. Let's talk about it tomorrow."

Aynur turned around, but stayed where she was. Her eyes smoldered in the semidarkness. "Why did the *Engliziya* wait until now to give you the child? Or did you not want the child?"

André tried not to groan. It was clear Aynur would not drop the subject until she had gotten answers.

"It's all very complicated, especially for Emily," he answered tentatively. "I brought her with me so that she could get some peace of mind."

"I understand. The *Engliziya* was angry when she saw me at Qasr el Bahia with you. She must have known then that she was expecting a child. I had thought that foreign women were more careful than that." A catlike smile flashed across her face. "You betrayed her love. That is why you deserve to feel her wrath. I would also let you feel my wrath if you betrayed my love."

Before André had a chance to answer, she blew out the lamp and darkness engulfed the room. He heard her naked feet softly padding on the floor. When she sat next to him, he could feel her breath on his neck. She smelled like the roses growing outside in their garden.

"Do you share her bed when you are in Mogador?" Aynur whispered in his ear.

In all the years they had been together, she had never asked him this before, but when he heard the quiver in her voice, it dawned on him how much the uncertainty must have tormented her. He felt for her hand. "My bringing Emily here has nothing to do with Sibylla and me. It concerns only Emily and me."

She withdrew her hand. "You haven't answered my question."

"I do not share my bed with her. Never. Not once since you entered into my life!" he answered more vehemently than he had intended. "Are you satisfied?"

Aynur leaned over his ear. "That depends . . ."

He pulled her into his arms. "Don't worry. You are the best companion I could wish for. Without you, I would not have my other wonderful children and Qasr el Bahia would not be what it is today. Do you think I could forget that?"

Appeased, she placed her cheek on his chest. "I believe you, beloved. Your daughter shall want for nothing here. Please forgive me for violating the holy laws of hospitality. It will not happen again."

He lifted her chin and kissed her. She deftly pulled his shirt over his head, then kneeled behind him on the bed and began massaging his back. "Hard as a rock. It must be painful, beloved. But I will make the pain go away."

He leaned forward and surrendered to her even, powerful ministrations. "*Ç'est merveilleux*. You have magical hands, Aynur."

Her hands slid over his chest and stomach, slipped under his waistband, and grasped his member. "You want me," she declared with satisfaction.

Instead of answering, he turned and gently pressed her onto the mattress.

Mogador, end of April, 1861

The crowd in front of the Bab Doukkala grew silent as the funeral procession neared. Four pallbearers entered first, Samuel Toledano's coffin on their shoulders. They were followed by the mourners: first, the rabbi; followed by Aaron Toledano, the eldest son and new patriarch;

Samuel's widow, who was being supported by her daughters; and the rest of the family. Last came more relatives, friends, business associates, and neighbors from the Jewish community of Mogador.

Sibylla took a deep breath. The long procession of silent, darkly attired people depressed her. André had been in Mogador three weeks earlier. Although he had conveyed greetings from Emily, she suspected that he had made that up in order to console her. At any rate, he had not brought the letter from her daughter that she so longed for.

Emily had been gone four months now, and Sibylla could not remember a more joyless Christmas season. It was now the end of April and still she felt just as sad and despondent as if their falling-out had come just yesterday.

"She will return to you," André had said when he left. "Be patient and don't worry! I am taking good care of our daughter."

If only patience were not so difficult, she thought and looked across the funeral procession to Qaid Samir, who was standing on the other side of the city gate, surrounded by his entourage, to pay his last respects to the dead *tujjar al-sultan*. Next to her, two traders were engaged in a conversation under their breath.

"To think a simple box with a body is all that is left of one of the country's most influential men," one of them whispered, looking at the humble wooden casket, adorned by neither picture nor ornaments nor flowers. Only the dates of Toledano's birth and death according to the Hebrew calendar were engraved on the lid.

"The man was eighty years old. I hope I can reach such a venerable age," said the other and reverently doffed his hat.

Sibylla thought about Benjamin. He'd have been fifty-one years old now, had he not died a gruesome death. The secret he'd left still cast a shadow over Sibylla. For his part in things, Toledano had gotten off lightly. Too lightly, in Sibylla's opinion, and she had stubbornly refused to do business with him all these years.

She turned to John and was about to tell him that she wanted to go home when Victoria accidently met her eyes, then quickly lowered her gaze.

Victoria had apologized, but the relationship between the two remained strained. The peace was superficial and, in her heart, Sibylla had not yet forgiven her. She knew that John had had a very serious talk with his wife and told her that under no circumstances was she to tell outsiders either the reason for Emily's sudden departure or her whereabouts. Since then, Victoria had hardly left the house and Sibylla assumed that the young woman felt lonelier and unhappier in Mogador than ever.

The funeral procession had now gathered around the grave in the Jewish cemetery, a dusty, untended piece of land. The rabbi was reading aloud from the book of Genesis, and Qaid Samir and his entourage returned to the city. The traders too began to leave.

"Hello, Mrs. Hopkins. This weather is perfect for a funeral, is it not?"

Sibylla turned around in surprise. Sara Willshire stood behind her, smiling nervously.

Sibylla muttered a greeting and turned to leave, but Sara quickly asked, "Where's Emily? I do hope she's not ill. I haven't seen her for such a long time."

Sibylla felt herself growing angry. Where did this woman get the nerve to ask such a question when her gossiping was the reason that Emily was gone!

"I'm sorry, but did you just inquire about my daughter?"

"I was merely trying to fulfill my neighborly duties and inquire about Emily's well-being." Sara sounded aggrieved.

"Well, in that case, allow me to answer your question." Sibylla gave her a withering look. "Emily is with her father."

"With her father?" Sara stammered. "What do you mean? I mean, how is that possible?"

"Why, Mrs. Willshire, you amaze me. You know very well how that is possible. After all, you yourself contributed to it!"

Sara blushed and looked away. "Your reproach is unfair. Everyone in Mogador knows the truth. Sooner or later, your daughter-in-law would have found out anyway, and Emily too."

Sibylla's nostrils quivered. "I have only one thing to say, Mrs. Willshire: don't you ever again pour poison in my family's ears!"

Chapter Twenty-Six

Qasr el Bahia, early summer 1861

At breakfast, André announced, "Today, the women and the older children are going to work the upper terraced field. You will take out all the plants that have more than three bulbs and separate and replant them."

After half a day, Emily furtively massaged her aching back. She wanted no one to know how exhausting the work in the field was for her. Aynur noticed, however. She could imagine how the city girl was feeling. After all, she herself had once been a pampered little thing whose most arduous task had been to pick flowers in the harem garden.

André had paid little heed to her laments and tears in the beginning. He was not even bothered when the sun burned her delicate skin and her soft hands blistered.

"You can return to your tribe anytime you wish," he had said. "But if you wish to stay, you must share my life with me. I have no use here for a harem princess. What I need is a woman who is going to farm this estate with me."

He had not spared her in the beginning and she knew it was his way of punishing her for driving the Englishwoman away. But it had only served to motivate her. She wanted to prove she could win the good-looking foreigner for herself, even if he carried the Englishwoman in his heart. She made sure he never saw how she cried with exhaustion or loneliness. She persevered and fought for his respect. With time, she came to realize that she much preferred this life to the idleness of the harem. She reflected on her Glaoua heritage, the pride of her tribe, its longing for freedom and love of the land, and she wondered how she had survived so many years of a walled-in life.

As her pregnancy became visible, André was careful not to overwork her. Then came the day when the child moved. She took his hand and placed it on her belly and he smiled at her for the first time. But only when Tamra placed the newborn Malika in his arms and he looked at the baby with tender, surprised eyes did she know that he would not send her away.

She had been fearful for a long time that the Englishwoman would return and claim André for herself. But strangely enough, she had never been seen at Qasr el Bahia again. Aynur now had to witness every day how much the Englishwoman's daughter meant to her husband, but she did not complain. Maybe he had loved the Englishwoman more than her, but he loved all his children with equal devotion. She also knew she had become indispensable to André. The Englishwoman was a spoiled city dweller who was probably ill-suited for life out here. But her daughter, she had to admit, put up a good front. She never complained or shirked her work, and she tried to keep up with her half siblings. She tried to emulate Malika, who picked up bundles of saffron bulbs from the freshly plowed furrow and threw them into the basket on her arm without breaking the rhythm of her walk.

The little *Crocus sativus*, whose minuscule pistils make the world's most precious spice, stayed in the same field for four years. After that, the bulbs had to be taken out of the soil, divided, and replanted elsewhere. André hired Ait Zelten for that work, the saffron harvest, and many other jobs on the estate.

Christian had attached a mule to a simple plow consisting of a wooden rod with an iron hook on the end. He followed the plow and directed the mule with reins and voice commands as the crocus bulbs were exposed. The women gathered them up and threw them in the baskets over their shoulders. Once the baskets were full, they were placed on the field, the children carried them to the edge, emptied them, and separated the bulbs. Then the bulbs were taken to be stored in a dry, dark, and well-ventilated storage facility until the end of July, when they were planted in different fields after the barley harvest.

The Ait Zelten women in their colorful skirts looked like splashes of bright paint on the brown soil. Emily had already captured their suntanned faces with charcoal or oil color and brush. Mothers with their babies strapped on their backs, children bustling about and playing catch or petting the mule in between doing their chores. Emily's only regret was not being able to depict the sounds and smells on her canvas: the melodious singsong of the language, the children's laughter, the soft jingling of the women's silver jewelry, and the smell of the earth.

Canvases, paint, charcoal pencils, and sketchbooks had been the first things she packed for her move to Qasr el Bahia. She had been uncertain at first if André's family and the Ait Zelten would allow her to draw. After all, Islam prohibited the depiction of any part of God's creation. But neither André's family nor the Ait Zelten were bothered when Emily painted them. They were pleased to look at themselves in her pictures and proud when they were chosen as models. In the countryside, far removed from the guardians of the faith in the cities, people made religion their own. The Ait Zelten maintained their traditional faith in nature spirits, omens, and symbols as firmly as their faith in Islam. But André and Aynur's children observed their prayer times only for their mother's sake, as Frédéric confided in Emily, and André himself said that he would rather put his faith in good old common sense than in any deity.

Emily had been living here for six months now and had immortalized everyday life on the estate in many paintings and drawings: her father and Frédéric shoeing a horse in the threshing area in front of the stables; André Jr. proudly perched on a branch of the blue-silver Atlas cedar in the courtyard; old Tamra dozing in the sun on a bench in front of the house; two barefoot Berber boys driving a herd of goats along the old mud wall. She had sketched Aynur decorating the graves of her two little daughters under the gnarly old holly oak in her garden with the delicate first flowers of spring, and Malika, one evening in April, when a troupe of jugglers and storytellers had come by and she had danced with them in front of the campfire.

"This crocus gathering is obviously your favorite kind of work, Sister." Malika brought Emily back to reality. "Just wait until Baba's new field has been cleared. You won't know how to climb into bed at night, you'll be so sore."

In appreciation of André's translation of a military text into Arabic last year, Sultan Sidi Mohammed had given him another piece of land bordering the east side of the estate. He planned another saffron field there. But for now, the Ait Zelten men were busy clearing the underbrush and digging out the rootstock.

"You just wait yourself! All that bending will make you as hunched over as old Tamra and then I'll paint you like that!" Emily threatened.

Malika laughed. She was aware of her own beauty. "I have a better idea. But you have to promise not to tell anyone about it." She looked around for her mother, but Aynur was busy admonishing Christian for daydreaming instead of tending to the mule.

Emily nodded. "What is it?"

Malika quickly moved next to her. "You'll paint me lying on my bed in my room," she whispered mysteriously.

"All right, but why are you whispering?"

"I don't want it to be an ordinary painting . . ."

"What do you mean?"

"Oh, you know!" Malika looked over at her mother again. Then she whispered, "The only thing I would be wearing is a shawl."

"Oh, you mean a nude. Why didn't you say so?"

Aynur turned around to check on the girls.

"What is a nude?" Malika whispered as soon as Aynur bent over the furrows again.

"It's a painting or drawing of a naked person," Emily explained in a patronizing tone. "It's common in European art." While she had never seen a nude, let alone drawn one, she had read about them in an art history book Uncle Oscar had sent her from England.

"Then you'll do it?" Malika urged her. "And I can keep it?"

Emily frowned. "I have rarely given away any of my work. I need it for the portfolio I'm going to submit to my teacher at the art academy in London."

She stopped abruptly, remembering that she had forfeited her studies as a result of her quarrel with her mother. The thought hit her in the pit of her stomach.

"Are you planning to give the picture to someone?" she asked. "Perhaps a young man?"

Malika shook her head. "I want it just for me so I can look at it one day when I'm old and fat. I also want it as a memento for when you become a famous artist. And you won't be doing it for free. I'm going to pay you."

"Oh?" As far as Emily knew, Malika had no money of her own any more than she did.

"I'm going to read your palm."

"Oh." Emily was disappointed. "You know I don't believe you can see my future in my palm. That's hocus-pocus."

"You can't be serious! Your life, every twist of fate, is written in the lines of your palm. You just have to know how to decipher them. So, what do you say?"

Emily turned her hands over to examine them, but try as she might, she could see only lines, some long, some short, some more deeply furrowed than others.

"Let me have a look!" Malika demanded. "I'll prove to you how good I am. Tamra taught me palm reading, and she knows everything about it."

Before Emily could stop her, Malika took her by the arm and led her to the edge of the field.

"Sit!" When Emily hesitated, Malika gave her a little shove. "Oh, come on! I know you want to find out about the man that fate has chosen for you."

Emily immediately thought of Sabri. Was there a future for them even though his parents had already chosen a bride? She took a deep breath, then stretched out her hands. "Here we go!"

Malika took her left hand and looked at it seriously. Emily smiled shyly when the young Berber woman sitting near them and nursing her child nodded encouragingly.

"What? What is it?" she asked nervously after Malika had stared at her hand for what seemed a very long time.

Malika looked up with a tiny smile. "Well, well, little sister! Who would have thought?"

"Who would have thought what? Don't make me beg you for every little word!"

"You've already found him, Sister, and yet you have not breathed a word. Aren't you ashamed?" Malika sounded very pleased with herself.

Emily wrenched her hand from Malika and hid it under her tunic. "You couldn't possibly know that from a few lines on my palm."

"Yes, I could, and it's as sure as the next sunrise. And even if I could not, you have betrayed yourself by now. Now give me back your hand. I'm going to tell you exactly what I am seeing." Malika took Emily's left hand, opened it, and stroked gently with her fingers.

"This is the heart line. It tells me about your fate in love." Using her index finger, she pointed to the upper of two thin horizontal furrows on Emily's palm. "Your line begins near the fourth finger. This means that you will be jealously vigilant that your man does not desire other women. But the line is also close to the third finger and that tells me you derive great pleasure from feeling your man's body. And in that, you are much like me."

"I have never felt a man's body!" Emily yelped. Her face was deeply flushed.

"Really?" Malika was astounded. "I have."

"Excuse me?" Emily thought she had misheard. "Does Father know?"

Malika dreamily stretched out her hand toward a lizard sunning itself nearby. "Of course. I was married and celebrated my wedding at a tribal meeting of the Glaoua three years ago. Together with twenty other couples, a young Glaoua man and I were married by the *qadi*."

"What? Where is your husband now?"

Malika poked the lizard gently with her forefinger and it darted away. "The *qadi* dissolved our union a year later. In Father's language, it is called divorce. Now I am free to choose a new husband whenever I want."

"Did you not love your husband?" Emily marveled.

"Of course I did. For almost an entire year." Malika was indignant.

"Did you . . . ahem . . . marry again after that?" Emily felt a bit envious of her sister for having had such experiences already.

"No. I don't like Arab men, and I don't like Berber men either. I don't like their scruffy beards and how they dress, those long tunics." She shook her head. "I would like to marry a foreigner, from my father's country, but foreigners don't come to Qasr el Bahia. So I would have to leave, and I don't want to do that."

Come with me when I go to the art academy in London, Emily wanted to cry. But then, for the second time, she remembered that she had given up her place at the academy and that it was unlikely she would ever travel there. She bit her lips and stretched out her left hand. "Come on, let's get back to work."

Malika pointed to a spot below Emily's forefinger. "Two lines make a cross here. That means you already know your great and eternal love. The heart line is long, clear, and red. You will always be true to your chosen one and you will love him wholeheartedly and passionately." She lifted her head and smiled at Emily. "Who has captured your heart, Sister?"

Emily could feel her pulse in her throat. She instinctively looked around, but no one was paying any attention to them. Not even the young woman, who was humming softly to her baby.

"You don't know him, he lives in Mogador," she whispered to Malika. "He is the *hakim* in the city."

Malika whistled softly. "An Arab man!"

Emily nodded. "But he has been in England and studied medicine there."

Sabri's image appeared before her mind's eye, the way he had looked that day when he spoke of taking her out. She had often wondered what else he might have said had not Thomas burst in. Her brother had spoiled everything, not only the wonderful moment with Sabri but all of her happiness!

Emily drew a quick breath. "Do the lines say that we have a future together?"

"You will have problems," Malika answered with a serious look. "There will be disappointments, but if you stay strong—"

A shadow fell over the two girls. "So this is where you are—startled like thieves caught in the night! Well, I hope that is because of your guilty conscience for shirking your work!" André stood before them, his hands on his hips, but his eyes were twinkling.

"Father!" Emily quickly withdrew her hand from Malika. "What are you doing here?"

"I wanted to ask you if you felt like coming with me. We are going to take lunch to the men who are clearing the field and then we're going to ride out."

"I'd love to!" Emily jumped up.

The new field lay on a sunlit plateau bordering Aynur's vegetable garden and an orange grove with scattered beehives. Behind it, the slopes of the Atlas rose to bluish, snowcapped peaks. The men had burned off the brush, but now they had to painstakingly hoe the roots out of the soil. Emily saw the large heap of roots lying by the side of the field. Bleating goats were jumping around on the area strewn with charred branches, rocks, and deep holes, with André Jr. and his playmates supervising. Emily thought about how much time and sweat it would take the men to transform this cratered landscape into a tillable field. And then there were irrigation ditches and retaining walls still to be constructed.

They dismounted just as the workers were finishing their midday prayer. There was no *muezzin* on Qasr el Bahia, so people determined prayer times according to dawn and dusk, the position of the sun, and the length of shadows.

Emily led the pack donkey over to some olive trees where the men were sitting and unpacked flatbread, vegetables in olive oil, goat cheese, dried meat, and oranges.

After their meal, one of the men pulled a flute from his tunic and began to play, another struck up a song, and the rest of them clapped their hands in time and sang the refrain. Emily still couldn't understand much of the Ait Zelten dialect, but André explained to her that the song told of an old legend of the Imazighen—the "free people," as the Berber referred to themselves.

"A long time ago, God revealed knowledge of agriculture and weaving to the free people. The plow and the loom were His gifts. The Ait Zelten sing praise to agriculture, which they consider a holy activity much like the art of weaving. When they plow the new field, you will notice that they always dig the furrows at right angles. In that way, they recreate the pattern of a woven rug's warp and weft. They thus serve God and protect the land from the powers of demons." He touched Emily on the shoulder. "Shall we?"

"Gladly!" She got up.

"Baba!" André Jr. shouted. "Look! Over there!"

A band of six riders came galloping out of the orange grove uttering ugly cries and waving their guns aloft. Suddenly, a shot rang out, the sound reverberating off the rocks. André Jr. screamed and covered his ears. Men and children jumped up and ran around in confusion.

André felt for his gun and cursed when he realized that it was hanging from his saddle several strides away. He quickly looked around to make certain no one had been hurt. Emily had had the presence of mind to throw her little brother on the ground and cover him with her body. The Ait Zelten men had formed a circle around the other children, but they were almost completely unarmed. Some had grabbed hoes and shovels, others had ripped their knives out of their belts, but no one had a gun.

"Father!" screamed Emily. "Look out!"

The riders were heading straight for André. Horrified, she watched as he did not take even one step back. At the last second, the group pulled up short. Even when their horses reared above his head, André did not budge.

Emily cradled her terrified little brother and eyed the troublemakers. They were young Ait Zelten men, most no older than she was. Only their leader was a little older. His eyes glowed and he had a port-wine stain running from his left eye across his whole face. He sat proudly on his horse, holding the reins with one hand and brandishing his gun with the other.

André took one step in his direction. "What a heroic deed it is to shoot at children and unarmed people! And you call yourselves men?"

"Filthy foreigner!" the man hissed. "Your greed devours our land like the desert devours a fertile oasis! Take your brood and go back to the infidels!"

"Shame on you for tainting our friendship with the *faransawi*! You're not a man but a dishonorable coward. Go home and crawl back into your mother's lap!" The sheikh of the Ait Zelten stepped up next to André and shook his soil-stained fists.

Loud, angry muttering came from the group of riders. The leader aimed his weapon at the man. "You son of a dog! You're betraying your own people to an infidel!"

"Enough!" André shouted. "Put your weapons down! Those barrels may be crooked as the horns of a mountain goat, but you could still hit an innocent with them. And now"—he turned to the leader—"you listen to me: the Ait Zelten and I have been good neighbors for more than twenty years. Do you really think that you can command me to leave the land that has been given to me by two of Morocco's sultans? Who do you think you are?"

"The *faransawi* is right," the sheikh said. "He helped us when we lost the greater part of our herds and were starving. Without him, your wretched bones would have turned to dust long ago! He may be an infidel, but he is a friend and you are showing your gratitude with hatred. Shame!"

"If he hadn't stolen our land, we wouldn't have lost those herds in the first place. Here"—the leader drew a wide circle with his arm—"is where our goats once grazed. No sultan can give this land away. It was ours long before the Arabs arrived!"

"Ay, ay!" the riders shouted approvingly.

"I listened to your ramblings twenty years ago. At that time, this land no longer belonged to your herds," André countered. "But now it feeds many people. Get off your horses and help feed your people instead of being a burden to them!"

The leader waved his gun in the direction of the Ait Zelten workers, who had been silently following the altercation.

"What are you? Are you free people, or are you old women who will take orders from anyone?"

The men responded by gathering behind André and their sheikh, like a silent, menacing barricade.

"Shame on you for breaking your backs for the infidel!" He spat on the ground in front of André, then pulled his horse around and galloped away through the orange grove, followed by his band.

After the excitement had died down and André had made sure that the young agitators were not still lurking nearby, he and Emily rode to a high plateau half an hour up the mountain.

From there, Emily could see across a sparse forest of cedars up to where the Oued Igrounzar and Oued Zeltene merged. Qasr el Bahia, looking massive and unassailable with its mighty donjons and sturdy gate, was situated between the two areas. One of the two towers was accessible only by means of retractable ladders. André had shown her the small rooms with the sleeping mats, torches, water, and several days' worth of provisions. He kept his saffron inventory hidden in the tower in a locked trunk behind some sacks of grain and rolled-up rugs. In the event attackers were to break through the gate, the residents had a nearly impregnable shelter in the towers.

Terraced fields lay spread out around Qasr el Bahia, some a reddish brown, where the saffron bulbs still lay submerged in the soil, and some golden, where the ripe barley stood ready for harvesting. In between were dots of green from the orange, lemon, pomegranate, and olive trees. Emily spotted the new field in the east. From here, the men clearing it looked like tiny ants.

"I was afraid," Emily confessed.

André, who had just finished tying the horses to a jujube tree, turned around. "Of those pretend warriors? I've known almost all of them since they were born. I put their leader in his place my very first day on the estate. I'm not afraid of them, and you shouldn't be either."

"I'm not afraid for myself, Father, but for you, my brother, and all the others."

He came over and took her in his arms. She nestled up to him and he led her to a sunny spot. "We can sit and talk here," he suggested and moved a few stones out of the way with the tip of his boot. "We've been living under the same roof for half a year now, but we have many years to catch up on, *n'est-ce pas*?"

They sat down on the warm, dry ground. He had retrieved two oranges from his saddlebag; now he peeled them and handed her one. "Are you happy at Qasr el Bahia, or are you homesick for Mogador?"

Emily's first—and longing—thought was of Sabri. Her second—and sorrowful—was of her mother. She furrowed her brow, just the way Sibylla always did. "No, I'm not homesick. I would like to stay with you for a while longer."

"I'm happy to hear that. Of course, you can stay as long as you like." He took a segment of orange and chewed it.

Emily leaned her head back and watched a pair of falcons circling high above them in the sky. Did Sabri think of her? Did he miss her? It had been so long since they had last seen each other that their encounter seemed like a dream. She stifled a sigh. There was a sharp-edged rock lying on the ground not far from her. She used it to scratch an image of the falcon pair in the dirt with just a few strokes. Next, she sketched the horses standing calmly under the jujube tree, chasing away flies with their tails. And finally, as though her hand had a mind of its own, Sabri's eyes appeared in the dust, looking just the way they had that day at the *maristan*: warm and loving.

"Who is that?" André leaned forward and looked at the sketch with interest.

"Nobody." She hastily wiped away the image with her hand.

"Is that the young man you're in love with? Does your mother know about him?"

She hesitated and then shook her head. "Father, please don't be angry, but I'd prefer not to talk about it."

"You've done a lot of painting since you came here. I'm very pleased that there are now such beautiful pictures of Qasr el Bahia. They will tell our story even after you and I are long gone. That's why it would be a great shame if you gave up your chance to study at the Royal Academy of Arts. Just think how few women are considered good enough to study at this renowned academy."

Emily did not answer but scribbled a wavy line on the ground.

André continued, "I myself have certainly not seen much art or many famous paintings, but I know you well enough to see that you're not happy unless you can paint or draw."

She pouted. "Are you chastising me, Father?"

He laughed. "A bit. I just wish for you not to waste such talent."

"I was looking forward to London," Emily admitted hesitantly. "Not just the academy but meeting the rest of my family. My brothers and Victoria have told me so much—I think life there must be quite different. But I'm not allowed to travel alone like John or Thomas. Mother would accompany me and that—"

"I too insist that a young lady not travel alone from one continent to another. So, you see, you will have no alternative but to reconcile with your mother. Why don't you let me take a letter to her the next time I go to Mogador?" He winked encouragingly, but she dropped her gaze and said nothing.

"Emily, are you determined to be upset with your mother forever?" he asked her gently. "She asked about you when I was in Mogador. She misses you."

"I miss her too," she admitted reluctantly. "I don't want to be angry with Mother forever. But if it hadn't been for Victoria, she would have kept the truth from me until this day. She has lied to me and to you, and has kept us from each other for so many years!"

"That's not entirely true. I saw you whenever I was in Mogador. And on your birthdays, I brought you presents."

"That's not the same," Emily replied stubbornly and regarded him warily from the side.

He lifted his hands in jest as though she were pointing a weapon at him, and they both had to laugh.

"I understand that you need some more time to forgive your mother," he said finally. "She lied to you. But you should never forget that she had no choice. What would you have done in her place?"

"I don't know," Emily muttered.

André put his arm around her. "Understanding is at least a good beginning."

She squeezed him. "Father?"

"Yes?"

"Did you love Mother?"

He cleared his throat. "Yes, I did."

Emily thought of Aynur, and of her sister, Malika, who was a mere six weeks younger than she.

"Then why did you . . . ?"

Her father's face went blank, his eyes staring back into a time she did not know. She regretted having brought up the past.

"Please don't be upset, Father. It's none of my business."

Chapter Twenty-Seven

Mogador, October 1861

Firyal was dreaming that she was eating couscous. She had almost finished, but she was still hungry, so she scraped the bottom of the bowl impatiently with her spoon until the noise awakened her.

It took her a few seconds to realize she'd been dreaming. Then she became aware that the scraping sound had not stopped. She sat up in bed and listened. It was coming from the inner courtyard. She carefully slipped out of bed, tiptoed to the door, and peered around the door she always left ajar to let fresh air in.

The moon was high, full and round, and its silvery light illuminated the courtyard, the leaves on the olive tree, the swing hanging immobile from the sturdy branch, and the bronze hinges on the sundial that had been her master's pride and joy. Directly in front of the foundation that the master had built, not ten yards away from Firyal, she saw something that made her hair stand on end.

A black shadow was crouched on the ground. At first it was perfectly still, then it suddenly teetered back and forth, up and down, before sinking onto the ground. All the while it whimpered so ghoulishly that Firyal's heart almost stopped.

"A *djinn*!" she screamed. "A demon! God help this house!"

The shadow spun around and stared in Firyal's direction. She slammed the door shut, locked it, and went to take refuge in bed. But she stumbled over a stool and cut open both knees. When she at last made it to her bed, she wrapped herself in the blanket, clutched the amulet she wore around her neck, and began to recite the Koran in a quivering voice: "There is no true god but God! The Ever-Living, the Eternal Master of all. Neither drowsiness nor sleep overtakes Him. His is all that is in the heavens and all that is on earth—"

There was rumbling, crashing, and noise throughout the house, and she again screamed in fear. The doors on the second floor, where the masters lived, were flung open, and footsteps echoed. Then Firyal heard her mistress's voice.

"Thanks be to God! We're saved!" she whispered and broke into tears.

"An evil spirit? Nonsense! There are neither good nor evil spirits!" John stood in front of Firyal's room shaking his head. His hair rumpled, barefoot, and wearing a long white nightshirt, he almost looked like a ghost himself. Victoria stood behind him looking over his shoulder. She was holding a flickering lamp. Her long hair had come out from under her nightcap. Her eyes wide with fright, she watched Sibylla and Nadira as they sat next to Firyal on her bed and tried to calm her. The servant was sobbing loudly and, upstairs, Charlotte and Selwyn had awakened and were howling just as piercingly.

"I'm going to look after them," Victoria said, and disappeared.

"Can you show me where you saw the ghost?" Sibylla asked Firyal. The servant only looked at her in horror and shook her head.

Sibylla placed her hand on her arm. "Have no fear. We're here with you. No one is going to hurt you."

"Yes, my lady." Firyal rose and went to the door of her chamber. "There," she said, pointing to the sundial. "That's where he was."

Sibylla stared at her. "Are you sure?"

"Yes, my lady." Firyal nodded emphatically. "Over there by the sundial is where the demon was and where he performed his horrific dance."

Sibylla stepped outside and squinted into the darkness. At first glance, the place looked the same as always. What if Firyal had just had a bad dream?

At that moment, the gatekeeper came around the corner, followed closely by the cook. "My lady, master, there was a burglar in the house. Someone broke in through the kitchen door. I found this on the floor." Hamid showed Sibylla and John a crowbar.

"So it was a burglar, and he used this to break open the door!" John took the crowbar and turned it over in his hands. "Damn it all, what good are you?" he shouted at Hamid.

"Hamid's chamber is on the other side of the house, next to the front door. He couldn't have heard the burglar any more easily than we," Sibylla said. "The burglar probably fled when Firyal screamed." She was trying her best to appear calm, but she was deeply troubled by the incident. Nocturnal burglaries were infrequent in Mogador because the city gates were firmly bolted and carefully watched—although, she supposed, a determined burglar could easily slit the throats of the watchmen. "Don't you find it strange that he went to the courtyard?" she asked her son. "Why didn't he go after the valuables in the rooms?"

"That's a good point," John answered. "I'm going to look through everything with Hamid. Perhaps something is missing. I'll send Victoria down with the children. It's safer if you all stay together. You'll be responsible for the women and children." He pointed to the cook.

Sibylla went over to the sundial and looked at the ground with a furrowed brow. There was no doubt. Someone had begun to uncover parts of the foundation. But why? Something flashed in the moonlight. She kneeled down and discovered a small shovel that the intruder had left behind. As she looked at it, she realized that the intruder had been looking for something specific and had known exactly where to find it. She had the feeling of an icy hand brushing against her back, of falling into a bottomless abyss.

This cannot be, she thought. *I'm the only one who knows what was buried here, and I have not told a soul. The person who buried the gold, the only other person aside from me who knows about it, is dead!*

But the uprooted soil and forgotten shovel said otherwise. Sibylla scanned the garden, squinting into dark corners, up the wall to the flat roof, while a voice inside her insisted, *How can you be so sure that Benjamin is dead? Did you see his body? Did you bury him?*

She looked over at the small group of frightened people in front of Firyal's chamber. She cared about these people. They were her family and she wanted to protect them from this unidentified danger that had crept into her house.

Be sensible, she told herself. *Stay calm! You saw with your own eyes that the fortress on the Island of Mogador burned down to the foundation walls after the bombardment. No one could have survived such an inferno.*

She pensively stroked the cold, shiny blade of the shovel with her finger. Who had trespassed into her home? Who, except she and Benjamin, knew about the slave gold?

Mogador, November 1861

Sibylla watched as the pale veils of steam gathered under the blue, white, and green tiles of the dome and floated away through the vents in the walls. It was an honor to bathe with the wives of Qaid Samir el Tawfiq in their *hamam*. She enjoyed the scent of frankincense, cloves, and sandalwood wafting from the coal pans, the warmth of the heated marble bench on which she sat, the women's voices that rippled like a soft melody through the room, and the muffled clatter of their clogs on the stone floor. Not far from her, there were three young concubines splashing in a large, round water basin, naked as the day they were born. Despite their nakedness, all the women here moved about without any shame, and they all looked beautiful in their own way. It did not matter if they were young and slender like gazelles, or whether their bodies showed the signs of age or numerous pregnancies, whether their breasts were like round little apples or like big, heavy pears. Only the slaves, who tended to, washed, and cared for their mistresses, were wrapped in thin cotton robes.

One of them sat behind Sibylla and massaged a paste made of salt and fragrant honey into her back.

"Ouch, that hurts!" she complained.

"Pardon me, *Sayyida*, but your back is harder than the bench I'm sitting on. You have too many worries," the slave explained as she kneaded Sibylla's muscles with expert hands.

"That may well be," she mumbled, thinking about the mysterious break-in three weeks earlier. She and John had made inquiries, but to no avail, and the uncertainty was weighing on her.

"Just let her do her job, Mrs. Hopkins," Lalla Jasira, sitting on an adjacent bench, interjected. "She will help you feel better. After all, a visit to the *hamam* should enhance not just one's beauty but one's health as well."

"I don't know how I ever lived without this pleasure," Sibylla agreed. "It is like heaven on earth."

"And the perfect way to end a successful business transaction, don't you think?" Lalla Jasira added with satisfaction.

She had sold Sibylla a consignment of silk pillowcases for a very nice commission. Her nephew Sultan Sidi Mohammed's three hundred wives had embroidered them with pearls and gold cords using ancient techniques.

Sibylla had been delighted when Lalla Jasira had shown her the samples. She was sure to get an excellent price for this charming work.

More than a public bath for women, the harem *hamam* represented a world of seclusion. The only way a little bit of light could enter was through the solitary window in the dome. Sibylla, Lalla Jasira, and all the concubines and wives, small children, and slaves melted like shadows in the warm, foggy steam.

The slave standing behind Lalla Jasira was holding a thin loop of thread she used to swiftly pluck her mistress's eyebrows into gently curved wings. Meanwhile, the slave tending to Sibylla had filled a wooden bucket with warm water, and began to rinse her back in gentle, even motions.

Sibylla looked up when a eunuch opened the door leading to the antechamber of the *hamam*, where the women undressed. Wahida came in with a very young, strikingly beautiful woman. As soon as she clapped her hands, two slaves rushed over to her.

"Here, cleanse and wash this kitten from top to bottom and in all orifices. I want my son to discover a fragrant flower in his bed!" Her shy young companion cast her eyes down as Wahida pushed her forward.

Wahida had been emancipated ever since the death of Qaid Hash-Hash and, as the mother of the reigning governor, was the highest-ranking woman in his harem. She took her role very seriously and controlled not only her son's love life but also his wives and concubines.

"We have heard you and will obey, Umm Walad." The slaves took the young woman to lie upon a large oven, the top of which was covered in smooth marble and overlain with sparkling quartz stones. They got out a bowl with fragrant lather and sponges made of palm fibers and began lathering the concubine from top to bottom.

"That's Bahar, our lord's new favorite," Lalla Jasira informed Sibylla in a low voice. "For three weeks, he has wanted only her in his bed. That worries some of the others, especially Sukalina, the mother of Rami, his favorite son." She sighed. "I thank God that those days are behind me. It was stressful, having to contend for the lord's favor all the time. And I don't envy Wahida for being in charge of the harem. I appreciate my peace, my poetry collection, and my business. Oh, here comes Sukalina with little Rami. Just look at her face, how she resents Wahida devoting her attention to the new favorite and no longer to her!"

Sukalina strode into the room like a queen, followed by her entourage of slaves and allies. Her jewel-studded clogs clacked provocatively. Throwing an angry look at Bahar, she slid her sublime body on the warm oven top and snapped her fingers. A slave rushed to her side.

"Where is the soap?" Sukalina hissed. "Why do I have to wait?"

The slave stammered an excuse and scurried away. Sukalina's son, three-year-old Rami, toddled up to Wahida with a happy squeal. She bowed down to him and smiled. "Hello, my little prince, have you come to see your grandmother?"

"Rami, come here!" Sukalina commanded from the other side of the oven.

"That sounds very familiar," Sibylla muttered. "Wahida has my deepest sympathy."

A slave came over with a tray full of colorful glasses containing an ice-cold delicacy called sorbet, a mixture of pureed fruit and crushed ice. Lalla took two glasses from the tray and handed one to Sibylla. "What aggrieves you, my honorable friend? Certainly not the conclusion of our business, I trust?" she inquired with a smile.

"Oh, goodness, no. Please don't worry." Sibylla gloomily poked at her sorbet. She had been thinking of Emily again. She missed her terribly. It was almost a year since they'd seen each other. Was she well? Did she miss her mother sometimes? And most of all: When was she coming home?

"Lalla Jasira." Sibylla turned to the other woman. "May I ask you a question?"

"But of course." Lalla Jasira signaled the two slaves, who had begun combing their hair, to leave them alone. "Now we are undisturbed, my friend."

Sibylla took a deep breath, struggling to find the words. "Am I a woman who cannot forgive?"

Lalla Jasira pensively ran her fingers through her long silver hair. "I am not in a position to judge that. What I do know is that we are all capable of change—perhaps from a person who does not forgive to one who does."

"But are there certain things that are too grave to be forgiven?" Sibylla probed.

Lalla Jasira looked at her with her dark, kind eyes. "Only God can decide how grave a transgression is. Only He knows the innermost nature of all human beings and their deeds." She tapped her pearl-studded wooden clogs. "I can sense that your heart is weeping, honorable friend. If you will allow me, I will tell you a story about forgiveness."

"Ouch! By all the saints!" Bahar's scream shattered the air. Qaid Samir's favorite concubine was completely washed and rinsed and lying on a silk rug. A slave had spread a paste of sugar and lemon juice all around her genitalia. Once it had dried, the slave pulled off the crust together with the undesirable pubic hair.

Sibylla could sympathize. She remembered all too well the burning pain of her first hair removal. Back then, she had been in Morocco only a short time and had had no idea of what went on in a *hamam*. She had been horrified when the *hamam* worker had busied herself with her most intimate body parts—a ritual that she now would not do without.

"Now, now!" Wahida calmed the young concubine. "You must be able to suffer a little pain. After all, you don't want to go before your lord like a hairy bear!" She sat next to Bahar and sniffed at the different perfume bottles being offered on a silver tray. "Musk," she decided. "We'll take musk for Bahar. My son is like the Prophet: he loves prayer, women, and fragrance."

Sibylla turned to Lalla Jasira again. "I would very much like to hear your story, Princess. Please tell it!"

Lalla Jasira placed her sorbet glass next to her on the marble bench. "Many years ago, two young women lived in the harem of a powerful man. One was a noblewoman from the ruler's house, raised in luxury and wealth and destined to become the man's chief wife. The other was a poor slave, kidnapped and forced to leave behind her family and her faith. Both women were beautiful and both were determined to win their master's favor. Initially, the man was just. He divided his attention between them and summoned them to his bed an equal number of times. Before long, the slave became pregnant. The man was overjoyed. Over the years, she bore him more sons and daughters and he loved her more for each child she gave him.

"But the chief wife's womb remained empty. She sought the advice of doctors, sages, and witches, made pilgrimages—all to no avail. She became sad and embittered. The angrier she became, the less frequently the lord summoned her, until, at last, he ignored her altogether. In her sorrow, she became angry with God for trying her so severely, and slowly her bitterness turned to hatred. Hatred against herself, her husband, and against the slave who had risen to become the lord's favorite wife and who had everything she herself desired.

"When she had lost all self-respect, God took pity on her. He came to her in a dream and said, 'If too much pressure is exerted on you, you become hard like dry wood that splinters and breaks. Be like a reed that gently sways in the wind and you will regain your happiness. Follow my example, for I, the Eternal One, am also forgiveness and reconciliation.'"

Lalla Jasira fell silent and her gaze was lost in the bath's twilight. Sibylla looked over to the two slaves who had begun making up Bahar's eyes with crushed green malachite and black kohl. Sukalina sat glowering on the opposite side of the *hamam*, smoking a water pipe.

Sibylla thought about Emily and André, about Victoria and Sara Willshire. The number of people she resented had grown over the years. And for the first time, she began to consider the possibility that there were, likewise, a good many people whose forgiveness she needed. She sighed. "Thank you for telling me this wonderful story. It's quite complicated, isn't it?"

Lalla Jasira looked at her in surprise. "Did not your prophet Isa ibn Maryam, whom you call Jesus Christ, also preach love and forgiveness? I want to tell you how the story continues after the powerful man's chief wife accepted that it was her fate never to bear children. She forgave herself and thus found peace. And in doing so, she regained the respect of the women in the harem as well as that of her lord. He did not take her to his bedchamber very often, but he valued her wisdom and her kind heart more than he had ever valued her body, and he sought her advice more and more frequently."

"And that is the end?"

Lalla Jasira gave her a dreamy little smile. "The story of love and forgiveness never ends, does it, my honorable friend?"

"Good evening, Mother. Do forgive me for making you wait. I simply had so much to do. It wasn't until Aladdin reminded me that I remembered my promise to pick you up." John leaned forward to kiss Sibylla on the cheek.

"Not at all, darling. I had a wonderful afternoon." She returned her son's kiss.

He offered his mother his arm. As they walked through the dark alleyways, he told her about his day, of the two ships of theirs that had left the harbor. He also told her that he had spoken with several more people about the break-in, among them the harbormaster and Consul Willshire. But all claimed not to have noticed a thing amiss. There had been no other break-ins in the foreigners' quarter. Whoever the intruder was, he seemed to have vanished from the face of the earth.

"A very troubling notion." Sibylla thought about the scattered dirt around the foundation of the sundial.

"Isn't it, though? If he hadn't left traces in our garden, one might think we'd imagined it all."

"I wish we had," she sighed.

"My lady! You're back at last!" Hamid said, relief all over his face.

"Why? Has something happened?" Sibylla asked anxiously. "Another break-in?"

"No, my lady, no break-in, but—"

"My lady!" Nadira called. "Thank goodness you're back!"

"What's happened?" Sibylla scrutinized both of her servants.

Nadira took her coat. "You have a visitor from Qasr el Bahia. He is waiting in the drawing room."

"I hope nothing has happened to Emily!" Sibylla took off running, followed by John. When she pushed open the door to the drawing room, the guest hastily rose from the divan and bowed awkwardly. Sibylla stopped dead on the threshold. "André?"

After a few confusing seconds, she realized that, although the young man looked like André, he did not look like the André she knew, but André as he must have looked as a very young man.

"Mrs. Hopkins?" The stranger looked at her uncertainly. "My name is Frédéric Rouston. Emily has sent me. She said that you would help us. Qasr el Bahia was attacked this morning!"

"Good Lord!" Sibylla felt her knees giving way. She felt John's hand supporting her back and heard his voice as if from a distance. "I am Emily's brother John. Please take a seat, Frédéric."

Frédéric Rouston collapsed onto the divan and ran his fingers through his tousled black hair.

"Bring something to eat and drink for our guest," Sibylla ordered Nadira, who was waiting by the door. When the servant returned with a tray, Frédéric reached for the water jug, poured himself a goblet, and drank greedily. "Please excuse me!" he said and wiped his mouth with the back of his hand. "I've been riding nonstop since morning."

Sibylla looked at him anew and took in the man's exhaustion, his filthy, scraped-up hands, the crusted blood. "I am grateful that you found your way to us. Once you have eaten something, you will tell us what happened on the estate."

Frédéric devoured the couscous, meat, and bread Nadira had brought. He washed it all down with two more goblets of water. Then he began gloomily, "It was terrible, it was just a stroke of good luck that they didn't murder us all . . ."

Chapter Twenty-Eight

Qasr el Bahia, the same morning

The first blue-gray light of day was shimmering across the peaks of the High Atlas when André stood in front of the big cedar in the middle of the courtyard and clapped his hands. "Today we are going to break our backs for the last time this season, and tomorrow we are going to celebrate the best saffron harvest in years!"

"Ay! So be it!" The sixty Ait Zelten men, women, and children sitting on rugs laughed and clapped in agreement. They had been camping in the courtyard in their *khaimas*, tents made of goat's hair. They had just eaten breakfast with André and his family, as they did every day, and now it was time to go out into the fields. Even old Tamra was present. Frédéric and Christian had carried her in her armchair to a spot under the cedar tree, where Aynur had draped a woolen blanket over her to protect her from the cool morning air.

"I'll take the teapots to the kitchen!" André Jr. eagerly ran over to the large fire pit in the middle of the camp, where several large brass pots were resting on the warm stones.

"I suppose I'll start breaking my back as well, then." Malika began stacking the empty couscous bowls. "What do we have here?" She held up one hand. A brown, spotted insect with long legs, round black eyes, and spiderweb-like wings was dangling between her forefinger and thumb.

"A locust! Eeeh!" Emily, who had been collecting the baskets with the remnants of flatbread, grimaced.

"What are you saying?" André crossed to Malika and looked at the insect for himself.

"Ugh! One has landed on my shoulder!" Emily shook herself. The locust fell to the ground and she stomped on it with her boot.

André stared at the dead insect for a few seconds and then looked out at the horizon. A rosy golden light above the High Atlas announced the sunrise. However, a thin dark-gray streak hung between the mountain peaks.

He strained his eyes, but could not make it out.

"Is everything all right?" Aynur looked at him quizzically.

"I'm not sure." He showed her the locust.

Aynur's eyes grew large. "The wind's teeth, a bad omen." She beat her breast with her fist. "On the day when the caller calls for evil occurrences, they will come from their graves. May God help us!"

"Stop that! Are you trying to frighten everyone?" André took hold of her. "We'd better see to it that the rest of the saffron is harvested as quickly as possible."

"Frédéric!" He motioned to his eldest son. "Go open the gate with Christian. And then everybody off to the fields!"

He threw the locust to the ground and trod on it the way Emily had. "Don't worry," he reassured Aynur, who was watching wide-eyed. "You're too superstitious, that's all." He put his arm around her. "Let's go and see if the saffron we plucked yesterday has dried already."

They went off to the barn where the saffron from the day before was being stored, untold numbers of tiny thin threads glowing orange in the light of the oil lamp.

He placed the lamp on the floor, leaned over the saffron, and inhaled that strong, aromatic scent of sun and earth. Gently, as though caressing a woman, he lifted a few of the thin threads, crushed them between his fingertips, and tasted them. The saffron tasted slightly bitter, slightly sweet, slightly like the pungent smoke of a wood fire.

"Wonderful!" he said with satisfaction. "I can't wait for your roasted beef marrow bones with saffron gravy!"

"Then we can put the other threads together with the rest of the harvest in the tower?" Aynur asked eagerly.

"Yes. I'm riding to Mogador next week and I shall get a wonderful price for our red gold." Out of sheer joy over the exceptionally good harvest, he grasped Aynur's waist, lifted her up, and spun around with her. "What shall I bring from town for you? Indian silk for a new dress? Or a nice piece of jewelry?"

"Can I have both?" She smiled mischievously.

He set her down. "Anything you want. I know well that Qasr el Bahia would not be what it is today if it weren't for you. Day in, day out, you see to it that everything gets taken care of."

She smiled and felt flattered, but she knew that his praise was justified. Every morning, she went out to the terraced fields with the Ait Zelten and painstakingly picked thousands of lilac crocus blossoms until her back was so bent that she could hardly stand. Still, the harvest had to go quickly. For once the sun had risen over the fields and the blossoms opened up in its warmth, the hidden threads lost their precious aroma.

The most pleasant part of the harvest would begin later. They would all sit in the courtyard together, singing songs and telling stories while they deftly plucked the tender threads out of the blossoms. The children would mill around and pick up the empty blossoms to feed to the cows and goats later on. Aynur would see to it that there was an ample supply of fresh, sweet peppermint tea available and would watch with great vigilance to ensure that not a single one of the precious pistils surreptitiously disappeared in the women's wide skirts.

"Here." André handed her a linen sack.

She filled it with saffron from the rack and tied it carefully. "I shall accompany you to Mogador this year."

He stared at her incredulously. "You have never wished to come before!"

"Well, I've changed my mind. I would like to choose my own silk and jewelry. We could also visit Emily's mother together. We are all family, after all." Aynur sounded a little unsure.

André was delighted. "What a wonderful idea. For that, you'll get another present!" He had been wondering for a long time how he could bring Emily's family and his together.

"I'll hold you to that!" She disappeared from the barn swinging her hips.

"Baba! Help! Ahhh!" The rest of the scream was drowned out by a desperate cry of pain.

"By God! Away with you, rogues!" André heard Aynur call out.

Screams and the clatter of galloping horses drowned out everything else. André grabbed a shovel. The sack of saffron lay in front of the barn door where Aynur had dropped it. Before he knew it, André was pushed aside by one of the onrushing riders. He stumbled and fell and, as he scrambled to his feet, he saw the rider lean down and snatch the sack.

"Villain!" André yelled. Then he saw the other riders rushing through the half-open gate. He guessed there were ten, maybe twelve. He recognized the leader immediately by his port-wine stain.

He ran toward him angrily, holding the shovel. "Damn it! What do you want now? Can't you leave us in peace?"

There was pandemonium in the courtyard. The Berbers guided their horses ably through the narrow spaces and ruthlessly rode over anyone who did not jump out of the way in time. The men bellowed, the women screeched, children bawled, cries of fear mingled with cries of pain, and panic-stricken people ran into each other.

"Christian! Watch out!" André watched in horror as his son stumbled and fell. But Frédéric pulled him out of the way of the horses' hooves.

"To the tower! Quickly!" André bellowed against the din and gesticulated with his shovel. Frédéric seized his younger brother by the arm, raced with him to the donjon, and pushed him up the ladder ahead of himself.

André frantically looked around. Where were his other children, where was Aynur? He tried in vain to find the rest of his family amid the people, horses, tents, gunshots, and screams. Then he saw Emily and Malika. They were standing as though paralyzed by the entrance to the kitchen.

"Come on!" André screamed frenetically.

But they were much too far to hear him.

"Imma! Imma!" André Jr. had spotted his mother in the chaos and was trying to squeeze past his sisters. Fortunately, Emily and Malika grabbed the little boy's shirt just in time, dragged him into the house, and slammed the door shut.

André had also spotted Aynur. Tamra had been pushed from her armchair and was lying helplessly on the ground. The two riders, coming from behind at full tilt, did not notice Aynur trying to help the old woman.

"Over there! That's the little one! She's the one I want for myself!" yelled the first of the two men. "And afterward—" He made a jagged motion in front of his throat. "Then we'll collect our reward!" He laughed as he jabbed his heels into his horse's flanks.

"Wait!" the second one replied. "That's the wrong one! We're supposed to kill the merchant woman's brat!"

"Who cares? Everyone on this accursed estate is a traitor!" His companion aimed his gun.

André let loose an earsplitting scream and threw himself forward with desperate courage. His concern for Aynur lent him tremendous speed, and he succeeded in cutting off the first of the two riders.

At that moment, a gun rang out next to him. Aynur screamed and slumped down on Tamra's body.

"No!" André bellowed. He swung his shovel high in the air and hit the rider who had fired the shot. There was a crunching sound. The attacker dropped his gun, his neck snapped to the side. As the man plunged off his horse, André noticed his expression of surprise, frozen in death.

A loud howl erupted next to him. "You will pay for that, infidel!"

André spun around and dodged the hooves of a rearing horse. The hideous face of the rider was distorted with bloodlust, but the jagged port-wine stain across his face was still clear.

André felt a hatred the likes of which he had never before experienced in his life. He was going to kill that man if it was the last thing he did! He swung the shovel again, but the younger man was quicker and pushed his horse against him. André stumbled and lost his shovel. He pulled out his knife, but before he knew it, a rifle butt came crashing down. Tremendous pain flashed through his skull. He covered his head with his hands and swayed. Above him, he could see the leader's face, his triumphant grimace. There was a growing buzzing in his ears and, above him, a shimmering, dancing cloud rose over the walls of Qasr el Bahia and darkened the sky.

Locusts, that's all we need, he thought before falling into a fathomless darkness.

Tears ran down Frédéric's face. "The teeth of the wind did destroy part of our harvest, but they also saved us. If God had not sent them at that moment, we would all be dead." He reached for his goblet and gulped some water. Sibylla refilled it with trembling hands.

Finally, John cleared his throat and asked, "What do you mean by the 'teeth of the wind'?"

"Locusts," explained Frédéric. His eyes lost focus as he relived the events of the terrible day. "The largest swarm I have ever seen. They came across the mountains like a storm cloud and blocked out the sun. More of them fell from the sky than there are grains of sand in the desert. And the noise! Crows and ravens diving at the insects and all the people screaming. Christian and I were safe in the donjon, but in the courtyard, people were running for their lives. But when the locusts came, the attackers' horses took fright and they had to flee. It was a miracle! As soon as the attackers were gone, I climbed out of the tower and barricaded the gate. And then I saw my parents—" Frédéric's voice broke. "I'm not even sure they're still alive. My father was unconscious when I left. He had a terrible head wound and my mother had been shot. Tamra is dead for certain, killed by a bullet. I must go back! Who knows how my brothers and sisters are, all alone like that." Frédéric pressed himself up from the divan although he was unsteady on his feet from exhaustion.

Sibylla rose. "That's not a good idea, Frédéric. You were very brave today, a hero. But now you must rest. Nadira has prepared a room for you."

He was about to protest when she placed her hand on his shoulder. "If I could, I would go immediately myself. But we'll be of no use to anyone if we fall off our horses in the dark. I am certain that Emily and Malika have bolted the gate well after your departure. For tonight, the people inside the walls of the estate are safe. And tomorrow morning we shall ride to Qasr el Bahia together."

"I'm going to pack my things," Sibylla announced after Frédéric had reluctantly withdrawn to the room that had been made ready for him. "We should also alert Thomas, as there are wounded on the estate. We may be gone for quite a while, so I'm afraid you will have to handle all the business for me in the meantime, John."

"Of course. Think nothing of it," he assured her. "But under no circumstances can you ride to Qasr el Bahia alone. I'm convinced that those villains are lurking near the estate. I'll ask the *qaid* to provide an escort." He hastened to his study and returned a short while later with a sealed envelope. By then, Sibylla had fetched Hamid.

"And as soon as you have a reply from the *qaid*, go to the doctor's house and tell him to come here!" John directed the man, who nodded earnestly.

"I'm so glad that you are here," Sibylla confessed with relief. "There is so much going on, I can hardly think clearly."

"Anything you need, Mother," John said as he embraced her.

The door to the drawing room opened and Victoria entered carrying a tea tray. "Nadira told me what happened. I hope Emily is all right," she said as she poured.

"A cup of tea is exactly what I need right now." Sibylla gave her daughter-in-law a look of gratitude and Victoria blushed.

She poured John a cup as well. Then she sat down on the divan and looked from one to the other. "I hope no one's been seriously hurt."

John stirred his tea. "That's what we're all hoping."

Half an hour later, Hamid returned with the message that the *qaid* would have an armed escort waiting in front of the city wall shortly before sunrise.

With the gatekeeper came not only Thomas but also Sabri. Both physicians inquired immediately about the number of wounded and what types of injuries had been sustained, but neither Sibylla nor John could tell them.

"I'll return to the *maristan*," said Sabri, "and load a mule with medicine, bandages, and surgical instruments. That way you can stay with your family, Thomas. We'll all meet by the city gate in the morning."

"You wish to accompany us?" Sibylla asked.

"Of course," Sabri answered, tormented with worry about Emily. "We have no idea what to expect. One doctor may not be enough."

Early the following evening, Sibylla, Frédéric, Thomas, and Sabri, together with the *qaid's* six armed cavalrymen, arrived at the gates of Qasr el Bahia. Anxiety had hastened their journey. They had stayed in the saddle all day and paused only to let the horses have a drink of water. Both humans and animals were utterly exhausted.

The closer the group got to its destination, the lower morale sank. Thomas and Sabri conferred softly about what sort of medical emergencies they might have to deal with. Frédéric's expression was gloomy. Sibylla's thoughts were with Emily and André. Still, she noticed how desolate the countryside they were traveling through looked. Swarms of crows and ravens were circling in the sky and devouring the locusts as though they were at a banquet. Sibylla had never seen so many insects and could not help but shudder at the sight. They were on the ground, in the shrubs and trees, buzzing through the air in swarms, and falling into her hair, into the folds of her clothing, and onto her increasingly unsettled horse. Two shepherds they met told them that this was merely a remnant of the huge swarm now on its way to the ocean, darkening the sky along its way. The bare landscape suggested an infestation of biblical proportions. The trees and shrubs were bare and leafless and there was not a single leaf of grass for the horses to eat. Fortunately, John had insisted on packing fodder for them.

Qasr el Bahia looked forbidding in the evening light. No torches burned in either of the two donjons or in the iron brackets framing the gate. Everything seemed eerily still, almost uninhabited.

Frédéric jumped off his horse and pounded on the gate with both fists. "It's me! Open up! I've brought help! Can you hear me? Open up!"

Sibylla's heart was racing. What would they find inside? Had Emily really not been hurt? And what about André? She could not bear to think about the possibility that she had come too late and he had died of his wounds.

Creaking and scraping sounds came from the other side. A bolt was moved aside, a chain was loosened, and finally, the gate was opened just enough to allow one rider at a time to pass through. Once the last of the riders had entered, the slender adolescent bolted and barricaded the gate again.

"Frédéric! I'm so glad you're back!" The boy scrutinized the newcomers cautiously.

Frédéric embraced him. "Christian! Did you take good care of everyone? How are Baba and Imma?"

"Not well." Christian shook his head despondently.

"Where are the injured?" Thomas inquired. Sabri had already begun to unload the mule. Some farmhands came to take care of the horses.

Sibylla slid out of her saddle and looked around. Low tents were ringed around a flickering fire in the middle of the courtyard. Men were sitting together in small groups and talking quietly while smoking a water pipe. A servant distributed bowls with food and tea. Women were taking care of the younger children. Sibylla looked around for Emily, but could not find her anywhere. People came to greet the new arrivals. Some were limping, some had their arms in a sling, some using branches as crutches. An old man with a dirty bandage wrapped around his head said to Sibylla in despair, "How could our own flesh and blood abuse us in this way?"

"Mummy!" Emily came running out of the house and threw herself into her mother's arms. "Finally, Mummy! I've been waiting for you!"

Tears streamed down Sibylla's face. Emily had been a little girl the last time she had called her that.

"Promise me that we will never again let a whole year pass without speaking!" Sibylla implored her and stroked her daughter's hair.

"Never again, Mummy!" Emily promised.

"Little sister, I'm so glad that you're all right!" Thomas also embraced Emily.

Then came Sabri.

"I thank God that nothing has happened to you," he said quietly and squeezed her hand.

"I've been told there are two dead. Is that right?" Thomas asked.

Emily nodded. "One of the attackers. Frédéric and Christian saw Father strike him with a shovel after he shot at Aynur. And Aynur's servant, Tamra. The bullet that grazed Aynur struck Tamra in the heart."

"Where were you during the raid, Miss Emily?" Sabri asked.

"I hid in the house with Malika and my youngest brother."

"Good," Sabri replied. Their eyes locked for several seconds.

Then Sibylla asked, "How is André?"

"Father is still unconscious. I'm very worried."

Sabri took charge. "Thomas, I suggest you go inside and treat Monsieur Rouston and his wife. I'll take care of the injured out here."

"Good idea. Afterward, I'll come and join you," Thomas agreed. "Emily, can you take me to them?"

"I'll come with you!" Sibylla hastened after them. "To help."

Christian, Emily, and Malika had carried their father into a small room normally used to accommodate passing travelers. He lay motionless on the bed draped in a woolen blanket. The right side of his face was bluish red and severely swollen. He had a gaping wound on his temple, two fingers wide and one finger long. The margins were black with dried blood.

"My God," Sibylla muttered. She leaned forward and placed her hand on the uninjured side of André's forehead. His skin felt cold and waxy.

"If I am to examine him, you'll have to make room, Mother." Thomas sat down on the bed. He palpated André's face while Sibylla watched intently.

"The skull is not broken," Thomas finally determined. He took the oil lamp from the nightstand and held it over André's face. "The wound looks bad, but it's already begun to heal and the bone is intact. I'm going to clean and bandage it. We can treat the swelling with cold compresses. And the rest we shall have to leave to time."

"The rest?" Sibylla probed. "Do you mean if he's going to wake up?"

Thomas gently opened André's eyes with his thumb and forefinger, and examined the pupils under the light. "The loss of consciousness is profound. I'll be able to tell whether he's suffered any brain damage only once he has awakened. I hope that that will happen within the next two days."

"And if not, *Hakim*?" a quiet voice asked. "Does that mean Baba will die?"

A dainty young woman dressed in traditional Berber attire was standing in the doorway. Emily introduced her. Thomas hesitated. Malika was certainly entitled to know her father's likelihood of survival, but at the moment, Thomas himself was uncertain.

Finally, he explained, "The sooner your father regains consciousness, the better his chances of a full recovery. But even if it takes longer, we shan't give up hope!" he added upon seeing Malika's horrified expression. "Your father is a strong man. His chances are good. Would you please take me to your mother now, Mademoiselle Rouston?"

Malika nodded. "She's in the bedroom she shares with Baba."

"Is there anything we can do?" Sibylla asked.

Thomas picked up his doctor's bag from the floor. "Get some hot and some cold water, soap, and clean towels, and bring everything here. I'll be back as soon as I've taken a look at his wife."

"I'll show you where everything is, Mother," Emily spoke up. "And then I'll see if Sabri needs help."

◆ ◆ ◆

The bedroom was empty when Thomas and Malika entered. The rumpled bedclothes indicated that Aynur had lain here, but she had vanished.

"I told her not to get up!" Malika became very agitated. "She has a fever and she's lost a lot of blood."

"Do you have any idea where your mother might be?"

"No doubt she's keeping vigil over Tamra, her servant. Tamra's death has devastated her. Christian and I had to drag her away from the body so that we could tend to her wounds." Malika rushed to lead the way to the adjacent chamber, a small room with a narrow bed against a brown mud wall, a woven rug, and a chest under the small window. A single candle stood on the ledge and its flickering light allowed him to make out the body of a very old woman on the bed and Aynur sitting on a stool next to her. Her back was turned and all Thomas could see was the long dark-blue veil that covered her hair.

"Imma," Malika began, "the *hakim* is here. He wants to treat your wound."

Thomas took a step forward. "Madame Rouston? I'm Dr. John Hopkins from Mogador. I'm told you were shot during the raid. With your permission, I would like to examine your wound."

Aynur turned partway around. "I've been waiting for two days to bury Tamra next to my little daughters. As long as she lies here, waiting for her immortal soul to rise to God, I am not going to leave her side, *Hakim*."

"The cemetery lies outside the walls," Malika quietly explained. "And we're afraid that the attackers are still out there." She turned toward her mother. "I have good news, Imma. Qaid Samir has sent soldiers to protect us. We will bury Tamra first thing in the morning. So, please, allow the *hakim* to examine your wound."

Aynur thought for a moment. Then she rose. "Very well then, *Hakim*. Examine me."

She led Thomas and Malika to her bedchamber and sat down on the edge of the bed. When Thomas examined the wound, he discovered that she had, indeed, only been grazed. Using a pair of tweezers, he debrided the necrotic wound margins and crusted blood, washed the wound with lukewarm water, and dabbed it with a solution of silver salts. Then he took out a small linen sack containing dressing made of small, soft balls of cotton threads, which he placed on the wound and gently pressed down. "This dressing will cushion the injured arm and absorb pus and moisture. As soon as you feel any pain, please let me know, and I'll give you some laudanum," he said to Aynur while he bandaged the arm with a clean linen cloth.

"God helps me to tolerate my wounds," she replied proudly.

Thomas could not help but admire her. In London, he had treated strong workers, seasoned men who toiled on the docks or operated dangerous machinery in factories, but none of them had tolerated pain with the same pride and determination as this small, delicate woman.

"I've got the water, soap, and towels ready for you," Sibylla said from the doorway. In a matter of seconds, she had taken in the furniture, mirrors, and candlesticks, and finally the bed, covered with silk and brocaded pillows. Yet her face did not betray her feelings about being in the very room where the man she loved had spent countless hours with the other woman in his life.

She greeted Aynur calmly and politely. "Good evening, Madame Rouston. I do hope my son is taking good care of you."

"He is an irreproachable *hakim*," Aynur replied with like equanimity.

The two women scrutinized each other for a few seconds. Then Sibylla turned to go. "I wish you a restful night, madame."

Chapter Twenty-Nine

"*Hakim*, please, you must to help! My son, he very hurt!" The Ait Zelten man tugged on the young doctor's sleeve. His Arabic was broken, his voice hoarse with worry.

Sabri looked up from the deep laceration on a woman's calf that he had just sutured with catgut thread and adjusted his glasses. Night had long ago fallen on Qasr el Bahia and it had become noticeably chilly in the courtyard. But Sabri was as unaware of that as he was of his own exhaustion. He worked untiringly, even after Thomas had come outside to assist him. Emily did not leave Sabri's side. She handed him the instruments he needed, fetched fresh water and clean towels, and acted as interpreter for the Ait Zelten.

Many people had sustained their injuries—luckily only minor—in their attempts to flee from the attackers. There were mainly contusions, bumps, cuts, and dislocated joints. People had stood for hours by the large fire Frédéric and Christian had lit in the center of the courtyard, warming themselves by the flames and patiently waiting until they could be seen by either the Arab or the foreign *hakim*.

"What kind of injury does your son have?" Sabri asked while he bandaged the woman's leg, but the man only pointed to the tents and urged repeatedly, "Please come, *Hakim*! There!"

"Would you accompany me, Miss Emily, despite the late hour? I fear I'll be needing your interpreting services."

"Of course."

He picked up his doctor's bag and they followed the man to one of the low tents.

Emily crawled inside behind the man and Sabri. It was warm here; it smelled of people and smoke. A boy aged no more than eight or maybe ten lay next to a small fire. Emily had often seen him in the saffron fields and knew him to be a happy, cheeky rascal. Together with André Jr., he liked teasing the little girls. But at this moment, he was lying under a blanket, his face tearstained, his right arm stretched away from him, whimpering with pain. His mother hovered next to him, stroking his hair. As soon as she saw Sabri, she began a tirade, sounding alternately concerned and angry.

"The boy fell when he was fleeing from the intruders," Emily translated, omitting the countless curses the woman uttered against the attackers. "Since then he hasn't been able to move his hand and his arm is getting more and more swollen."

Sabri smiled at the little boy and kneeled down next to him. But as soon as he tried to touch the arm ever so gently, the boy howled with pain.

"It does seem as though his arm is broken," Sabri said. "It would be good, therefore, if I could really examine him."

I would fight back too, thought Emily, *if there were so many grown-ups around and I were in terrible pain*. "Is there nothing you can give him to calm him down?"

Sabri thought hard. "I have neither ether nor chloroform with me and I don't really have much experience in the dosing of anesthetics."

Suddenly, his face lit up. “But what I could do is give the little one some greatly diluted laudanum to help him sleep through the treatment.”

However, when Sabri approached the boy with the beaker, he pressed his lips together and turned his head to the side.

“Would you let me try?” Emily took the beaker and squatted next to the child on the floor. “Why won’t you let the *hakim* help you?” she asked in Tachelhit. “He can make your pain magically disappear with the drink he has mixed for you.”

“So the *hakim* is an *asahhar*?” the boy wanted to know, half wary, half interested.

“That’s it.” Emily nodded. “He’s a magician.” She slowly extended her hand with the beaker. “All your friends will admire you for being so brave.”

“You were fantastic!” Sabri exclaimed when the boy fell asleep. Emily blushed with happiness and was glad for the dim light.

He turned his attention to the boy and carefully palpated his arm. “It’s a simple fracture of the radius. Quite common in falls like this. I have to set the bone and apply a firm bandage to immobilize it. Would you assist me, please, Miss Emily?”

“What do I need to do?” she replied warily.

“What we have here is two parts of the bone positioned next to each other. Our job is to place them on top of each other so that the pieces of the bone can heal and grow back together at the site of the fracture. To achieve this, I’m going to pull the lower part of the arm. You have to hold on tightly to the upper part. It’s very important that you hold it with all your might in order for the two pieces to fit into each other. Don’t be afraid of hurting the boy. He’s not going to feel a thing.”

“All right,” Emily replied, although she was feeling a bit queasy. But she did exactly as Sabri said and, with a few calm and confident movements, he had the bone set in no time.

“Next I’m going to apply a compression bandage to make sure the bone grows together correctly. Could you go get me some sheets of card paper, as well as a chaff pillow? I'm going to mix the paste in the meantime."

When Emily returned, Sabri had already prepared the sticky mass. Next to him lay several tin cans and linen bandages.

Emily peered into the bowl. "It looks like icing."

"Gum arabic with dextrin, a starch mixture. Please stir it until it's nice and thick while I apply the first bandage." Sabri handed her the wooden spoon.

As she was diligently stirring, she watched as Sabri pushed the chaff pillow under the boy's broken arm. He opened a can containing talcum and spread a thin layer.

"This keeps the skin healthy and prevents itching. While I'm bandaging the arm, you're going to tear the card paper into strips and wet them, but not too much," he instructed. He applied the bandage with a few deft movements, brushed it with the paste, and splinted the arm with the card paper.

All along, the parents had been watching with anxious expressions. The mother unceasingly stroked her sleeping child's tousled black hair.

"Finished," announced Sabri after applying another layer of bandage and card paper. "The whole thing has to dry for one to two days. During this time, the little one must keep his arm still," he explained to the parents while Emily translated. "This way, the bone can heal under its protective armor and, in six weeks, your son's arm is going to be fine again."

"*Rabbi akkisellem!* Thank you very much, Doctor!" The father embraced Sabri joyfully.

"That was the last patient," Sabri said as he and Emily walked in the direction of the house. The Ait Zelten's camp was quiet, the people fast asleep in their tents.

Emily stopped by the smoldering fire in the center of the courtyard. "You are a wonderful doctor, Dr. bin Abdul. People trust you. I would willingly entrust myself to your care if I were ever sick."

She shivered in the cool wind. Sabri put down his bag, took off his jacket, and placed it around her. "Would you also entrust yourself to me if you were not sick?"

"Yes," she whispered.

Sabri caringly smoothed down the jacket over Emily's shoulders. "You were a marvelous assistant, Miss Emily. But now you should lie down and rest." He hesitated, then stroked her cheek.

She leaned against the warm, soft palm. He was right, she was tired. But it was so wonderful to be standing here by the fire with Sabri, so close she could feel his breath on her neck. She could have spent the entire night watching the last little flames dance in his dark eyes.

"Emily," he sighed softly. "How perfectly your name suits you."

They were startled when Malika came running out of the house as though all the mountain demons were after her.

Emily froze in fear. *Father*, she thought.

"Emily!" Malika pressed her sister's hand. "Dr. Hopkins says that Baba is waking up! Dr. bin Abdul, thank goodness you're here. You must come as well."

Three days after the raid on Qasr el Bahia, in the cold, gray light of dawn, Tamra was laid to rest under the broad treetop of the old holly oak in the garden behind the estate. The old woman's body, draped in a linen cloth and borne on a bier by four Berber men, seemed tiny and light as a feather.

It is as though she would rather fly to heaven than be buried in the ground, thought André. He clutched the knob of the walking stick Frédéric had carved for him from the trunk of a young cedar tree. The strong scent of the wood made him feel nauseated despite the ginger-root tea Malika had brewed. In addition, he was afflicted by vertigo and a dreadful headache.

"Typical symptoms of a concussion," Thomas had explained. "They will subside soon. But only if you get sufficient bed rest."

Sibylla's physician son had been categorically opposed to his attending Tamra's funeral, but André knew how deeply his wife mourned the old servant and wanted to be by her side at this difficult hour. Tamra had been a mother to her, unconditionally devoted, had known her better and longer than any other human being.

He reached for Aynur's hand. Her fingers were like ice. She stood motionless next to him, never taking her eyes off Tamra's body as it was lowered into its narrow grave next to her children, Thiyya and Izza.

Frédéric, Christian, and André Jr. stood on Aynur's other side. Malika gently supported André's back. Very slowly, so as not to lose his balance, he turned and looked over at Emily and Sibylla. They hung back next to Thomas and Sabri bin Abdul under the arched adobe gateway leading to the garden. The Ait Zelten were also paying their last respects and had assembled in a silent semicircle around the holly oak.

Before the funeral, their sheikh had paid André a visit. "I am deeply ashamed that men from my tribe have brought death and destruction upon you and yours," he had said and bowed his head as a sign of his shame. "Today, my sons rode off into the mountains. I have ordered them not to return until they have killed every last one of those cowardly jackals!"

Qaid Samir's soldiers had already searched for the attackers without finding even the slightest trace. That did not surprise André. He was familiar with the mountains around Qasr el Bahia and knew there were many inaccessible caverns and hidden gorges. Had he been in better condition, he would have ridden off to confront the gang himself. But, he thought, the sheikh's sons might be able to succeed where Qaid Samir's men had failed.

André was startled when something fell on his left shoulder. A locust. He shrugged off the insect in disgust and stepped on it. The locust plague had prevented the worst from happening, but looking at the damage to his land made him want to weep. The saffron not yet harvested was lost. Blue-green stumps were all that was left of the plants. The pomegranate, orange, and olive trees were bare. The proud holly oak looked as though it had been plucked.

"When the wind blows through the leaves, that means the tree is singing," Aynur had always said of this old oak she loved so much. But now its constant, soft song had been silenced.

Aynur shuddered when some of the men began shoveling dirt on Tamra's body. Her body was racked by shivers. She moaned and began to sway. André thought that she was overcome by grief until he saw her face, covered in sweat.

"You're not well. Why don't you go and lie down again? I'll send Dr. Hopkins to you," he urged her, trying to support her even though he could hardly stand upright himself.

"Leave me be!" She resisted when he put his arm around her waist. "I just have a little headache."

"Baba is right, Imma, you belong in bed!" Malika insisted, but Aynur shook her off too. Only when the Ait Zelten had covered Tamra's body completely did she turn away.

Sibylla had been watching jealously. "I'm a little cold. I think I'll fetch a shawl from the house," she said, hurrying off before Emily or Thomas had a chance to react.

"When will you finally understand that Aynur is the most important woman in his life?" she scolded herself with clenched teeth. She pushed open the door to her bedroom and angrily shooed a cat off the bed. She would return to Mogador first thing tomorrow. And Emily must come with her. She had been at Qasr el Bahia long enough!

Sabri and Thomas also had noticed that Aynur was not well. "I'm concerned about you, Madame Rouston," said Thomas when they reached the arched gate. "I would like to examine you once more."

Aynur did not answer, but leaned against the mud wall, gasping and exhausted. Although she felt cold, sweat was running down her face and body. Her head pounded and she seemed to have lost control over the cramps making her back muscles shudder.

"Madame Rouston? Can you hear me?" Thomas was extremely worried. As André was slowly regaining his vigor, Aynur seemed to be losing hers.

"I just need to rest a little," she replied with a forced smile. "You may examine me again after midday prayers."

"*Hakim*, please, you must examine her now!" Malika whispered to Thomas.

Thomas watched Aynur stumbling toward the house and nodded. "I'll run and fetch my bag."

Sabri frowned. "Do you want me to come along?"

Thomas shook his head. "You go and take care of your patients."

Sibylla found André standing at the edge of his destroyed saffron field. She had been determined to tell him that she was leaving Qasr el Bahia, but seeing him so crestfallen, she did not have the heart.

"I am so very sorry," was all she could say and, after briefly hesitating, she placed her hand on his arm.

He turned his face, swollen and bruised, toward her. Dark stubble grew on his chin and a thick bandage circled his head. "Three days ago, there was a purple carpet of flowers blooming in this field. Now everything is destroyed. The locusts did not spare even one single plant."

"Don't forget that you have brought in most of the harvest already. And soon saffron crocuses will grow again."

"There is no certainty of that." André loosened some of the soil with the tip of his cane and kneeled down with great difficulty. "As I suspected, those pests have laid their eggs here."

He showed Sibylla the palm of his hand. A little perplexed, she peered at the whitish foam swimming among the pieces of dirt.

"Next spring, the larvae will hatch," André explained. "And the whole thing may happen again."

He threw the soil back on the field and struggled to get back to his feet. Sibylla quickly came to his aid.

"Thomas says that you must rest. Please listen to him, André. He is a good doctor."

André looked ruefully over his ruined saffron field. Finally, he sighed. "I must accept my fate. It was only a few plants. My family is alive. If I believed in a god, I would pray every day for Him to punish those criminals with all His wrath!"

Sibylla cleared her throat. "I'll be returning to Mogador tomorrow."

He spun around and tried to suppress a painful groan. His face showed surprise and, much to Sibylla's delight, regret.

"I'm strongly against it," he declared firmly. "As long as the attackers are still at large, the area around Qasr el Bahia is not safe."

"The *qaid*'s soldiers are returning tomorrow and I shall ride with them," she replied. "I can take your saffron with me. You're still too sick to ride and, as long as those thugs are still making trouble, the harvest is not safe on the estate. So, what do you think of my offer?"

He snorted angrily. "Offer! Don't make me laugh. This proposition is typical of you, Sibylla. You do everything exactly as you see fit and worry little about the feelings of others."

She squinted in the sun, now standing over the blue peaks of the Atlas Mountains and pouring its golden light over the black cedar forests. "There's nothing more for me to do here, André. But if I take your saffron to Mogador and keep it safe, then I have contributed something to helping you all recover from these terrible events."

He stared at his dusty boots. "Very well. I respect your decision."

"And I'm taking Emily with me."

His head jerked up. "Is that what she wants?"

Sibylla's back went up. "I have not asked her yet, but she will come."

"Our daughter is an adult. She knows what she wants and she is old enough to decide for herself," André remarked sharply.

"Are you going to teach me about my daughter?"

"Sibylla, you know I'm right. When will you honor Emily's wishes?"

She said nothing. It would have been so easy to finally let him have it: the indignation, the hurt, the jealousy she had bottled up all these years. But for Emily's sake, she said nothing.

"I would like to have Emily with me," she finally said reluctantly. "She's been gone a year now. Can you imagine how much I've missed her?"

"Oh, indeed I can!" he said emphatically.

She avoided his eyes and lowered her head. They stood next to each other for a while. At last, André took her hand gently. "When will we see each other again?"

"In Mogador, of course, to negotiate the price of your saffron."

"That's not what I'm talking about. Do you not at last wish to speak about those things that are still between us?"

Tears welled up in her eyes. "You have Aynur. I have seen how much she means to you. We cannot turn back time, André." She very gently caressed his bruised face. "I shall go find Emily now and tell her we're leaving."

"The paste is almost hard," Sabri said with satisfaction as he carefully checked the little boy's bandage. "Emily, please tell the parents that their son must remain lying down today. He may get up tomorrow. But they absolutely cannot return to their village. They have to remain on the estate until the arm has healed completely."

Emily lowered her charcoal pencil and translated for the mother, who paid close attention.

Meanwhile, Sabri looked at her sketch of the little boy with his arm in a sling. "I like your drawing," he said approvingly.

She smiled happily. She was always happy when Sabri spoke to her in a familiar tone. He did so only when there was no one else around or if those present, like the parents of the injured boy, understood neither English nor Arabic. "I promised him a drawing as a memento of his courage."

There was activity all around them. The Ait Zelten sheikh had refused the agreed-upon pay and informed André that the people were ready to return to their village. Now, there were pack donkeys all over the yard being loaded with tents, rugs, equipment, and cooking utensils. A group of children had gathered around the injured boy to marvel at his bandage.

"Emily?" the boy asked.

She was concentrating on capturing the folds of his mother's headscarf. "Yes?"

"Why do you look so strangely at the *hakim* when he speaks with you?"

"Pardon me?" She lowered her pencil.

"I want to know why you look at the *hakim* like that," the little boy repeated impatiently. The other children giggled. The mother too smiled at Emily.

"Look, I'll show you. Like this." He opened his eyes wide and stared into the air with a rapturous expression.

It made Emily laugh. "That's not true. I never make a silly face like that!"

"What's he saying?" Sabri interrupted. "Is he in pain?"

"Oh no! He wanted to know how much longer he'll have to wear the bandage," Emily fibbed.

"Six weeks exactly," Sabri told the boy with a firm look.

The boy turned his attention back to Emily. "My sister looks at her bridegroom the same way. Is the *hakim* your bridegroom?"

Embarrassed, Emily said nothing and busied herself with her sketch.

"Shush, *alemzi*, quiet!" The mother lightly smacked his bottom. She fiddled with the jewelry around her neck and handed Emily a silver chain with a pendant made of bright red coral. "For you, because you have helped my child. The coral glows with the color of love, like your heart. If you wear it, it will bring you fertility and many children." She ceremoniously hung the chain around Emily's neck.

"Thank you very much." Emily shyly looked over at Sabri and wondered if he had understood anything.

But he joked without any inhibition, "What did she give you? An amulet to cast a spell on me?"

Emily was relieved to see Malika coming toward them from the stable. "It's a good thing you're here, Sister. Do you think you could finish milking the goats for me? I want to be with Imma when the English *hakim* examines her wound."

"Of course! Pester my brother with questions all you want, and don't worry. Aynur will get better, just like our father." Emily hugged Malika.

"May God repay you for all your kindness, Sister!" She hurried away.

Emily gathered her drawing materials, said good-bye to the young family, and hurried off to the stable. This was where the horses and cows of the estate were kept and now, in the wintertime, the goats had their own fenced-off area as well. Malika had milked most of them already. Full earthenware dishes were lined up in the milking area, which was paved with mud tiles. André Jr. was pouring the fresh, foamy milk through a horsehair strainer into tin pots, which Christian then took to the rectangular cooling basin André had built in the courtyard next to the well. A pump made fresh, cold mountain water run into the basin and cool the warm milk. After that, the cook used the milk to make *laban*, a mildly acidic farmer's cheese that was eaten with olive oil and flatbread or with honey and fresh fruit.

"Your mother would love to see you," Emily said to Christian and André Jr. "Go ahead, I'll take care of the milk."

After the boys had left, she took a clean earthenware dish from the wooden shelf, fetched a rope from an iron hook on the wall, and went over to the goats. There were only five of them left with full udders, and they greeted Emily with their bleating. She looped the rope around the first goat's neck, fastened it to a ring on the wall, placed the dish under the udder, and crouched down on the floor.

"Might I help you?" a voice behind her asked.

"Sabri!" Emily had not noticed that he had followed her into the stable. "You know how to milk goats?"

He shook his head. "I'm afraid not. Will you teach me?"

"Why not? Come and sit down on the other side. Normally, they're milked from behind, but if you want me to teach you, it's better like this. We'll each take a teat and you shall do exactly as I do."

The animal's udder felt pleasantly warm and soft in Emily's hand as she expressed the milk. The goat turned her head and looked at her with large brown eyes as if to ask, *What's going on? Why are you working so slowly?*

Next it was Sabri's turn. But try as he might, he could only express a few paltry drops. The disgruntled goat tried to kick him, knocking over the dish.

"Do it with feeling, *Hakim*! Where are your sensitive physician's hands?" Emily convulsed with laughter.

"Go ahead and make fun of me!" He gave her a helpless look. "I have been living in Mogador all my life. How was I to know that milking a goat requires such finesse?"

"I'll show you once more," Emily said. Without taking her eyes off Sabri, she reached for his hands underneath the goat and placed them on the udder.

"There," she continued patiently. "And now you ask her with your fingers to give you her milk. But you must do it gently, lovingly. After all, you are asking her to give you her children's nourishment."

Steadily and evenly, her hands over his, Emily guided him through the pressing and stroking motions, and soon, a thin stream of milk squirted into the bowl.

"I can do it!" Sabri shouted enthusiastically.

"Really? You no longer need my help?"

"Well, yes, I do." He winked at her. "That would be nice."

Their eyes met and, slowly, their faces neared each other. When their lips touched over the goat's brown back, Emily closed her eyes and lost herself in the glory of her first kiss. Somewhere in her consciousness, she remembered something Thomas had told her, something about Sabri's being promised to an Arab girl in Mogador, but she blocked out that thought, especially when Sabri took hold of her face and kissed her more and more. It was only when the goat bleated loudly and jerked on its rope that they returned to the present moment.

"That was beautiful," Emily whispered as she untied the rope with jittery fingers.

"We could repeat it sometime," Sabri suggested hopefully.

She took a deep breath and looked into his warm, kind eyes. Perhaps Thomas had been mistaken. Perhaps there was no promised bride. Sabri was not acting as though there was another woman waiting for him.

"Why 'sometime'? We will be undisturbed over there." She took him by the hand and led him to an unused horse stall in the remotest corner of the stable. Sabri pulled her close and they were locked in a tight embrace when they sank to the thin layer of hay on the mud floor. André's horse in the next stall snorted. There was a warm smell of leather, hay, and animals, and Emily could not remember feeling as alive as she did just now.

Sabri kissed her for a long time with abandon and when he said, "Do you know that I love you, Emily?" her joy knew no bounds.

"I love you too." She took his hand and guided it to the neckline of her tunic. He flinched when his fingertips felt her naked breast, but she held his hand in place. "I want us to do what married people do when they love each other." She looked deeply into his eyes while she placed her hand on the crotch of his pants.

"Emily! What are you doing?" He tried to push her away. "And how on earth do you know that a man is, uh, sensitive there?"

"Malika told me. She's been married before and she told me everything." Emily felt very worldly and experienced.

She assumed that her own desire was not very different from Sabri's. He exhibited what Malika referred to as a "love column" in the same place where her "heavenly lips" were located. Emily did not have her own name for the place between her legs. Nor for that mysterious little organ that Malika called an "almond," which brought such wonderful pleasure if she massaged it gently.

"I wish you could crawl inside my body and experience all of my emotions for yourself!" she whispered and pressed herself against Sabri. When she felt how big and hard he became, her eyes grew wide. So that's why Malika had talked about a column! She forgot everything around her, felt only the two of them, their bodies filled with warmth and passion. She lifted her pelvis toward Sabri expectantly. But to her surprise, he pulled away from her a little.

"Emily, we shouldn't do anything we might regret."

"What do you mean, regret? Malika has told me that it's very beautiful."

She looked confused and hurt and that hurt him. He so wanted to make love to her, enter her body, melt into her soul. But, in the house of the *qaid* of Mogador, there was a young girl, his bride. He had never seen her, but it had been decided long ago that she would become his wife. That is what both sets of parents had determined when the little girl was born and he was a boy of twelve.

"We first have to be married to do what we both would like to do," he said to assuage Emily.

"Then let us get married!" She looked at him, her eyes large and full of anticipation like those of a child receiving a present.

But Sabri stayed silent, afraid to speak the truth and hurt this woman he loved.

She sat up and hugged her knees. "You want to marry me but cannot because your parents have already chosen a bride for you, is that it?"

"You know about that?" He was flabbergasted.

She nodded. "Thomas told me when he noticed that I liked you. He warned me to forget my feelings for you."

Sabri pulled Emily into his arms, rested his chin on her head, and caressed her curls. "I love you, Emily, and it is my greatest wish to spend my life with you. But it will not be easy. Your reputation and that of my bride are at stake. Her family will be insulted if I break the engagement and my parents will be shamed. We will have to pay a high price for our happiness. Are you willing to do that?"

She lifted her head and looked at him defiantly. "Your religion permits polygamy."

"You mean you would—" He was utterly taken by surprise.

"Of course, I insist on being your chief wife!"

"No, Emily, no," countered Sabri once he had recovered from the shock. "I love you and only you. I want to share my future with you."

"Emily? Where are you?" They heard Sibylla's voice approaching.

Emily felt as though she were being torn out of a beautiful dream. She reluctantly freed herself from Sabri's arms. "I have to go. Wait a little bit until I've distracted my mother. Then you can sneak away." She stood up and shook the hay out of her skirt.

"Wait!" Sabri held her back. "I want you to know one thing: I will find a solution."

She leaned forward and kissed him. "We will find a solution."

Chapter Thirty

When Sibylla stepped into the stable, Emily was standing in the milking area with a bowl full of fresh goat's milk in each hand. "Hello, Mother. Have you come to help me carry these?"

"Well, I've really come to discuss something with you." Sibylla took two more bowls and followed her daughter into the courtyard. Emily's hips swayed provocatively from right to left in front of her and her long curls bobbed up and down.

My little girl has become a woman. A beautiful, desirable woman, thought Sibylla, half in awe, half in shock. Then she spotted the straw. "How did you get that in your hair?" She placed the milk bowls in the cooling basin, plucked a piece of straw out of Emily's hair, and held it up.

"My goodness, Mother, you get dirty whenever you work in a stable!" Emily took the piece and threw it on the ground. "What did you want to speak to me about?"

Sibylla frowned. "You have to pack. We're riding back to Mogador in the morning."

"Excuse me?" Emily indignantly placed her hands on her hips. "Father is not even well yet!"

"And that's why I have promised your father that I would take care of something for him in Mogador."

"How nice," Emily countered stubbornly. "I'm staying here."

"It's really not necessary to be a burden to your father and Aynur any longer. They have enough on their hands in the aftermath of this terrible assault."

Emily glowered at her mother.

At that moment, Sabri peeked around the stable door. Seeing Emily and her mother, he was about to retreat when someone shouted, "Hakim bin Abdul!" André Jr. was leaning out of one of the living-quarter windows and gesticulating wildly.

Sabri froze. Emily bit her lips. Sibylla turned around, and her eyes grew wide.

"You must come! Hakim Hopkins needs to speak with you!" André Jr. continued to shout.

Sabri squared his shoulders, nodded to Sibylla, and walked toward the house in as dignified a fashion as he could.

"I'm beginning to see why you insist on staying here," Sibylla observed. "Yet another reason for you to ride home with me as soon as possible."

Emily was angry. "The only reason you want to leave is because you cannot bear that Aynur is Father's wife. You must have done something to make him choose her over you!" Shocked by her own words, Emily stopped abruptly. She had often had disputes with her mother, but had never been insolent before.

Sibylla was thunderstruck. For the first time in her life, she had the desire to spank Emily. Why did her daughter have to provoke her so? Thomas and John were not nearly so headstrong. She took a deep breath and struggled to regain her composure. She looked at her daughter, who was standing before her with a contrite look. What would Lalla Jasira have done in this situation? Would she have forgiven Emily for her outburst? Sibylla swallowed hard. "I treated you like a child, Emily. That was wrong." She swallowed. "Do you forgive me?"

"Won't you please forgive me?" Emily rushed into her arms with tears in her eyes.

Sibylla stroked her daughter's back. "The main reason I want you to accompany me is that this estate is not a safe place as long as those criminals are still about."

Emily snuggled up to her. "If that is so, Mother, then we will ride back to Mogador tomorrow."

There was a cool wind blowing down from the Atlas when Frédéric warily opened the gates the following morning. Christian led the horses out of the stable. They flared their nostrils and sidled about in an enterprising way. Emily looked up at the crystal-clear blue sky, which made the snow-covered peaks of the high mountains look close enough to touch, and blinked away a few tears. Parting with her other family after this remarkable year was difficult.

"When will you come back?" whined André Jr., who did not want to leave Emily's side.

"Soon." She stroked his hair. "I'll return to help you with the next saffron harvest."

Aynur had stayed in the house. Thomas had ordered absolute bed rest for her. Malika, who did not wish to leave her mother's side, was also absent. Emily fingered the soft leather of the jacket Malika had given her as a farewell present. It was colorfully embroidered and lined with lambskin, and would keep her warm during the long ride. "So that you won't forget me, Sister," she had said.

"Promise you'll come and visit me in Mogador soon," Emily had replied.

"For your wedding with the *hakim* at the latest. You remember what I read in your palm: if you two stay strong . . ." She had embraced Emily one more time and returned to her mother's room.

"May I help you into the saddle?" Frédéric stood next to Emily's horse. He leaned forward and held out his intertwined fingers. She stepped on them with her left foot, placed her hands on the saddle, and before she knew it, he had lifted her up.

"You're strong!" She sat upright.

He grinned mischievously and helped her put her boots into the stirrups. "Too bad you're my sister. I would like to have had someone like you for a bride."

André waved him over. "Frédéric, will you please fetch the saffron from the tower?"

He ran off and returned a short while later with four firmly closed linen sacks that he placed gingerly on the ground next to the pack mule. Two wooden boxes, padded with a woolen blanket to prevent pressure sores, had been attached with leather straps on both sides of the animal's back. Frédéric loaded the sacks in the boxes. When he was finished, André closed the tops and checked that the straps were secure.

"Thank you again for protecting my saffron. If I weren't still so dizzy, I would ride myself."

"I'll take your red gold safely to Mogador. After all, we have the protection of the *qaid*'s soldiers." She looked over at the six armed riders who had already mounted their horses and were waiting by the gate.

Leaning heavily on his cane. André went over to the captain. "I place in your hands not only the lives of these two women, Captain, but also the yield of an entire year of hard work," he said solemnly.

"The women and the saffron will be as safe with me as at their mothers' bosoms," the man assured him and patted the butt of his rifle. "Are we ready to leave?"

"We are." André returned to Sibylla. "It was so good to have you here, even if only for a short time." Fighting to conceal his emotions, he looked down and checked that the saddle girth on her horse was tight enough.

For a fraction of a second, her hand grazed his shoulder. "The estate is beautiful. The last time I was here, it was a ruin. You and Aynur have done much with it."

"Qasr el Bahia was to be your home," he could not prevent himself from whispering. "You know that was my wish."

Sibylla smoothed her riding gloves. "Yes, André, I know. But life decided differently. When Aynur is well again, I want your whole family to come and visit me in Mogador. You are all cordially invited."

Sibylla had taken her leave of André's wife and thanked her for her hospitality. But she was not sure whether Aynur had even been aware. Thomas had had her moved to the quietest room on the estate, as far from the noise of the yard as possible, because she had a high fever and was in severe pain. Thomas had confided to his mother that the wound refused to heal and he was gravely concerned. For all her own heartache, Sibylla sincerely hoped that Aynur, who had taken in her daughter so graciously, would soon be well again.

Thomas and Sabri were also in the courtyard to say good-bye. She beckoned her son. "Will you kiss your mother good-bye and help her into the saddle?"

"Well, now!" André called out at that moment. "What have we here?"

Sibylla and Thomas turned around and watched as Emily, leaning down from her horse, kissed Sabri on the mouth for all to see.

"Well, I'll be damned!" Thomas mumbled.

André turned to Sibylla. "Did you know about this?"

Her answer was a helpless shrug.

"And when," he grumbled, "had you planned to tell me?"

"I didn't know! I just suspected," she said.

"Women!" André snorted. "Always with their secrets!" He squeezed his cane and marched over to Emily.

Sibylla looked on with concern. "Thomas, did Dr. bin Abdul declare his intentions vis-à-vis Emily to you?"

"I think that's something he had better discuss with you and Monsieur Rouston. And I really must go check on my patient. Good-bye, Mother." Thomas helped Sibylla into her saddle and hurried away before she could ask any more questions.

Emily and her father said a tearful good-bye. André gave her horse a pat and followed the little group as far as the gate. He could no longer see the riders, but listened to their voices, the hoofbeats of their horses on the coarse gravel that rolled away down the hill. Then all was quiet.

Suddenly, he felt very much alone. He missed not only his daughter but also Sibylla. He remembered the elation when he had awoken from his unconsciousness and seen her sitting on the edge of his bed. For a few disorienting seconds, he had forgotten Aynur altogether. But Sibylla was right. They could not turn back time. He would continue to live on Qasr el Bahia with Aynur and their children and sometimes with Emily too, while Sibylla stayed in Mogador—his business partner, the mother of his daughter, the woman whose love he had lost.

When he turned around, the courtyard was almost empty. Only Sabri bin Abdul was still there, a forlorn expression on his young face. "Dr. bin Abdul, do you have a moment?"

"Of course, Monsieur Rouston."

André came straight to the point. "My daughter likes you, Doctor."

Sabri's eyes lit up. "I like her too. No, what I mean is, I love her."

"So you are serious about this love?"

"I am, Monsieur Rouston."

"And your family?"

Sabri did not hesitate for one second to give his answer. "It will not be easy to convince them, but I will find a solution. Emily is the woman I wish to marry."

André smiled with satisfaction. He liked the fact that this young man did not resort to excuses or subterfuge. "If Emily wants you—and that is certainly how it looked just a moment ago—you have my blessing." He patted Sabri's shoulder. "However, you may still have to persuade Emily's mother."

"I—" Sabri started to say.

"Father! Hakim bin Abdul!" Malika came running across the courtyard toward them. "You must come right away! Imma is worse. She's acting as though the Prince of Darkness has taken hold of her!"

"So you've fallen in love with Dr. bin Abdul," Sibylla stated firmly and handed her daughter a piece of flatbread.

Emily smiled broadly as soon as she heard his name. "Yes, Mother. And he loves me." She heaped some fresh goat cheese on her bread and took a hearty bite.

The small group of riders had made it halfway and was taking a break by the Oued Igrounzar. Its stony banks were strewn with the lifeless bodies of locusts that had died in the river swollen with winter rain. When the soldiers led the horses to the river to water them, the animals stood up to their fetlocks in dead insects. Sibylla and Emily shuddered at the sight, especially when the wind made the loricate bodies rustle and pop. They had seen only a few live locusts on their ride. The plague had disappeared at the same speed with which it had arrived.

Emily and Sibylla were sitting comfortably on a blanket, enjoying the warmth of the midday sun, and eating a meal consisting of flatbread, goat cheese, olives, and dried dates.

Sibylla threw a few bread crumbs to a foraging sparrow while she searched for the right words. "It is a beautiful thing when two people have found each other. But I want you to be certain of one thing, Emily. Even if the two of you are sure of your feelings for each other, many people will be against you."

"Including you, Mother?" Emily looked at her seriously.

Sibylla did not know whether to be annoyed or to laugh. With three little words, Emily had succeeded in cornering her. She found herself having to take a stand even though she had not even formed an opinion yet.

"Of course not!" she said emphatically. "Still, I am concerned. I don't doubt Dr. bin Abdul's intentions, but have you given any thought to the fact that you won't be marrying just him but his entire family? And this family has chosen another bride for their son. It is well known in Mogador. Could you accept his family's rejection?"

"You don't know that they will reject me!" Emily shot back.

Sibylla took a few dried dates from the napkin spread out between them and offered some to Emily. "Try some, they're delicious." She went on in a conciliatory tone, "I have met Sabri's father several times at the governor's palace. Haji Abdul bin Ibrahim keeps his distance from the infidels in this country. As the principal of the *madrassa* and a man who has completed the great pilgrimage to Mecca, he is especially bound. Furthermore, the *qaid*'s daughter is an excellent choice. Her family is the most distinguished in the city, and—"

"Stop it, Mother!" Emily held her ears. "Stop ruining my happiness!"

"But, Emily!" Sibylla was dismayed as she took Emily's arm. "That's not what I ever wish to do."

"Yes, Mother, it is. You are trying to take away the man I love. But you won't succeed!"

"I'm merely trying to make you understand that there is more to marriage than love. One's origin—"

"And that's why you married Benjamin Hopkins and saved your love for an affair with Father, is that it?"

"That was uncalled for." To conceal how much her daughter's words had stung, Sibylla concentrated on the food.

Emily's eyes welled up. Just a moment ago, she had been so happy and so much in love, but now doubts were creeping in. Did she and Sabri really have a chance, or were they deluding themselves?

"Sabri loves me!" she blurted desperately. "He doesn't want the *qaid*'s daughter, he wants me. Why won't you help us to be happy, Mother? You could talk to his family."

"Happiness is a funny thing," Sibylla mused quietly and thought of André. "One day you're certain that you can never again be happy without that one man, and the next you find out that fate had other plans for you."

"Please, Mother!" Emily pleaded again.

The captain approached them. "Can we go on, Mrs. Hopkins?"

"In a moment." Sibylla waved impatiently and the man withdrew.

Emily packed the leftovers in a sack. While Sibylla folded the blanket, she thought hard about how to convince her daughter that she would do her best.

"Once Dr. bin Abdul is back in Mogador," she began, "I am going to invite him over and talk to him about everything. If he can convince me that he will take good care of you and not break your heart, I shall do everything in my power."

"Thank you, Mummy!" Emily kissed her mother.

"In the meantime, you might go to London first, pursue your studies, and see something of the world," Sibylla could not stop herself from suggesting. And even though she could see how Emily's expression darkened, she added hopefully, "Distance can give one a little perspective."

"You can try, Mother, but you are not going to drive Sabri and me apart." Emily turned around and stomped to her horse.

"Sabri, please hold the candle closer."

Thomas leaned over Aynur and examined the wound on her arm as well as he could in the flickering light. It was a bright day outside, but he had closed the shutters.

"What's going on here? Why is it so dark? Why is she not getting any fresh air?" André panted.

His vertigo and headache had prevented him from keeping pace with Sabri. He had also stopped outside to console Malika, who was hysterical because Thomas had said that each additional person in the room was excruciating for her mother.

"Shush, Monsieur Rouston!" Thomas whispered. "Noise causes her pain, but tranquility and darkness do her good, don't they, madame?" He smiled at Aynur.

The cramps that had made her slender body twitch as André entered had subsided. She was lying still. However, her back was stiff as a board, as though stretched between two pegs.

André felt his way to the head of the bed. The sight of his wife, whose pretty face had been frozen into a ghastly mask, teeth bared, gave him a fright. He was only too familiar with this look. He had seen it often enough on his wounded comrades during the Algerian War.

"The doctor will help you, *ma chère*," he whispered. "Don't be afraid."

He gently caressed her sweat-beaded brow with his fingertips. Immediately, her neck went into spasms, bending her head all the way back. André quickly jerked away, shaken to the core. Only by her eyes was his wife still recognizable. Deep black eyes, in which her agony, which she could not escape, was written. Since he had entered the room, these eyes had followed him, had stared at him without blinking. She wanted to say something to him with that look. André sensed what it was, but was too terrified to accept it.

"Sabri, hand me the bottle of silver salts from my bag. I want to cleanse the wound again. And I also need fresh dressing material," Thomas whispered.

Sabri brought them over. "I got you some quinine powder as well, for the fever."

"Good idea." Thomas treated Aynur's wound with a few careful movements with Sabri assisting him and André holding the candle in his trembling hands. He carefully shielded her face from the light to spare her unnecessary agony. Still, her frail body was racked by spasms as soon as Thomas touched her ever so lightly.

André was haunted by long-forgotten memories of helpless surgeons on the edge of battlefields, of shocked and frightened soldiers having to witness the agonizing death of their comrades. Aynur's eyes with their dilated pupils were fixed on him as though in a silent scream. She knew what was in store, and she was begging him for help. His eyes welled up. He bowed his head and softly stroked her hair. "I know, *ma chère*," he whispered. "I know what you're asking me."

A short while later, he stood in front of the sickroom with Thomas and Sabri. He was white as a sheet and had to support himself against the wall. He had sent Malika away to make some tea for her mother. "I want you to be honest with me, Doctors. Is there anything you can do for my wife?"

Thomas looked gravely at Sabri. "What do you think, my friend?"

The young physician moved his head side to side. "Convulsions in the affected arm, *risus sardonicus*, musculoskeletal tension of the back, high fever, discolored margins, and greatly increased sensitivity. The wound is badly infected."

Thomas nodded slowly. "That's my diagnosis as well."

"So it's tetanus," André concluded. "Is it still possible for you to amputate the arm?"

The two physicians exchanged looks. "You're familiar with this, Monsieur Rouston?"

He took a deep breath. "During the war in Algeria, I became better acquainted with the deadly symptoms of tetanus than I care to recall. So, gentlemen, what is your opinion?"

Thomas cleared his throat. "I'm afraid it's too late for an amputation. I recommended it to your wife, but she wouldn't hear it. By now, the toxins have spread all over her body."

"Apart from that, the patient is weakened considerably. The danger is great that she would not survive such a procedure," Sabri added.

André lowered his head. His chest felt like it might split in two. Yet nothing compared to the pain Aynur was having to endure. "How much time does she have?" he finally managed.

"One day, two at most," Thomas replied, and Sabri nodded.

André thought about the look Aynur had given him. It was the last plea of a dying woman, and he vowed to comply with it, no matter how difficult it might be. He looked each of the doctors in the eye and said, "I know how this disease progresses and I have seen people die from it. But Aynur will not die that way. Her cramps will not break her bones. She will not suffocate from paralysis, drowning in fear. My wife will leave this world in a dignified and pain-free manner. That is her wish, and I will see it honored. My question for you, Dr. Hopkins, and you, Dr. bin Abdul, is the following: Can my wife count on your help?"

The three men were silent. Thomas and Sabri exchanged tense glances. Thomas's head was spinning. What about the Hippocratic oath that he and Sabri had taken, the holy oath of physicians to do no harm? For Thomas, that oath had been the solemn culmination of his medical studies, and he took it very seriously. He had seen much misery in the slums of London. He had personally witnessed the cruel death that a tetanus infection could mean. At times, he had caught himself quarreling with God and with himself when a patient had to die slowly and painfully, especially where children were concerned. Nonetheless, until now, he had not dared interfere with the Lord's decisions.

"I realize what I'm asking you to do." André's voice cut through the silence. "But my wife's death is certain, and you are asking much more of her than I am of you if you deny her peace."

Thomas looked intently at Sabri. "I believe that she should be allowed to die a peaceful death. What do you think, my friend?"

Sabri looked unblinkingly at Thomas. Then he said quietly, "*Amin*, so be it."

Thomas felt a profound sadness over his inability to save Rouston's wife. He cleared his throat. "I have belladonna extract and laudanum tincture. Both are anticonvulsants and analgesics but, like many other medications, they are poisons. Ultimately, their effect depends on the dosage."

André nodded.

Thomas took a deep breath. "Come to my room in one hour. I will give you a little bottle. You will administer its contents with a spoon. It is of the utmost importance that you give her all of it so that it . . ." He hesitated. "Works."

"I thank you both." André's voice sounded rough. He wiped his eyes with the back of his hand. "I will speak with the children now and prepare them to say good-bye to their mother. Then I will come to you, Dr. Hopkins."

The sun was sinking behind the western hills when Aynur died. Narrow beams of light were falling into the sickroom through the closed shutters and lent a warm shimmer to her pallid face.

Her children had been with her a short while before. They had cried a lot, particularly André Jr. But they had felt that their mother was no longer really with them, that she was already on her way to a place where they could not accompany her.

Now only André was with her. He looked at her, lying calmly on her back. Her chest rose and fell weakly under the blanket. Her head lay in his lap. He caressed her cheeks, her forehead, her eyelids. Her skin felt cold, but her features were relaxed and peaceful. Then he placed his hand on her lips and felt her breath becoming weaker. When it had become almost imperceptible, André, who had long ago stopped believing in a god, began to pray quietly as Aynur slipped gently away.

Chapter Thirty-One

Mogador, December 1861

Consul Willshire closed his Bible and rose. "My dear compatriots and friends, I wish you a blessed second Sunday of Advent. Until next Sunday."

"Advent under palm trees," sighed Victoria, drowned out by the noise of chairs being pushed back. She took little Charlotte by the hand. "I would so very much like to experience a winter season with snow and a service in a real church for a change!"

"I really can't see what you're complaining about," John replied, picking up Selwyn. "I'd much rather attend a service under the open skies of Morocco than freeze in a cold, drafty church in England!"

Consul Willshire and his wife held services among blossoming orange trees and fragrant oleander in their garden. While the sultan allowed Christians to practice their religion in his country, he insisted that they do so discreetly and prohibited worship services celebrated by priests in churches.

Victoria and John slowly made their way toward the exit. Sibylla and Emily were directly ahead of them, bidding the consul and his wife good-bye. Emily was wearing the embroidered jacket Malika had given her and a wide skirt that barely covered her calves. She wore soft leather boots and numerous jangling silver bangles on her wrists. She stood out like a cheerful, colorful bird among the dour Englishwomen in their corseted black Sunday dresses and stiff hats. Victoria overheard one of the wives whispering to another, "Ever since she returned, she's been dressing like a Berber woman. Very inappropriate indeed, especially on a Sunday!"

"Well, just look at the mother," the other whispered behind her hand. "The apple doesn't fall far from the tree."

"Indeed, my dear, indeed." They eyed Sibylla's purple silk pants, long silk shirt, and the embroidered scarf around her shoulders with a mixture of distaste and fascination.

Victoria looked over at John but he was sharing a joke with Selwyn and had not heard. She considered how to react. Deep down, she shared the women's opinion. However, her relationship with Sibylla had finally thawed, and it irritated her to hear outsiders making unkind remarks about her mother-in-law or Emily.

She cleared her throat. "Ladies, I'm certain I misheard you just now, or did you really speak disparagingly about two members of my family?"

The women regarded her uneasily.

"You can consider yourselves fortunate that my husband did not hear," Victoria went on. "He would not stand for having his mother and his sister spoken ill of. In order not to jeopardize the good business relations between the Hopkins family and your husbands, I am willing to overlook this rudeness—provided I do not hear of any further instances." Victoria was nodding condescendingly when she suddenly noticed that Sibylla was watching her.

"Well done! Thank you!" Sibylla mouthed.

Victoria blushed. Ever since she had caused such strife with her revelation about Emily's father, hardly a day had gone by that she did not regret her outburst. The idea that she had just atoned for it in a small way filled her with pride.

Now it was Sibylla's turn to say good-bye to Sara Willshire. "That was a lovely service," she said, and Sara replied eagerly, "I am genuinely pleased that you are attending our little gatherings again. Perhaps you, and, of course, Emily, will do me the favor of attending afternoon tea soon?"

That André Rouston—and not Benjamin Hopkins—was Emily's father was now an open secret. But no one spoke of this twenty-year-old scandal anymore. Emily was well liked and it was obvious that her family stood by her. And besides, Rouston was a reputable man, who, unlike Hopkins, had never been involved in any shady business.

"Thank you for the invitation. Perhaps we will do that soon," Sibylla replied with a smile. "Good-bye, Sara."

They joined John on the street. He was having fun with Selwyn by rubbing his stomach with exaggeration and announcing, "We're starving, aren't we, and we're looking forward to a lovely piece of roast lamb!"

His son nodded and mimicked the gesture with a giggle.

"You go on ahead," Sibylla said. "I'm going to stop by my office in the harbor to pick up a file that I want to go through this afternoon."

"I'll come with you, Mother. I feel like walking." Emily linked arms with Sibylla.

"Hurry!" John called after them. "I don't want to have to wait too long for my dinner!"

At the harbor, a strong wind off the ocean swept the last clouds from the bright blue sky and tousled Emily's curls.

No ships can come in today, thought Sibylla and held on to her shawl. Just that morning, John had once again been saying that days like this were far too frequent in windy Mogador and that the resulting delays were very costly for merchants and ship owners.

"That wouldn't happen in Tangier," he effused. "It doesn't get nearly so stormy nor so foggy there, and the harbor will connect the Pacific Ocean with the Atlantic, once the Suez Canal is opened."

Maybe he's right, Sibylla thought. The harbor in Mogador really was too small for modern ships, especially if steamboats were indeed the future. And fewer and fewer caravans were coming to Mogador. They went directly from Marrakesh to Rabat, Casablanca, and Tangier.

She looked at the harbor entrance, where the waves were breaking and foaming against the rocks. What would become of her if John moved the business to Tangier? Her children were grown and leading their own lives. If she stayed in Mogador, she would not even have her work to keep her busy.

And in Tangier you will be too far away from André, a voice whispered.

Sibylla pushed the thought aside. Yet something strange had happened since her return from Qasr el Bahia. She had dug out the worn edition of *One Thousand and One Nights* that she had buried under a pile of old files after her falling-out with André. When she was alone in her bed at night, she would furtively leaf through the stories and discover that they evoked the same confusing fantasies now as they had twenty years earlier. Ecstatic images of passion and lovemaking that followed her into her dreams and made her blush in the morning. She resolved to stash the book away, but then she would find herself reading it again, greedily, and with flushed cheeks, like a drunkard needing his spirits.

Sibylla sighed and looked out at the fishing boats moored to the pier. Some fishermen were using this time to mend their nets, while others repaired their hulls. The rest stood together, smoking *shisha* and complaining about the Almighty having created such weather when honorable fishermen wanted nothing more than to do their job.

"I feel sorry for those people out there," Emily shouted against the hissing wind and pointed to a few merchant ships dancing on the waves like nutshells and waiting for the wind to die down so that they could enter the harbor.

"When I came to Mogador, there was a storm," Sibylla reminisced. "And fog. We had to wait for two days before we came on land. The ship we sailed on, the *Queen Charlotte*, is in the harbor now. When she is fully loaded, she'll sail directly back to London. You could go along, perhaps with Victoria." The idea for making her homesick daughter-in-law happy had come to Sibylla when she heard Victoria defend her and Emily.

Emily, however, was not enthused. "You just want to keep me away from Sabri," she countered suspiciously.

Mother and daughter were standing in front of the warehouse of the Spencer & Son Shipping Company. Sibylla took out the key to the heavy gate, but found it already unlocked. "Strange," she muttered and peered inside. But the warehouse was quiet and empty; nothing seemed amiss, so far as she could tell in the semidarkness.

"What's the matter?" Emily asked.

"Oh, nothing. Perhaps Aladdin is here working. Sunday is for him an ordinary day, after all. Wait here, will you? I'll be right back."

When the sound of her mother's footsteps on the wooden stairs had faded away, Emily walked aimlessly through the large hall and looked at the variety of merchandise stored there. In front by the gate were piles of leather from Fez, which were first in line to be shipped. Behind, there were several rows of wooden barrels with palm oil and on the other side of the gate were crates in which smaller orders could be shipped. Emily was reading the labels when she heard Sibylla shriek.

"Robbers! Thieves!"

Without hesitation Emily grabbed an iron rod normally used to prop open the gate and rushed up the stairs. "Mummy! Where are you? Do you need help?"

She found her mother in front of the large oak cabinet in her office. The doors were wide open. One of the two large earthenware jugs Sibylla used to store the saffron lay shattered. She held the other in her hand.

"They stole all of the saffron!" she cried. She turned the jug over and one last dried blossom floated to the floor. "Everything in the jugs and the four sacks from André as well! I wanted to keep his harvest safe for him. And now this! The thief took the cash box too, almost a thousand English pounds plus as many pesetas and ducats! I had planned to give them to Comstock on the *Queen Charlotte*." Sibylla's voice faded. "But the loss of the saffron is much worse. Of course I'm going to—"

"Mummy!" Emily looked around nervously. "Maybe the thieves are still lurking. We should get out of here!"

Thomas was waiting for them in the salon when they arrived home half an hour later. Already overwrought, Sibylla feared another misfortune. "You're back already? Is Monsieur Rouston worse?"

"Would that be a reason for me to be here, Mother?" Thomas sounded surprised. "No, I can assure you, Monsieur Rouston is on the road to recovery. But his wife . . ." He paused, for he was still haunted by Aynur's cruel fate. "She has died."

"My God!" Sibylla sputtered. "Her poor children are all alone."

"So is Monsieur Rouston," Thomas replied. "He is grieving for his wife."

"Of course." Sibylla wiped her brow with her hand. Her head swam. She longed for André, wanting him to take her in his arms and console her. But André was mourning Aynur, and Sibylla had no one.

Thomas turned to Emily and kissed her on the cheeks. "Hello, little sister." He held her at arm's length and looked her over. "You look strange. Has something happened?"

Sibylla had told her that she wanted to be the one to share the news of the theft, so Emily said only, "Is Sabri back in Mogador as well?"

Thomas nodded. "He is with his family. But he instructed me three times to give you his regards. Also, he's brought along your little patient with the broken arm and his parents. They're staying at the *maristan* and we shall be looking after the little one until he is well."

The door to the salon opened and John stuck in his head. "Can we please eat now? I'm going to get very cross if I don't get my roast lamb soon!"

Sibylla cleared her throat. "First, I have something to tell all of you. John, please fetch Victoria! Something has happened at the harbor."

A few minutes later, the family had gathered. John, standing behind Victoria's chair, grumbled, "I can't wait to hear what can be so important as to keep me from my Sunday roast!"

Sibylla, fingers interlaced in her lap, looked first at Thomas and then at John before speaking. "Somebody has broken into the cabinet in my office. All of the saffron and the cash box are gone."

"Merciful heavens!" Victoria covered her mouth. "To think what might have happened had you caught the intruder in the act!"

"She's absolutely right. From now on, you should never go to the harbor unescorted," Thomas cautioned her.

Sibylla nodded.

"I'll go to the *qaid* and demand that he order an investigation," John decided. "Perhaps there's a connection to the attack at Qasr el Bahia. It could be that those thugs were trying again to steal Rouston's saffron."

"But how could they know that I had taken the saffron with me?" Sibylla objected.

"Yes, quite right." John furrowed his brow. "But what about the possibility that it was the same man who broke in here and frightened Firyal?"

Sibylla stared at him. Goose bumps rose on her skin as she thought of that night when she had stood in front of the dug-up dirt around the foundation of the sundial.

◆ ◆ ◆

Carefully, as though afraid of being followed, the man looked over his shoulder. Then he gently pushed down the handle of the blue wooden door leading to the Hopkins family's kitchen, but, of course, he found it firmly locked so late in the evening. The man pulled the hood of his *djellaba* even tighter over his face, stood close to the wall of the house, and waited.

A few minutes passed. Then he heard a soft sound. Metal scratched on wood, a heavy latch was pushed aside, the door was cracked open, and Emily stuck out her head. "Sabri? Are you there?"

"Yes," he whispered and moved away from the wall.

"Oh, I'm so glad!" She threw herself into his arms and covered his face with kisses. He pulled her close, nestled his face in the warm crook of her neck, and inhaled the sweet scent of her skin.

"You're all right! Thanks be to God!"

He had been worried since a messenger had delivered a letter from Emily that afternoon with news of the burglary. Had she not written that she would meet him after evening prayers by the back entrance of the house, he would have come earlier to see for himself that she was unharmed.

She set pillows on the threshold and they sat next to each other. Emily snuggled up to Sabri's shoulder. "I'm so glad you're here. The atmosphere in the house is horrid. Everyone is so nervous."

"Of course. I am too." Sabri looked at Emily. "You look very pretty."

All she wore was a long nightgown, slippers, and a shawl around her shoulders to ward off the cool air. During their embrace, he had felt her body through the thin cloth as though she were naked and the thought aroused him.

"Really? Shall I try to seduce you?" She coyly lifted the hem of her nightgown a little.

"Oh, stop it!" he countered throatily. "You're making me all muddled."

She smiled and let the hem fall. "Have you spoken to your family about us?" Her large dark- blue eyes looked at him, full of anticipation.

"Yes."

"And? What did they say?"

He stared at the ground and stayed silent.

"Oh," she mumbled. "It must not have gone very well."

"What do you expect? I don't imagine that a Muslim and Christian in Morocco have ever before wanted to get married!"

"Might not we hope to become the first?" Emily sounded disheartened.

He placed his arm around her shoulder. "If I didn't have hope, life would lose its meaning."

Sabri was grateful Emily hadn't pressed him for details.

"Marry for love? You deplorable fool!" his father had raged. "That is for stories and infidels! The woman is the man's seedbed—so it is written. She must obey you and bear sons to be your heirs and daughters to care for you in your old age. This infidel, this daughter of sin, has robbed you of your senses! I forbid you to mention her name in this house ever again!"

Sabri had pointed out that the Koran permitted marriage between a man who was a true believer and a woman of the People of the Book. After all, his father had married a Christian woman—Sabri's own mother, a native of Abyssinia.

At that, his father had turned red with rage. "You insolent boy! You dare oppose me? Your mother was a slave. It was my duty to marry her because it is written: marry the unmarried women among you as well as the righteous slaves. But now God is punishing me for allowing my only son to study among the infidels! Oh, Lord, smite me down, so that I no longer have to suffer the indignity of watching him besmirch the honor of his family!"

The fracas had attracted Sabri's mother and grandmother, his unmarried aunts and sisters, as well as his father's chief wife. As soon as they heard about the outrageous wish of the only son in the family, they began wailing. Sabri's mother shed bitter tears of shame, his aunts insisted he be punished, his unmarried sisters lamented the fact that no honorable man would marry them now, and the chief wife looked daggers at the Abyssinian woman and claimed to have seen this catastrophe coming.

It had taken all of Sabri's moral and intellectual strength to withstand this onslaught, but he had maintained his position: he was going to marry Emily and not some child he had never even seen before, even if she was the immaculate daughter of the *qaid*!

Once Haji Abdul had seen that his rage was having no effect, he became deathly calm. "Tomorrow morning, I will call on the *qaid* and have a marriage contract drawn up. You will be married by the end of the month. Should you dare to defy me," he had announced with an ominous flash in his eyes, "you will no longer be my son!"

Sabri felt like he was swallowing knives each time he recalled his father's words. He loved his family. He loved being in their company, eating, singing, telling stories, sharing tales of sorrow and success with them, and he wanted them to love Emily as he did. He could not possibly tell her of their horror and shame.

But she had already noticed how downcast he was. "They want nothing to do with me, don't they?" She sadly rested her head on his shoulder.

Gray clouds in the night sky began to obscure the moon, and Emily shivered at the thought of all the obstacles in their way. "Are you going to leave me?" she asked anxiously.

"Never! I would never think of doing that!" He kissed her passionately.

"I am so relieved," she whispered. "But what shall we do?"

He forced a smile. "I could abduct you. We have that custom. If the couples' families don't agree, the bridegroom abducts the bride and they marry in secret."

"So they elope," Emily replied. Suddenly, she sat up and grabbed Sabri's arm. "That's it! You'll abduct me. We'll run away together, we can marry, and then no one can keep us apart anymore."

Sabri's eyes grew large. "That is one option—not the best, but—"

"—but we don't have any choice!" Emily finished.

They talked for a while about where to go. Qasr el Bahia was out of the question because it would be the first place they would be sought. They dared not go to the mountains as long as the men who had assaulted the estate were still at large. Finally, Sabri suggested Cairo. "The mother of all cities is so large that they would never find us. And there is plenty of work for a physician."

But Emily had a better idea. "What do you think of London? Mother wants to send me there anyway. And I happen to know that one of our ships, the *Queen Charlotte*, is about to set sail."

Sabri thought about that idea. After his experience at Qasr el Bahia, he had toyed with the idea of returning to Charing Cross Hospital to study the medical art of surgery and better learn to treat bone fractures.

"London is good," he finally agreed. "But you do realize that we may never be able to return here?"

Emily swallowed hard. "Yes."

"And you still want to go with me?"

"I will tell Mother tomorrow that I plan to sail to London on the *Queen Charlotte*. You had best get a cabin right away. They don't have much space for passengers."

Sabri rose and lifted her. "I must go now. If someone sees us, our plan will be for naught." He embraced her.

She scrutinized his face. "You do mean it, don't you, Sabri?"

He kissed her one last time that night. "Send me word and I'll meet you at the harbor!"

Chapter Thirty-Two

Sibylla, Emily, and Victoria had tea in the courtyard of the *riad*. They sat on little chairs they normally took on picnics, and a pot of freshly brewed tea stood on a table next to small cakes filled with ginger jelly and candied oranges.

Sibylla, exhausted, massaged her temples with her fingertips and watched her daughter, who was showing Charlotte and Selwyn the drawings she had done at Qasr el Bahia. She had tossed and turned in bed all night, unable to shake off a shapeless fear.

Emily was just as unnerved. Her decision to elope weighed heavily on her. Sabri had certainly already paid for his passage on the *Queen Charlotte*. But now she felt like she was betraying her mother. Not for the first time, she opened her mouth but was unable to utter a single word. Charlotte was pushing against her knees and pointed to the drawing on her lap. "Ooh, what a big house!"

"This house is called Qasr el Bahia," Emily replied, "and it's in the mountains. Can you see those mountaintops? They're white because there's snow up there."

"What's snow?" Selwyn wanted to know.

Victoria smiled as she looked up from her embroidering. "In the winter, there was snow in London, and sometimes even ice on the Thames. But you don't remember that, do you?"

Selwyn's eyes grew large and he shook his head.

"Mother," Emily started, and once again she stopped short.

Her mother looked so tired, so worried. Emily thought about how devastated she would be to learn that her only daughter had deluded her, that her journey was only a subterfuge. Finally, in desperation, she blurted it out all at once. "I've been thinking, Mother, and I believe you're right. I will travel to London and start my art studies. I'll leave on the *Queen Charlotte* whenever she sets sail."

"But that's tomorrow!" Sibylla cried out. "How on earth are we to get everything ready?"

"We shall just have to be quick," Emily replied, her heart pounding. How she longed to tell her mother the truth!

Grateful for the diversion, Sibylla began pacing back and forth and pondering all that had to be organized in such a short time. "Nadira, fetch Firyal! She's going to accompany Emily to Europe. And she must help me pack."

"At once, my lady. I'll get the trunks out of the storage room and clean them." Nadira hurried away.

Victoria listened with mixed feelings. She was struck by a perfect yet unreasonable idea that she could not shake off.

"Who is going to accompany Emily?" Victoria cautiously inquired. "You, Mother?"

Sibylla smiled as she looked up from the list she was making. "Actually, I was going to ask if you might be so kind. You would be doing me a great service."

Victoria's eyes were brimming with tears. "No, you would be doing me one," she finally managed to say.

Then she remembered Charlotte and Selwyn. "I can't leave," she said sadly. "What about the children?"

Footsteps could be heard on the wooden stairs and, a short time later, John appeared. He had just come from Qaid Samir to inquire whether the thief or thieves had been apprehended.

"What was that about the children?" he asked and mussed Selwyn's hair. Then he spotted the tea table. "Isn't that my favorite type of cake? Surely you three weren't going to eat these all by yourselves?"

While Emily poured tea for him, Sibylla grabbed a plate and heaped numerous small cakes on it. "Here you are, my son. Enjoy!"

"You wouldn't be trying to bribe me by any chance, would you?" he asked, only half joking. "Out with it: What are you two plotting?"

Sibylla laughed sheepishly. "Emily has decided to travel to London tomorrow, and I have asked Victoria to go with her."

"Excuse me?" John froze, cake suspended halfway to his mouth. "What can you be thinking? Who's going to care for the children? Victoria cannot take them with her. The winter in England is bad for Selwyn's lungs."

"Victoria is not going forever. Emily's studies will take only a year. Charlotte and Selwyn are well cared for right here, and it's simply impossible for Emily to travel alone."

John resolutely shook his head. "No, I won't allow it."

"But, John," Sibylla tried.

"I'm going!"

Everyone's head spun around. Charlotte and Selwyn abruptly stopped their game of catch. Victoria had jumped up from her chair, her embroidering fallen to the floor.

"I am going to London with Emily. Tomorrow morning!" she announced. "Your mother is absolutely right, John. The children are well cared for. I'll miss them terribly, that's true." Her voice trembled and she furtively wiped her eyes with the back of her hand. "But I'm not leaving them forever. I'm coming back."

"You don't know what you're saying!" John was shattered. His wife had never before opposed him so resolutely.

"Oh yes, John Hopkins, I know exactly what I'm saying!" Victoria's cheeks were burning. "For the past two years, not a day has gone by that I have not been homesick. Now I have the chance to see England again, and I will go whether you like it or not!"

John could only stare at her, speechless. Sibylla bit her lips to hide a smile, but Emily clapped her hands and shouted, "Bravo, Victoria!"

"You women always stick together!" John snapped at her angrily.

Victoria went to him and put her hand on his arm. "I believe that I will find life in Mogador easier if I can spend a little time at home," she explained quietly.

"Your home is here," he grumbled and then, when she did not say anything, added uneasily, "Who knows, if you go, maybe you won't want to return."

"But of course I'll come back. Surely you don't think that I'll leave you and the children!"

John struggled for several moments before forcing out the words, "All right then, go, for God's sake."

After another long silence, Sibylla asked, "John, what did Qaid Samir say? Does he have any information on the thieves?"

"He's posted guards at all the city gates as well as at the harbor, but there's no trace so far. I still have work to do, so if you'll excuse me." A few moments later, the front door was loudly pulled shut.

"Perhaps I shouldn't—" Victoria started awkwardly.

"Of course you should!" Sibylla said. "My son will have to get used to the fact that, every now and then, his wife makes her own decisions."

Late that night, there was a soft knock on Sibylla's bedroom door. Emily's voice whispered timidly, "Are you still awake, Mummy?"

"Come in!" Sibylla hastily stuffed her tattered edition of the *One Thousand and One Nights* into the drawer of her nightstand and sat up on her pillows.

Emily slipped inside the room. She was barefoot and, despite being almost twenty-one, her wide nightgown and long curls made Sibylla think wistfully of the little girl she had been. She felt a rush of sadness at the thought that her youngest was about to leave for faraway England.

The day had ended in a mad rush. The news that she would accompany Emily and Victoria had caused Firyal to panic. "Please don't do this to me, my lady, I beg you!" she had implored. "The ocean's evil spirits will devour our ship and we will all drown!"

She had only given herself over to fate after much cajoling, many tears, and the promise of extra pay.

Then they'd realized that neither Emily nor the servant had clothes suitable for the English winter. Victoria offered some of her own, and Nadira altered them as best she could. Still, Emily's dress was too short and Firyal's too tight. But they would have to do until a new wardrobe could be acquired in London.

And then the messenger Sibylla had sent to the *Queen Charlotte* to reserve two cabins had returned with bad news. Because she was a cargo vessel, the *Queen Charlotte* had few passenger cabins and all but one were occupied. Emily, Victoria, and Firyal would have to share one cabin. Knowing how cramped conditions on a ship were, Sibylla could only hope that the two very different sisters-in-law would not have a complete falling-out before they had berthed in London.

"You're excited, aren't you?" she asked her daughter.

Emily nodded.

"I feel the same." Sibylla pulled back her bedspread and patted the mattress. "Come here, little one."

Emily happily slipped in next to her mother. Sibylla tucked the covers in around them and put her arm around her daughter. The dimly flickering light of the oil lamp danced on the dark walls and furniture.

Emily snuggled up to her mother. "Almost like the old days, isn't it, Mummy?"

Sibylla smiled. "You mean when Firyal told you stories about the *djinn* that skulked around our house at night and you wanted to sleep with me because you were afraid?"

"She used to do that to punish me whenever I snuck sweets. But now she's afraid that Satan's son, Zalamur, is going to drag our ship down to hell." Emily giggled.

"And what about you?" Sibylla stroked her daughter's hair. "Are you afraid of your trip to England?"

Emily was silent, and Sibylla was surprised to see tears in her eyes. She had thought that Emily's curiosity and love of adventure would overpower any fear of the unknown.

"You're going to have a wonderful time in England, my sweet girl. I'm going to give you a letter for your uncle Oscar to explain the reasons for your unannounced visit, and I'm quite sure that the family will be delighted to meet you. And I will inform your father of your departure as well."

Emily began to cry. "Oh, Mummy, I shall miss you and Father so much!"

"And I you, dear child. But I know that you'll have so many wonderful experiences. There's no reason to cry." Sibylla opened her nightstand and pulled out a handkerchief to wipe Emily's nose the way she had done in years past.

"Mummy! I'm not little anymore." Emily managed a crooked smile. She took the handkerchief from her mother and blew her nose noisily. "I have something I want to ask of you, Mummy. Do you promise not to be angry with me no matter what happens?" She seemed tense.

"What do you imagine could happen? Is something weighing on your mind?"

Emily avoided looking at her. "Oh, nothing. A lot can happen in a year."

Sibylla took Emily in her arms. "Don't you worry! You and your brothers are the most important people in the world to me, and nothing and nobody can change that."

On the Queen Charlotte, *December 1861*

After finishing his breakfast of hard dry rusks, tea, and corned beef, Sabri stepped from the mess hall onto the deck of the *Queen Charlotte* and looked up at the azure blue sky. A strong wind hurried along the puffy white clouds. The Atlantic rushed, lifting the ship up and dropping it back down on the waves. With one hand, Sabri held his turban firmly on his head and clutched the railing with the other.

It was their third day at sea and he had yet to catch a glimpse of Emily. But the steward had assured him that Miss Rouston and Mrs. Hopkins had indeed come on board.

"With this kind of swell, the ladies are not feeling well," he had informed Sabri as he swayed to keep his balance on the unsteady surface, carrying a metal bucket from which the smell of vomit emanated.

The *Queen Charlotte* had only been at sea for a few hours when the trade winds had worked themselves into a mighty storm. The sailors had managed to tie down anything that might be swept overboard, but the cow meant to provide fresh milk for the thirty passengers had fallen and broken a leg, so Sabri had had to assist the ship's doctor with emergency butchering during the heavy storm.

He was among the few passengers not afflicted with seasickness. During the day, he sat in his cabin listening to the creaks and squeaks of the wooden hull, the roaring winds, the crashing waves, and the shrill sailors' whistles. At night, he lay awake and tried to forget the pain of the separation from his family. If he did nod off for a little while, he would invariably be awakened from restless dreams by the ship's bell announcing the change of guards.

Mealtimes were a welcome distraction, even though only a handful of passengers appeared at the captain's table. The steward had tied down cotton strips crosswise on the tablecloths. This way, the dinnerware and glasses would not empty their contents into the passengers' laps.

There had been decidedly more people at breakfast this morning, but Emily and Victoria were not among them. Captain Comstock had good-humoredly announced that the storms were now behind them—they had reached the more temperate westerly winds at last.

Now Sabri spotted the captain standing on the stern next to a sailor who was measuring the ship's speed using the Dutchman's log. He tossed a log attached to a rope knotted at regular intervals into the water and counted the number of knots that passed through his hands. A second sailor stood on the other side of the captain with a sand timer.

"Four knots!" the sailor called when the sand had run through the timer.

"Hmm," Comstock grumbled and chewed on the mouthpiece of his pipe. "The *Queen* should easily manage nine knots in this weather." He rubbed his hands together. "Into the shrouds, men. We're going to pick up some speed! The group to finish first gets extra tots of rum!"

The boatswain blew his whistle and boots rang out across the deck. The sailors quickly and nimbly scaled the masts.

Sabri rubbed his chin and grinned. Many years at sea had made the captain of the *Queen Charlotte* hard and gnarly like an old Atlas cedar. But his crew obviously respected him. The passengers told stories of how he had courageously stopped a mutiny on this very ship many years ago. It had cost the former captain his life, but Comstock, who was only a helmsman at the time, was rewarded for his valor by being put in charge of the *Queen*.

Sabri leaned his head back and watched the sailors balancing above him at dizzying heights. Soon, the first sails were unfurled and began to flap in the wind. The sailor on watch turned the hourglass and rang the ship's bell three times: half-past nine and still no sign of Emily. Sabri sighed longingly and looked out at the ocean.

"Where are you going?" Victoria asked her sister-in-law. She sat on the edge of her bed in her dressing gown, brushing her hair.

The cabins for passengers who could afford the afterdeck were tiny and separated by thin canvas partitions. Beds hung from the ceiling by ropes to compensate for the ship's rolling, but the table, chair, cabinet, and washstand were bolted to the floor. Still, traveling like this was considerably more comfortable than on the lower decks, where the poorer passengers slept together with animals and freight in unventilated, tight, frightfully damp spaces.

Emily turned around, her hand already on the door handle. "I want to go on deck. When three persons have spent days vomiting in an extremely confined space, the only thing to do is get some fresh air. I also want to ask the steward to bring us something to eat."

"You might also ask for some tea," Victoria suggested. Like Emily, she was wan with dark circles under her eyes, but compared to Firyal, they were in excellent condition.

Poor Firyal was incapable of helping her mistresses. Whenever she was not vomiting, she would curl up and recite verses from the Koran, certain that they were all doomed. After several days of this, she had finally fallen asleep and was snoring softly on her berth.

Emily slipped out. Food and fresh air were, of course, not as pressing as finding Sabri. She had spent these terrible days tormenting herself with the notion that he had changed his mind and decided to yield to his parents' wishes and marry the *qaid*'s daughter.

The fresh, salty air helped Emily overcome her queasiness, but she was still not accustomed to the swaying of the ship. She anxiously pressed her back against the wall behind her while her eyes scanned the deck. The sailors were cleaning the *Queen Charlotte* after the storm. With buckets and brushes, some scrubbed the wooden planks while others polished the brass fittings on the railing, and still others pumped out the water that had been swept into the lower decks. Suddenly, Emily spotted Sabri and her heart started beating faster. He stood at the railing looking eastward, where somewhere in the blue haze lay the coast of Morocco. He had not noticed Emily, but she could see the melancholy on his face. She understood all too well the sadness he felt at leaving behind his family and home, perhaps forever.

She ran toward him, overcome by the need to feel his arms around her. But the ship swayed and the wooden deck was slick with sea spray and soapsuds. She slipped and fell on her bottom with a loud cry. Sabri spun around and rushed toward her. He almost slipped himself but was able to catch himself just in time and help Emily to her feet. The sailors roared with laughter.

"Finally!" Sabri put his arm around Emily's shoulders and led her away to the bow, which offered a little privacy thanks to its thick foremast and large sails.

Sabri pulled Emily close to him. "How are you? You look very pale."

Instead of answering, she put her arms around his neck and kissed him. "Nothing and no one can separate us now!" At this moment, the joy and relief of being with him outweighed her guilty conscience about having lied to her family. She looked at him carefully. "You look well. Didn't the storm affect you?"

"Other than that the shield in front of my porthole came off during the night and I got a face full of ice-cold seawater, I'm fine."

"Oh dear, you poor thing!" She kissed the tip of his nose.

He beamed at her. "The sight of you makes me so happy that I could sing. Although I must say, you look a little different in Western clothing."

"I feel different too," she replied with a laugh and looked down at herself. Under Victoria's form-fitting blue wool coat, she could see a pair of her mother's old lace-up boots. Her curls were gathered in a bun. "These European clothes are rather stiff and uncomfortable." Emily grimaced.

"Now it's my turn to feel sorry for you!" He kissed her tenderly.

"So that's why you were suddenly in such a rush to go to London!" shouted an irritated voice behind them.

Emily and Sabri nervously let go of each other and turned to see Victoria glowering with her hands on her hips. "Am I correct in assuming that this trip is all some sort of ruse?"

"I don't wish to be lectured by you, who, of all people, would accept any excuse to get to England!" Emily shouted.

Victoria ignored the objection. "I take it your mother is not cognizant of the fact that Dr. bin Abdul is also on board?" she inquired frostily and, when Emily said nothing, raised her eyebrows histrionically. "And how do you two conspirators intend to proceed from here?"

"I understand your anger, Mrs. Hopkins," Sabri began. "But Emily is not to blame. I begged her to elope with me. You have to understand that my family is absolutely opposed to our liaison."

"Victoria, please understand! Sabri's family will disown him if he doesn't marry the bride they have chosen," Emily added, moved at Sabri's attempt to cover for her. "You see, we had no choice."

Victoria swallowed hard. How cruel to be disowned for loving the wrong girl!

"So you shall never return to Mogador?" she gasped.

Sabri shrugged helplessly. Emily nodded, tearing up at the thought.

"I don't like this at all," mumbled Victoria, thinking of both the elopement and their plan never to return. They may have been the same age, but Sibylla had appointed her Emily's chaperone and Victoria intended to fulfill her duty as such.

"I have no idea how to explain this to Mother. It will surely break her heart. Have you not thought about that?" she wanted to know.

"I've thought of little else." Emily wiped her eyes. "But what are we to do?"

"Well, you are going to write to her and confess everything. Your mother will be disappointed, but I'm sure she will do everything in her power to ensure you two can return home. But first of all," she closed with all the authority and dignity becoming a chaperone, "you two are going to get married!"

"We are planning to be married by a clergyman as soon as we reach London," Sabri assured her.

"And until then, you expect me to be your chaperone?" Victoria again put her hands on her hips.

"Upon my honor, you can trust me, Mrs. Hopkins!" Sabri replied with dignity.

Victoria thought of the passionate embrace she had caught them in. "No, I don't like it, but"—she paused and gave them a sly look—"I have another idea. Don't move from this spot—I shall be right back!"

Chapter Thirty-Three

Mogador, February 1862

"Do you think that Miss Emily and Miss Victoria will have reached London by now, my lady?" Nadira asked.

"Pardon?" Sibylla replied absentmindedly and took a sip of mint tea.

A pale yellow sun was rising over Mogador. Sibylla was already dressed and sitting at her vanity while Nadira pinned up her hair.

Sibylla had moved jars, bottles, and hairbrushes aside to make room for a tome the size of an *Encyclopedia Britannica*. Every year, Lackington Allen bookstore in London published their book catalogue, and Sibylla had been waiting impatiently for it.

The catalogue had finally arrived yesterday together with her book trunk and several editions of the *London Times*. Ever since then, she had been leafing through it every free minute she had and marking all the titles that interested her.

The servant knew her mistress disappeared into another world whenever the Lackington Allen list arrived. But the house had changed, become empty and quiet since Emily, Victoria, and Firyal's departure. Nadira missed their faces.

"It was two months ago today that Miss Emily and Miss Victoria went on board," she started again as she took the two mother-of-pearl combs lying on the table and pushed them into Sibylla's hair. "How long did you say until they arrive in London?"

"If the weather is good, they should arrive any day now. I'm sure Emily will write to me immediately. But it will take several weeks more before her letter reaches Mogador." Sibylla again leaned over her catalogue.

"Astonishing that the *qaid*'s soldiers haven't found the saffron thief yet. I'm sure he's long gone by now," Nadira remarked.

That got Sibylla's attention. "I hold out hope that he's caught and receives his proper punishment!" she said.

Neither the break-in at her home nor at her office had been solved, a fact that caused her great distress. Almost every night, Sibylla was tormented by nightmares about a black shadow that followed her through the alleys of Mogador and lay in wait in the rooms of her house.

"Who are you? What do you want from me?" she would demand. The shadow would whirl around and throw back the hood of his cloak, but before she could recognize him, he would vanish and she would awake, drenched in sweat. After that, she would wander restlessly through the house, look into every room, and make sure that all the doors were bolted.

"All finished, my lady." Nadira was smoothing a few wrinkles in Sibylla's tunic when there was a knock at the door.

Sibylla closed the catalogue and rose. "That must be John. We plan to have breakfast and go to the harbor together."

But it was the voice of the gatekeeper who called. "My lady, a messenger has brought a letter for you!"

Sibylla's heart began to beat faster. Perhaps André had finally written to her! How she longed for news from Qasr el Bahia. But since Aynur's death, André seemed to have withdrawn completely.

Nadira went to the door and took the letter from Hamid, who waited respectfully on the threshold.

"It's from Emily! She posted it in Lisbon," Sibylla said in surprise, taking the envelope in her hands. She opened it, unfolded the long letter, and skimmed it in joyous anticipation. Her eyes grew wide.

"Oh, my lady! Did you receive bad news?" Nadira asked.

Sibylla stared at her numbly. "I cannot call it good."

"What do you mean, my lady?"

Sibylla took a deep breath and swallowed. "Emily and Dr. bin Abdul have married. The captain of the *Queen Charlotte* married them—three days after they left Mogador."

"God be praised!" Nadira was delighted, but when she saw her mistress's expression, she fell silent. Sibylla looked shattered.

"You are not happy, my lady," Nadira observed.

Sibylla raised her shoulders. "Is there reason for me to be happy when my daughter elopes as though she did not trust me? Is there reason for me to be happy when she marries in secret and presents me with a *fait accompli*? And to think Captain Comstock was complicit in this plot! The next time he comes to Mogador, I shall have a serious talk with him."

She looked again at the sheet of stationery. The tearstained words swam in front of her eyes. Her servant placed a cup of steaming tea in front of her, but Sibylla did not touch it as she processed more outrageous news still.

Emily revealed that not only had she and Sabri eloped, but they planned never to return to Mogador because Sabri's family was so vehemently opposed to their union.

She thought back on the evening before Emily's departure. She had intuited her daughter's aggrievement and now she reproached herself bitterly for not having pressed her about it. What if she could have prevented this precipitous flight?

She quickly reread the end of her daughter's letter.

Sabri and I left the Queen Charlotte *in Lisbon. We know that we shall be happy together, Mummy, but we cannot bear the thought of forever being separated from you. I beg you to help us, even though I know that I have disappointed you terribly. But if you go to Sabri's family and convince them to forgive, we will be able to return home. If anyone can persuade them, then it is you, Mummy. Please help us! Sabri and I love each other; we have not committed a crime!*

Dearest Mummy, I will wait in Lisbon with Sabri and pray that you send us good news soon!

P.S. Victoria is with us. She wishes to forgo London and return to Mogador because she misses Charlotte and Selwyn too much. But she has said that she will stay here until we get word from you.

Sibylla took a breath, folded the letter, pushed it away from her, and groaned as though struck.

"My lady!" Nadira cried in alarm.

"Emily writes that she might never be able to return home."

"Almighty God!" Nadira gasped. "But our little girl cannot leave her family!"

Sibylla thought frantically. "I wonder," she finally said, "if the Abdul bin Ibrahim family have received a similar letter. Sabri is their only son. I cannot imagine they will so readily renounce him just because he's married a Christian girl. Sabri too has a mother who is about to lose her child and surely she is as unwilling to accept that as I am!" Sibylla stood and pushed her chair back forcefully. "I shall go speak to Sabri's mother at once. Nadira, you're coming along. Together we will find a way to help our children!"

◆ ◆ ◆

"I always thought I knew Mogador well, but I have never been in this alley before," Nadira told her mistress.

The closer they drew to the mosque, the clearer it became that they were in the quarter of religion and scholarship. Booksellers and bookbinders, calligraphers and miniaturists had their small stores and workshops here. A merchant offered prayer rugs and embroidered prayer caps for sale by the entrance to the house of worship. Opposite, an instrument craftsman had set up his stand. Contentedly smoking his water pipe, he stood among large and small drums, flutes, zithers, and lutes the faithful could purchase for holiday processions.

The two women walked around the mosque and came to a house. The holy green of Islam on the door and roof tiles indicated that this was the *zaouia* of the city. A sign reminded visitors to enter this noble place only in accordance with religious rules—abluted and with respectful demeanor. Through an open window upstairs, Sibylla and Nadira heard a man's deep voice reciting from the Hadiths: "Sometimes a revelation comes to me like the sound of a bell, and that is, for me, the most difficult form . . ."

"If Haji Abdul only knew how true his words are," Sibylla remarked drily and looked up at the window from which a chorus of young boys repeated the teacher's text.

The house of the Abdul bin Ibrahim family was adjacent to the *zaouia*. Like Sibylla's, it was two stories, brilliantly whitewashed, with no windows facing the street and a blue wooden front door.

Nadira knocked. "El Sayyida Sibylla wishes to speak with Sayyida Almaz," she told the guard looking through the hatch.

He disappeared and, a short time later, they were received by a female slave who led them across the inner courtyard to the women's quarters.

Unlike the *qaid*'s harem, this private area was very plain. The living room was square and not particularly large. A stodgy cast-iron chandelier hung from the ceiling and quotations from the Koran on the walls were evidence of the inhabitants' deep devotion. Woven rugs lay on the dark wood floor, sofas stood along the walls, and there was a low table with a ceramic bowl of dates and candied almonds. The only luxury was an artfully carved cedar table bearing a leather-bound and gold-embossed edition of the holy book. The silk rugs, silver chandeliers, elaborately glazed wall tiles, and crystal mirrors that made Qaid Samir's harem so decadent and carefree were absent.

Sibylla recognized Sabri's mother right away by her tawny skin, large brown eyes, and classically beautiful Abyssinian features. Consequently, the plump little Arab woman, whose gold-laden hands belied her demure black garment, had to be Haji Abdul's first wife. The two wives sat as far apart as the small room would allow and did not deign to look at each other.

Three young women sat between them on a divan. They were wearing colorful garments and watched the visitors curiously with their kohl-rimmed eyes. Sibylla took them to be three of Sabri's six younger sisters. The oldest was probably Emily's age. She held a baby on her lap, and a toddler sat by her feet, contentedly sucking on a date. Lastly, there was an old woman wrapped in a blanket sitting in an armchair and staring at Sibylla with opaque, blind eyes: Sabri's grandmother. Her nostrils vibrated with suspicion.

The women received Sibylla in silence and reservation compared to the exuberant welcome that she was accustomed to in Arab households. After all, standing before them was the mother of the girl who had turned their son's head so much he had thrown honor and propriety to the wind. But Sibylla was determined not to let the cool reception discourage her.

"Assalamu alaikum," she said pleasantly and stepped toward the old woman's armchair to pay her respects. In doing so, she tripped over a baby's rattle lying on the floor.

Sabri's sisters giggled behind their hands and, finally, the first wife rose and came toward Sibylla. "*Wa-alaikum salam*, Sayyida Sibylla. My house is also your house."

"Please give me the honor of presenting my modest gifts." Sibylla signaled Nadira to present the silk shawls. She noted with satisfaction that the women's eyes lit up with interest. It was obvious they would have liked to put them on immediately instead of placing them aside as etiquette demanded.

"Please allow me to share the foods of my home as a way of expressing my thanks." The first wife clapped her hands and ordered slaves to bring tea and refreshments. Then she invited Sibylla to sit next to her. Nadira stood by the door.

While two slaves served fragrant tea, sweet almond pastry, and fresh *labneh* with pomegranate jelly, a third brought a basin with water and towels for hand washing.

The women ate, drank tea, and exchanged some small talk, but Sibylla knew that was only because hospitality here was sacrosanct. Once politeness had been established, one would come directly to the point.

And indeed, the first wife soon said, "To what do I owe the honor of your visit, Sayyida Sibylla?"

Sibylla slowly set her tea glass on the table. She had thought carefully about how best to reach her goal and had come to the conclusion that it was best to speak mother to mother, even though it was impolitic to pass over the first wife.

"Honorable Sayyida Almaz." She turned and looked at Sabri's mother directly. "My daughter has gone away, and I am afraid that I will never see her again."

Almaz's eyes grew wide. She sat bolt upright on the sofa and Sibylla had the feeling she knew exactly what she was trying to say.

"Well, she's not here," the first wife said snidely, obviously feeling insulted.

Sabri's grandmother chimed in as well. "That infidel girl has destroyed our domestic peace!" She beat the armrest of her chair with her bony hand.

The three daughters of the house were silent, their eyes flitting back and forth between Sibylla and Almaz.

At last, Almaz spoke up. Her voice was not loud, but calm and dignified. "No mother should have to give up her child, Sayyida Sibylla. But what does my son have to do with your fear?"

"My daughter and your son boarded a ship to England. I have just learned that they have gotten married on board this ship. They are now in Lisbon and fear the wrath of their families."

The first wife wheezed in surprise and the old woman lamented, "Oh, that seductress! More treacherous than a mirage in the desert sand, she has lured the son of this house to his ruin!"

Almaz uttered a distraught cry, but one of Sabri's unmarried sisters sighed longingly, "By God, how great a love that must be!"

Sibylla looked at Almaz. "Did you know about their plans?"

Sabri's mother shook her head. "My son left a letter for his father in which he told him that he was returning to England to further his medical studies. He wrote that he did not wish to marry the bride his father had chosen for him. But he did not mention another bride."

"Our lord is very angry about this letter," the first wife interjected with a hint of triumph in her voice. "It was extremely humiliating for him to tell the *qaid*. Our lord managed to postpone the wedding, but he had to increase the *mahr* for the bride by several *dirham*."

"Sabri is already married. The wedding to the *qaid's* daughter will not take place," Sibylla countered firmly. "Do you agree with me, Sayyida Almaz?"

"The opinion of the Abyssinian concubine means nothing. The master of this house will decide!" the old woman croaked.

"Then I will never see my daughter again, and you, Sayyida Almaz, will never again see your son. My daughter has written that she and

Sabri will return to Morocco only if Haji Abdul accepts their union." Sibylla signaled Nadira. She gave her Emily's letter, which she read from aloud.

There was silence when she finished, then Almaz sobbed loudly. Sabri's sisters sat frozen in their seats. Only the baby gurgled, unperturbed by the general tension, and reached for his mother's dangling earrings.

Sibylla said emphatically, "Our children love each other, and if we do not show them that we love them too, they will leave us!"

"Love! Such a big word," the first wife snarled. "But honor is a big word as well. And the honor of the *qaid*'s own daughter has been besmirched by these two unfortunates!"

"Please, Sayyida Almaz," Sibylla urged, suddenly fearing that Sabri's mother might surrender to the first wife. "You want to see your son again, and I don't want to lose my daughter. Please let us write to our children to assure them that they will always be welcome in their parents' homes!"

"We do not wish to lose our dear brother," the eldest sister declared and the other two nodded emphatically.

Almaz wiped her eyes with the corner of her veil. "You're right, Sayyida Sibylla," she managed to say at last. "I want to see my son again. We will write this letter at once."

"The wedding of our son, Sabri, with the daughter of the *qaid* will not take place, my husband. But there will be another wedding," Almaz announced that evening. She was heeding Sibylla's advice to simply present him with facts and doing her best to sound resolute.

Haji Abdul, wearing only a long white shirt, reclined on a cushion-covered bed and smoked *shisha*, watching appreciatively as his wife undressed.

Now, however, a deep furrow of irritation developed between his eyebrows. "Has God robbed you of your senses, woman? What are you saying?"

He did not wish to think about his son right now. Sabri's flight had hurt him badly and caused a lot of unpleasantness. In the *souk*, the *hamam*, the mosque, no matter where he went, other men gave him contemptuous looks. He had the impression they were whispering behind his back and, in the tearoom on Friday, after the last prayers of the day, the *qaid* had let it be known that another bridegroom might be more suitable for his daughter.

He had a nerve to say that, considering I doubled the mahr *for his daughter*, thought Haji Abdul as he sucked grimly on his pipe. And now Almaz was talking nonsense!

"Be silent, woman, and come to me!" he demanded and patted the bed invitingly with his free hand.

But Almaz, his gentle, favorite wife, would have none of it. The flickering light of the candle made her beautiful face appear like a mask of stone. "I had a visit today from Sayyida Sibylla. We spoke about our children and decided that, as soon as they are back from Lisbon, there will be a big wedding celebration."

"Excuse me?" Haji Abdul was confused. "Who is celebrating a wedding? And why Lisbon? Sabri is in London."

"Your son and the English girl Emily are going to marry."

"Stop!" Haji raised his hand. "What are you saying? Are you feverish?"

Almaz crossed her arms. "Sabri and Emily have eloped. They saw no alternative because some fathers are more willful than a mule and more stubborn than a camel. Now they are waiting in Lisbon until they are allowed to return to the bosom of their families."

Haji Abdul gasped. Not only had his only son taken an infidel for a wife, he was also threatening to live abroad forever. The thought almost broke his heart. At the same time, he was furious to learn that every single member of his household was apparently acting without regard for propriety and morals.

"Never!" he screamed when Almaz informed him that the women, his own mother included, were conspiring with the infidel merchant's wife to host a wedding celebration. "I will never permit this madness!"

"According to the law of the infidels, they're married already. And Sayyida Sibylla and I do not want to lose our children. We have written a letter in which we ask them to return and celebrate a real wedding in Mogador according to our customs and with their parents' blessing. The honorable first wife has already summoned an astrologer to determine the best date, and your daughters are going to the *souk* tomorrow to choose material for their dresses. Surely you cannot have any doubts now!"

"Doubts?!" Haji Abdul bellowed. "Our son has a bride! I just had to double the *mahr* to make sure she'll still have him!"

"But she won't have him, my lord," Almaz told him quietly. "You'll have to go to the *qaid* and speak with him. If he announces that his daughter is breaking the engagement because she has found a better husband, her honor will not be blemished."

The first wife had thought of this solution. Once everyone had assimilated the outrageous news of the elopement, Sabri's sisters had announced that their brother and his wife must celebrate a real Arab wedding. Everyone had liked the idea, even the first wife and Sabri's grandmother. A wedding would bring welcome distraction from their monotonous, circumscribed lives. By the time Sibylla left that afternoon, the planning was well underway.

Almaz had accepted the terrible task of informing the man of the house. But now that she saw him before her, confused, angry, and hurt, she felt sorry for him. Her lord was not a bad husband. He had always provided for her and had never beaten her, not even when she was still his slave, and he was a tender and considerate lover. If only he could bring himself to understand and seize this opportunity to regain their beloved son.

But on the contrary, Haji Abdul snorted angrily, "You women are like cats that lie in wait for their prey just for the pleasure of playing with it. If you think that I'm going back to the *qaid* to make a fool of myself, you're all sadly mistaken!"

"But there is no other way, my lord." Almaz sat down on the edge of the bed. "Do you want your family to fall apart? Do you want to lose your only son? Never play with his children on your lap? Not see them grow up?"

Haji Abdul drew on his pipe and was silent. His family meant everything to him. He had been so proud of Sabri when he became a doctor, but now he was horribly disappointed. For years, he had been watching the infidels creeping into Morocco with their consulates and commercial settlements, with their money, with their modern weapons and armed fleets. Twenty-two years ago, the French had aimed their cannons at Mogador, and two years ago, after some bloody battles, the Spaniards had annexed the city of Tétouan in the north. The infidels were gnawing like rats at his beloved country and dictating the ruler's every move. He ran into them everywhere in Mogador: the *qaid*'s palace, the *hamam*, some of them even trespassed at the mosque, and now his own son had brought them into his family! And his wives had helped him do it!

Almaz watched him silently. She gently took his right foot, placed it on her lap, and began delicately massaging it. "God is merciful. He wants you to forgive your son and his wife. Remember: the worst man is he who accepts no apology, forgives no sin, and excuses no mistake."

"Don't try to teach me wisdom, daughter of infidels!" he growled.

Almaz did not reply and continued massaging his foot.

Haji Abdul sighed. "You'll find out soon enough what your intrigues bring, woman!" He placed his other foot in Almaz's lap. "Every mother-in-law gets the daughter-in-law she deserves."

Qasr el Bahia, May 1862

André squatted next to the furrow Christian had just plowed and crumbled a handful of dirt. "Again, no larvae. It really looks as though we've overcome the infestation." A smile spread across his emaciated face. He stood up and patted his son on the shoulder. "This deserves a celebration! Malika has made something special: shoulder of lamb with caramelized onions."

The fifteen-year-old turned away and busied himself with the mule's harness. "Imma's was better."

André laid his hand on his back. "I'll tell you what, we'll have a glass of French wine with dinner. I'll get out a bottle from my stash. You're working like a man and that kind of work needs to be rewarded."

Christian did not turn around. "Are we done here, Baba? Can I unhitch the mule?"

"Go ahead." André watched the boy leave, trudging next to his mule in the direction of the main gate, his shoulders pulled up.

The assault on Qasr el Bahia six months earlier had changed them all. Christian was quiet and withdrawn, Frédéric directed his anger into working furiously on the estate, André Jr. had lost his childlike cheerfulness, and Malika tried with all her might to replace Aynur.

André looked past the estate to the old holly oak. Malika visited the graves of her mother, her sisters, and Tamra every morning and left little nosegays made of fragrant herbs and flowers that André Jr. had picked. The young boy spent a lot of time with his sister. Together, they had created fieldstone borders around the graves.

We are all looking for ways to come back to life, thought André. *And sooner or later, we will succeed.*

The terrible events had left a mark on him as well. Outwardly, not much was visible aside from a narrow scar on his forehead. Like his eldest son, he sought oblivion in his work. But his children were not alone in missing Aynur.

André knew he would never truly make peace with her agonizing death. But he hoped that life could return to Qasr el Bahia now that the last of the locust larvae had hatched and flown away.

Normally, they should have begun harvesting the barley next month, but this year, he had not sown any to avoid providing nourishment to the larvae. In the humid warmth of late spring, they had hatched in huge numbers like a terrible ghost of the previous fall. But after just a few days, the infestation was over. Without sufficient nourishment, they had to move on and soon disappeared in the direction of the sea.

"So you really didn't find any more larvae?" Frédéric had come from the stables to make sure it really was true. He was eighteen now, taller than his father, muscular, with broad shoulders.

André nodded with a smile. "We can plant the saffron bulbs soon."

"That's good." Frédéric placed his fists on his hips. "We can't keep on living off our savings."

He had accompanied his father to Mogador that winter. They had bartered part of their saffron supplies for provisions, seeds, and grain for the horses before returning directly to Qasr el Bahia. André had not visited Sibylla. He was not up to answering her questions or enduring her scrutinizing, pitying looks. He wanted to be alone, to take care of his children and his land.

"Someone is here." Frédéric looked nervously toward the south. A rider was climbing the hill, still too far away to be recognized. André instinctively felt for his gun over his shoulder. Since the assault, he was careful to have his weapon within reach at all times. But as the rider came closer, he relaxed and went toward him. *"Asselama en ouen,"* he welcomed the sheikh of the Ait Zelten.

"Asselama." The sheikh looked closely at André. "You don't look well, my friend. If a man lives without a woman for such a long time, his loins dry up. I've always told you that one woman is not enough for a man. You," he said, pointing a bony finger at Frédéric, "should start

out with two. There are many beautiful girls in my village who would love to get a strong young fellow like you!"

"Good advice!" Frédéric smiled.

"What have you brought us?" André pointed to the bulging linen sack hanging from the sheikh's saddle.

The man's suntanned face turned serious. "I have long been in your debt because those ignoble bastards from my people attacked your home and brought misery to your family. I swore to you that I would atone for this sin, and now the day has come at last: my sons have ended the lives of those good-for-nothing criminals. They tracked them down and killed them the way they deserved. Now vultures pick the flesh off their bones and their souls rot in the pits of hell!" He waved André nearer. "Here, my friend, I want to prove to you that I am speaking the truth." He loosened the lacing of the sack.

André carefully peeked inside and pulled back immediately. "My God, that stinks to high heaven!"

Yet he had seen enough to recognize the leader's stained face, despite the decomposition and the maggots. His eyes began to water and he was forced to support himself against the horse's shoulder. His rib cage quivered as he took a deep breath and felt the leaden weight that had been pressing on his shoulders ever since the robbery slowly lift.

"I thank you, my friend," he whispered quietly. "You have given me back my peace of mind."

"What is it?" Frédéric asked, wrinkling his nose. "It smells like three-week-old carrion."

André stepped aside so that his son could look inside. An expression of grim satisfaction appeared on Frédéric's face. "Thanks be to the justice of God!" He raised his clenched fist to the heavens.

"Where was the murderous gang hiding?" André asked.

"Those villains had hidden high up in the mountains, but not too high for my sons," the sheikh declared with pride.

André smiled. "You have brought us good news, my friend. Please be our guest. Malika has made a delicious lamb roast. And that," he said, pointing to the sack, "will be thrown to the vultures."

Frédéric roared with laughter, but the sheikh raised his hand. "I have more important news for you: when they were tortured, the bastards confessed that there was someone else. Someone who instigated the attack against your estate."

"What are you saying?!" André grabbed the reins of the man's horse. "Who was it? Is he still alive? Where is this fiend?"

The sheikh shrugged sorrowfully. "Before my sons could beat that information out of those villains, the weaklings were already dead! The only thing they know was that the stranger came from Mogador."

"Mogador! And I was sure they just wanted to drive us off their land!"

The sheikh's revelation changed everything. André tried to think who in Mogador could possibly have become his enemy. He shook his head in confusion. What if this unknown man should strike again? He needed to find him as quickly as possible.

"Frédéric!" He turned to his eldest. "You'll have to look after your brothers and sister for a while. Always keep the gate closed and never leave the house alone or unarmed. I'm riding to Mogador to hunt down this devil, whoever he is."

Chapter Thirty-Four

Mogador, May 1862

"My brother writes that you are planning to begin your well-earned retirement when you return to London, Captain Comstock," Sibylla said as they looked at the *Queen Charlotte*, anchored far out in the harbor basin.

A light wind off the ocean mitigated the heat and heavy gray rain clouds were piling up. The sun appeared intermittently, transforming the water into a silvery mirror. Alongside the great West Indian ship, a skiff was bobbing in the waves. It was ferrying the last packages to the *Queen*: wall hangings from Fez, earthenware amphorae, silver teapots, colorful tea glasses, and filigree lamps. These special orders had been brokered by Lalla Jasira, who was happy as always to earn good commissions thanks to the growing enthusiasm of European ladies for all things Oriental.

Captain Comstock took his pipe out of his mouth and stroked his white-gray whiskers. "Yes, Mrs. Hopkins, it's time for saying good-bye. My faithful old *Queen* and I are getting scrapped. Speed's what counts in modern times. 'Time is money,' your brother told me when we left London. 'Can't afford to be sentimental,' he said. 'If we want to keep up, we have to use more modern ships.'" Comstock sighed sadly. "I know full well what he meant: soon, steel beasts will rule the oceans instead of the wind and true sailors."

"But progress brings benefits for many people," Sibylla tried to console him despite feeling nostalgic herself. Had it really been more than twenty years since she had arrived in Mogador on this very same ship? Now the *Queen Charlotte* was going to be decommissioned. Nothing and no one was immune to the passage of time.

Comstock watched another small skiff approach. It was heading for the quay to take him on board. "Well, it's time to say goodbye to Mogador."

"I wish you an easy adjustment to life on land." Sibylla chuckled.

"If I have a hankering, I'll head down to the Thames and greet the ships from all over the world and remember at least I don't have to deal with bad winds or lazy sailors anymore!" He studied Sibylla for a moment. "Aren't you ever homesick for England, Mrs. Hopkins? Don't you want to go home?"

She shook her head with a smile. "My dear Mr. Comstock, I've lived here for so long, Mogador is my home."

The skiff arrived at the quay wall. As the helmsman threw the mooring rope, the harbormaster approached. "Your ship is ready to leave, Captain. Here are your customs papers." He handed Comstock a leather portfolio, nodded politely to Sibylla, and left.

The captain of the *Queen Charlotte* adjusted his bicorne and straightened his shoulders. "All right, Mrs. Hopkins—" He was about to bow, but Sibylla raised her hand.

"Just a moment, Mr. Comstock." She handed the old mariner a flat box that she had been hiding behind her back. "As a memento of your years at Spencer & Son."

When he opened the box, a beautiful pocket watch on a gold chain was revealed. Sibylla had had his years of service engraved on the watch's cover.

"Mrs. Hopkins, this is much too elegant for an old sea dog like me." His voice failed. He took off his bicorne and pressed it against his chest.

"As one of the most loyal captains this company has ever had, especially after the mutiny on the *Queen Charlotte*, you have truly earned this. Although," she added sternly, "at the very end, you did cause me some anguish."

He looked at her with such embarrassment that he completely missed the playful sparkle in her eyes. "Are you talking about Miss Emily? I only meant well, Mrs. Hopkins, you have to believe me! And, with all due respect, it was a great honor for me to wed your daughter and the Arab gentleman. Life on board is rather hard, no room for feelings, if you understand what I mean. And if a chance comes along unexpectedly to be a part of so much happiness . . ." He cleared his throat. "That is something you never forget."

"I doubt I'll forget it soon myself," Sibylla replied dryly. "Fortunately, everything is turning out well now."

Emily, Sabri, and Victoria had been back in Mogador for ten days, and Emily was bursting with enthusiasm over her trip.

When the *Queen Charlotte* had arrived in Lisbon, the rainy winter months had just come to an end, and she had greeted the hilly city on the Tagus wearing a spring dress. Emily was enchanted by the flowers on the balconies of the bourgeois houses, the green parks, and the boulevards with their modern gas lamps. She had admired the splendor of the royal palace and visited churches, monasteries, and cathedrals. Victoria had taken her to exhibitions and elegant shops and, in the evenings, the three of them had attended theater and opera. One weekend, they had made an excursion to the fashionable resort of Estoril and, another time, they had taken a trip by train. During her two-month stay in the

Portuguese capital, Emily had experienced countless things for the first time.

But now she was happy to be home again and was consumed by preparations for her wedding, assisted by all the Hopkins women as well as the bin Ibrahims. This morning, right after breakfast, she had gone with Victoria to the seamstresses and embroiderers to try on her wedding dresses. Victoria had been a bit envious when she discovered her sister-in-law was getting not one but ten dresses for the three-day celebration. Sabri's sisters had explained it was simply the custom in this country. A bride should feel like a princess out of *One Thousand and One Nights* on the day of her nuptials.

While Emily was trying on dresses, Sibylla had auditioned musicians. And, after prayers, she was to meet Almaz and Haji Abdul's first wife in order to taste a few of the abundant dishes that were to be served at the feast. In between, she'd found time to stop by the harbor to bid Captain Comstock farewell.

"Mummy! Here you are!" a voice behind her called out. "We have to hurry if we want to be on time to meet Almaz and Sabri's father's first wife!"

She shook the veteran mariner's hand. "Fair winds and following seas, Captain. That's what you say, isn't it? I wish you many happy years!"

He beamed and bowed awkwardly. "Always an honor to work with you, Mrs. Hopkins!"

Mother and daughter headed to the warehouse together. It was almost noon and the *muezzin* would soon call the faithful to prayer. But for now, the quay buzzed with life. Ships were being loaded and unloaded. Sailors scrubbed decks, mended sails, checked anchor cables and ropes. Workers were hauling sacks and rolling barrels back and forth between ships and warehouses, and the harbormaster was standing next to the captain of an American frigate and checking whether the number of bales of cotton on the paper corresponded with the actual number delivered.

"I miss Sabri," Emily sighed. Since their return from Lisbon, his family had insisted that they live separately in their respective family's homes until the wedding. They were not even permitted to visit each other.

"If you hope to have a peaceful relationship with your future family, you will have to endure this yearning, whether you like it or not—watch out!" Sibylla grabbed Emily's arm and pulled her away from a suspended crate spinning dangerously on its way off a Danish ship.

"I'm so happy that Uncle Oscar and his family are coming for our feast!" Emily said once the danger had passed. "It's all right if Grandmother Mary finds the journey too strenuous, because I'm going to meet her soon anyway." Emily and Sabri were planning to travel to London for their honeymoon and stay there for one year so that Sabri could further his medical training and Emily could finally undertake her art studies.

"The rooms for Oscar's family still have to be made ready. I really don't know how we're going to get everything done in time!" Sibylla sighed as they entered the warehouse. "Wait here. I'll be right down."

As Sibylla ran up the stairs to the second floor, the *muezzin's* call to prayer came from the minaret; the hall rapidly emptied out, as did the entire harbor, with the exception of a few Christian sailors.

Emily leaned against a pallet of leather and dreamily stroked the smooth material. She thought of Sabri and how much she loved him. So much that she would have endured anything, even leaving Mogador forever.

She had sensed it immediately when they first met on his return from London. Now that they were married, she was sure: he was the one. She had never thought that it would be so wonderful to be man and wife—one flesh, as Captain Comstock had read from the Bible when he married them. She closed her eyes and thought back to their first night together in the captain's quarters, which Comstock had lent them for the occasion. She thought of Sabri's arms, which had held her so tightly and told her that she belonged to him from now on; of his mouth, which had caressed not only her mouth with his lips and tongue but also all the other areas of her body, especially those where her most overwhelming sensations lay hidden. A strange, greedy desire had taken hold of her when he tenderly touched her in these hidden places . . .

The warehouse gate creaked on its hinges. Emily turned around and watched it being opened slowly, stealthily. A shadow lingered a moment, then entered. A tall man in a black *djellaba* and a black turban crossed the hall and climbed the wooden stairs so rapidly that he did not notice Emily standing there in the semidarkness. He hurried toward her mother's office. Emily stayed quiet as a mouse next to the pallet. The hairs on her neck stood on end when she saw that the stranger had covered his face except for a small slit for his eyes. Who was this man? He wore Arab clothing and yet he had not answered the call to prayer. She held her breath and watched as the stranger raised his hand and knocked. She could hear her mother's muffled voice telling the man to enter. He opened the door and disappeared.

Emily had a tingling sensation in her stomach, half frightened, half curious. Without making a sound, she climbed the stairs and tiptoed to the closed office door. She hesitated, but her curiosity won out. She crouched down and peered through the keyhole. The stranger was standing with his back to the door, so Emily's view was partially blocked, but even so, she could see the unspeakable terror on her mother's face.

"Hello, Sibylla. Why are you looking at me like that? Do you no longer recognize your husband?" The stranger removed his scarf.

"Benjamin?!" Sibylla stammered and then again, "Benjamin?" She recognized his voice, that slightly nasal, haughty voice, like an echo from times past, and his icy blue eyes. And still she could not believe it—she had thought him dead for twenty-two years, burned to death in a blaze no one could have survived. But there he was, standing before her, pale and shrunken, his face covered in scars and bulges as though liquid wax had hardened, no eyelashes, eyebrows, or proper nose. She had the feeling a ghost was standing in front of her, and she shuddered with fright.

Benjamin pulled his lipless mouth into a hideous, knowing grin. "I've changed a bit, haven't I, my dear? But the same is true of you. You have aged." Before she had a chance to react, he was by her side, touching her hair, now more white than blonde, with fingers that resembled claws, bulging and fissured. She recoiled full of disgust, but he quickly grabbed her wrist. "Go ahead and look at me, look at my new skin! It took me one whole year to grow into it."

"Let go of me at once!" Sibylla freed herself with one lurch and sought refuge behind her desk.

"Oh, calm down, Sibylla! I have always found your money far more attractive than you. But then, you always loved your books more than you did me."

He stepped over to her abacus, which stood in front of the wall in a large wooden frame on a movable table, and idly moved some beads along the wires.

"How did you survive? I saw the ruins. No one could have made it out alive." She stared at his back, still struggling to understand that it was really and truly Benjamin standing there.

He moved awkwardly, not because of her question but because his cloak scraped against his scarred skin. He would never get used to this feeling of being sewn into a suit that was too small for him. He pushed one of the wooden beads. It glided silently along the wire and crashed against the frame.

He was tormented by more than his deformities. The horrific images of the bombardment haunted him as clearly and vividly as if he had escaped the inferno yesterday and not many years ago. He could still hear the earsplitting crash of the cannonballs, the impact of the incendiary projectile that swallowed his screams of fear. He could still feel the sand and dust, mortars and small rocks raining down on him, and he still had to force himself not to fall on his knees and whimper, covering his head with his arms whenever the air around him shimmered with heat or smelled of gunpowder and sulfur.

His fingers clenched the wooden frame of the abacus.

"Where have you been all these years?" Sibylla asked. "Why did you never get in touch or come back?"

"Be quiet!" He spun around, making his cloak fly, and she flinched. "Do you want to make me believe that you've missed me? Don't bother. I know that you let that Frenchman kiss away your tears before even the first month of mourning had passed. I know that and then some!"

She clutched the edge of her desk and shuddered to think that Emily might enter at any moment to find out what was taking so long. She did not even want to imagine what Benjamin might do if he discovered Emily and began asking questions.

But for now, Benjamin was not asking anything. He was absorbed in memories. Almost a whole year of darkness lay between his old life as the respected businessman Benjamin Hopkins and his new existence as a nobody disfigured by fire. This new life had begun with unspeakable pain in the naval hospital in Gibraltar. Military doctors and nurses had told him what he no longer remembered: that French soldiers had found him lying on the beach after the bombardment. Unconscious, naked, and covered in terrible burns, he was found between two dead French soldiers. The French had taken him for one of theirs, carried him on board one of their warships, and transported him with other casualties to Gibraltar. He had been expected to die, but—to the great astonishment of all—he had grimly clung to the little bit of life left in him.

By the time he was finally better and the physicians cautiously began speaking of survival, he knew that he would have to start a completely new life. If he returned to Morocco, he would surely be arrested again. So he caught a ship headed to London, went underground in the large city, and built a small import-and-export business. His talent as a businessman was all he had left. He did well in his business and could have lived undisturbed until the end of his days. But thoughts of the fortune hidden away under a sundial in Mogador ate at him. Only after twenty years had he finally summoned the strength and courage to retrieve it.

"You could have come back, Benjamin." Sibylla's voice intruded into his reminiscences. "I had gone to see Abd al-Rahman, don't you remember? He pardoned you. You were free!"

The ground under his feet swayed as Benjamin realized that he had been living in hiding for nothing.

"Is that true?" he asked flatly. "You really convinced the sultan all by yourself?"

"Well, I had help." She thought of André.

"Yes, right!" he sneered. "You went with Rouston to see the sultan. And I'm quite sure you compensated him generously for his support."

"How dare you?"

"Why so virtuous all of a sudden, my dear?" The hem of his *djellaba* undulated through the air as he took a quick step toward her. "You mean it's not true, what everyone in Mogador is saying?"

Sibylla was speechless as he went on. "That you squandered my gold by giving it to these good-for-nothing Moors? That you had houses, schools, and even a water-supply system built for those who had me arrested? I wouldn't have thought that you were so stupid and sentimental."

Benjamin struck the desk angrily with his fists. Oh, how he had dug, first with a shovel, then with his bare hands, only to discover that everything was gone, that not a single gold sovereign was left under his sundial! Afterward, he had returned to the tiny room he had rented in the *fondouk* and sat and brooded until he realized that only Sibylla could have found his gold. He himself had given her a clue during her visit to his cell on the Island of Mogador when he had asked her how much money Qaid Hash-Hash's soldiers had found and where they had searched. The bitch must have turned the whole house upside down until she had finally found it.

"You were the intruder in my house!" she whispered. "You wanted to retrieve your bloody slave gold."

He gave her a hateful look. "Enough talk! Let's get down to business: How do you plan to compensate me for my loss?"

Sibylla desperately searched for an answer, an escape from this nightmare. Then she recalled the weapon in the desk drawer: André's old service revolver that he had given her for protection in a warehouse chockful of valuable merchandise. If she could get ahold of it, she would be able to keep Benjamin at bay and yell for Emily to summon help. It was risky, but it was her only chance. Her fingers felt for the drawer handle. When she pulled it, the wood creaked. She froze, but Benjamin, still basking in his triumph, had apparently heard nothing.

"I want 16,625 English gold sovereigns! And not one penny less. Consider yourself lucky that I'm not charging interest. Borrow the money from the Toledanos or one of the other moneylenders in town. You have until tomorrow morning."

Sibylla carefully slipped her right hand into the drawer until her fingers made contact with cold metal.

"Why only until tomorrow morning?" she asked to stall him.

"That's when my ship leaves."

"Your ship?" She almost let go of the revolver in surprise.

"If everything had gone according to plan, I would be long gone. I'm stuck here only because you had to give away my gold. But at least I learned a few interesting things while I waited." He shook his head slowly to mock her. "*Tsk, tsk, tsk*, Sibylla, who knew you were so wanton! You let that Frenchman knock you up and then had people believe the bastard was mine." He gloated over her shocked expression. "Surprised, are you, Sibylla? For a few *dirham*, people will tell you all kinds of things. For example, that Rouston had trouble with some

Berbers. In exchange for some weapons, they were happy to attack his estate and shoot your brat. I'm sure you can understand I couldn't have you passing her off as my child with all of Mogador—from the *qaid* to the beggars by the city gate—laughing about how I was cuckolded!" He smirked. He had waited so long for his revenge, had imagined it a thousand times, but now the reality of it was even sweeter than he had hoped.

"You were behind the assault on Qasr el Bahia?" Sibylla stammered. "You hired killers to murder my daughter? No, that can't be true! You wouldn't!"

He didn't flinch. "It's your own fault. If you had just left my gold under the sundial, I would have left town without learning about your sordid escapades. Well, I shouldn't keep you any longer, seeing as you don't have much time to get my money. And don't mourn that child too much. She was only a bastard." He took a mocking bow and turned to leave.

"Don't move!" Sibylla's voice whipped through the room. Benjamin turned around in surprise and looked down the barrel of the revolver. The hammer clicked as Sibylla pulled it back. However, before she could fire, he hurled himself toward her. She stumbled and fell hard, the revolver slipping from her hand. There was a deafening *bang* as it fell to the ground and the shot went off, wood splintering as the bullet hit the desk. Then there was another *bang* as Emily flung the door open. Sibylla wanted to reach down to pick up the revolver, but the pain in her back made it almost impossible for her to move. Benjamin grabbed the weapon and pointed the smoking barrel at Emily.

"Run!" Sibylla panted, although the pain almost took her breath away. "Get help! Quickly!"

But Emily was paralyzed by fear. She saw only her mother, doubled over in pain as though she had been hit by a bullet. "Mummy!" she screamed before Benjamin grabbed her by the hair and pulled her so forcefully that she fell to her knees.

"Mummy?" He leaned over her and stared at her face. "You're not dead? So who the devil did those good-for-nothings shoot?"

"Hel—" Emily began to howl before he pistol-whipped her in the neck and she collapsed with a groan.

"Please, Benjamin!" Sibylla pleaded. "I'll do anything. Anything you want, just don't hurt her!"

Without releasing Emily, he turned around and grinned at her. "All the Muslims are at the mosque praying. No one is going to come to your aid, Sibylla."

There was a moment of silence. Sibylla struggled for words. Then she heard footsteps running over the stone floor beneath them. A man's voice called, "Sibylla, Emily! What's going on?"

Benjamin's grin dissolved. He knew it was too late to flee. He looked at Emily, lying motionless on the floor, and bit his lips. Then he took a deep breath, cocked the gun again, and pressed the barrel against Emily's head.

"No!" André burst in through the open door, his scream reverberating through the entire warehouse.

Now Benjamin pointed the weapon at the Frenchman.

"André, look out!" Sibylla shouted.

Benjamin pulled the trigger.

Sibylla covered her eyes, but no shot rang out. The old gun had jammed. Cursing, he threw it down. As it hit the ground, it slid along the floor and out of his reach. Sibylla lowered her hands just in time to see André charging Benjamin, lifting him up by the hood of his *djellaba*, and throwing him out the office door. Sabri, who had been right on André's heels, managed to jump out of the way as Benjamin smashed against the railing. The wooden banister broke apart with a great crash, and he plunged into the darkness with a bloodcurdling shriek before landing with a thud on the stone floor of the warehouse below. John and Thomas, who were still on the stairs, gawked in disbelief at the motionless body with the black cloak still billowing over it like a sail.

"You go to Mother and Emily!" Thomas panted. "I'll see if he's still alive."

John ran up but stopped on the threshold. His sister lay on the floor just as still as the stranger in the warehouse. His mother was holding her head and gently stroking her pale face and closed eyes, André was squeezing her limp hands, and Sabri had placed two fingers on her neck.

"Is she . . . ?" John swallowed.

Sabri wiped his brow. "She's alive," he said in a choked voice.

"Dieu *merci!*" André's voice broke.

"Thanks be to you." Sibylla laid one hand on his tearstained cheek. "If it hadn't been for you, Benjamin would have killed us both."

"Benjamin?" André stared at her. "Do you mean that man was—"

"—our father?" John finished flatly.

Emily groaned softly. She moved her head and cried out in pain. Then she opened her eyes and tried to understand why four people were surrounding her with worried expressions. "What's going on?" Then she remembered. "Mummy! He didn't shoot you!"

There were steps approaching the office. Emily flinched. "We have to get away! He has a gun!" She tried in vain to sit up.

"It's all right!" André helped her up. "I have it." He had tucked it away even before seeing to Emily—a precaution in case the intruder was not alone.

"Emily! Dear God!" Thomas stood in the doorway, looking as shocked as John had a moment earlier.

"She's fine. She was hit in the neck with the revolver, but all she will suffer is a bruise," Sabri quickly assured him.

"The intruder who did that to her was our father," John informed his brother with a husky voice.

Thomas stared first at him, then at his mother. Sibylla just nodded.

"Is he still alive?" André inquired with concern.

Slowly, as though in a trance, Thomas shook his head. "The fall broke his neck."

Thomas examined his mother's back to make sure there was no serious injury from her fall. While he was gently palpating her, Sibylla informed the others that Benjamin had been behind not only today's attack but also the break-in at the *riad* and the raid on Qasr el Bahia—and that the shots that had cost Tamra and Aynur their lives had been meant for Emily.

"Maudit soit le diable!" André cursed. "That devil! I don't regret that he died by my hand. Even if he was your father," he added, looking at John and Thomas.

They were all silent for a few seconds. "The criminal who tried to murder our sister is no longer my father," John calmly stated. Thomas nodded emphatically, but there was profound sorrow in his eyes.

Sibylla's heart broke to see her sons so confused and humiliated. She wanted to embrace them, dry their tears the way she had when they were little, but John turned his face without a word and Thomas gently pushed her away.

"Perhaps one day it will be possible for us to remember the father of our childhood instead of the monster he became."

It was at that moment that she decided to reveal Benjamin's last secret to her family, to have everything aired out at last. But she would do so at home—Victoria also deserved to know the whole truth.

She felt for André's arm. "Let's go home. I don't wish to stay here any longer."

When she saw the splintered banister, Emily pressed her face into Sabri's shoulder. She stifled a gasp at the sight of Benjamin's motionless body under the blanket that Thomas had found.

John cleared his throat. "We have to lock the warehouse. Mother, please give me the key. I'm going to go inform the *qaid*."

The peaceful atmosphere outside seemed at odds with what they had left behind. Out here, the sun was shining in a clear blue sky, seagulls sailed screeching over the harbor, and the masts of the anchored ships bobbed gently in the breeze.

They all jumped when a little boy's voice squeaked behind them, "Is the gentleman coming out too?"

A little Arab boy approached. He was holding the reins of a mule carrying two packing crates.

"What gentleman are you talking about?" André asked.

"Why, the tall one, with the black *djellaba*. I'm watching his mule," the little one replied earnestly. "What was all that noise inside?" He tried to peer inside.

Emily gasped.

But John replied, "Something fell over, that's all," and quickly closed the door.

Sibylla looked at the mule. "Benjamin mentioned that he was leaving Mogador tomorrow morning. This must be his luggage."

"Then we had better take a look inside," said André.

"I'll take care of that." John fished a few coins out of his jacket pocket and held them out to the boy. "The gentleman is not coming. But I'll give you these if you'll run to the governor's office. Tell the guard that John Hopkins must meet Qaid Samir in the harbor regarding some important business."

"But what about the mule?" the boy objected.

"I'll take care of it. Now run along!"

"It must have been providence that brought all four of you at just the right moment," said Sibylla when they sat in the salon having tea and biscuits and waiting for John.

She was sitting on the divan, propped against several cushions, next to Emily, who had a cold compress on her neck. Sabri had placed it there for her. The young physician had not left Emily's side and continued to give her concerned looks.

Victoria sat up very straight, trying to maintain her composure. Only her fingers, which kept turning her teacup, betrayed how difficult it was for her to comprehend the outrageous news she had just heard.

"You were providence, Monsieur Rouston." Thomas smiled at André.

When Sibylla looked confused, he explained, "Monsieur Rouston came here to visit Emily. When he ran into John and me, he suggested that we all go to meet the two of you. And on the way, we met Sabri coming from his office." Thomas nodded to Sabri.

"I missed you so much that I didn't care that we weren't supposed to see each other," Sabri confessed and lovingly caressed Emily's curls.

"Thank goodness!" she answered softly.

Sibylla kept stirring her tea. "What could have brought you to Mogador before the wedding?" she asked André.

"Ah, yes!" He nodded. "The sheikh of the Ait Zelten came to tell me that his sons had killed the men who attacked the estate. They also found out that there was a mastermind behind the assault and he was hiding somewhere in Mogador. I immediately came to see the *qaid* and ask for his help. But, of course, the mastermind is now dead."

They heard voices and steps outside. John entered. "The packing crates have revealed some surprises," he announced and gestured to Hamid, directly behind him. The gatekeeper was carrying four linen sacks, which he placed in the middle of the room.

"I cannot believe it!" André cried. "Benjamin stole my saffron from your office!" He had immediately recognized the Qasr el Bahia imprint on the sacks. He quickly opened one and took out a handful of tiny red-gold pistils while shaking his head.

Sibylla was thunderstruck. Yet another disgraceful deed of her husband's.

Then John placed the cash box on the table in front of his mother. "The lock was broken, but I've counted the money. Most of it is still there. I also found this." He pulled a leather portfolio out of his jacket and handed it to his mother.

"I hope this is not another nasty surprise!" she muttered.

"Take your time," he said.

She opened the portfolio and found several papers with the letterhead of a well-known London law firm. The top page had the words "Sales Contract" written in large letters and bore many stamps and signatures. She immediately recognized Benjamin's.

"Well, Mother, what is it?" Thomas inquired anxiously.

"It's a contract for a sugar plantation in Cuba that Benjamin purchased." She took another piece of paper with an outline map of Cuba with a large *X* marked to show the location of the plantation and handed it to Thomas. There were also inventories: lists of equipment and lists of slaves.

"It appears to be a large plantation. He had, however, made only an initial payment," Sibylla concluded. "Benjamin was going to pay the balance once he arrived in Cuba."

"I've taken the liberty of looking at the papers as well, Mother," John interjected, "and I questioned a few sailors at the harbor right away. At this time, there is only one ship anchored in the harbor destined for Cuba: the *Infanta Isabella*, a Spanish ship that is leaving early tomorrow."

"I know the ship!" Sibylla exclaimed. "She set sail just before Christmas, got caught in a storm, and only just made it back to Mogador. One of the masts was broken, the sails were torn. And she had sprung a leak. It took all winter to make her seaworthy again."

"And if he had not been forced to wait these months, today's terrible events would not have transpired," André added. "I only wonder where he's been hiding all this time."

"Qaid Samir is starting an investigation," John reassured everyone. "And he's also having the body buried in the Christian cemetery in front of the city wall. That's what you want, isn't it, Mother?"

Sibylla cleared her throat. "Yes, yes, of course. You did the right thing."

"As his widow, I suppose you are now the owner of a sugar plantation in Cuba," Thomas declared.

"A sugar plantation that has not been paid for yet," Sibylla corrected him.

"Why did Hopkins not travel directly from London to Cuba?" Sabri wanted to know. "Did he expect to come by some money here to finance the plantation?"

"I believe I can explain that." Sibylla took a deep breath, steeling herself to divulge the secret she would rather have kept buried forever. "Your father traded not only in leather, spices, and ivory, but also in human beings."

Little by little, she told the whole story. She began with Benjamin's arrest by Qaid Hash-Hash, then told how André had managed to get her an audience with Sultan Abd al-Rahman and that she fought for Benjamin's release because she had believed in his innocence, and how, only a short time later, she had learned the terrible truth when Thomas's marble fell under the damaged foundation of the sundial.

"Then, last October, he came back for his blood money."

"You told us at the time he was on a business trip," Thomas marveled. "When he was really in prison on the island. So that's how he came to die in that fire! I remember you said something about him stopping at the island on his way back from his business trip, but that never quite made sense . . ." He looked exhausted as he ran his fingers through his hair. "But what came of the money, Mother?"

"You were so little—I had to shield you from the truth. And I could never keep money that had caused so much suffering. That's why I donated it for the reconstruction of Mogador. In return, Qaid

Hash-Hash let it be known that all accusations against your father were false."

"I always wondered where you got all that money for the reconstruction!" John said, shaking his head.

"I wanted you two to grow up unburdened and with fond memories of your father. Unfortunately, it appears as though I've failed," Sibylla replied sadly.

"You're the best mother there is, as far as I'm concerned," Emily declared firmly and kissed her.

"I would have tried to shield my children as well," Victoria affirmed.

"You carried a heavy burden for all of us, Mother," Thomas added and John nodded in agreement.

Sibylla wiped her eyes with a corner of her shawl. She had kept Benjamin's dirty secret for more than twenty years. Only now did she realize how onerous it had been.

André went to her, took her hands, and pulled her up from the divan. "The past is behind you now," he said and tenderly enfolded her in his arms. "You are free."

Chapter Thirty-Five

Mogador, June 1862

"I don't want to go to bed, Mummy!" Charlotte made a face. Selwyn copied her and whined, "I'm not sleepy at all, Mummy!"

Since Victoria's return from Lisbon, the two of them had managed a couple of times to wear their mother down with persistent whining, but tonight she was steadfast. "If you don't go to sleep, you're not going to go to the wedding tomorrow. Now kiss your aunt Emily good night."

Nadira came to take over for her, but Victoria stopped her. She wanted to tuck the children in herself. She had missed them terribly during her six-month journey and now spent every available moment with them.

She took Charlotte and Selwyn by the hand and crossed the roof garden of Sibylla's *riad* to Emily, who was sitting on a cushion surrounded by Sabri's sisters and Malika.

Charlotte regarded her with curiosity. "Why are you holding your fingers like that, Aunt Emily?"

"Because the design on my hands has to dry. See?" She held her palms out to show them the swirling henna painted on them.

"It's very pretty," Selwyn squeaked in his little voice. "Just like the princess in my fairy-tale book."

Emily laughed. "At my wedding celebration tomorrow, I'm going to be a princess too. Good night, you two!" She waved after the twins. "Sweet dreams!"

"Are you thirsty? Would you like some tea?" asked Malika.

Emily's half sister and Sabri's eldest sister were her *negafas*, her indispensable helpers during the three-day festivities that had begun yesterday with a visit to the *hamam* and would end tomorrow with a lavish feast on the beach.

Emily nodded gratefully and Malika ran to Firyal and Nadira, who stood next to a table with cake, fruit, and sweet sorbets, and retrieved a glass of green tea.

"Here you are, Sister!" She handed Emily the glass. "But not too much. You know you mustn't go to a certain place while the henna on your hands is still wet."

Sabri's unmarried sisters giggled and Emily sighed. "I doubt that Sabri has to suffer so much pain and inconvenience to marry me!"

At the *hamam*, attendants had cleaned and scrubbed her from head to toe, removed all hair save that on her head. They'd also given her the extra bridal treatment: a bath in donkey's milk, so that she might enchant her bridegroom with especially soft skin.

Today was the *beberiska*, the henna ceremony. No men were allowed. They had assembled at Consul Willshire's to fete Sabri while the female guests—an unusual confluence of Arab women, the wives of European and Jewish merchants, and Emily's half sister, Malika—celebrated in Sibylla's rooftop garden. Emily was particularly happy to have her extended English family there. Oscar had left the business in the hands of his son, Edward, and taken the first trip of his life with his wife, Eugenie, and their adolescent daughter, Arabella. The three of them were enjoying their adventure to the fullest and were already making plans for an extended tour of Morocco.

The women had been sitting together since late that morning, keeping the bride company while she rested on a cushion and the *hennaya* painted ancient symbols of good luck and magic on her hands and feet. As they passed the time enjoying tea and delicious food, music, song, and dance, evening had come, the sky above Mogador turned dark blue, and the stars sparkled in the warm early-June air. Now, Nadira and Firyal were lighting torches, and voices, laughter, and instruments could be heard, accompanied by the hoarse singing of Sabri's old grandmother.

The *hennaya* had mixed a fresh paste called earth of paradise using the ground leaves of the henna bush, black tea, and tamarind juice, and filled a piping bag with it. She was an old Arab woman, a widow who lived in a modest hut by the city wall and who also made her living as a matchmaker, arranging marriages between the affluent Arab families of Mogador. Malika held up a lamp to provide light while the *hennaya* bathed Emily's feet in a bowl of orange-blossom water.

"The attendants in the *hamam* have done good work. Your skin is as smooth as silk, my little dove," the *hennaya* said with satisfaction.

"You should see her Venus mound!" Haji Abdul's first wife cackled. "Sweet and fragrant as a rose blossom. But how she squealed when the servant pulled off the sugar paste! Like a puppy taken off the teat."

"There are no *hamams* in Lisbon." Emily laughed. "Yet somehow we managed without it!"

"My poor son!" Almaz exclaimed with exaggerated concern. "How on earth did he find the path through all that thorny briar?"

It was part of the *berberiska* ceremony for married women to initiate the bride into love's secrets by telling lewd jokes. It did not bother anyone that Emily was already familiar with these secrets.

When the laughter died down, the *hennaya* said, "If you will permit me, my little dove, I am going to paint the magic signs of good fortune, love, and prosperity on your feet now and interweave them with the name of your beloved."

"Rather paint the signs for desire and fertility," Sabri's eldest sister piped up. "They've been sharing the same bed for months already, and her belly has not grown fat!"

"How could it, if I've had to be separated from my husband since our return?" Emily sassed back. "Good thing the astrologer recommended we wed in early summer. We surely would not have been able to forgo the pleasures of love much longer!"

The women appreciated Emily's ready wit, which, much to her relief, distracted them from her childlessness. There was a simple reason for that: small sponges, soaked in lemon juice, which she inserted into her vagina before lovemaking. Malika had told her this secret during her stay at Qasr el Bahia.

"Tell us about your first night!" Sabri's youngest and still-unmarried sister begged, casting a furtive glance in her mother's direction. But Haji Abdul's first wife was too engrossed in a conversation with Sibylla, Eugenie, and Almaz to notice.

Emily looked dreamy and smiled. "It was terribly romantic. All the other passengers congratulated us. The sailors serenaded us and the captain let us have his quarters for the first night. But that's all I'm going to share with you."

Sabri's youngest sister looked at her with deep disappointment.

"When you celebrate your own wedding, you'll understand," Emily consoled her. "The memory of our first night belongs to my husband and me. But I will tell you this: it sealed our love more profoundly than any wedding vow ever could."

"And you lovebirds have had to live abstinently for a month now, oh dear, oh dear! You will have to be doubly careful not to be consumed by your own fire tomorrow night," the eldest sister jested.

Almaz added with dignity, "May the fire of your love always be stronger than the wooden log that turns to ash, and may you, Emily, be the water for my son that keeps him from dying of thirst."

Sibylla smiled to herself. Just one month earlier, Almaz would never have uttered such a wish, but ever since Benjamin had attempted to kill Emily, Sabri's family had forgotten what remained of their reservations about the Christian bride and the wedding. Almaz and the first wife had even called Emily their beloved daughter. For his part, Haji Abdul had been very impressed with André's bravery. He had Sabri describe to him again and again how André had grabbed Benjamin and thrown him through the banister. He would nod his head and ceremoniously announce, "The daughter of such a man shall bear strong and healthy sons. You made a wise choice, my son."

Early on the morning of the tenth of Dhu al-Hijjah of the year 1278 after the Prophet's departure from Mecca—June 8, 1862, in the Western calendar—music and singing enticed the inhabitants of the *medina* from their homes. A bevy of women, diaphanous muslin veils wafting around them like a silvery morning mist, danced through the alleyways to Sibylla's house to collect the bride and adorn her for her great celebration.

Musicians played flutes and *vihuelas*, beat tambourines and plucked the lute. Young girls sang about the bride being sweeter than honey and lovelier than the full moon, and children scattered rose petals and jasmine blossoms along the path. Four sturdy eunuchs in baggy pants and multicolored turbans carried an empty palanquin on their shoulders. Next came the solemn bridegroom and his father, dressed in white *djellabas*, belts with decorative daggers set with precious stones at their hips, and red *tarbooshes* with black tassels atop their heads. They were followed by servants carrying baskets and boxes with the morning gift for the bride, then Sabri's uncle, his brother-in-law, and his cousins.

Victoria, who had been watching the procession from the roof garden, ran to Emily's bedroom and flung open the door. "They're coming! Hurry up!"

"Did you see Sabri? How does he look?" Emily called from the edge of the bed. Malika was in the process of removing the muslin bandages that had protected the henna overnight.

There were loud knocks on the front door and voices calling, "Open up, we've come to collect the bride!"

"Are you happy?" Malika asked, while Victoria wanted to know, "Are you nervous?"

Emily's eyes shone and her cheeks glowed rosily. "Of course I'm happy!"

The door opened again and Sibylla entered. She was wearing her best dress and a fringed shawl that shimmered in all the colors of the rainbow, and she looked every bit as excited as her daughter.

"Good morning, my little girl!" She kissed Emily. "I'm sure you've heard that the bin Ibrahim women are here. Nadira is giving them tea, but they'll come to get you any minute. You'd better get dressed quickly unless you want to be carried through Mogador in your nightie."

André received the gentlemen in the large salon with his three sons, as well as John, Thomas, and Oscar by his side. Sabri beamed from ear to ear and embraced everyone while his father looked on, bursting with pride. The uncles and cousins supervised the bearers as they unpacked Emily's morning gift and placed the items on display in the middle of the room.

When the door swung open and Sibylla entered with Eugenie and Victoria, André's heart skipped a beat. He thought that Sibylla, with her silvery hair and sparkling blue eyes, was the most impressive person in the room. He was beside himself with joy when she gave him a special smile before greeting everyone else.

"*Assalamu alaikum*, gentlemen! May I offer you some refreshment?"

She signaled Firyal, who had been waiting by the buffet, and who began pouring tea. A young boy who often helped out in the kitchen offered flatbread, fresh yogurt, dates, and plums.

Eugenie and Victoria fairly gaped at the gifts, Emily's *mahr*. They picked up the precious gold jewelry, sniffed the valuable perfumes, fingered the bright fabrics, silk rugs, porcelain, and silver candlesticks. Haji Abdul really had spared no expense, even though, according to custom, he was responsible not only for the *mahr*, but also for the cost of the feast. André and Sibylla were not allowed to contribute, because that would have called into question the bride's virtue. Their wedding gift was a house for the young couple. Consul Willshire and his wife were returning to England in a few weeks, and André had used his ties to Sultan Sidi Mohammed to enable him and Sibylla to buy the Willshires' house.

But for now, Sabri and Emily had no idea.

After the guests had partaken of food and drink and André expressed his thanks effusively to Haji Abdul, Sabri and André left to go to the *qadi* to sign the marriage contract. Sibylla proceeded to the party tent on the beach in order to supervise the preparations there.

The tent held two hundred guests. It was turquoise like the sea, and with pennants and ribbons blowing in the wind it resembled a fairytale palace. It was filled with thick rugs, soft sofas, and leather floor cushions. Coal basins on low tables emitted the scents of frankincense and amber, cinnamon and cloves.

The guests trickled in, listened to the musicians, chatted, or tasted from the overwhelming abundance of delicacies.

Three sheep and a large swordfish were roasting on spits in front of the tent and, for those whose faith did not prohibit it, there was wine and champagne that André had bought from the French consul. For the rest, there was orange-blossom water, almond milk, and tea. The other concession to the Christian and Jewish guests was that men and women would celebrate together. For now, though, there was little evidence of that. The Arab women gathered behind the screens set up for them on the left half of the tent, with most of the Christian and Jewish ladies keeping them company. The men, meanwhile, were buzzing around the bridegroom on the right side of the tent, slapping his shoulder and making jokes about the pitfalls of married life.

Sabri had changed and was now wearing his most resplendent *jabador*. He sat on one of the two decorated armchairs that had been placed in the middle of the tent and did his best to appear dignified and relaxed. He knew it was the bride's prerogative to keep her groom waiting, but the tension was almost too much to bear. To calm himself, he counted the eggs that his sisters had arranged in an elaborate pyramid—one of many symbols of fertility and good fortune that were part of the celebration. He could hear the women chatting behind the screen. André paced in front of him in his Chasseur d'Afrique uniform, looking as nervous as if he were the groom himself. Outside the tent, a horde of children ran back and forth, screaming that they still could not see the bridal procession.

"You look like you could use something to calm your nerves." Thomas held out a porcelain cup to Sabri.

"Thanks, that's very nice of you, but I really don't feel like any tea."

"Take it and drink up!"

"Doctor's orders?"

Thomas grinned.

Sabri put the cup up to his mouth and sniffed. "Ah, I see," he said and grinned back at Thomas.

"Hurry up. Your father is right over there."

Sabri put the cup to the lips and emptied it in one go. "Ah, that feels good. Thank you, my friend!"

The children stormed into the tent led by André Jr. "She's here! She's here!" they screeched, dragging Sabri out of his chair. "Come! Emily looks beautiful!"

◆ ◆ ◆

The *negafas* had helped Emily into her most precious garment, a *takchita* consisting of floor-length red brocade, which the embroiderers from Fez had turned into a veritable piece of art with lace, pearls, and trim. It had long, wide sleeves but was form-fitting on the torso and had a broad sash around the waist.

Emily's black curls fell over her shoulders. She wore heavy gold earrings and the coral necklace given to her by the mother of the little Berber boy with the broken arm.

She was an attraction the likes of which had not been seen in Mogador for quite some time, arriving in the palanquin carried by four splendidly dressed black slaves. The many curious onlookers who had followed her to the beach clapped their hands and cheered. Now Malika and Sabri's eldest sister were walking directly behind her, singing verses from the Koran, followed by Almaz, Sabri's other sisters, and Haji Abdul's first wife.

It's really happening, thought Emily as the reflecting midday sun seemed to transform the dome of the tent into liquid gold. She took a surreptitious glance at the fine lines on her left palm. Almost two years ago, Malika had read those lines and foretold that she would experience passionate love. Sabri and she had overcome obstacles just as Malika had predicted, but not until today had her prediction really come true.

The four slaves carried Emily into the tent, and now the ladies ventured out from behind the screens to cheer her on. Emily saw her mother and her father, her brothers and Sabri's sisters, Victoria, Oscar, Eugenie, and Arabella, their many friends and acquaintances. Everyone was beaming at her.

Then she spotted Sabri stretching out his hands to help her out of the palanquin. Next to him stood Nadira with a pitcher of almond milk. After Emily had alighted, Sabri took her right hand and gently turned it over to make a bowl. Nadira handed him the jug and he poured a little almond milk into Emily's palm, then leaned forward and drank from it. She took his hand and repeated the ritual.

"Now we are forever united," Sabri whispered to her.

"*Ana behibak*, I love you," she replied, deliriously happy.

Next, the *negafas* helped Emily into another of her ten gowns behind the screens. Meanwhile, outside the roast sheep and fish were taken off the fire and carved. Sabri's sisters giggled at Eugenie's and Victoria's clumsy attempts at eating with pieces of flatbread instead of silverware, and Haji Abdul gave a long speech about the virtues of a married woman. After that, André rose and declared that the moment had come for the bride to receive her dowry according to Christian custom.

He threw a long, loving look at Sibylla and announced, "We, as Emily's parents, have decided to give the newlyweds a home of their own."

He paused for effect and to enjoy the look on Emily's and Sabri's faces.

"You will not only live in the Willshires' lovely house," Sibylla continued, "it will really be yours. Sultan Sidi Mohammed has sold it to us." She smiled at Sara, who looked almost as emotional as the bride and groom. "When you return from your honeymoon in London, everything will be ready for you to move in."

"By God, what a wonderful gift!" Sabri muttered, moved.

"You could not have given us anything more beautiful!" Emily was fighting back tears. She had feared having to live under Haji Abdul's roof, where she would have been under the thumb of not only Sabri's grandmother, but also his mother and the first wife. But now she would have her own house, in which she could do as she pleased.

Haji Abdul's expression was sorrowful. *I should never have allowed Sabri to travel to the land of the English*, he thought sadly. *He has adopted the foreigners' customs more and more. His Christian bride will be a good wife to him, but will she raise his sons in the true faith outside of his parental home?*

He was startled to see Almaz standing in front of him, smiling under her thin muslin veil.

"Their own home, how wonderful!" she said dreamily. "I wonder if Emily will furnish it in the European style. I will, of course, gladly be on hand to give her advice—"

"Your place is in my house!" he snapped more harshly than he had intended.

Almaz looked as though she'd been struck. "Do you mean to break my heart? Will you stop a mother from visiting her son's home?"

Looking sour, he turned away from her to look for his first wife. As one born into the true faith, she, at least, was loyal to God's laws! Poor Haji Abdul froze in horror. There was his first wife next to the *Engliziya*, seemingly unconcerned that she was exposed to the gazes of all the men. She was handing the bride and groom a glass of tea with a large cube of sugar.

"Drink up!" she cried for all to hear. "Drink up and let your mouths find sweet words for each other!"

Gnawa musicians were moving through the tent making a deafening clatter with their *qarqabas* and bass drums. They were a group of freed slaves who lived in shacks outside the city gates and entertained people at festivals and processions. Children swarmed around them excitedly, stuffing silver coins in the pockets of their garments adorned with cowrie shells and crying, "*Yalla, yalla!* Faster, faster!" as the men turned in circles to the beat.

After the *gnawa* came a group of nomadic Marrakchi people, who breathed fire and swallowed swords. They were accompanied by Berber women who danced with snakelike agility. Malika jumped to her feet and joined them. The men gave her admiring—and the women shocked—looks as the silver coins she had woven into her hair jingled and her embroidered skirt whirled around her legs.

Emily could not dance because her dress was too heavy. She sat on a round leather pouf next to Sabri's grandmother's chair and helped her spoon quince puree and chopped lamb onto a small piece of flatbread.

"My grandson was right to take you," said the old woman and patted Emily's cheek with shaky fingers.

Sabri stood with Oscar, André, John, and Thomas in the back of the tent. Oscar had already drunk plenty of the heady French wine and was describing at length how he had, at the tender age of sixteen, helped Eton beat Harrow in a legendary cricket match.

"Cricket is a sport that you in the East really must adopt," he decided and slapped Sabri's shoulder. "That's how a man learns team spirit, fair play, and seizing your chance at the right moment. Just the qualities a good businessman needs!"

"That's all well and good, Uncle Oscar, but Sabri is a doctor." Thomas chuckled. "Has he told you that we plan to take the empty rooms at the *maristan* and turn them into modern operating rooms?"

"Has Uncle Oscar told you that we are planning to visit Tangier together?" John interrupted.

Thomas held out his champagne glass for a servant to fill. "So you really mean to leave Mogador?"

His brother shrugged. "Businessmen need to be wherever their business is. Trade is shifting to the north of Morocco, where Europe and Africa, the Atlantic and the Pacific intersect."

Oscar nodded. "We're going to explore the possibility of establishing a trading station in Tangier."

"First we must see that the port there is suitable for steamships made of steel," John added with a sparkle in his eyes, thinking of his father-in-law's steelworks.

But Thomas seemed doubtful. "Does Mother know of your plans? I cannot imagine that she'll agree."

"Our mother is a clever woman," John replied firmly. "She is well aware that the Europeans are putting pressure on the sultan to open Morocco even more to international trade. And that, of course, is going to happen first in the northern cities, where our influence is greatest."

"It seems that all of us have new challenges to face," Sabri said and looked over at André. "What are your plans, Ab?" Since his return from Lisbon, he had been addressing André with the Arabic word for father.

"I shall transfer more responsibilities to Frédéric and Christian to prepare them for the day when they must run Qasr el Bahia by themselves. I would like André Jr. to attend school in Mogador. He has a sharp mind. And further than that . . ." He stopped. Since Aynur's death, he had lived from day to day and avoided looking too far ahead. It was as though his old place in life was gone and he had not yet found a new one.

His eyes fell on Sibylla. She was laughing and applauding the dancers. He thought how wonderful it had been to spend a few days and nights before the wedding as a guest under her roof. He had been conscious of her nearness the whole time, even when she was in a different room. He stifled a sigh when he realized how much he would miss her when he returned to Qasr el Bahia.

At that moment, she turned around and looked over at him with a little smile on her face, and André knew what he wished for his future.

As the sun went down, Emily and Sabri snuck away. While the festivities inside the tent were still in full swing, they stood together on the beach and watched the orange ball of light slowly sink into the ocean. Finally, there was nothing left but a glimmer of light on the black water.

Emily had taken off her shoes and wriggled her toes in the sand. The wind smelled of salt, and laughter and music from the tent mingled with the steady rush of the waves.

Sabri put his arm around her and pulled her close. "Are you happy, Emily?"

"Deliriously, my love." She clung to him. "This is just the beginning!"

André took a bottle of wine, two glasses, and an oil lamp from a table in the back of the tent. It was the same dark wine that he had drunk with Sibylla many years before in the ruins of the Portuguese church.

"I want to show you something," he told her. "Will you come?"

She looked at him from the side and noticed the smile wrinkles that danced around his eyes, the curly hair now streaked with gray, the narrow scar on his temple. The last two years had left their mark on him, and she felt their connection more deeply than ever.

"I would love to," she replied.

André's smile deepened. He placed his hand on her back and guided her through the throng of partiers.

Outside, it was almost dark. Torches were burning around the tent. In the day's last light, Sibylla saw a man and a woman standing close to each other on the beach. She nudged André and whispered, "Look, it's Emily and Sabri."

He looked in the direction she indicated. "It seems they won't be needing us anymore today."

"And you?" she asked with a throbbing heart. "What is it you wanted to show me?"

Grinning sheepishly, he pointed to the neck of the wine bottle protruding from his pocket. Then he turned away from the water and pointed to the city wall, where the ruins of the old Portuguese church rose above the flat roofs of the houses. The destroyed walls of the steeple were black against the dark blue sky. "Do you recall that we were once very happy there?"

"How could I ever forget?" she whispered.

He took her hand and raised it to his lips. Then he led her away from the beach and the tent, in which the wedding guests would celebrate Emily and Sabri's future life together until daybreak.

The hinges of the door to the old church creaked as they opened. The interior was completely black. There was a smell of dust and the refreshing coolness of stone. Stars twinkled through the broken roof. André slipped off his jacket, laid it on the ground, and pulled Sibylla down with him. She heard a cork pop, then smelled the delicate aroma of the wine.

He handed her a glass. "I want to drink a toast with you, Sibylla. To the years to come, to the future, and to life, whatever it may yet bring us."

"I don't quite know what that will be for me," she said after taking a sip. "My children are grown and it is time to turn over my work to them. I fear I shall have a lot of time on my hands." She took another sip. "I could write my own story, perhaps. You know—the true, one-of-a-kind adventures of an English merchant's wife in Morocco."

"A marvelous idea, but you can do that later," he countered. "First, I think you ought to go on a journey."

"A journey?" she echoed. "Where?"

"You have inherited a plantation in Cuba, have you not?"

"Oh my goodness, yes!" she exclaimed. "A plantation and slaves! But why do you say I should go there? Rather I should get rid of all that as quickly as possible."

"Sometimes it's better to take a careful look before making a decision."

"Perhaps you're right," she replied. "But I shall not be a slave owner."

"It's possible to run a plantation with paid laborers, you know."

"Still, that's not an easy decision," she muttered.

André held his breath, but Sibylla said nothing more for a long time. His heart sank.

At last, she asked very softly, "Suppose I do travel to Cuba. Would you come with me, André?"

"I feared you'd never ask! Do you really still want me, Sibylla?"

She put her hand on his cheek. "I've been missing you my whole life."

Afterword and Acknowledgments

Mogador, present-day Essaouira, was founded in 1506 as the Portuguese fortress of Magdoura and today is a small coastal town. In 1765, Sultan Sidi Mohammed Ben Abdallah expanded it into Morocco's largest seaport at the time. Until the middle of the nineteenth century, it was Morocco's gateway to the world, from which approximately forty percent of Moroccan commodities were exported. However, the emergence of the steamship and the disappearance of caravans during the nineteenth century led to its decline.

A few historical facts were altered for the benefit of the novel's plot, especially the French bombing of Mogador, which did not take place in 1840 but in 1844.

We wish to thank the research fellows of the Übersee-Museum Bremen and the German Maritime Museum for their help in answering our questions, as well as Henk J. Vroom of Sunshine Art BV and Dottore Alberto Peroni of Castello Del Trebbio. We would like to express our particular thanks to Zahira Efeturk for enlightening us about the Arabic language. If by any chance our readers come across any mistakes, we ask their pardon. They are solely our fault.

About the Authors

Photo © 2016

Julia Drosten is the pseudonym for a two-person writing team based in Münsterland, Germany. This novel was originally published in German under the title *Die Löwin von Mogador* and was an Amazon bestseller in Germany.

The authors have written many other works of historical fiction in German, and they greatly enjoy conducting research for their novels, diving into history and making the past come alive. They count flying in a historic biplane, watching butchers work in a butcher's shop, exploring Egypt, and being pampered by a beautician among their research pursuits. *The Lioness of Morocco* is their first novel translated into English.

About the Translator

Photo © 2014 Paul Galvani

Christiane Galvani is a professional translator and an adjunct professor at Houston Community College. She earned her bachelor of arts degree in French and German at the University of London and her master's degree in German at Rice University. Galvani is a licensed court interpreter and an ATA-certified translator. She currently resides in Texas.